You are an enemy here," Melantha protested, desperate to keep the lines between them clean and deeply cut. "A Mac-Tier."

"That is true," Roarke agreed, moving toward her.

"You came to crush my band, and if you'd been able, you would have killed me that day we fought in the woods," she continued, backing away from him. The cool stones of the wall pressed into her, arresting her retreat.

"You were every bit as determined to kill me." He reached out and gently brushed a dark strand of hair away from her face. "Remember?"

His fingers were warm against her skin, warm and filled with gentle strength. It was wrong to stand there and endure his touch, and yet she found she couldn't move, could scarcely even draw a breath as he held her steady with nothing more than the raw desire emanating from him. . . .

THE ROSE AND THE WARRIOR

Karyn Monk

Bantam Books
New York Toronto
London Sydney Auckland

THE ROSE AND THE WARRIOR
A Bantam Fanfare Book / April 2000

ISBN 0-553-57761-1

Published simultaneously in the United States and Canada

Bantam Books are published by Bantam Books, a division of Random House,
Inc. Its trademark, consisting of the words "Bantam Books" and the portrayal
of a rooster, is Registered in U.S. Patent and Trademark Office and in other
countries. Marca Registrada. Bantam Books, 1540 Broadway, New York, New
York 10036.

PRINTED IN THE UNITED STATES OF AMERICA

OPM   10   9   8   7   6   5   4   3

FOR MY BEAUTIFUL LITTLE GENEVIEVE,

WHO CAME INTO MY LIFE AS I WAS WRITING
THIS BOOK,
FILLING IT FOREVER WITH MAGIC.

ALL MY LOVE,
MUMMY

CHAPTER 1

The Highlands of Scotland

summer 1216

Every step of his mount was agony.

It is nothing, Roarke told himself harshly, shifting his weight to ease the torturous pressure on his spine. But the relentless throbbing in his muscles continued, an incessant reminder that his body no longer enjoyed the hard resilience he had once known.

It was a bitter realization.

" 'Tis getting late," observed Eric, urging his horse alongside Roarke. The enormous, fair-haired warrior studied the fading light. "We should make camp."

Roarke shook his head.

Eric stared at Roarke, his blue gaze penetrating. Roarke returned his friend's scrutiny with rigid indifference.

"As you wish," said Eric after a moment, shrugging. "I was only thinking of the horses."

"We will go farther." He resisted the urge to shift his weight yet again, for fear it might betray his fatigue. "We may still find him today."

"Strange that there's been no sign of him yet," remarked Donald, idly stretching his arms over his head. He yawned. "Perhaps the elusive Falcon and his charming band will be more apt to introduce themselves once we've settled for the night."

"That's what they did to the last men Laird MacTier sent to capture them," growled Myles. The heavyset warrior spat contemptuously on the ground. "Attacked them as they lay snoring after knocking out the men assigned to keep watch."

"Stripped them bloody naked and stole their horses," Eric added. "The fools had to walk back to the holding wearing nothing but a few strategically placed branches. Laird MacTier was furious."

Donald arched one brow in bemusement. "Now, that doesn't seem very sporting. Stealing weapons and valuables is one thing, but why would the Falcon steal their plaids?"

"To humiliate his enemies." Roarke was unable to contain his disgust. Better to slay one's opponent, quickly and with honor, rather than strip him like a bairn and send him limping naked back to his clan. "The Falcon and his men prefer the weapon of shame to the clean cut of death. If they make MacTier look like a fool, then other clans will view us all as fools. That is why we must crush this band of outlaws."

"Yet MacTier wants the Falcon taken alive," mused Donald.

"He wants to kill the troublesome bastard himself," Roarke explained. The Falcon had been a festering thorn in his laird's backside for months now, and his patience was at an end. "MacTier also needs him alive so he can learn where the Falcon has hidden the fortune he has stolen from us."

"We needn't drag him all the way back to our holding just for that." Eric's massive hand clamped the hilt of the heavy dirk strapped to his waist. "A few strips of flesh peeled away, and he'll tell us exactly what we want to know."

"Our orders are to bring him back alive, Eric," Roarke reminded him.

The warrior reluctantly released his weapon. "I prefer battle to this tedious business of hunting," he complained darkly. "In battle I don't have to choose between whom I kill and whom I maim."

"By God, that's an inspiring reflection!" said Donald, chuckling. "No doubt when we return home you will enchant many a fair maiden with your gallant philosophy."

Eric snorted. "I leave the enchanting of maidens to you. You have the pretty face for such idiocy."

" 'Tis not my face that wins their hearts," Donald maintained, although with his elegantly carved features, there was no denying his appeal to women. " 'Tis simply that I know how to put a gentle maiden at ease—unlike you, who with that fearsome Viking scowl manage to send them screaming home to their mamas before you even bid them good day."

Eric's expression darkened. "Women are feeble, silly creatures."

"Eric's right," agreed Myles, scratching his shaved head. "Fawning over women is a sport for fools." He belched.

Donald sighed. " 'Tis clear you both have been removed from the company of lasses too long," he mused. "Tonight I will begin your lessons on how to win a maid's attentions, and soon you'll have them flocking to you like starving birds to ripe berries."

"I have no desire for women to flock to me," Eric replied. "Women sap a man's strength and waste his time, which is better spent training for battle."

"Ah, but there's nothing sweeter than the softness of a lass pressing tightly against your hardness," rhapsodized Donald dreamily, "or the velvety caress of her moist, parted lips grazing upon your—"

"There is a clearing ahead," interrupted Roarke. "Go and see if it is a satisfactory place for us to make camp."

"Gladly," Eric growled. "Anything to escape Donald's infernal chatter." He dug his heels into his mount and cantered toward the clearing.

"The day will come when you beg me for advice on winning a lass's heart," Donald shouted cheerfully, riding fast behind him.

"Go with them, Myles," ordered Roarke, "and try to keep Eric from killing Donald before I get there."

"It won't be easy," Myles muttered, heading toward the clearing.

Roarke watched as his warriors disappeared into the shadowy veil of trees. Certain he was alone, he slowly bent his head from side to side, groaning with relief at the ripple of cracking sounds that rewarded his effort. Then he raised his arms and flexed them, easing the painful knots of tension in the damaged muscles. He grunted and stretched forward on his horse, trying to loosen the stiffness in his aching back. The movements did little to alleviate his discomfort, but even a marginal improvement was better than none at all. Now he would be able to feign a modicum of ease as he dismounted before his men, rather than succumbing to the treachery of his weary, battered body.

"Look here," called Donald, seeing Roarke approach. "It appears someone has been here before us." He yanked a shimmering dirk from the earth at the base of a tree. "Someone with a penchant for lavish weaponry," he added, turning the heavily jeweled hilt over.

Myles's eyes grew wide. "Bloody hell, that must be worth a fortune."

"It is not the weapon of a warrior," scoffed Eric. "Only a fool would trust his life to such a clumsy piece."

Uneasiness flashed through Roarke. Dusk had withered to a smoky caul, making it difficult to see through the shadows of the thickly entwined pine and rowan trees. A whisper of sound caressed the stillness, barely more than the flutter of a wing, but a sound that somehow struck him as out of place in the sweetly scented arbor of these woods. He narrowed his gaze and fought to distinguish between the shifting shapes surrounding them, straining to hear beyond his warriors' irritatingly loud ruminations on the dirk.

There was nothing except the occasional twitter of a bird, and the soft rustle of a small animal as it skittered across the loamy ground.

You are being foolish, Roarke told himself impatiently. *It is nothing.*

In that instant a giant net dropped from the trees, trapping his startled men like rabbits.

"Got them!" shouted a voice gleefully from above. "Three fat flies in one sticky web!"

"Good work, Magnus!" called another, "but there's still one left!"

Roarke jammed his heels into his mount and flew forward, barely evading the second net.

"You missed, Lewis!" shouted a tall fellow who dropped from the trees with feline agility. He regarded Roarke with cool wariness, considering his next move.

"Sorry!" apologized a chastened voice over Roarke's head.

"Not yer fault, lad," the first voice assured him. "He's as slippery as a fish on a fire, that one is!"

"Never mind that, somebody get him!" commanded the tall one, who had now been joined on the ground by a stocky man with wildly curling hair. Ignoring Roarke, they grabbed the ends of the net and began racing in a circle around his bellowing warriors, who were swearing and knocking each other over as they vainly attempted to free themselves.

Suddenly another warrior burst from the trees upon a magnificent steel-colored charger, his sword a flash of silver against the swiftly waning light. The new attacker wore a dark, battered helmet and a coat of finely wrought chain mail over coarse woolen leggings. His eyes were two black slits, but the grim determination with which the warrior gripped his weapon left no doubt as to his intent.

Roarke charged forward and met the first thrust of his opponent's blade, edging him back, but only for a second. The warrior instantly raised his sword and thundered toward him once more, thrusting before Roarke could better his own position. Roarke whipped up his own blade in a powerful arc, ably deflecting the warrior's blow in a golden burst of sparks. The clang of steel mixed with the ignoble swearing and howling coming from his now hopelessly entangled soldiers.

His attacker was no match for Roarke's size and strength, but what the fellow lacked in power he more than compensated for with deftness and speed. Roarke thrust again and again, each strike edging his opponent back a little farther, until finally they were beyond the clearing and he sensed the advantage was his. Utilizing every shred of his strength Roarke swung his sword high into the air, preparing to hack off his opponent's head.

Pain suddenly lanced his buttock, reducing his triumphant roar to a startled bellow. Another arrow sliced the air beside his ear and flew toward his adversary, who lurched to one side, then flapped his arms helplessly as he toppled off his horse. A third shaft whistled past, causing Roarke's mount to rear, which had the distressing effect of driving the iron point buried in his bum even deeper. Cursing savagely, he released his reins and sword to grab at the blasted arrow, then flailed at empty air before crashing unceremoniously beside his helmeted attacker.

"Move so much as a whisker, ye great hulkin' beast, and I'll plant this arrow straight in yer shriveled, greedy heart!" declared a voice from above.

Roarke glanced at his sword, which lay impossibly beyond his reach. Summoning the mangled remains of his dignity, he gritted his teeth and eased himself onto his good buttock.

"Not so bold now that ye've a shaft up yer arse, are ye?" His captor cackled. "Let that be a lesson to ye, for darin' to tangle with the mighty Falcon!"

Roarke stared at the ancient old man with the quivering bow and arrow aimed none too steadily at his chest. "You're the Falcon?" he demanded, unable to conceal his astonishment.

The snowy-haired thief's eyes narrowed. "If ye're thinkin' to make sport with me, ye should know I've killed dozens of men for less." He stretched the string of his bow to a menacing tautness. "Were ye wantin' another arrow in ye?"

"I meant no insult," Roarke assured him, eyeing the trembling arrow precariously gripped in his captor's gnarled hand. "It's just that you have a band of men working with you." He glanced at the three who now had his bellowing warriors trussed in their net. "I assumed you were their leader."

The old man regarded him warily, evaluating his explanation. Suddenly his wrinkled mouth split into a yellow smile. "No harm done, laddie," he said, striking a jaunty pose. " 'Tis easy enough to see how ye might be confused, facin' such a formidable warrior as myself. That's the Falcon lyin' there beside ye," he continued, waving his weapon at the fallen warrior. "An ye'd best hope he's not sorely injured, or I'll be buryin' another shaft in ye!"

Roarke glanced at his opponent, who hadn't stirred since hitting the ground. Clearly the fellow's fall had dazed him. Infuriated that he had been trapped by the very prey he stalked, Roarke reached over and roughly knocked off the Falcon's helmet.

"My God," he drawled hoarsely.

The dazed warrior's eyes opened and stared at him in confusion. Their color was a brilliant swirl of emerald and gold, like a Highlands forest in the shifting sunlight. The infamous Falcon studied Roarke a moment, the fine crescents of her brows arched, as if trying to remember how she had come to be lying upon the ground beside him. She showed no sign of fear but merely childlike curiosity, as if his proximity to her was entirely acceptable, if only she could recall the explanation. Roarke studied the delicate perfection of her in awe, wondering when he had ever seen such silky skin, a nose so elegantly sculpted, or lips as full and invitingly curved. Her hair spilled across the ground in a glossy dark cape, its tangled strands rippling over the crushed grass like fine dark ale. He wanted to say something, but his ability to speak had deserted him, and so he simply stared, lost in the guileless depths of her gaze.

"Ye took a wee tumble, Melantha," said the old man. "A good thing ye were wearin' yer helmet, or ye'd have cracked yer head like an egg," he added, chuckling. "Are ye all right?"

Melantha's gaze remained fastened upon the stranger staring down at her. "I fell?"

Roarke nodded. Had the arrow in his backside arrived but a fraction of a second later, he would have severed this magnificent creature's head from her neck. A woman. Little more than a girl, really. Shame sluiced through him, making him feel sick.

How he ever would have forgiven himself for performing such an atrocity, he had no idea.

Melantha studied the handsome warrior looking down at her, confused by the concern she saw etched in the lines of his weathered face. Her mind was wrapped in a gauzy shroud, but it was clear that this man was most troubled by her fall.

"I'm fine," she assured him, reaching up to lay her hand against the roughness of his cheek. The intimate gesture seemed to surprise him, but she did not withdraw her palm. Instead she pressed it against the warmth of his skin, fascinated by the hard contour of his jaw against her slender fingers.

"I doubt this brute is overly concerned about how ye're feelin'," interjected Magnus, "seeing as he was just about to cut yer head off when I shot him in the arse."

The veil cloaking Melantha's mind instantly disintegrated, releasing her memory in an icy rush. She snatched back her hand and rolled away to grab her fallen sword before nimbly rising to her feet.

"Who are you?" she demanded, pointing her blade at Roarke's throat.

He winced as he tried to balance himself on his good hip. "My name is Roarke."

"Now, that's a fine name," observed Magnus, leaning casually against his bow. "It means 'outstanding ruler.' Are ye a laird then, laddie?"

Roarke shook his head, his gaze still fixed on Melantha. Her loose-fitting coat of finely wrought chain mail and her shapeless leggings effectively concealed any hint of her feminine figure, yet Roarke found himself stirred by the lean, willowy grace of her as she stood over him.

"I am a warrior," he said.

"From which clan?" Melantha's sword was poised to slash his neck if he so much as breathed the wrong way. "And spare me your lies, for if I hear a different answer from one of your fine soldiers, my men will enjoy slowly flaying each of you until we have the truth."

"From the Clan MacTier." Roarke watched in fascination as her eyes narrowed.

"You're rather far from your holding," she observed tautly. "What are you doing in these woods?"

"We are on our way to the MacDuff lands," Roarke lied. "We have been entrusted with a message to be delivered to their laird."

She eyed him suspiciously. "What message?"

"The message is for Laird MacDuff's ears alone."

"He lies."

The tall, agile fellow who had first leaped from the trees approached. He did not appear to be much past twenty-two, but the hard set of his face indicated he had long since lost the whimsy of youth. His shoulder-length hair was of brown and gold, and he bore a neatly shaped beard to match, which served to obscure his relative lack of years.

"They carry no message." He regarded Roarke with contempt.

"How do you know, Colin?" asked Melantha.

"Because the others have already revealed that they were coming here to capture the Falcon," he replied. "It seems we have caught four more of Laird MacTier's finest." His tone was heavily derisive.

Melantha pressed the point of her sword into the base of Roarke's throat. "Be warned," she said ominously, "I have no patience for men who lack the courage to speak the truth."

"And you be warned," Roarke growled, shoving her blade away, "that I will not be prodded like a slab of stringy meat with this rusty sword of yours."

Colin sprinted forward and jabbed his own weapon at Roarke's chest. "Do that again," he invited with deadly calm, "and I'll make certain it is the last thing you ever do upon this earth."

"Here, now, lads, that'll do," objected Magnus. "There's no call for more fighting today, to my way of thinking. These MacTiers have been caught with little harm done save for an arrow in this big beast here, and while that might sting a bit, I don't believe 'tis going to kill him."

"A pity," Colin snapped, his sword still prodding Roarke. "Perhaps I should remedy that."

"That's enough, Colin," said Melantha. "Take him over to the others and bind him. Lewis will watch them while we talk."

"On your feet, MacTier," ordered Colin, keeping his sword at Roarke's chest.

Roarke awkwardly rose and limped toward his men, clenching his jaw against the pain streaking through his buttock. His warriors watched him glumly through the tangled prison of netting.

"Is your injury serious?" demanded Eric, unable to see the arrow projecting from his backside.

"No," Roarke replied shortly.

"Where is it?" Donald asked.

Roarke hesitated. Realizing he could hardly walk around with an arrow sticking out of his backside and not have them notice, he turned.

"That's—most unfortunate," managed Donald, trying his best not to laugh.

"Don't believe you've been struck there before," Myles commented.

"It will need stitches," Eric said. "The flesh there is soft and easily torn—"

"It's nothing!" Roarke snapped, wishing they would all shut the hell up. "Forget it."

"Give me your wrists," ordered Colin, brandishing a length of rope. "And don't try anything, or Lewis will gut you like a fish."

A gangly, awkward looking youth with blood red hair and freckle-spattered skin nervously stepped forward. Roarke doubted young Lewis had much experience gutting anything that wasn't small and already dead, but he refrained from commenting on this. Instead he obligingly held out his wrists and permitted Colin to secure him to a tree.

"Lewis, you watch over them while the rest of us talk," instructed Colin. "If any of them gives you any trouble, kill him."

Lewis glanced apprehensively at Roarke. Roarke glowered, causing the poor lad to stumble back. Roarke rolled his eyes, unable to believe he had permitted himself to be captured by such a ridiculous band of misfits. If only his hands were free and he did not have this goddamn arrow stuck in his ass he could easily overcome the whole bloody lot of them.

As it was, there was little more he could do than scowl as the other members of the Falcon's band gathered just beyond the clearing.

"They're a surly lot, that's for sure." Magnus chuckled, shaking his head. "Let's see if a nice walk back to Laird MacTier without their plaids takes some of the snap out of them."

"We can't let them go," Colin objected. "They came here looking for us, and they bloody well found us. If we release them, they'll fetch an army and lead it right back here."

Finlay drove his sword deep into the ground and spat beside it. "Let's finish them off."

Magnus's crinkled eyes rounded with shock. "Y'er not suggestin' we kill them?"

Colin regarded him soberly. "I don't see any way around it, Magnus."

"But that's not our way," protested Magnus. "We're thieves, lads, not cold-blooded murderers."

"This isn't murder," Colin countered. "We're protecting ourselves and our clan from another attack. Besides, they've seen Melantha. We can't let them go, knowing who the Falcon really is."

"This is terrible," fretted Magnus. "Ye know I've no great love for the MacTiers, but till now our only crime has been to rob them, and chafe their pride a wee bit. 'Tis far more serious to slaughter these lads like trapped deer."

"It's no worse than what MacTier did to our people the night he attacked us," retorted Colin furiously. "We lost over two dozen men to the savagery of his warriors. These four were probably part of that slaughter. It's time we repaid the MacTiers in kind—with their own blood."

"Colin's right." Finlay jerked his sword from the ground. "Let's get it over with."

"No."

Colin regarded Melantha in disbelief. "But if we let them go—"

"If we let them go, they will bring more warriors back to find us," she acknowledged. "But if we kill them, MacTier will be enraged. He may not know who is responsible for the deed, but he will make sure his wrath is felt by all those clans whose lands border these woods. Our people cannot withstand another attack, Colin. We cannot kill them."

"If we can't release them and we can't kill them, then what the hell are we to do with them?" he demanded.

"We have to take them with us."

"Take them with us?" Magnus repeated blankly. "Ye mean as prisoners?"

She nodded. "They're worth more to us alive than dead. We can ransom them back to MacTier—their lives in exchange for money and goods."

"That's madness," Colin objected. "Even assuming Mac-Tier cares enough about these warriors to actually pay the ransom, once we release them he'll just attack our clan and steal it back, and more besides."

"That depends on the size of the ransom," countered Melantha. "If we demand enough money to buy us the protection of an army, MacTier won't dare attack us after we have released them."

Finlay regarded her in confusion. "What army?"

"The MacKenzies have a powerful army," Melantha explained. "They are close enough to us that they could arrive quickly if we sent a message saying we needed them."

"Y'er not thinkin' clearly, lass," Magnus objected, "because of that wee tumble ye took off yer horse. The MacKenzies have no interest in helpin' us."

"We went to Laird MacKenzie for help after MacTier attacked us," Colin reminded her. "The old bastard refused."

"He refused because he said we had nothing to offer him in return. The MacTiers had stripped us of everything, so we had nothing with which to barter. But if MacTier is willing to pay us in gold for the return of these warriors, then we will be able to buy the MacKenzies' protection."

"The lass may have a point." Magnus thoughtfully stroked his white beard. "Old MacKenzie has always been a greedy bastard. I'd not think him one to refuse a sack of gold in exchange for the occasional use of a few of his warriors. Those lads are always spoilin' for a fight, anyway."

"I don't like it," said Colin. "This takes our battle with MacTier out of the woods and leads him straight to our holding."

"We don't have a choice," Melantha argued. "We can't let these warriors go, and if we slay them, MacTier will end up at our castle demanding to know who is responsible. At least this way he will be forced to pay, and we have some chance of arranging for our protection."

"Very well," relented Colin. "We take them with us. But realize this, Melantha. If the council does not agree to ransom them, we will have no choice but to kill them."

"The council will agree to it," Melantha assured him, "once they understand how much we have to gain by keeping these MacTiers alive."

"Y'er in luck this day, lads," declared Magnus cheerfully as they returned to the clearing. "We've decided to let ye live, though 'twas by no means a united decision. I was all for having ye chopped into wee morsels and fed to the wolves."

"An excellent decision," remarked Donald from the confines of his rope prison. "I commend all of you on your exceptionally sound judgment."

"We will camp here for the night," Melantha announced. "Lewis and Finlay, remove the net from those men. Secure their wrists and ankles so they aren't tempted to run away. Magnus, build a fire. Colin, take the first watch. I'm going to walk the horses to the stream." She gathered the mounts' reins as her men moved to carry out her orders.

"I do hate to be a bother," Roarke drawled, "but do you intend to leave me standing beside a tree with this arrow sticking out of me all night?"

Melantha shrugged. "The thought had not troubled me. If you are uncomfortable, Magnus will take it out."

Roarke scowled. "No offense, but that old man's hands shake so much he can barely keep his fingers attached to them. If it's all the same to you, I'll have one of my men remove it."

Melantha regarded him coolly. "I'm not such a fool that I will free one of your men and permit him to pull a weapon out of you. Magnus will remove it, or you can suffer until the wound festers and poisons your entire body. If you die, it merely saves me the trouble of killing you myself." She began to lead the horses away.

Roarke stared after her, infuriated. Had he actually thought there was something even vaguely attractive about this ridiculously attired slip of a girl? She was a hard little bitch, and if he weren't tied up he would take her across his knee and give her a sound thrashing.

"Come, now, lad, ye've no cause for alarm," Magnus assured him. "I've pulled out many an arrow in my day, and most have lived to tell the tale. Then again, ye might not want to be tellin' others that ye ended up with yer plaid pinned to yer arse!" He slapped his thigh and laughed, vastly amused by Roarke's predicament.

"Just see that you pull the bloody thing out straight," muttered Roarke as Finlay released him from the tree. He lowered himself onto the ground.

Magnus knelt beside him and placed his gnarled hand upon Roarke's throbbing buttock. " 'Twill be as straight and true as the shot that landed it there," he promised.

"You mean you were actually aiming for my backside?"

"Don't be daft," Magnus chided, grasping the arrow. "If not for these quiverin' hands of mine, I'd have hit ye squarely in yer heart." He jerked his hand up, releasing the shaft in a gush of blood.

Roarke swore.

"Look at that!" cried Magnus, elated. "I'll be able to use this again!"

"I'm delighted to hear it," managed Roarke tersely. "Tomorrow you can shoot it into the other side."

"Only if ye give me reason to." Magnus tossed the shaft on the ground. "Now, then, let's have a look at the damage." He eased Roarke's bloodied plaid up and clicked his tongue. "Well, 'tis not the worst I've seen, but I'm afraid 'tis going to need a stitch or two. Have no fear, lad, I'll make it so tidy ye'll be proud to show the scar to anyone."

"Somehow I doubt that."

"Finlay, bring me needle and thread, and a scrap of linen for mopping up the blood. And see if these lads had any ale with them," the old man added hopefully. "Ours is all gone."

"There is no ale," Roarke informed him.

Magnus sighed. "Now, that's a sorry thing—I always stitch better when I've had a wee drop."

"I shall try to be better prepared next time," promised Roarke dryly.

Finlay returned a moment later bearing the requested items. Despite his determination to remain relaxed, Roarke found himself tensing his buttock muscles as he waited for the needle to pierce his skin. Nothing happened. Wondering what the hell the old man was waiting for, he turned his head.

Magnus's white brows were scrunched into one as he struggled to bring needle and thread together. Try as he might, he could not steady his shaking hands enough to see the deed done. Finally, in a moment of pure exasperation, Roarke grabbed the needle and threaded the damn thing himself.

"Here," he said, thrusting it into Magnus's hands.

"Why, thank ye, lad. My eyes are not what they once were." Magnus squinted at the needle, making certain he actually held the sliver of iron between his fingers, then peered down at Roarke's wound. "This won't take a moment," he declared cheerfully.

Roarke gritted his teeth and silently endured Magnus's fumbling stitches. After what seemed an eternity of pricking and pulling, the old man finally had closed the wound to his satisfaction.

"There, now," he said, admiring his handiwork. "I think ye'll be most pleased."

"I'm sure it's magnificent," Roarke drawled sarcastically, jerking his plaid down to cover himself.

Melantha tossed another stick onto the fire she had built. "If you're finished, Magnus, then Finlay can bind his wrists and feet for the night."

Roarke yawned. "That won't be necessary. I'm not going anywhere."

"You're right," Melantha agreed, "you're not."

He gave her a black look as Finlay secured his wrists and ankles.

"I'll take the watch after you, Colin," she said, settling herself upon the ground with her sword at her side. "Wake me before you become overly tired." She flung her arm over her eyes.

Roarke watched as the rest of the thieves settled for the

evening. Eric, Donald, and Myles lay bound a few feet away from him, regarding him intently, waiting for him to give them some sign. Roarke shook his head. There was nothing more they could do this evening except get some sleep. Eric stared at him in frustration, then finally lay back and closed his eyes. Roarke adjusted his position on his stomach, contemplating their situation.

Whatever the intentions of this ludicrous assemblage of outlaws, Roarke felt relatively certain that they did not plan to kill him and his men—at least not on purpose. They probably intended to keep him and his men prisoners for the night, then strip them of their belongings and send them limping back to their holding in the morning like the disgraced Mac-Tiers before them.

Roarke did not intend to let that happen.

At the first opportunity he would overwhelm one of his captors and demand that the others release his men. Then he would take the whole damn lot of them prisoner and escort them back to Laird MacTier.

His orders had been to crush the band and return with only the Falcon, but Roarke did not relish the idea of killing these men. Poor Lewis was little more than a stripling, and quivery old Magnus was far too ancient to merit slaying. Finlay was rough and brash, but these were qualities Roarke admired in a young warrior, so he hated to snuff them out. As for Colin, he was a hotheaded fool, and Roarke would cheerfully skewer him with his sword, if not for the fact that Colin was so fiercely protective of Melantha. It was clear the lad was in love with her. Roarke turned his head to study her, wondering if she could actually be interested in such a callow, posturing boy.

She lay facing the fire, one arm pillowing her head, the other clutching her sword. Her ale-colored hair rippled over her in a tangled cape, and Roarke found himself imagining what it would be like to touch something so silky and fine.

Firelight played across her skin, highlighting the chiseled contour of her cheek, the elegant curve of her nose, the feathery sweep of lashes against her eyes. She seemed impossibly vulnerable as she lay there, like a child who had fallen asleep and needed to be carried to bed.

How had this strange girl forged such a formidable reputation as the Falcon, who was renowned for his clever and daring feats as he preyed upon those who crossed his path? Roarke thought of her galloping toward him through the woods, her sword raised high as she battled an opponent nearly twice her size. The courage she had demonstrated in that moment was impressive. Impressive and appallingly stupid. He had nearly lopped off her head.

He shoved the thought from his mind and continued to study her. What had driven her to dally in such a dangerous game? Simple greed, or perhaps boredom? He recalled the intensity of her gaze when she learned he and his men were MacTiers. A terrible fury had shadowed those green-and-amber eyes, a bitter loathing that went far beyond mere contempt.

Whatever her motivation for stealing, this was not a girl who was merely in search of pretty baubles for sport.

A small moan escaped her lips. Roarke watched in fascination as her grip on her sword tightened and her jaw clenched.

" 'Tis all right, lass," said Magnus, his voice low and soothing. "Ye've naught to fear, Melantha, everyone is safe. Go back to sleep."

She did not waken, but hesitated, evaluating his words.

And then she sighed and curled her head protectively in toward her body, her thin hand still clutching the battered hilt of her sword.

CHAPTER 2

Roarke wakened with a filthy curse.

"Here, now, there's no cause for foul language," scolded Magnus. "If my fair Edwina were here, she'd make ye hold soap in yer mouth till ye vowed never to speak so again. And I warn ye, she'd not be swayed by yer uncommon size or the black look yer givin' me now," he added, chuckling.

"Are you sure you didn't get confused last night and stitch the head of that bloody arrow into me?" growled Roarke irritably.

Magnus proudly held up the arrow he had been cleaning. "Here's the whole shaft right here. I've put a wee notch on it, so I'll know it from the others. That way I can save it for a special occasion."

"Wonderful," Roarke muttered, awkwardly easing himself onto his good hip.

He glanced moodily around the campsite. The cool gray of dawn had spilled into the clearing, causing his men to stir. The Falcon's band, however, was already wide awake. Finlay was seated on a rock with his sword in his lap, honing the broad blade against a small stone, while young Lewis was meticulously repairing some minor tear in the net that had trapped Roarke's men. Melantha and Colin were nowhere to be seen.

"Where are the other two?" asked Roarke.

"They went hunting," Magnus replied, vigorously shining the head of his prized arrow with a tattered corner of his plaid.

"Excellent." Donald yawned. "I'm famished."

Myles grunted and stretched his bound arms. "So am I."

"Warriors do not eat from the hands of their enemies." Eric cast them a dark look.

"Now, Eric, I see no reason to starve just because we are sharing company with this fine band of outlaws." Donald smiled pleasantly at Magnus.

"Absolutely right," agreed Myles. "No point in going hungry."

"You're both weak." Eric snorted, disgusted. "Hunger makes a warrior strong."

Donald could not help but laugh. "Is that so? I'll be sure to remind you of that the next time I watch you devour an entire leg of venison."

Roarke studied his men, considering. With two members of the Falcon's band gone, this was a good opportunity to overwhelm these remaining outlaws. The fact that he and his men were bound and weaponless put them at a disadvantage, but Magnus's advanced age, Finlay's brashness, and Lewis's fearful cowering made the odds much more equitable. He cleared his throat and glanced meaningfully at his men. Donald responded with a barely perceptible tilt of his head.

"I hate to be a bother, Magnus, but my men need to relieve themselves," Roarke said. "Perhaps they should do so before Melantha returns, to spare her any embarrassment."

Magnus's eyes crinkled with amusement. "Melantha is scarce likely to be bothered by the sound of ye draining yer ballocks. The lass could hardly live in the woods with the rest of us and worry about such triflin' matters."

"Nevertheless," Roarke persisted, "my men would rather see to their needs without a woman watching."

"Shy, are ye?" Magnus chuckled. "Very well, laddie. Finlay, take these blushin' lads one at a time and let them water the woods. Not far, mind ye. Just over by that tree will do fine."

Finlay hopped down and pointed his freshly honed sword at Donald's chest. "Try anything and I'll skewer you like a rabbit on a spit."

"That won't be necessary," Donald assured him, looking more amused by his threat than concerned. "I do believe I will need to have my legs freed if I am expected to get up."

"Lewis, quit fussin' with that net and help Finlay," ordered Magnus.

Lewis hesitated, eyeing Donald uncertainly.

"Now, lad, ye needn't be afraid," Magnus soothed. "Finlay here will make sure he doesn't bite you."

Not looking terribly reassured, Lewis carefully laid down the strands of net he was working on and slowly moved toward Donald.

Donald smiled and bent his knees, ostensibly to scratch his bound ankles. Once Lewis was close he would kick the unsuspecting boy in the chest, knocking him onto his back. Then Donald would spring to his feet, place his booted foot on the lad's neck, and threaten to crush his throat if Finlay didn't lay down his sword.

"I'm thinkin' ye should stretch those legs of yours out a bit before Lewis unties them, laddie," Magnus said, blithely polishing his arrow with his plaid. "Ye'd not want to accidentally kick poor Lewis, now, would ye?"

Donald managed to look credibly affronted. "Good Lord, Magnus, what kind of a warrior do you take me for?"

"Forgive me, lad," he apologized. " 'Tis just that ye're a MacTier, and as such we have to be extra careful."

Roarke kept his expression indifferent, but inside he felt a stab of admiration. Clearly Magnus was not quite as naive as he appeared.

"That'll be Colin and Melantha," Magnus said, returning his attention to his arrow.

Roarke scanned the surrounding woods. He strained to hear, but could not detect the faintest crush of a twig or the rustle of branches to signal that someone was coming.

"You're mistaken, Magnus. There's no one there—"

"Good hunting?" asked Magnus as Colin and Melantha suddenly emerged through the trees.

Colin tossed a coarse brown sack onto the ground. "A few skinny rabbits and some small birds. If they're made into stew and stretched with some vegetables, they should last a while."

"That sounds absolutely wonderful," said Donald, returning to the clearing with Finlay. "But please, don't trouble yourself making a stew—roasted on a spit will do just fine."

"They aren't for you," Colin snarled.

"Are we not to be fed, then?" enquired Roarke mildly.

Finlay snorted in disgust. "You came here to kill us, and now you expect to have your bellies filled?"

"Starve me if it pleases you," returned Roarke, "but at least feed my men. They have not eaten for nearly a day."

Melantha tossed him a look of contempt. "A day without food is nothing. Your men are strong and can easily endure it."

Golden petals of sunlight had filtered into the clearing,

and as they flickered across her fury-clenched face Roarke was suddenly struck by the pale fragility of her. Melantha's shapeless chain mail and leggings effectively concealed the curves of her body, but Roarke did not need to see her waist or hips to know that this girl was intimately acquainted with the hollow ache of hunger. Last night in the soft glow of the fire her cheeks had seemed high and elegantly sculpted, but in the harsher light of day her beauty was revealed to be a little too lean. Her cheeks and jaw bore the sharply cut contours of deprivation, and the delicate skin beneath her dark eyes was shadowed by sleeplessness and months of insufficient nourishment.

"Well, now, I'm not sure 'tis a good idea not to feed these big brutes," interjected Magnus. "After all, we don't want them fallin' ill."

"Magnus is right," relented Colin. "I suppose if we're not going to kill them, we have to feed them."

"Fine," Melantha snapped, turning away. "Feed them something—but not the meat."

"Oatcakes all round, then," declared Magnus brightly, rubbing his hands together in anticipation. "Lewis, fetch some from yer bag and give them to our prisoners."

Lewis obediently went to his horse and retrieved a worn leather satchel from which he produced a number of hard, lumpy biscuits. Scurrying about like a skittish hare, he somehow managed to distribute them among Roarke, Donald, and Myles. But as he approached Eric, the gigantic blond warrior gave him a murderous scowl, causing poor Lewis to stop dead in his tracks.

"Keep your food," Eric growled.

Roarke sighed. "Just eat it, Eric."

Eric adamantly shook his head. "The biscuits are poisoned. In a moment you'll be screaming in agony as your guts boil up into your mouths."

Donald and Myles stopped chewing and stared at their half-eaten oatcakes in dismay.

"Good God, lad," sputtered Magnus, slapping his knee with amusement, "if we wanted ye dead, we'd not waste perfectly good oatcakes on ye to see the job done!"

Finlay raised his blade so that its wickedly sharp edge glinted in the sun. "I'd just cleave you wide with my sword and let that be the end of it."

"There, you see, Eric?" said Roarke, his tone placating, "if your guts are going to come out, it will be through your belly, not your mouth."

Eric stubbornly shook his head. "They lie."

"Then don't eat it," snapped Colin. "Our food is too precious to be wasted on you. Lewis, finish giving out those damn things and let's be on our way."

Lewis hesitated, then broke off a piece of the oatcake he was holding out to Eric and ate it himself.

Eric's expression twisted into a hideous mask of fury. *"Do you dare to taunt me, you skinny, spineless pup?"*

The blood drained so completely from Lewis's face Roarke was certain the lad would faint. Nevertheless, he did not retreat—perhaps because his fear had paralyzed him.

" 'Tis . . . 'tis safe to eat," he stammered, meekly offering Eric the remainder of the biscuit.

Eric's enraged expression froze.

"Take it," Lewis urged. "You'll be hungry later."

The enormous warrior stared in complete bemusement at the thin, outstretched hand trembling before him.

Finally, acutely aware that everyone was now staring at him, he grudgingly accepted the oatcake.

"Is he always this hard to feed?" asked Magnus curiously.

Having taken care of Eric, Lewis tentatively approached Melantha and held a biscuit out to her.

"You have it, Lewis," Melantha said. "I'm not hungry."

"Eat it," ordered Magnus sternly. "Ye've put nothin' in yer stomach since yesterday morn'.'"

"I'm not hungry."

He snorted in disbelief. "No, of course not—ye're never hungry when ye think there might be someone else needin' it more than you. But if ye starve yerself to death, what good will ye be to us then?"

"The day is nearly half gone," she said, abruptly changing the subject. "Get them on their horses and let's go."

"That's it, try to turn my attention to something else," muttered Magnus, shaking his head. "But when ye're too weak to climb up on Morvyn and lead us, don't be bellyachin' to me about how unfair it all is."

"Come on then," said Finlay, bending to untie the rope binding Roarke's ankles. "Up with ye and onto yer mount."

"It's generous of you to allow us to keep our horses," observed Roarke, suppressing his grimace as he slowly rose to his feet.

"I would have taken great pleasure in making you walk barefoot." Melantha swung herself lightly up onto her horse. "Unfortunately, I cannot permit you to slow us down."

Roarke frowned. "Slow you down?"

"We can hardly have ye trailin' after us on foot, now, can we?" said Magnus, leading Eric's and Myles's horses to them. "Especially with that backside of yours laced full of stitches. It would take us over a week to get home."

"Home?" Myles looked uncertainly at Roarke.

" 'Tis not that far," Lewis assured him as he freed the warrior's ankles. "Two days' journey at most."

"Why in the name of St. Columba do you want to take us there?" asked Donald. "You've taken our weapons and our valuables. What more do you want?"

"They intend to slaughter us like helpless animals before their people," Eric surmised direly. "Then they will spear our heads on pikes to rot as a warning to others!"

"Good Lord, lad, wherever do ye get such foul notions?" wondered Magnus, looking genuinely horrified. "I'll have ye know we're God-fearin' thieves, not heathen savages."

"Then why are you taking us with you?" demanded Roarke.

"We want to see how much you're worth to your laird."

Roarke looked at Colin in disbelief. "You intend to ransom us?"

"You MacTiers have stolen much from our clan. We intend to use you to get some of what belongs to us back."

Roarke tightened his jaw, struggling to keep his sorely frayed temper under control. It was bad enough that he had been shot in the arse, robbed, and made a prisoner by the very outlaws he had been sent to capture. But to be imprisoned and held for ransom by this preposterous little party was more humiliation than he could bear. He could just imagine MacTier's reaction when his laird received the missive from the Falcon demanding payment. Once he recovered from his shock, his laird would be infuriated that his finest warrior had failed in what Roarke had assured him would be a childishly simple mission. After years of brilliant service, in which Roarke had successfully led scores of men into the bloodiest of battles and on the most harrowing of raids, he had come to this. He had been captured by an asp-tongued wisp of a girl in coarse leggings and a battered steel helmet, a decrepit old man who looked as though he might trip and impale himself on his own sword at any moment, and three striplings who barely qualified as grown men, never mind warriors.

Everything he had fought so tenaciously to procure for himself these past twenty years would be completely, irretrievably lost.

"You have no hope of securing a ransom for us," he said flatly. "Laird MacTier will not pay."

Magnus scratched his white head. "Why not, lad? Does he not like ye?"

"To pay for our return would subject all of his warriors to the risk of being trapped and ransomed in the future," Roarke explained. "MacTier cannot possibly agree to your demands."

"You had best hope that you four hold a special place in your laird's heart," Melantha warned, "or there is no value to our letting you live."

"He will not pay," Roarke insisted. "You should take what you want and release us. I give you my solemn word that we will not seek you out, but will simply return to our holding."

"Now, that's a joke," scoffed Finlay. "Expecting us to trust the word of a MacTier."

"You came here to kill us, yet you expect us to release you?" A bitter laugh erupted from Colin's throat.

"I am trying to prevent you from doing something that will only endanger you and your people," Roarke replied. "By ransoming us, you will infuriate Laird MacTier, and I warn you, his wrath will be awesome."

"We are well acquainted with MacTier's vile ways," Melantha snapped. "Now get on your horse, or I shall have Magnus shoot another arrow into you to get you moving."

Magnus fitted his prized arrow against the string of his bow. "Take yer time decidin', laddie. Truth be told, I'm curious to see how this shaft flies."

Roarke muttered a curse, then reluctantly limped to his horse and heaved himself up, gritting his teeth against the pain the movement cost him.

Realizing they had no choice, his men did the same.

"My men will form a ring around you at all times," Melantha informed her prisoners. "If any of you try to break from the group, you will be shot—is that clear?"

"If I am shot, I will kill two of you with my bare hands before I hit the ground," vowed Eric darkly.

Magnus chuckled. "Got a real fire in yer ballocks, don't ye, laddie? Ye remind me of myself when I was a lad. What ye need, if ye don't mind my sayin' so, is a good, strong woman to put out some of those flames."

"I was just saying the very same thing," said Donald, amused.

"I could tell ye tales that would make yer eyes pop right out of yer heads!" bragged Magnus, pulling himself up onto his horse. "I'll have ye know that in my youth, I was known all across Scotland for the glorious feats I performed." His eyes twinkled with pleasure as he settled into his saddle and urged his mount forward. "Of course in those days, I was known as Magnus the Magnificent. . . ."

She hated them.

Her animosity festered like a weeping wound, filling her with such acrid loathing she was scarcely aware of anything else. Not hunger, nor weariness, nor even the pain of her aching muscles could detract from the emotions roiling through her as the little party rode north.

There was bitter irony to the fact that she was taking these MacTiers to her holding, as opposed to trying to drive them away. Here she was, leading this murdering scum back to the very place where they had already inflicted horrendous misery and destruction. MacTier had sent his forces once before. For one hideous day they had held her people in the jaws of terror, slaughtering men, terrorizing the women and children, and stripping the cottages and castle of every object of beauty or value. It had been the end of Melantha's life, or at least the end of the life she had known. In those agonizing hours she went from being a laughing girl, who had lived safely sheltered within the glorious heather-covered mountains that surrounded the MacKillon lands, to being an inferno of pain and rage that threatened to consume her within its flames if she but let it.

Her people would be terrified when they arrived, of that there could be no doubt. But once they understood that these despicable warriors were the key to forcing Laird MacTier to make restitution for all he had wrought upon them, her clan would see she had made the right decision. The only other choice was to murder these men, and despite the suffering the MacTiers had so cruelly inflicted upon her and her people, somehow she could not bring herself to do that. Magnus was right—she and her men were thieves, not cold-blooded murderers. Her loathing of the MacTiers was absolute, but she would not permit them to turn her into one of them. To do so would be to let them wrest away the last few shreds of her integrity, leaving her but a cold, vacant shell of the girl she had once been.

She would not let them have that final victory.

"The light is falling," observed Colin, riding up to her. "We should find a place to make camp."

Melantha studied the soft glaze of slate and peach seeping through the canopy of trees overhead. Afternoon had melted into early evening, and the air was cool and fragrant with the scent of crushed pine and sweet earth. It was as good a moment as any to stop. But she had been away from her younger brothers for well over a week, and she was longing to see them again. The prospect of closing the distance between her and Daniel, Matthew, and Patrick, even by just a few more miles, was far more enticing than the promise of rest.

"Do you think Magnus is tired?" Her voice was low so the old man would not hear her.

"He doesn't seem to be," Colin replied, glancing back at the white-haired elder.

". . . and then I raised my rusty sword," Magnus was boasting, lifting his sword in the air for effect, "which was so blunt ye could scarce have used it to carve butter, and with my broken arm hanging at my side, I cut down every one of those murderin' rascals, till all eight of them lay in a twitching, bloody heap before me...."

The MacTier warriors kept their expressions politely composed as Magnus recited his wildly exaggerated tale. Magnus mistook their skeptical silence for rapt fascination, and immediately launched into another story.

"We will ride on," Melantha decided. "That way there will be less of a journey tomorrow."

"It has been a long day, Melantha," Colin reminded her gently.

"I'm fine, Colin."

"I wasn't thinking of you—I was thinking of me having to endure another hour of Magnus's outlandish stories." He smiled, then turned his horse and rode back to join the others.

"... and then there was the time I had to battle a terrible, two-headed beastie," Magnus continued excitedly, "with naught but my trusty sword, which nearly melted when the horrible creature breathed its ghastly fire upon it...."

Melantha inhaled deeply, savoring the spicy tang of pine and earth. The smell of life, her father used to call it. *Breathe deep, lass,* he would say, thumping his great barrel of a chest. *Breathe deep, my bonny Mellie, and know that the woods and meadows and sky and dirt of this blessed place are part of you. Never forget that, my sweet lass. God has blessed you by making you part of the most glorious place on earth.* And Melantha would puff out her skinny little chest and draw in a great gasp of air until she thought she would surely burst, and as she held it her cheeks would swell into two bulging apples, which would always make her father laugh.

She would have given anything to hear her father's laughter again.

A rustling sound tore her from her thoughts. Looking ahead, she saw a deer burst from the trees, then disappear.

Melantha instantly bent low over Morvyn and urged him into a gallop as she freed an arrow from her quiver. There was no time to inform the others—the deer was moving too fast. She could not risk losing it to the thick forest and the rapidly fading light. She and Morvyn thundered in and out of trees, heedless of the branches that clawed at them. Morvyn snorted with excitement as he pounded through the woods, sensing Melantha's urgency and eager to please her.

It had been a long time since her people had enjoyed the taste of venison, for the animals that had once crowded the woods on their lands had been all but eradicated by a devastatingly cold winter. By the time spring finally arrived, most of the poor beasts lay frozen and starved, their bodies shredded by wolves. Hunting parties had only produced small game, which was scarcely adequate to feed her people, especially since the MacTiers had either stolen or slaughtered all their livestock. This single deer could not begin to feed Melantha's entire clan, but its precious meat and hide would be a welcome treasure nonetheless. She thought of her brothers with their thin little arms and rawboned legs, and the pleasure that would light their gaunt faces when she returned home with a fine deer.

"Faster, Morvyn," she urged. "Come on, faster!"

Morvyn snorted and flew forward. The light dulled to a flat gray as they pressed deeper into the woods, but Melantha's hunting senses were keen and she knew the deer was not far ahead. Another few yards and they were nearly upon it. She took careful aim, guiding Morvyn with her legs as she kept her gaze locked upon her prey.

A massive fallen tree suddenly obstructed their path. She scrambled to grab the reins and pull Morvyn back, but he had already begun to jump. Melantha clutched wildly at his thick mane as he struggled to heave his massive body over the unexpected barricade.

His right foreleg slammed into the heavy trunk, making

an ugly crunching sound. Morvyn screeched in agony while Melantha cried out and vainly tried to shield herself as they crashed to the ground.

"... and then there was the time I had to rescue my fair Edwina from a rascal band of Campbells," continued Magnus excitedly, "who were so bewitched by her comeliness that I had to hack them into bloody, steaming chunks of—here now, what's that noise?"

"Sweet Jesus!" swore Roarke, hearing Melantha's cry. He kicked his heels deep into his horse and galloped into the woods ahead.

"Here, now, ye can't be ridin' off like that!" protested Magnus, fumbling for his bow and arrow. "Ye're a prisoner!"

"You'll have to forgive him," apologized Donald. "I'm afraid he doesn't have much experience with being held captive."

"Stay with the others!" snapped Colin to Lewis and Finlay before thundering after Roarke.

Roarke tore through the woods as fast as his mount would carry him, heedless of the pain of his wound. A trail of broken branches and freshly churned earth indicated the path Melantha and her horse had taken, but the light had waned, making it difficult to follow the course at such a reckless speed. After a few moments he cursed in frustration and abruptly stopped, uncertain which direction to pursue. A pain-filled whicker reverberated through the trees. Roarke urged his charger forward again, crashing through the forest like a madman. Finally he saw her horse lying helplessly on the ground, whinnying in pain. Melantha lay in a crumpled heap beside him, unmoving.

Roarke dismounted quickly and limped toward her. Kneeling down, he grasped her shoulders with his bound hands and turned her over. Her face was pale and still, save for a crimson stream leaking from a deep gash in her forehead. A faint gust of breath trickled from her, thin and shallow as a baby bird's, but there nonetheless.

"Melantha."

Her eyes flickered open. Once again the hard edge of her anger had softened, transforming her into a far different girl from the one who had snapped that if he died it would merely save her the trouble of killing him. The woman he held in his lap was as beautiful and enigmatic as she was fragile. They were enemies, but in this shadowy, stolen moment, as she gazed up at him with those magnificent forest-colored eyes, he found he was drawn to her.

It had been nearly two years since he had touched a woman, for the coarse, unwashed whores who had been available to him and his army as he fought on behalf of his clan and King Alexander had held no appeal to him whatsoever. He had all but forgotten what it was like to feel the soft silk of a woman's lips caress his own, to know the sweet pulse of her breath as it fluttered against his cheek, warm and filled with promise. He longed to touch the creaminess of Melantha's earth-smudged cheek, to trace his fingers along the delicate line of her jaw, and rake his fingers through the dark tangle of her hair.

Unable to control himself, he bent his head and captured her mouth with his.

The whisper of her breath froze and her body stiffened, but she did not push him away.

"*Get the hell off her, you bastard!*"

The words crashed over them like freezing water. Roarke shifted Melantha off his lap and clumsily rose, preparing to face Colin's rage.

"*No!*" shrieked Melantha, scrambling to her feet. She threw herself against Roarke, knocking him back a step before turning to face Colin.

"I'm going to kill him!" he vowed savagely, his sword raised.

"It isn't what you think, Colin!"

His eyes grew wide. "My God, Melantha, you're bleeding!"

She raised her hand to her forehead, then stared in confusion at the scarlet staining her fingertips.

"You fell from your horse," Roarke explained. "You must have struck your head in the fall."

Melantha turned her gaze to the injured beast. "Morvyn!"

Her mount attempted to rise, then whickered in pain and collapsed to the ground once again.

"Oh, God," cried Melantha, racing over to him. "You're all right, my sweet lad, you're fine," she crooned, gently stroking the animal as she surveyed his legs, trying to ascertain which one he had injured. "Colin, please help me with Morvyn," she pleaded brokenly.

"If you try to escape, I will slaughter your men," Colin promised Roarke. "Do you understand?"

Roarke nodded.

" 'Tis his right foreleg," Melantha reported as Colin knelt beside her.

Colin expertly ran his hands over Morvyn's rapidly swelling leg. The horse whinnied with pain and tried to pull away.

"Easy, now," said Colin, stroking the horse to calm him. "Rest easy."

Morvyn studied him a moment, his velvety nostrils flaring with each rapid breath, his eyes dark and filled with suffering. Colin continued to stroke the animal's neck, murmuring low words of reassurance. Finally Morvyn lay back against the ground and permitted Colin to finish his examination.

"Is it bad?" asked Melantha, biting her lip.

Colin eased the horse's swollen foreleg onto the ground. "I fear it's broken, Melantha."

"No." She shook her head.

"Poor Morvyn must have struck it very hard when he

tried to clear this tree." Colin's tone was low and soothing, as if he were speaking to a distressed child. "His bones are not as strong as they once were, and his leg just cracked."

"It isn't cracked," Melantha insisted, laying her hand protectively on Morvyn's sweat-soaked shoulder. "It's just sore and swelling a bit, that's all."

"He cannot stand, Melantha," Colin pointed out, gently placing his hand over hers. "He cannot move." He hesitated a moment before quietly stating, "We've no choice but to end his pain."

"*No!*" She knocked Colin's hand away. "You'll not touch him, Colin, do you understand? Not you, nor anyone else. It's my fault he's injured. I'll tend to him."

"We've no time for that, Melantha. We have to get these MacTier prisoners back to our holding—"

"The MacTiers can wait," Melantha interrupted. "It will soon be dark, so we have to stop anyway. We'll make camp right here, and I'll tend to Morvyn, and by morning the swelling in his leg will have eased and he'll be fit enough to stand."

Colin regarded her with aching regret. "He'll never stand again, Melantha. You must accept that."

"You're wrong. And I'll not let you kill him when it's my fault for riding him so fast when the light was falling and he was tired. I caused him to miss that jump, Colin," she said, her voice nearly breaking. "I'll not let you slay him for something that was my fault."

Roarke studied her. He had thought her cold and unfeeling, but he had been mistaken. The same woman who had shown not the tiniest fragment of concern for him when he had been wounded was now almost shattered by the possibility of losing her beloved horse.

At that moment he would have let her build a cottage around the damn animal and stay here for as long as she wished, as long as it made her happy.

"Very well, Melantha," Colin relented. He laid his hand with tender familiarity upon her cheek, a gesture that Roarke found both telling and a little irritating. "We will make camp here, and you can tend to him."

Melantha swallowed thickly. "Thank you."

"But if he cannot stand come morning," Colin continued seriously, "we have to end his misery."

"He will stand," Melantha assured him in a small, fierce voice. "I will see to it."

"So this is where ye be hidin'," said Magnus, emerging through the trees. "We've been searchin' all of God's green earth tryin' to find—good Lord, lass, what's happened to yer head?"

"It's nothing," Melantha assured him.

"Ye've cracked yer pate and ye're halfway to bleedin' to death, and ye call that nothing?"

"It's Morvyn who has been injured," Melantha said adamantly. "I need some strips of linen or wool to bind around his leg to stop the swelling. Lewis, have you any extra fabric in your bag?"

Lewis shook his head. "You're welcome to have my plaid, Melantha."

"Now, there's a sight I don't much care to see," said Finlay. "Little Lewis's freckled arse polishing his saddle all through the mountains."

Lewis regarded Finlay with irritation. "Melantha needs some fabric. Besides, my shirt is almost long enough to cover me."

"I've a better idea, Lewis," said Colin. "Each of you take your dirks and cut a length off your plaids, but not so much that you can't secure them around your waists. Between the four of us, we should have enough cloth to bind poor old Morvyn's leg."

"You'll have more than enough between the eight of us," interjected Roarke.

Melantha looked at him in surprise. "You would spare us some of your plaid?"

Roarke shrugged. "I hate to see an animal in pain."

"Of course you do." Colin's tone was flagrantly sarcastic. "That's what you MacTiers are known for—your soft hearts."

Roarke ignored him and kept his gaze fixed on Melantha. "You may take whatever you need from our plaids."

"You seem to forget, you're our prisoners," pointed out Finlay. "We don't need your permission to take something from you."

"Now, Finlay, let's not be rude," scolded Magnus. " 'Tis most obliging of Roarke here to make such an offer. Most obliging."

Melantha stared at Roarke a long moment. His expression was utterly composed, revealing no trace of the kiss they had shared moments earlier. Her body stirred at the memory. Shame washed through her, making her feel small and soiled.

Had her father been alive to hear that she had not resisted the touch of her clan's sworn enemy, he would have been mortified.

"I don't want your plaid," she said coldly.

Roarke shrugged. "If you change your mind, my offer stands."

"She won't be changing her mind," Colin snarled, glaring at Roarke. "Lewis, cut the plaids and help Melantha tend to Morvyn. Magnus and Finlay, get these MacTiers secured to trees so we can make camp. We will stop here for the night." He shoved Roarke toward a tree.

Pushing aside her shame for the moment, Melantha focused on the task of helping Morvyn. She ordered Lewis to cut the swaths of fabric he collected from the other men into narrow strips while she went to a nearby stream and filled a leather pouch with water. Then she tied the strips of wool together, dipped them into the frigid water, and carefully wrapped the sodden bandage around Morvyn's swollen leg. He endured her ministrations stoically, although it was clear it pained him to have his foreleg handled. Once the leg was thickly sheathed in cold wrapping, Melantha poured more icy water on it, trying to chill his throbbing flesh and keep the swelling to a minimum.

"Shall I fetch more water for you, Melantha?" asked Lewis.

She nodded. "Fill this pouch, and empty my saddlebag and see if it will hold water as well. Morvyn must be thirsty by now, and I'm going to have to keep chilling this bandage through the night if I'm to get the swelling down. The cold will help to ease his pain as well."

"How's he farin', lass?" asked Magnus, going over to join her as Lewis left.

"Better." Melantha gently stroked her horse's neck. In truth she could not discern any improvement, but she was not about to admit that. "I'm certain by tomorrow he'll be able to stand."

"Of course he will, lass," Magnus agreed. "A few hours of rest, and old Morvyn will be as fit as ever. A true warrior can't be kept down by something as paltry as a banged shin, ye know. Why, courage runs thick as oatmeal in his veins, just as it did in yer father's."

Melantha nodded.

"Well, then, how about I clean that nasty nip on yer head?" he suggested brightly. "It seems to have stopped bleedin', so I'm thinkin' I can spare ye my stitches—though I'm happy to give ye a tuck or two if ye'd like."

"I'm fine, Magnus," said Melantha, wholly uninterested in the state of her forehead.

"Ye're not ridin' home sportin' a mess like that, or old MacKillon will have me hauled before the council demandin' an explanation." He dipped the frayed end of his plaid into the pouch of water Lewis deposited beside them. "First they'll be wonderin' why yer helmet wasn't on yer head where it's supposed to be."

Melantha winced as Magnus daubed at the dried blood. "I was hunting a deer. I only wear my helmet for raiding."

"Seems to me ye nearly bashed yer skull in, all the same," Magnus observed. "Which suggests yer helmet should have been on yer head."

Melantha sighed. It was useless to argue. Ever since she had agreed to let Magnus be part of her band of thieves, the aged warrior had appointed himself Melantha's guardian. Whether they were raiding sheep or attacking a party of unsuspecting travelers, Melantha could always be sure that Magnus was near, ready to fly to her rescue if he decided she needed him. Although often this resulted in his charging forward at inopportune moments, occasionally he actually did help her.

His presence had certainly been beneficial when Roarke was about to cut her head off.

"There, now," Magnus said, surveying his work with satisfaction. "If ye're lucky, ye'll not have a scar."

"I don't care if it scars."

"No, of course ye don't." Magnus chuckled, shaking his head. "That's because ye're too busy thinking of ways to rob MacTier to be concerned with yer own appearance. If yer father could see ye gallopin' around the woods in leggings and chain mail, he'd be wonderin' just what kind of wild lass he'd raised."

"He'd be proud," Lewis interjected loyally as he dropped an armful of grasses by Morvyn's head. "Proud."

"Well, I suppose he might be at that," allowed Magnus, his mouth curved in a reluctant smile. "There, now, ye'd best leave poor old Morvyn to rest and get some sleep yerself, lass. There's naught more ye can do for him tonight."

"I have to keep wetting his bandage to keep the swelling down—but I'll get some rest," she promised quickly, seeing Magnus was about to argue.

"See that ye do. And eat somethin', " he added sternly, "or I'll open yer mouth and cram the food in for ye." With that unlikely threat he went and stretched out by the fire.

Roarke lay on his good side with his arms and legs bound, watching Melantha. Despite her assurances to Magnus, she did not eat. Instead she remained by her horse, crooning to him in a low, gentle voice as she squeezed cold water on his injured leg and tried to coax him to eat.

The night deepened to a silver-flecked cape of black before she finally yielded to her weariness. Still, she did not find a place for herself beside the low flames of the fire. Instead she withdrew her sword and curled up beside Morvyn's head, keeping one hand ready upon her weapon and the other lightly resting upon her horse's neck.

It was much later when Roarke finally spoke, sensing that she, like he, could not sleep. "Even if his leg is not broken, it is certain he is finished with riding," he observed quietly.

Silence stretched between them.

"I know," Melantha finally admitted, her voice barely a whisper.

"Then why do you fight so hard to save him?"

He could not see her clearly through the darkness, but he knew she had begun to stroke her horse. "One does not reward a friend for years of loyalty and service by getting rid of him the minute he is no longer of value. Morvyn deserves more than that."

"But if tomorrow he cannot stand, what will you do?"

"He will stand," Melantha assured him fiercely. "And then I will take him home, where he belongs."

"To what end?" persisted Roarke, trying to understand. "His days of carrying you on his back are finished."

"He will rest until his leg has healed," Melantha replied,

"and then he can spend the rest of his days grazing in meadows, feeling the sun warm his coat, and watching as one season turns into another. That is far more fitting than to cut his throat and leave him to rot alone in these woods."

"He will slow your journey to your holding."

"I don't expect a MacTier to understand," she retaliated scornfully. "You would leave one of your own men to die, if taking him with you meant you would be inconvenienced."

"I am a warrior. I do not have the luxury of fretting over one injured soldier or horse. I make my decisions based on the greater benefit to my men and my clan. That is what a leader does."

"I am also a leader," Melantha informed him coolly. "Don't forget, MacTier, I am the infamous Falcon your laird sent you to capture. I have led my men on dozens of raids, and each time we have all returned safely. And I would no sooner leave one of my men behind, or my horse, than I would take out my sword and run them through with it. To do so would not only be despicably selfish, it would also be cowardly."

Roarke closed his eyes, dismissing her as he prepared to get some sleep.

The lass was scarcely more than a child, an unruly girl playing at being a brigand and a thief, so she could bring some pretty treasures home to her clan and impress them with her prowess. She could not possibly understand the unfathomably ugly decisions a warrior had to make as he fought to honor his clan and protect the men fighting alongside him.

But as he listened to the gentle whisper of her voice soothing her injured horse, he could not help but be moved by her misguided compassion.

And feel strangely guilty that tomorrow he would seize her and drag her back to his laird for retribution.

CHAPTER 3

"By God, lass, ye've got the touch!"

"He's not fully standing yet, Magnus," said Colin, watching as Melantha slowly coaxed her horse to his feet. "We don't know if he can walk."

"You'll walk, won't you, lad?" asked Melantha softly as she rubbed the animal's injured leg. "You're just afraid to put your weight on your leg because you remember how terribly it pained you yesterday—but you're better now, aren't you?" She eased his heavy foot to the ground. "There, you see? That barely hurts at all."

Morvyn gingerly shifted some weight on his tightly bandaged limb.

Then he whickered and drew it back up again.

Roarke cursed silently.

"Now, that won't do," Melantha admonished, laying her hands firmly upon Morvyn's leg. "I know it's sore, but the swelling is down and we've got to get moving, so I need you to be a brave lad and endure it until we get home. Come, now, I'll help you, all right?" She eased the aching limb to the ground once more.

Everyone held their breath as Morvyn tentatively placed his hoof on the ground, keeping all of his weight on his other legs.

"There's a good fellow," praised Melantha, stroking his silky nose. "Now let's try a little step."

She took hold of his bridle and slowly walked forward. Morvyn stretched his neck as far as he could without actually moving. When Melantha kept walking, he had no choice but to take a faltering step with her.

"Look!" exclaimed Lewis. "He's walking!"

"Melantha said he would, didn't she?" demanded Finlay, as if there had never been any doubt.

"Aye, she did!" Magnus slapped Colin heartily on the back. "And when that lass makes up her mind about something, there's no use tellin' her she can't have it!"

Roarke watched with relief as Melantha led her beloved horse in a circle through the trees. The poor beast was slow and limping, but his tightly swathed leg was taking the burden of his weight relatively well, which meant the bone was not broken after all.

"I was sure that horse was finished yesterday," mused Donald, shaking his head in amazement. "I'd have wagered money on it."

"As would I," admitted Myles. "But she was determined he would walk, wasn't she?"

"Aye," said Roarke. "She was."

"That horse is a warrior," observed Eric with gruff

approval. "A warrior forces himself not to think of his pain."

"That's a good lad," murmured Melantha, caressing Morvyn behind the ears. "That's my good, brave lad." She gave Colin a triumphant smile. "As long as we move slowly and give him time to rest, he'll be fine."

Colin nodded. "Then let's be off. At this rate it will take us all day to get home."

"I'll ride with you," said Melantha, leading her horse over to him. "Morvyn can follow behind us."

"All right, then, lads, up ye go," said Magnus, gesturing to Roarke and his men. "There's a long ride ahead, but fear not—I've plenty more tales to keep ye entertained!"

"Wonderful," Roarke muttered, awkwardly hoisting himself up onto his horse.

The little party set out, its cumbersome pace dictated entirely by Morvyn. This meant they plodded along at scarcely more than a walk, stopping every couple of miles to enable the limping beast to rest. Not once did any of Melantha's men complain or question the wisdom of her decision. Instead they seemed genuinely delighted that the hobbling creature was faring as well as it was, and took turns assuring Melantha that once they were home Morvyn would soon be as fit as ever. Whatever weaknesses the Falcon may have had as a leader, it was clear her men respected her enough to abide by her decisions, even when it meant saving a crippled horse that would never be of use to anyone again.

Had the decision been his, Roarke would have cut the limping creature's throat and left it to die in the cool, fragrant green of the forest.

"They're back!"
"The Falcon has returned!"

The first excited cries startled Roarke as they reverberated from high within the branches over his head. Melantha's people had a decided propensity for hiding up in trees, he reflected.

Curiosity to see the Falcon's holding, coupled with a lack of opportunity to escape, had ultimately made Roarke resign himself to the prospect of being presented to Melantha's clan as a prisoner. This had the benefit of enabling him to lead a force back to retrieve all of the valuables that had been stolen from his clan. Within minutes the news of their arrival was rippling far beyond the woods, and by the time they emerged from the forest people were racing toward them, their smiling faces flushed with excitement.

" 'Tis good to be home again." Magnus sighed happily.

Roarke stared in confusion at the castle rising before him.

He had not wasted any time contemplating the appearance of the Falcon's holding. Nevertheless, he was completely unprepared for the crumbling pile of stones standing precariously in the middle of a scrubby field. He scanned the rest of the meadow, searching for the keep that was actually being used by these people. There was nothing more except a scattering of small, bleak cottages dotting the dry grasses. At least a half dozen of these had been reduced to roofless walls and blackened rubble, apparently consumed by fire. The other cottages were a patchwork of old stone and new, with fresh thatch covering the rooftops. Evidently these huts had also recently been claimed by fire, but Melantha's people had managed to salvage them.

"Recognize this place?" demanded Colin sarcastically.

Roarke rode slowly toward the forlorn looking castle, saying nothing.

It seemed the stronghold had once been an attractive structure of salmon-colored stone that was quite different from the bleak gray fortresses to which Roarke was accustomed. Enormous care had been taken to quarry rock of this pleasing color, and the effect was a building that rose warmly against the lavender and slate of the early evening sky. He could easily imagine how handsome the holding had been before it fell into such sad disrepair, especially when the surrounding fields were green and the sun lit the stone to a fiery glow. The rock itself had been neatly cut and artfully pieced together around many large windows, which although attractive, instantly struck Roarke as a weakness. Even the gate was handsomely framed with an intricate arch of beautifully arranged stone, giving the entrance an elegant, welcoming look, as opposed to the forbidding countenance it should have manifested. There were four high, rounded towers of handsome proportions, but like the rest of the fortress they were scarred and decrepit—the result of too many attacks and the unforgiving wear of time. It baffled Roarke that no one here had thought to orchestrate the castle's repair. Perhaps these people lacked either the skill or the initiative to undertake such a mammoth task.

They rode through the black jaws of the gate and entered the courtyard, where Melantha's people were excitedly scrambling to assemble themselves. Their ruddy faces were bright with pleasure, making it clear that the return of the Falcon and her band was cause for celebration. Some of them had raised cups of ale into the air, while a bent, white-haired fellow who looked even more ancient than Magnus had balanced himself precariously on a small platform and was now awkwardly struggling to hoist his bagpipes onto his bony shoulder. There was a palpable energy to the people as they poured from the castle, hastily adjusting their gowns and plaids in a valiant attempt to improve their rather peculiar appearance.

They were clad in gowns, shirts, tunics, and plaids of every quality and description, from the absolutely threadbare to the costliest and finest. Men were dressed in tattered brown

and green plaids that had been paired with intricately embroidered, ill-fitting shirts, or handsome plaids of varying
colors were draped over tunics that seemed little better than
rags. The women were predominantly garbed in drab gowns
of worn wool, over which many of them had tied colorful
sashes and shawls of rare silk. Several older women even wore
elegantly stitched gowns of exquisite beauty, but it was
eminently clear from their poor fit that these dresses had
not been created with the present wearer in mind. Roarke
noticed that most of the clan's footwear was cracked and
worn, but there were a number of men sporting heavy deerskin boots that seemed a size or two too large, and some
women garbed in tattered dresses had squeezed their feet
into richly ornamented slippers. All the men had dirks
strapped to their waists and handsomely crafted swords
gleaming at their sides. But a closer inspection revealed that
the hilts were pocked with gaping, empty sockets where jewels had once nested.

The children also wore ragged plaids and gowns, and
had either bare feet or rough scraps of leather bound to their
soles with thin cord. It was the children's faces, however,
that most disturbed Roarke. Although well scrubbed and lit
with anticipation, they invariably bore the same hollowed
cheeks and sharply defined jaws that Roarke had noticed in
Melantha. These children also knew the cruel ache of hunger,
at a time in their life when they needed wholesome food
in abundance.

A few members of the clan suddenly noticed the bound
wrists of Roarke and his men. Their expressions grew wary,
and some of the women grabbed their children and moved
protectively in front of them. Roarke wondered at the obvious alarm. Certainly in their current position, stripped of
their weapons and with their hands bound, he and his men
posed little threat to them.

"Good Lord, Melantha," sputtered a tiny, shriveled-looking

man who shuffled forward from the crowd, "what in the name of St. Columba have you brought home this time?"

"I bring you two sacks of hares and birds, Laird MacKillon," replied Melantha, climbing down from Colin's horse and tossing the sacks onto the ground. "And four pairs of boots, eight dirks, eight leather satchels, five pounds of oats, two good blankets, two wooden cups, and four good swords." She retrieved two more sacks from Finlay and Lewis and threw them down. "Magnus will see to it that it is divided as fairly as possible."

Roarke recalled how Melantha had refused to sample even a small portion of the meat she and Colin had killed. As he looked at the thin faces of the children staring hungrily at the bags filled with game, the reason for her restraint was amply clear.

Everything the Falcon's band either killed or stole was brought here and divided among the members of their clan.

"Well, now, that's splendid," praised Laird MacKillon, bobbing his white head happily. "Simply splendid." He turned to his people. "Let's raise a cheer to the Falcon and her men, who have once again brought us wonderful gifts."

A restrained cheer rose into the air, tempered by the crowd's concern over Roarke and his warriors.

"Splendid!" praised Laird MacKillon, apparently oblivious to his people's lack of enthusiasm. "Thor, are you ready?"

"Aye." The old man on the platform took his mouthpiece between his lips and inhaled a wheezy breath.

An unbearable whining blasted through the air. Mercifully, the piece was cut short when the elder suddenly broke into a phlegmy fit of coughing. While this was infinitely better than the screech of the pipes, Roarke grew concerned that the ancient musician was going to expire from lack of air, topple off the platform and smash his head open.

"Here, Thor," called a scrawny young boy who rushed toward him with a cup.

The old man grabbed the goblet and greedily downed its contents. Then he wiped his mouth on his sleeve and released an impressive belch.

"Thank you," he said, cheerfully waving up at the sky. "You know I'll not mind going when my time has come, but t'would be a wretched shame for it to end in the middle of such a glorious piece of music." He belched loudly again. "That ale has nearly done the trick, Keith," he said to the lad, "but I'd best have another cup just to be safe."

The boy took his goblet and ran off to fill it again.

"You must be tired after such a long and perilous journey," said Laird MacKillon. He began to shuffle toward the main entrance of the castle. "Come inside and have something to eat."

"Forgive me, MacKillon," apologized a balding man whose tailored shirt of fine linen strained so tautly across his chest and belly Roarke was certain it was about to burst. "Don't you think we should inquire about the prisoners?"

Laird MacKillon stopped and scratched his head. "Prisoners, Hagar? What prisoners?"

"The men Melantha has brought with her," Hagar explained, pointing.

Laird MacKillon squinted at Roarke and his men. Suddenly his white brows shot up. "God's bonnet," he said, shocked. "Melantha, why do our guests have their hands bound?"

"Unfortunately, Laird MacKillon," she began, "we ran into a little trouble—"

"A little trouble?" interrupted MacKillon. "I think not. These big brutes look as though they could give you a great deal of trouble." He waved a gnarled hand at Roarke, beckoning him to approach.

Roarke obligingly eased himself off his horse, trying to minimize his limp as he approached the aged laird.

"Tell me, lad, are you from the Sutherlands, then?"

"No," said Roarke.

"I thought not," MacKillon hastily assured him. "Not even the Sutherlands grow them as big and ferocious looking as you young wolves." He scratched his nose thoughtfully, considering. "You're from the Murrays, aren't you?" he exclaimed suddenly, pleased that he had sorted it out.

"No."

"No, no, of course you aren't," MacKillon agreed, waving his hand dismissively in the air. "Melantha would never be so foolish as to take a Murray prisoner—why, to do so would be seen by Laird Murray as an act of war." He shuffled over to Eric, who glowered down at him. Laird MacKillon's crinkled eyes widened like two great cups.

"Sweet saints, Melantha," he squawked, hastily stepping back, "this fellow looks like a Viking. You haven't gone and kidnapped some of MacLeod's warriors, have you?"

"They are not MacLeods," Melantha assured him.

"Excellent," said Laird MacKillon, clearly relieved. He winked at Eric, as if the two of them shared some private joke. "Forgive me, big fellow—didn't mean to insult you—'tis just that blond hair of yours—quite shocking, really. No doubt you've some Viking blood roaring through those veins of yours, eh? Reminds me of a lass I knew in my youth—a comely little thing she was. Then she married and grew to the size of a cow, with hands and feet like fat loaves of bread. Of course you wouldn't take a MacLeod prisoner, Melantha," he finished, smiling fondly at her. "Now that that's all settled, let us go inside."

"But who are these men?" persisted Hagar.

Laird MacKillon regarded him in confusion. "Didn't we find out?"

"They're from the clan MacTier," supplied Colin.

The crowd gasped.

"MacTiers?" repeated Laird MacKillon blankly. "You've brought MacTiers back to our holding?"

Melantha hesitated, wishing they could discuss the matter elsewhere. "Unfortunately, Laird MacKillon, I had no—"

"By God, *let me at them*!" roared Thor with murderous fury. "I'll strip their flesh from their miserable, thieving bones and grind them up for haggis! Here, Keith, help me off this platform, take my pipes, then run inside and fetch my sword so I can get started."

"They cannot be harmed," Melantha protested. "They are to be ransomed."

Laird MacKillon blinked. "Ransomed?"

"That is our suggestion," qualified Colin, giving Melantha a warning look. "Perhaps we should go inside to discuss this matter."

"Yes, of course," agreed Laird MacKillon, nodding sagely. "Inside is a much better place to attend to a matter of such grave importance. All right, everyone, back to whatever you were doing." He flitted his hands in the air, shooing away his people. "The council and I will consider this important situation and tell you what is happening—as soon as we know ourselves."

"Lewis, take Morvyn to the stable and douse his bandage with cold water," Melantha instructed, handing him her horse's reins. "See that he is given ample fresh water and hay, and that his stall is thick with clean straw. I'll be along to tend to him later," she added, gently stroking Morvyn's nose. "Finlay, you take care of the other horses, and then both of you join us in the great hall."

"Do you think Laird MacKillon will be angry with us for bringing these MacTiers home?" asked Lewis worriedly.

"I will make Laird MacKillon and the council see that we have much to gain from these prisoners. Now go."

Laird MacKillon's order had not caused the crowd to disperse, but it did part to permit Melantha's prisoners entrance into the castle. As Roarke limped forward he was aware of everyone staring anxiously at him. It was clear the MacKillons feared him and his men. He glowered as he passed them, causing some of the women to gasp and step back.

"Here, now, lad, that's no way to act amongst women and children," admonished Magnus sternly. "Shame on ye."

Roarke said nothing. It was not his custom to intimidate women and children, but when the time came for escape, their fear would be a powerful weapon.

The interior of the MacKillon castle was little better than the exterior. Huge chunks of stone were missing from the walls of the great hall, and the holes had been only crudely patched with mud and straw to keep out the wind and rain. The wooden shutters over the windows were smashed, and pitiful shreds of embroidered cloth hung limply from nails embedded in the walls, the sad remnants of rich tapestries that had once decorated the salmon stones. The room was furnished with dark oak tables and benches, most of which were broken and somewhat haphazardly repaired.

Despite its dilapidated state, there was a remarkable aura of cheer in the room. Fires blazed in the massive hearths at both ends of the hall, and coppery flames fluttered from handsomely wrought torches, banishing the grayness of the day's fading light. The tables were neatly set for dining, and although the wooden platters upon them were only sparsely filled with bread, oatcakes, cheese, fish and fruit, massive pink and purple bouquets of heather bloomed everywhere, giving the hall a gay, festive air.

"So here you are, home at last." A short, amply proportioned woman bustled across the hall, impatiently drying her hands on her apron. Her dark hair was liberally striped with gray, and her plain but pleasant face bore the creases of many sleepless nights.

She went straight to Colin and grabbed his beard, handily pulling him down to her level so she could examine him.

"You're thinner than when you left," she observed critically. "Are you hungry? I've a nice broth simmering on the fire if you can't wait for dinner—"

"For God's sake, Beatrice," growled Hagar, "he's a full-grown man, not a squalling bairn. He scarcely needs you coddling him as if he were barely weaned."

"You needn't tell me when he was weaned, Hagar," returned Beatrice, her hand clamped protectively on Colin's shoulder. "I all but gave my life to bring him into this world and I'll do no less than see that he's well looked after while he's in it, and if you don't like it you can just—"

"I'm fine, Mother," Colin interjected, uncomfortably aware that Roarke and his men were watching him with amusement.

"You look terrible," she countered, pinching his cheek. "Scrawny as a starved rat, with dark circles under your eyes that I could see from across the hall. And you, my lass," she railed on, turning to Melantha, "are even skinnier than before, if such a thing is possible. If your dear, sweet mother could see you now, she'd lock you in a chamber and not let you out until you'd put some flesh on those bones, and I warn you I'm strongly tempted to take such a measure. Strongly tempted."

Melantha gazed at Beatrice fondly. She had been subjected to her fretful mothering from the time she was seventeen, when her own mother died. Although Colin found Beatrice's fussing tiresome, Melantha secretly enjoyed it. The burden upon Melantha's young shoulders had grown even heavier when her father was killed the previous autumn, and she often felt impossibly overwhelmed. It was nice to come home and have Beatrice worry about whether she had eaten enough or felt tired.

" 'Tis just these shapeless garments that make me look thin," Melantha protested.

" 'Tis your face I was looking at," objected Beatrice, impatiently dismissing her explanation. She planted her work-reddened hands on her hips and stared at Melantha and Colin with maternal disapproval. "Obviously you two children cannot be trusted to feed yourselves once you're out of my sight."

"I have just the thing for them," announced an attractive, silver-haired woman who appeared from behind the wooden screen leading to the kitchen. "A nice warm cup of my special posset." She smiled, then looked expectantly back at the screen. "Come, now, Gillian, don't be shy."

A pretty girl of about nineteen tentatively emerged, carefully carrying a heavy tray. She kept her gaze fastened on her burden, as if she feared she might spill a precious drop from one of the many cups balanced upon it, but even with this limited view it was obvious to Roarke that the girl was exceptionally lovely. Her skin was as pale as fresh milk, and her features were small and delicate. Her hair was neatly combed and woven into a soft, loose braid, which shone of copper and coral in the flickering torchlight.

"I—I helped Edwina make it," she stammered shyly.

"Did you, now?" said Hagar. "Well, daughter, that's a fine accomplishment indeed. 'Tis not every day a man gets to enjoy a tasty cup of warm posset, now, is it, Colin?"

"No," Colin agreed, smiling at his sister.

"Bless my eyes, Edwina," burst out Magnus, "I swear ye're more beautiful than when I left!"

A rosy flush colored Edwina's wrinkled cheeks. "Foolish talk from a foolish man," she chided, giving Magnus an exasperated look.

"Here, now, I want ye to meet our prisoners," said Magnus, taking no mind of her embarrassment. "This is Donald, that's Myles, and that tall, scowling fellow with the pretty hair is called Eric. And this great big chap is Roarke, who was unlucky enough to receive one of my arrows in his backside. I did a fine job of stitching him closed, though," he boasted, slapping Roarke amiably on the back. "Lift his plaid and look for yerself."

"You've no business stitching with those feeble old eyes of yours," scolded Edwina. "You'll ruin what little sight you have left. Come, lad," she said, sighing. "Let's have a look and see if I need to fix it." She reached for Roarke's plaid.

"Perhaps later," said Roarke, dodging her grasp.

Edwina chuckled. "Ye needn't be shy with me, my lad. I'm too old for such nonsense. Try my posset," she invited, offering him a cup from Gillian's tray. "It will slay your hunger and heal whatever ails you in the bargain."

Roarke obligingly accepted the goblet with his bound hands. "Thank you." He tilted his head politely at Gillian.

Gillian blushed to the roots of her hair.

"Ye're best to toss it down in one gulp," advised Magnus surreptitiously as Edwina offered her posset to Roarke's men.

Roarke frowned at the foamy brew. "Isn't it just warm milk curdled with ale?"

" 'Tis my own special recipe," boasted Edwina, smiling as she distributed the milky concoction among the rest of the group. "I'm teaching Gillian how to make it, so the secret is not lost after I'm gone."

Laird MacKillon raised his cup. "To our brave Melantha and her clever band, safely home once again." He drained the contents of his goblet.

Satisfied that the drink was harmless, Roarke and his men all took a hearty draft.

"By God!" roared Eric, spewing his mouthful onto the floor. "*It's poison!*" He threw down his goblet, splattering its contents all over Gillian's gown in the process.

Gillian stared in horror at her hopelessly ruined gown. Slowly she raised her shimmering eyes to Eric, who glared at her as if she were the deadliest of foes. She cried out in wounded dismay and fled the hall, dropping her tray in the process.

"There, now, swallow and you'll be fine," instructed Edwina to Roarke and his men, who were still choking on the vile mixture. "Perhaps the lass was a wee bit generous with the fish bile in this batch," she acknowledged, sniffing Magnus's cup, "but you'll be glad of its effects later."

Myles wiped his mouth on his sleeve as he manfully tried to keep from retching. "What effects?" he demanded.

" 'Tis marvelous for cleansing the bowels," Edwina reported gaily. "Just the thing a man needs after a long journey and irregular, poorly cooked meals."

Donald looked utterly revolted. "No doubt."

"You will apologize to my sister at the first opportunity," ordered Colin, glaring furiously at Eric. "Although I should have expected such brutish behavior from a swine like you."

"I thought it was poison," Eric said sheepishly. He looked with regret at the screen Gillian had disappeared behind. "I didn't mean to frighten her."

"I'm afraid the lass's feelings are rather tender," explained Hagar. "We all try to be extra gentle with her."

"Well, now, Melantha," said Laird MacKillon, who was digesting his posset without apparent difficulty, "tell us about these prisoners of yours."

"*By God, they're evil, thieving, cursed MacTiers!*" raged Thor, entering the hall with his sword dragging behind him. "What more do you need to know?" His arms quaking, he struggled to lift his weapon.

"Well, I should like to know why Melantha has brought them here," said Laird MacKillon reasonably.

Thor's eyes crinkled with anticipation. "She brought them here so we can hack them to pieces and feed their foul, mangled bodies to the wolves."

"Actually, I brought them here so we could ransom them back to Laird MacTier," Melantha clarified.

"Ransom them?" repeated Laird MacKillon, looking

astonished. "Oh, no, I don't think that's a good idea. Absolutely not."

"Have you completely lost your senses, lass?" demanded Hagar. "To ransom them would make MacTier fearfully angry."

"So I'll chop them up like stewing meat!" offered Thor, hacking at the floor with his weapon. "Then we'll grind their bones to dust, bake it into bread and eat them, so there's no trace of them ever to be found."

"If we just kill them, what will we have gained?" asked Melantha.

"Honor," supplied Laird MacKillon.

"Vengeance," added Hagar.

"Bread," finished Thor.

"I don't know how you can speak so in front of our guests," scolded Edwina, casting the three men a disapproving look. "These look like pleasant enough lads. Have they tried to harm you?"

Magnus shrugged. "Roarke tried to chop off Melantha's head, but I stopped him with an arrow in his arse. Other than that, they haven't been too much trouble."

"I should like to point out that Melantha was trying to kill me at the time," interjected Roarke, sensing that an explanation was needed.

Laird MacKillon raised his white brows in shock. "And that's how you treat a wisp of a lass who is only trying to defend herself?"

"I didn't realize she was a woman—she was dressed in that ridiculous outfit and her face was completely hidden by her helmet. And besides," he finished, "she attacked me first."

"Good gracious, Melantha, were you trying to kill this nice young man?" asked Beatrice, appalled.

"We were robbing them," explained Melantha, "and he had managed to avoid the nets."

"He's a slippery one, all right," agreed Magnus. He winked at Roarke.

"But why have you brought them here?" wondered Hagar. "You never bring prisoners home with you."

"Unfortunately, we learned that these men have been sent by MacTier to crush the Falcon and 'his' band," explained Colin. "As they intended to kill us, that made releasing them somewhat problematic."

"Then it's a bloody, agonizing death to the lot of them!" concluded Thor, ecstatic. "Stand still, you MacTier wretch!" He grunted with effort as he hoisted his sword and took a faltering step toward Roarke.

"Here, now, there'll be no killing without my consent, Thor," said Laird MacKillon, frowning at the elder. "Cease your nonsense and let's hear what Melantha has to say about this ransom business."

Thor huffed with irritation and lowered his weapon.

"As I see it," began Melantha, "we gain far more by ransoming these warriors than we would by killing them—"

"I don't know why you would think that." Thor eyed Eric speculatively. "A big chap like that would make a lot of bread."

"I propose that we use them to regain some of what MacTier has stolen from us," she continued, "and show him we are a force to be reckoned with at the same time."

"But we're not a force to be reckoned with," objected Laird MacKillon. "MacTier already knows that well enough."

"Perhaps we haven't the strength to face MacTier in battle," allowed Melantha, "but it is clear that the Falcon's band has troubled him enough these past few months to make him feel our sting. That is why he sent these warriors to capture us."

"But he doesn't know the Falcon is from this clan," pointed out Hagar. "If we ransom these nasty-looking fellows, he'll have to know that it is we MacKillons who have captured them."

"And he'll be terribly angry with us," added Beatrice worriedly. "I'm afraid I cannot see how that will benefit us at all."

"It will benefit us to regain that which he has stolen from us," explained Melantha. "We will exchange these warriors for food, livestock, clothing, weapons, and gold—all things that were taken from us by the MacTiers when they attacked us last autumn."

Hagar regarded her doubtfully. "What if MacTier agrees to pay us this ransom, and once he has these warriors he turns around and attacks us with his army?"

"The gold must be paid in advance of the release of these prisoners," Melantha explained. "We will use it to buy the alliance of the MacKenzies and the protection of their army."

"Not even MacTier will dare attack us again if he knows that we have such a powerful force ready to come to our aid," said Colin.

Laird MacKillon looked intrigued by the possibility. "An army, you say?"

Hagar stroked his chin. "That would come to our aid whenever we need it?"

Magnus smiled fondly at Melantha. "The lass is just like her father—always thinking."

"Does this mean I don't get to kill these chaps?" grumbled Thor.

"If we ask enough for these warriors, and we secure an alliance with the MacKenzies, then we need never worry about being vulnerable to attack again," said Colin.

"Not only from the MacTiers," finished Melantha, "but from anyone else."

"There is just one small problem."

The little group regarded Roarke in surprise.

"Laird MacTier will never agree to your demands," he informed them seriously. "Other than the issue of his pride, which is considerable, the man is exceptionally fond of his possessions—especially his gold. And as I have already explained to you," he continued, regarding Melantha intently, "to pay a fee for our return would put all his warriors at risk of being ransomed."

Laird MacKillon looked troubled. "Have you considered this, Melantha?"

"These warriors were sent to capture the Falcon's band and are most anxious that their laird not learn that they failed miserably in their mission and are suffering the indignity of being ransomed as well. This is why they would have us believe that there is no point in holding them prisoner." She tossed Roarke a look of contempt. "Besides, how will it appear if MacTier fails to intervene on behalf of his own clansmen?"

"The lass is right," Hagar concurred. "MacTier may be a greedy bastard, but he's not likely to let four of his own be killed just to save a few coins. I say we keep these big chaps for a while and see what MacTier says when he gets our message."

"Very well," said Laird MacKillon. "But what are we to do with them while we wait to hear from MacTier?"

"Throw them in the dungeon and let the rats gnaw on their hot, stinking entrails!" blazed Thor. "A few weeks in the dark with nothing but mossy bread and dank water, and we'll have them telling us what we want to know!"

"Your pardon, Thor, but what is it we want to know?" wondered Laird MacKillon.

"All enemies have secrets," Thor assured him. His face lit up. "If they won't tell us, we shall have to torture them!"

"We don't have a dungeon," Beatrice objected firmly. "And we certainly don't have rats."

Thor's expression fell. "Couldn't we get some?"

"All we have are the storage chambers," reflected Edwina, "and they are a terrible mess. It will take several days to clear one of them out."

"Are there any spare chambers available?" Laird Mac-Killon asked.

Beatrice shook her head. "Every room in the keep is occupied, I'm afraid, and many of the cottages are already housing two families. Someone will have to move out to make room for these gentlemen, or agree to share their chamber."

"Share a chamber with these thieving MacTier cutthroats?" Thor looked outraged by the suggestion. "*Never, I say, never!*"

"If we don't have a dungeon for them and there aren't any spare chambers, where are we to keep them?" Hagar wondered.

"Why don't we just keep them here?" suggested Magnus.

Hagar regarded him in confusion. "In the great hall?"

"Seems to me ye couldn't find a better place to keep a steady eye on them," Magnus reasoned. "After all, there's always someone in here. Should they try to escape, the place would be swarming with men in no time."

Laird MacKillon's expression brightened. "We can set up an area for them down at that end, with beds and a table and a washbasin—"

"—of course we'll need to put up a screen, so they can have a little privacy when they need it—" added Hagar.

"—and a few chairs for sitting upon—" Magnus suggested.

"—they'll be close to the kitchen, so it will be easy to bring them food—" pointed out Edwina.

"—and the fires will keep them warm at night—you know that storage room is rather chilly—" Beatrice added.

Roarke listened in bemused silence as the MacKillons made plans for imprisoning him and his men. It was clear the MacKillons despised the MacTiers, and apparently they had good reason. Yet here were the laird and his closest advisors fussing over Roarke and his men's comfort. It would be most convenient to be held in the main room of this dilapidated castle, where Roarke could witness the activities of the clan and overhear their conversations. Not that these MacKillons seemed the least bit concerned about their prisoners knowing exactly what their plans were. Roarke had no doubt he and his men would be able to escape with little difficulty. The sight of the MacKillon children in their ragged clothes, their faces hollowed by hunger, had given him pause, however. He decided he would delay his departure until he learned more about what exactly had happened here.

"It's all settled then, lads," said Magnus, interrupting his thoughts. "Ye'll stay in the hall for now, and as soon as we can make arrangements for yer comfort downstairs, ye'll have a chamber all to yerselves."

"Do let us know if there is anything else you need," invited Laird MacKillon graciously.

Eric glowered. "I need nothing from the hands of my enemies," he said savagely. "Not food, nor water, nor even—"

"Your concern for our comfort is most appreciated," interjected Donald. "Now that you mention it, a hot bath might be rather pleasant—"

"What time is dinner?" wondered Myles, hungrily eyeing the food on the table.

"They aren't guests," objected Melantha, "they're prisoners."

"Even worse, they're MacTiers!" bellowed Thor.

"Nevertheless, they deserve to be treated with decency," Laird MacKillon said. "I'll not have them being mistreated while they are in our custody—is that clear?"

Thor scowled.

"Thank you, Laird MacKillon," said Roarke, unable to resist casting an amused look at Melantha. "You are a most gracious captor."

"Not at all, lad." He smiled, clearly pleased by the compliment. "Now that that's settled, let's sit down and eat, shall we? Colin, invite the others in. We will tell them of our plans to ransom these fine fellows and gain an army in the process, over dinner."

"You're not suggesting the prisoners should eat with us?" Melantha demanded, appalled.

Laird MacKillon regarded her in confusion. "Have they already dined?"

"As a matter of fact, we haven't," said Roarke cheerfully.

Melantha sent him a glare that could have frozen fire. "As prisoners, they should be fed somewhere else. Perhaps in the kitchen."

"Absolutely not," Beatrice objected. "It's crowded enough in there without these four big brutes getting in everyone's way."

Hagar scratched his balding head. "I don't see why they should have to go somewhere else, Melantha. After all, the great hall is already set up for dining."

"Come then, lads," invited Edwina, ending the debate. "Sit down and have something to eat."

"Thank you." Roarke gave Melantha an infuriating grin as he made his way to the table.

"You must sit at the laird's table, Melantha," said Beatrice, "so you can tell the clan all about the Falcon's latest adventures."

"I'm not hungry."

"Yes, ye are," countered Magnus. "Ye've scarce eaten a bite in more than three days, so sit yerself down and eat."

"No," she managed, feeling bile rise in her throat.

With that she wheeled about and fled the great hall, unable to bear the sight of MacTier warriors comfortably dining in the chamber where but a few months earlier they had wrought such terror and destruction.

Roarke lay on his side, contemplating the languid flicker of the dying torches.

His buttock was throbbing, as was much of his body, but the pain had been dulled somewhat by the enormous quantity of ale he had consumed during dinner. His men had also imbibed heavily, which accounted for the swiftness with which their snoring had rumbled through the hall, even though they were bound hand and foot. Unfortunately, the sanctuary of slumber had long been elusive for Roarke, and despite his profound weariness, tonight was no exception. The relentless ache of his battered bones and muscles, coupled with the melancholy wanderings of his mind, made it difficult to release himself to that quiet refuge. And so he lay in silence, staring at the fading light of the torches, wearily aware that he was only tormenting himself further as he studied their red-gold hue, which in that ale clouded moment exactly matched the color of his beloved daughter Clementina's hair.

It had been several days since the memory of either his little daughter or his wife had permeated his thoughts. The realization filled him with guilt, for it demonstrated that he had abandoned them in death the same way he had abandoned them in life. He had not meant to, but there it was. He was a cold, unfeeling bastard—salubrious traits in a warrior, but utterly despicable in a husband and father.

I am sorry.

He knew his apology was pathetically insufficient. Not that they could hear him, anyway. They lay cold and stiff under the ground, forever sealed in a simple pine coffin, with Muriel holding their tiny daughter in her arms, their faces pale but serene. At least that was what Laird MacTier had told Roarke on that terrible day he returned from his raiding to find his small family dead and buried. *They are at peace,* his laird had assured him. *They are with God.*

Roarke had failed to see how his wife could be at peace. Despondent after the loss of her beloved three-year-old child to a fever, she had taken her own life by eating poisoned berries. But at the time he had not questioned MacTier's description. There had been a modicum of comfort in imagining sweet Muriel at peace, with little Clementina safely wrapped in the loving hold of her mother's arms. He still tried to imagine them lying so, as if they were merely sleeping, and would open their eyes and smile at him if he but chose to wake them. It was ridiculous, of course. A life of raiding and battle had left him intimately acquainted with death, and he knew its foul stench and rotting ugliness too well to believe such a fanciful tale. But during those first few months the image of his wife and daughter lying in gentle slumber had soothed him, and helped to alleviate the unbearable guilt that had threatened to crush him from within.

He swallowed thickly, watching as the torchlight blurred to a watery wash of gold.

All his life he had longed for nothing other than to be a warrior. And that was exactly what he had become, God help him. As a lad it had seemed a life of unparalleled wonder, filled with adventure, daring, and exotic travel. From the time he had first swung the crude wooden sword his father crafted for him, he had known that he was destined for greater things than staying caged within the boundaries of his clan's land. Farming held no appeal for him, and the idea of living his life trapped in a dark, smoky cottage with a shrewish wife and squalling babes had terrified him. And so he had pursued his training with relentless determination, excelling at every exercise, until finally Laird MacTier realized there was nothing to be done except send him off to fight. Over the years Roarke had grown from a green, arrogant lad with more strength than brains into an experienced, arrogant warrior, who loved battle and thought no further than the next conquest. His sworn duty was to his laird and clan. All who knew him understood that. Even Muriel, who had fallen in love with him at the tender age of seventeen and begged him to marry her. Roarke had been all of twenty-nine, and had just been given command of a small army of a hundred men, which at the time was heady stuff indeed. He had informed Muriel that life as a warrior left him no time for the burden of a wife and family, and that he could not possibly be expected to stay at home to tend to them. Muriel assured him that it did not matter, for she loved him and wanted to be his wife.

To have you with me some of the time is far better than not sharing my life with you at all, she had said.

And so he married her, planted a child in her belly, and left, foolishly believing that all was well and she would be content.

Instead he had destroyed her.

"Be quiet, Patrick, or they'll hear you and cut off your head with a giant sword!" whispered an agitated voice.

Suddenly alert, Roarke shoved aside his thoughts and quickly scanned the dimness of the hall.

Three small shadows of varying height were tentatively creeping toward him. It was clear by their careful, if not entirely graceful, movements, that they were trying to make as little noise as possible.

"Why would they do a mean thing like that?" asked the smallest figure. "I haven't done anything."

"They're thieving, bloodthirsty MacTiers, aren't they?" demanded the tallest of the three shadows. "That's what they do for sport—chop the heads off small boys and take them home and eat them!"

Both the middle and small shadows halted.

"H-how small?" stammered the middle shadow.

"You needn't worry, Matthew," the tallest shadow said. "You're too quiet for them to take any notice of you. It's Patrick here who had better watch out!"

"You said it would be safe to look at them, Daniel," the small shadow protested accusingly. "Now you're saying they're going to eat me!"

"I didn't say that," snapped the tall shadow. "I just said you have to be quiet!"

The midsized figure banged into a table, sending a pitcher crashing to the floor.

All three shadows froze.

The racket was enough to rouse the dead, but miraculously, Roarke's men continued to snore. Evidently the ale had impaired their hearing along with all their other senses.

Stricken with terror, the three small shadows remained rooted to the spot. Finally, unable to detect any movement from either Roarke or his men, they exhaled the breaths they had been holding.

"That was close," breathed the tallest shadow. "Do that again, Matthew, and we'll all be dead!"

"We shouldn't have come, Daniel," Matthew whimpered. "Melantha told us not to go near the prisoners!"

"Melantha never lets us do anything," complained Daniel. "If she had her way we'd be locked in our chamber until we were old men!"

"She just wants us to be safe," Matthew countered loyally.

"Fine," said Daniel, exasperated. "You two stay here and be safe. I'm going to look at these MacTier murderers."

"I want to see them as well," chirped Patrick, which struck Roarke as remarkably courageous, given that this little one believed he was in danger of being eaten.

"I—I do too," stammered Matthew, although he didn't sound entirely sure.

Daniel sighed. "Very well—but don't make a sound!"

A little late for that, thought Roarke, watching with amusement as the three shadows began to creep toward him and his men once again.

"Are you sure they're asleep?" whispered Matthew worriedly.

"Of course they're asleep," said Daniel. "You don't think they snore like that when they're awake, do you?"

"They sound just like Thor does when he's sleeping," Patrick observed. "I thought he made that disgusting noise because he's so old."

"All men snore when they sleep," Daniel declared authoritatively. "Even our da used to."

Matthew giggled. "It sounds like they've got something stuck up their noses."

"Why doesn't the noise wake them up?" wondered Patrick.

Daniel shrugged. "I expect they're used to it."

They crept a little closer. Roarke lay perfectly still, watching them through a barely cracked eyelid. Patrick emerged from the darkness into the wavering torchlight first. He looked to be about seven years of age and sported a wildly disheveled bush of bright red hair.

"Which one do you suppose is the leader?"

"It must be that fair-haired one," decided Matthew, inching hesitantly beside him. "Just look at what a great giant he is!"

This light-brown-haired lad seemed a little older than Patrick, although his frame was slight and his legs were painfully thin, making it difficult to assess his age. Nine, Roarke decided—certainly no more than ten.

"That isn't the leader," scoffed Daniel, joining the other two.

He was lean and long limbed, with sable hair and elegantly arched brows that struck Roarke as oddly familiar. Roarke guessed his age to be about thirteen, though it was possible he was older and a lack of food had arrested his development. Given sufficient quantities of meat and exercise, the boy might grow to an impressive size.

"Melantha said the leader's name is Roarke, and he has hair as black as night, with horrible eyes as cold and lifeless as two frozen stones. And she said when he looks at you he can make your heart stop," he warned direly, "so hideous is his face."

Now, that was a bit insulting, Roarke decided. Although he had never wasted much time considering his appearance, he certainly didn't think he resembled a gargoyle.

"I'm leaving," said Matthew, afraid. "I don't want to see him."

"Stay where you are, Matthew," ordered Daniel. "If you knock into something else you'll get us all into trouble."

"I don't want my heart to stop," he squeaked.

"Melantha just said that so we wouldn't come down here and try to get a look at them," Daniel assured him impatiently.

"How do you know?"

"Because Melantha is always making things sound much more dangerous than they really are, so we won't do them. Remember when she told us we couldn't try archery because we were likely to shoot each other?"

"But when she finally said you could, you did almost shoot me," pointed out Matthew.

"That was an accident," Daniel scoffed. "It never would have happened if Melantha hadn't kept yelling at me to be careful. She ruined my concentration."

"But then you shot Ninian's cart and startled his horse, so it ran off and the cart turned over with Ninian still in it," Patrick added. "He was sorely mad."

"Ninian shouldn't have driven his cart in front of me."

"The cart wasn't moving," countered Matthew.

"Do you two want to see these murdering MacTiers or not?" huffed Daniel, irritated at having his past transgressions recounted.

"I do," Patrick chirped.

"Then keep quiet!"

The two smaller boys obediently fell silent.

Roarke shut his eyes and lay motionless as the three lads cautiously approached.

"Look at the size of this one," Daniel whispered.

"Do you suppose he's the leader?" asked Matthew.

"His face is mean enough," Daniel decided.

"If he's the leader, then this is the one Magnus shot in the bum," said Patrick.

"That must have hurt," reflected Matthew sympathetically.

"He deserved to be shot in the heart." Daniel's voice was tight and savage. "And he's lucky he's sleeping, or I would take Da's sword and spear it through his evil, murdering—"

Roarke's eyes snapped open.

Except for the terror clenching their white faces, one might have thought the three lads were about to burst into song, so wide did their mouths gape. Roarke waited for them to flee. Instead they remained frozen to the spot, apparently paralyzed with fear.

"Well? Any of your hearts stop?"

Confusion marginally eased their terrorized expressions.

"Since you remain standing, I shall assume that your hearts are still beating," Roarke continued, amused. "It's a relief to learn that I am not quite so hideous as you were led to believe."

Daniel found his voice first. "Don't try anything, Mac-Tier, or I'll skewer you with my sword!"

Roarke raised a quizzical brow. "What sword?"

The boy groped vainly at his side. Realizing he carried no sword, he clenched his small hands into bony fists. "The sword I'm going to get and drive through your foul, rotting heart!"

"Now, that hardly seems a fair encounter," mused Roarke, "since I am lying here bound hand and foot, and could not so much as lift a finger to defend myself."

At the mention of his helplessness, the three boys visibly relaxed.

"It's a lucky thing for you that you're bound," Daniel told him, "because if you weren't, you'd be dead by now."

Little Patrick eyed Roarke nervously. "Are you going to cut off my head and eat it?"

"Of course not," replied Roarke, sounding offended by the suggestion. "I'm a warrior, not a wild animal. Whoever told you such a ridiculous thing?"

Patrick cast an accusing look at Daniel.

"Don't try to make us think you aren't evil," said Daniel. "You MacTiers attacked us last autumn and tried to butcher every last one of us, so we know exactly what kind of vile savages you are! You deserve to have your eyes burned into steaming black holes with a hot shaft, and then be slowly flayed until you're begging for death!"

Laird MacKillon had forbidden anyone to discuss the subject of the MacTier attack during dinner, deeming it too unpleasant for dining. This had prevented Roarke from learning any further details. But it had been clear from the animosity he had encountered since meeting Melantha and her band that the attack had been brutal. The dilapidated state of the castle and the near-starving condition of most of the people here further demonstrated that the MacKillons had suffered greatly, and continued to suffer. He endured Daniel's glare with something akin to shame, as if he were somehow responsible for the lad's misery. That was ridiculous, he told himself impatiently. He and his men had been far to the south at the time of this attack. He was guilty in that he shared responsibility for the actions of his clan, but he could not be held personally accountable for what had transpired here.

He had been too busy raiding other holdings on behalf of his laird and clan.

"You're lucky Melantha didn't slay you, because that's what she has sworn to do to all MacTiers, until every last one of you lies drowning in your own blood, and our brave da's murder has been avenged!" hissed Daniel fiercely.

Our brave da.

Of course, Roarke thought, studying the boy's finely chiseled face, his elegantly winged brows, and the dark fury smoldering in his eyes. Standing before him was a smaller, younger version of Melantha. He shifted his attention to the other lads. Matthew's features were softer, but his eyes were the same, although they lacked the bitter hatred that burned in his brother's. Little Patrick, however, was a mystery. His hair grew in a thick, wild tangle, and although it was dark Roarke could see that his skin was generously splattered with freckles, which bore no resemblance to the milky clear faces of the other two.

"Are you all Melantha's brothers?"

"Aye." Daniel's bony fists remained balled menacingly at his sides. "And if I ever hear of you trying to harm her again, MacTier, I swear I'll kill you."

His voice was deadly soft, his boyish face twisted with raw hatred. He was only a child, yet Roarke knew loathing and anguish simmered just beneath his skin, making him capable of almost anything. In all his years as a warrior, he had never seen a lad so completely stripped of every remnant of innocence, and the sight cut him to the bone. Roarke had fought in countless battles, and had led massive assaults on scores of holdings in the name of his laird and his king, but somehow he had always thought of it as a fight against other warriors, not women and children. Of course he had never tarried long once a holding had surrendered. After all, his skills were best utilized where there was another battle to be fought. And so he had always moved on, never permitting himself to dwell upon the terrible suffering he left behind.

"Does your mother know you're down here threatening the prisoners?" he enquired with uncustomary gentleness.

Little Patrick shook his head. "She died a long time ago."

"Only two and a half years ago," Daniel corrected tautly. "That's not so long."

No, Roarke agreed, that was not so long. Muriel and Clementina had been dead five years, and their absence still carved a deep abyss in his soul. He could well imagine the terrible pain experienced by these boys at losing both their mother and father in such a brief span of time. And so Melantha had been forced to assume responsibility for her younger brothers. Roarke had never been home enough to play a significant role in his daughter's upbringing, but he knew it would require enormous energy and patience to be both mother and father to these three lads. Melantha had strictly forbidden them to come here tonight, and they had recklessly defied her, just as he would have done at their age.

If she rose during the night to find the three of them missing, she would be overcome with fear.

"You lads shouldn't be here. If Melantha finds you with me, she will be very angry with you for disobeying her."

The boys exchanged uneasy glances. It was clear they had completely forgotten about this possibility.

"H-he's right," Matthew stammered nervously. "Melantha will be awfully mad when she finds out."

"Melantha won't find out." Daniel hurled a contemptuous look at Roarke. "Unless you tell her."

"I see no reason to tell anyone of your little visit," said Roarke. "Other than your threats to drive a sword through my foul, rotting heart and burn my eyes into steaming holes, I found your company quite pleasant."

Daniel eyed Roarke doubtfully, debating whether or not to trust him. "Come, then, lads," he finally said. "We've seen enough of these butchering MacTiers for one night."

Matthew eagerly turned, but young Patrick lingered a moment longer, his little red brows scrunched together.

"Did Magnus really shoot you in the bum?"

Roarke nodded.

"Did it hurt?"

"Yes."

"Does it still hurt?"

"A little."

"Once I fell and cut my forehead, and Melantha made me lie in bed while she pressed cold cloths on it, and she even let me drink some wine. You should ask her if she will do the same for you."

"Somehow I doubt your sister is overly concerned

about my pain," said Roarke dryly, "but thank you for the suggestion."

"We have to go, Patrick!" snapped Daniel.

"I have to go now," Patrick informed Roarke, "but I'll see you tomorrow."

"I shall look forward to that."

The lad gifted him with a smile.

And then he turned and scampered toward his eldest brother, who cast one last look of utter loathing at Roarke before melting into the shadows.

CHAPTER 4

"That's it, Lewis . . . ye've almost got it . . . there, now! Bang her in, she's as straight as can be!"

Roarke watched as Lewis obediently positioned a nail over the damaged shutter, gave it a meek tap with his hammer, then withdrew his supporting hand.

The shutter crashed to the floor.

"For heaven's sake, lad, ye can't expect to secure a heavy slab of wood with just one nail!" said Magnus, exasperated. "And ye must strike the nail as if ye mean to kill it, not as if ye're trying to rouse it from slumber!"

Lewis gazed down apologetically from his precarious perch of stacked benches. "Sorry."

Magnus sighed. "Never mind, lad. It's not yer fault ye've

no gift for fixing things. Climb down from there and let's see if we can't find something else for ye to do."

The great hall was teeming with men balancing on benches, tables, and chairs, their mouths crammed with iron nails as they awkwardly attempted to repair the damaged shutters dangling from the windows.

"Excellent job, lads!" praised Magnus, who was directing the activity from the center of the hall. "A few more hours work here, and those wily MacTier dogs will never be able to breach the windows."

"Forgive me, Magnus," said Roarke, "but why are all these men working in the great hall when there are so many repairs to be done to the outside of the castle?"

"I know 'tis a wee bit noisy, lad," Magnus acknowledged apologetically, "but until we get that storeroom ready for ye, I'm afraid ye'll just have to put up with us."

"I'm not complaining about the noise," Roarke clarified. "I'm wondering why you aren't securing the curtain wall and the gate instead of fixing a few broken shutters in here."

"There are plenty of men working outside, make no mistake," Magnus assured him. "And they've got matters well in hand. It may interest ye to know that we MacKillons have a long and splendid history of castle building—"

"For God's sake, Ninian, can you not tell the difference between a nail *and a man's bloody finger!*"

Roarke glanced across the hall to see a short dumpling of a man with blazing cheeks standing on a table, angrily shaking his stubby hand in the air.

"If you'd only watch what you're doing and keep your fat fingers out of my way, that wouldn't have happened, Gelfrid!" snapped Ninian testily from his seat atop several unevenly stacked stools. His skin was stretched taut over the bones of his face, giving him a sallow, almost cadaverous appearance that perfectly complemented his shrunken build.

" 'Tis you who needs to watch what you're doing," blustered

Gelfrid. "Any damn fool can see this is flesh and bone, not a piece of bloody iron!"

"You'd best let your wife take a look at that for you," said a fellow with a wild flurry of red hair. "It may need to be splinted."

"I'll be lucky if a splint is all that's needed, Mungo," Gelfrid complained irritably. "But while I'm at it, I'll ask my Hilda to make a potion that'll sharpen Ninian's sight!"

Ninian whirled around, waving his hammer. "There's nothing wrong with my sight! You put your great, fat finger right on top of the bloody—" Suddenly his eyes grew round and he began to flap his scrawny arms in a vain attempt to regain his balance.

Roarke winced as the poor fellow crashed to the floor.

"That must have hurt," reflected Donald, who lay comfortably stretched out upon his pallet watching the MacKillons make their repairs.

" 'Twas nothing," Eric scoffed, unimpressed. "I've fallen from twice that height and barely felt it."

"That's because you landed on your head," said Myles, lazily polishing his arm bands against his plaid.

Eric scowled. "You're just jealous of my superior strength."

"His head may tolerate the odd blow well enough, but I warrant this morning it is throbbing from the vast quantity of ale he drank last night," Donald teased. "No doubt that accounts for his surly disposition today."

"Perhaps Gillian should dose him with another cup of her posset," suggested Myles. "That would really put this superior Viking strength of his to the test."

"I thought it was poison," Eric grumbled irritably. " 'Twas the foulest brew I have ever tasted."

"I don't think you need worry about the lass going near you with one of her brews again," Myles reflected. "Judging by the haste with which she quit the hall, I'd say you've terrified the poor maid."

"Now, that's a pity." Donald idly examined the rope around his wrists. "She was a comely little thing."

"She was weak and afraid," Eric countered. "She would not make a fit mate for a warrior. A warrior needs a woman who is strong and fearless."

"I shall settle for a lass who is pleasing upon the eye, and soft and willing in my bed."

"It is a woman's duty to be willing," Eric replied brusquely. "My wife should be proud to take my seed and bear strong children."

Donald regarded him with amusement. "I really must spend some time educating you on the ways of women, my friend, before these barbaric ideas of yours get you into serious trouble." He sat up, pleased to have found something to keep himself occupied. "Now, then, your first lesson is how to look at a woman without sending her into fits of hysteria."

Eric glowered.

"Excellent. That is exactly how you don't want to look. Now that you've mastered that, let's move on. The next lesson is: when a woman offers you something to drink, which she has obviously gone to a great deal of trouble to make, try to refrain from spitting it out and accusing her of trying to kill you."

"If you don't cease this drivel I'm going to kill you," Eric warned ominously.

"You may think that now, but there is going to be a moment where you will actually want to thank me," replied Donald, unconcerned. "Women love to be complimented on their appearance, so try to think of something nice to say."

Myles stopped polishing his arm bands. "Like what?"

"That depends on what stage you are at in your seduction. For instance, if you have only just met, 'tis good to remark on something relatively safe, like comparing her hair to the dark of the night sky, or saying her eyes are the color of sapphires."

Eric snorted in disgust. "I have never seen a woman with eyes like sapphires."

"It doesn't matter whether they are actually that blue or not," explained Donald patiently, "you flatter her by telling her it is so. She is certainly not about to contradict you when you point out her more comely attributes."

"What about her arms?" asked Myles.

Donald frowned. "What about them?"

"Is that a good thing to compliment her on?"

"In truth, I can't recall meeting a woman who particularly wanted to hear about her arms. Besides, there are so many other wonderful things to remark on, like her creamy skin, her rosy lips, her tiny waist, her soft cheek—"

"I like strong arms," interrupted Eric. "That means she will be able to carry a heavy load of wood without complaining."

Donald sighed. "Fine. Mention her strong arms if you like, but be sure to add something else, like the delicate shape of her—"

"Broad hips," suggested Myles.

Donald raised his brow in exasperation. "You actually believe a woman wants to be told she has broad hips?"

"That means she will be able to bear many children with ease," explained Myles.

"Myles is right," agreed Eric, nodding with approval. "It is a good thing for a woman to have solid, broad hips."

"And a good pair of stout legs," added Myles.

"I don't think you two are going to get very far in your courting if you remark on the stoutness of a woman's hips and legs," reflected Donald doubtfully.

"Well, I'm not marrying any foolish wench who wants to be told some nonsense about her eyes being like blue rocks," snapped Eric. He heaved himself against his pallet and turned away from Donald, indicating the lesson had come to an end.

Ignoring the bored discourse of his men, Roarke watched

in frustration as the MacKillons continued their bumbling repairs of the great hall. He did not know if Laird MacKillon had sent a ransom message to Laird MacTier yet, but one thing was certain. If fixing these broken shutters was the extent of the MacKillons's preparation for an attack, then the outcome would be both swift and brutal, regardless of which clan assaulted them.

The thought did not please him.

"I'm afraid we need to work down at this end of the hall now," said Magnus, approaching Roarke. "If ye lads would be so kind to move toward the center of the room, I'm sure we'll have ye back in yer space in no time."

"It seems my men and I are just in the way, Magnus," Roarke remarked, determined to see what other preparations the MacKillons were making. "Perhaps it would be best if we went outside for a while, and left you and your men to finish the repairs."

Magnus cocked a white brow. "Ye're not thinking to try to escape, are ye, lad? Because I've no time to waste today on chasing after ye, do ye hear?"

"I can hardly see how that would be possible," returned Roarke. "It is the middle of the day, we are unarmed, our hands are bound, and the courtyard is filled with your people. And my arse still throbs from your arrow, which makes the prospect of a long chase wholly unappealing."

Magnus chuckled. " 'Twas a fine shot, there's no denying it." He considered a moment, then sighed. "I suppose there's no harm in ye lads takin' a bit of fresh air. But I'll have to send someone to watch over ye all the same." He turned to Lewis, who was kneeling on the floor, completely absorbed in the task of piecing together the fragments of his broken shutter. "Lewis, quit playing with that and take the prisoners outside for some air."

"I've nearly got it," murmured Lewis, completely absorbed by his task. "All I need is to find one more piece—"

"Leave it, lad," said Magnus impatiently. "We're better off building a new one anyway."

"But we don't need to," replied Lewis, sliding the last piece of his wooden puzzle into place. "See?"

Roarke looked down in amazement. In mere minutes Lewis had managed to completely reconstruct the badly broken shutter.

"Yes, yes, I see," Magnus said. "And in the time it takes to have a man put all those wee bits together, he can build two new shutters from good, strong wood and have them hung. Can ye not see how that makes all yer fussin' about with things a waste of time?"

Embarrassed to be chastised in front of Roarke and his men, Lewis nodded meekly.

"Be a good lad, then, and take these MacTiers out into the courtyard for some air. I'm not thinkin' they'll be giving ye any trouble. If they do, just shoot one of them in the arse," he instructed, chuckling. "That'll bring them around quick enough."

"That won't be necessary," Roarke assured him. "My men and I merely wish to get some fresh air and a little exercise, nothing more."

"Off ye go, then," said Magnus. "Just see that ye don't get in anyone's way while ye're out there—here, now, Mungo, what in the name of St. Andrew are ye doin' with that—watch out!"

Roarke winced as the tower of benches supporting Mungo crashed to the floor, with poor Mungo following.

The courtyard was roiling with activity as Roarke and his men stepped into the damp morning air. Men, women, and children were scrambling in all directions carrying rocks of varying sizes, which they were arranging with great care along the walls of the keep. Others were toting heavy buckets of water from the well and dumping them into enormous troughs and barrels in which a gray, claylike compound was being mixed.

"That's it, Finlay," said Laird MacKillon. He watched from his seat in the center of the courtyard as the stocky warrior gathered an armful of heavy stones from a cart and dropped them on the ground. "Fifty or so more cartloads, and we'll have more than enough stones to restore these magnificent walls to their former glory!"

"This one won't do," declared Thor, his forehead furrowed with disapproval as he examined one of the rocks. "Won't do at all."

Finlay wiped the sweat from his brow. "Not big enough?"

Thor shook his head. "It's big enough, all right."

"Not heavy enough?" suggested Laird MacKillon.

Thor grunted as he attempted to lift the stone from the cart, then abandoned his efforts and shook his head again. "That's a sound, heavy stone. Can't fault it for that."

"Is its shape uneven?" wondered Hagar, coming over to inspect the offending rock.

Thor ran a gnarled hand over the stone. "Smooth as a bairn's backside," he announced, patting it with approval. "Nothing wrong with its shape."

"What's wrong with it then?" wondered Laird MacKillon.

By this time the entire clan had halted their work and curiously focused their attention on Thor.

There was a moment of cryptic silence as he eyed his audience, immensely pleased to have so much attention directed at him.

"It's not *pink* enough," he finally announced gravely.

The clan stared at the stone in shock.

"By all the saints, you're right," said Hagar, bobbing his balding head in agreement. "It's not nearly pink enough!"

"Now, Finlay, I don't mean to criticize, but you are taking care to pick only stones of the rosiest color, are you not?" queried Laird MacKillon.

"Aye," grunted Finlay, carelessly depositing another armload of rocks onto the ground. "I am."

"Then how do you explain this one?" demanded Thor.

Finlay shrugged. "Must have looked pink when I picked it up."

The council members contemplated this explanation a moment.

"A perfectly reasonable answer," decided Laird Mac-Killon, nodding.

"Things often look pink to me one minute, and then an entirely different color the next," added Hagar. "It's a common problem."

"That's because your eyes are weak," scoffed Thor. "I can certainly tell the difference between something that is pink, and something that is decidedly not pink."

"But if you look closely at this stone, you can see that there are actually shades of pink running through it," pointed out Hagar. " 'Tis merely the intensity of the color that makes it unacceptable."

"The intensity of color is everything!" argued Thor. "That's the very attribute for which the MacKillon castle has been famous these past hundred years—its remarkable color! If we allow our keep to be repaired with just any shade of stone, we will have lost our proud heritage!"

"Of course I'm not suggesting we actually use this stone," Hagar assured him. "I'm only saying that the lad should not be overly criticized for thinking it was pink when he picked it up. Why, just look at all the other fine stones he has brought to us today!"

"Never mind, Finlay," said Laird MacKillon. "Everyone makes mistakes. Just see that you're more careful with the next load. Everyone back to work," he instructed, waving at all the MacKillons. "Everything is fine now. All sorted out."

"Great God in heaven!" burst out Thor, suddenly noticing Roarke and his men. "Those MacTier scoundrels have escaped!" He fumbled awkwardly for his sword and charged toward them. "Back, vile miscreants!" he raged, flailing his blade in front of him. "Back to your rat-infested prison, before I carve you into a thousand bloody pieces and mash your steaming entrails into the ground!"

Roarke calmly waited for Lewis to inform Thor that in fact they were not trying to escape. But poor Lewis was so startled by Thor's sudden attack, he actually stepped backward, bumping into Roarke.

"We aren't trying to escape," Roarke assured Thor, trying to steady Lewis as best he could with his bound hands.

Thor's eyes rounded with horror. "My God, they've taken Lewis hostage! I'll not stand by and let them get away with it! Prepare to die, you depraved curs!"

Roarke instantly pushed Lewis behind him, afraid the lad might actually get injured in Thor's misguided attack. "We aren't trying to escape, Thor," he repeated loudly, thinking perhaps the elder was hard of hearing.

"Back, foul pillagers of castles and ravishers of women!" raged Thor, poking the air just in front of Roarke's belly with his sword. "Back to your damp, dark hole, where you will rot in misery until the devil himself claims your wretched, stinking souls to burn for all eternity!"

"Here, now, what's all this fuss about?" demanded Magnus, appearing at the castle entrance. "A man can scarcely think straight with all this shouting."

"I've just saved the clan from another MacTier attack," boasted Thor, "and now I'm going to chop these MacTier villains into wee bits and feed them to the fish in the loch!"

"Attack?" repeated Magnus, confused. "What attack?"

"Thor seems to think we were trying to escape," Roarke explained mildly.

"That's ridiculous," scoffed Magnus. "The lad gave me his word that escape was the furthest thing from his mind—all he and his men wanted was a wee bit of air."

Thor kept his weapon trembling menacingly before Roarke. "If they aren't trying to escape, then what were they doing racing across the courtyard?"

"Actually, we weren't moving," pointed out Roarke. "We were watching you debate the matter of Finlay's stone."

"You were deciding how to steal our weapons and mounts and slay us all before you returned to your clan!" thundered Thor.

"Now, that would be quite a feat," Roarke agreed, "considering there are only four of us against hundreds of MacKillons."

"The lad's got a point, Thor," said Magnus. "Besides, can ye not see that I've got young Lewis guarding them?"

Thor blinked. "Lewis is guarding them?"

"Aye," said Lewis, sheepishly stepping out from the protective shield of Roarke's body. He cleared his throat and groped at his side for his sword. "I am."

"No offense, lad," said Thor, "but I scarcely think a skinny stripling like you is capable of guarding four savage brutes like these. Why, just look at the size of them compared to you! They'd eat you in the blink of an eye if they thought you had any meat on your bones!"

A stain of humiliation rose to Lewis's freckled cheeks.

"Don't be deceived by Lewis's slender build," interjected Roarke, disliking the way Thor was embarrassing the lad before his own clan. "When we were captured, he nearly hacked one of my men in two with that sword of his."

A gasp of awe rose from the clan.

"He did?" exclaimed Hagar, clearly impressed.

Roarke nodded. "Of course, Donald was weakened by the heavy blow Lewis delivered to the back of his head first. The lad has a powerful right arm."

Laird MacKillon regarded Lewis in amazement. "He does?"

"He most certainly does," agreed Donald, rubbing his

head for effect. "Left a lump on my skull the size of a goose egg. I expect I'll be feeling it for days yet."

"Are you trying to tell me that our Lewis here actually attacked this savage warrior of yours?" demanded Thor, gazing at Roarke in bewilderment.

Roarke nodded.

" 'Twould seem I've misjudged ye, laddie," acknowledged Thor, shaking his head. "I'd have never thought you capable of such a deed."

"Of course Lewis is capable of such a deed," declared a hard voice. "As part of the Falcon's band he performs acts of great courage and daring all the time."

Roarke turned to see Melantha and Colin standing behind him, with young Daniel, Matthew, and Patrick lined up between them. Melantha was dressed in a coarsely woven brown shirt, a dark leather jerkin, earth-colored leggings and deerskin boots, with her cumbersome sword weighing heavily at her side. Evidently she preferred the unfettered movement this attire afforded her to the awkward constraints of a gown, mused Roarke. Either that, or her exploits as the Falcon had stripped her of any desire to appear even remotely feminine, at least where her garments were concerned. Her shapeless clothes could not mask the delicate beauty of her face, although her rigid expression did little to suggest that there might be a softer side to her.

For a moment Roarke feared she had learned of her brothers' clandestine visit to the great hall the previous night. It was impossible to tell from Daniel's expression, for the boy glared at him with the same disdain as his sister, which had the unsettling effect of making their resemblance even more profound. Roarke shifted his attention to Matthew. The youth uneasily latched his attention to the ground, but Roarke sensed Matthew was always uneasy, so there was no help there. Only red-haired little Patrick regarded him with a sunny, untroubled look, complete with a crooked smile. A peculiar sensation of warmth seeped over Roarke. Feeling somewhat fortified, he returned his gaze to Melantha.

The coolness was still there, but he detected something else in the depths of her eyes. Frowning, he tried to discern what it was.

She abruptly tore her gaze away, as if he did not merit further scrutiny.

"Well, then, it's all sorted out," declared Laird MacKillon happily. "Everyone back to work," he instructed once more, shooing at his people. "There is still much work to do on these mighty walls."

"Forgive me, Laird MacKillon," said Roarke, "but why are you spending so much time and effort repairing the walls of your keep?"

"Why, to keep the MacTiers out, of course," Laird Mac-Killon replied, as if the answer were obvious.

"You don't think we're so naive as to believe your greedy, black-hearted laird won't be tempted to attack us again, are you?" asked Thor. "But this time we'll hack his army to bits as it stands, strip the flesh from its bones, and feed it to the wolves!" he threatened grandly. "And then we'll grind it's bones for bread!"

"Well, now, I don't know about that," fretted Laird Mac-Tier. "No offense, Thor, but I can't help but think that to grind the bones of an entire army would take an inordinate amount of time and effort."

"Besides, who wants to eat bread made out of Mac-Tiers?" wondered Magnus. "It's bound to be tough."

"If it's tough, we can feed it to the fish," Thor suggested. "They won't care."

Hagar scratched the shiny top of his head. "That seems like an awful lot of work to go to, just to feed fish. Couldn't we just bury their bones?"

"The whole idea is to destroy them without a trace!" argued Thor. "If we're just going to bury them, then there's no point in stripping their flesh off either!"

Roarke struggled for patience. "What I am trying to say is, if Laird MacTier sends an army to retrieve us, you really don't have a hope of holding them off."

"Do you think we should just sit and placidly wait for your clan to arrive?" demanded Colin sardonically.

"Don't forget, we're going to enlist the assistance of the MacKenzies' army," said Hagar, "and they're as strong and nasty a group of warriors as one could ever hope not to meet."

"But we must do what we can to keep your warriors at bay, at least until Laird MacKenzie arrives with his army and makes your laird realize he should just pay your ransom and take you home," Laird MacKillon added.

"It is good that you are making preparations for the event of an attack," acknowledged Roarke, ignoring Colin's hostility. "Your clan should be better prepared to defend itself regardless of whether MacTier sends an army or not. But the preparations you are making will ultimately have little effect. You cannot stop an army by replacing a few shutters and repairing the holes in your keep with pink stones."

"Your concern for my people's welfare is touching," Melantha observed icily. "No doubt you think we should just release you and your men to prevent further bloodshed."

"That would be the most prudent course of action," agreed Roarke. "But since you are so stubbornly committed to this notion of ransoming us, at least let me make a few suggestions for strengthening your holding."

"We're not interested in your suggestions."

"Actually, Melantha, it might be interesting to hear them," Laird MacKillon interjected. "After all, Roarke here is an experienced warrior, and has probably raided dozens of castles—haven't you, lad?"

"Of course he has," Melantha agreed caustically. "And our home counts among his many foul, depraved victories."

An uneasy hush fell upon the courtyard.

Roarke regarded her intently. "My men and I were not a part of the raid on this holding, Melantha. I swear it."

A bitter, half-choked laugh escaped her throat. "Even if that were true, it doesn't matter. You're still a MacTier."

"Yes," he agreed quietly. "There is nothing I can do to change that. But just because I'm a MacTier doesn't mean I can't offer your people a few suggestions on how you can fortify your holding."

"He's right, ye know, lass," said Magnus. "There's no harm in listening to what he has to say."

"Quite so," agreed Laird MacKillon.

"This is absurd!" snapped Colin. "He has no reason to want to help us. He'll try to trick us into doing something that will actually help his army when it comes."

"You don't have to actually do anything that I suggest," Roarke pointed out. "Unless you think it makes sense."

"Now, that sounds fair enough," said Hagar. "What suggestions did you have in mind?"

"The walls of your keep will eventually have to be repaired, but for now you should be devoting your energy to preventing an attacker from ever reaching the keep." Roarke studied the gate a moment. The heavy iron portcullis appeared to be structurally sound, and the thick wooden gate beyond it had not been damaged by a battering ram. "How did the MacTiers breach the castle?"

"They crawled up the curtain wall on ladders, like bugs on a tree," Laird MacKillon explained. "Then they came down here and opened the gate for the others."

"Didn't you have men on the wall defending it?"

"We had a few," supplied Hagar, "but only enough to keep watch."

"The cowardly scum attacked in the middle of the night, and we weren't expecting it," Magnus added. "They just appeared out of nowhere."

"Like foul, murdering demons," growled Thor, "sent by the very devil himself!"

Laird MacKillon shook his head, his eyes shadowed with sorrow. "The lads on the wall head fought them as best they could, but they were no match for such a dreadful attack."

"By the time we realized we were being invaded," Hagar continued, "the men on watch were dead and the MacTiers were already swarming the castle."

Roarke absorbed this information in grim silence. It was a long-favored method among his clan: to attack an unsuspecting castle in the dead of night, quietly disposing of the guards and then entering the castle unchecked. Few strongholds could resist for long once the gate was open and the rest of the army surged inside. It was a technique he had used himself countless times.

Guilt gnawed uncomfortably at his conscience.

"If the warriors were able to take control of the castle with such ease, then how was all this damage done?" He gestured at the crumbling keep, the badly pocked curtain wall, and the charred remnants of the cottages beyond.

"Surely you recognize the handiwork of your own clan?" Melantha's query was laden with bitterness. "No? Then permit me to enlighten you. After slaughtering any man who dared stand in their way, the MacTiers occupied themselves by terrorizing everyone and stealing all they could lay their hands on before attempting to reduce our home to a pile of rubble. They slew every cow, goat, and chicken they couldn't take with them, destroyed our fields of grains and vegetables, then burned the cottages of those who had the courage to plead with them to at least leave something for the children to eat." Her voice was flat and void of emotion as she finished,

"At the end of it twenty-six brave men lay dead or dying, our homes were stripped bare, and we were left to starve through the winter."

Her expression was composed, except for the loathing with which Roarke was becoming well acquainted every time she looked at him. But her hand was gripping the hilt of her sword and the skin of her knuckles was drawn so taut Roarke thought it might split and expose the bone. A terrible fury flailed within her, fury and pain and overwhelming hatred. Roarke could see it was taking every shred of her self-control not to lash out and kill him or simply sink to the ground and weep.

She had failed to mention that her father had been one of those brave men who had been slain that night, but Roarke could see by the wash of pain filling her eyes that she was thinking about him. Perhaps she did not want to ascribe more importance to her loss than to those suffered by the rest of her clan. Or perhaps she did not want to reveal this personal detail to Roarke and his men, for fear she might be exposing a weakness that could later be used against her. Daniel moved protectively to her side, as if he were trying to shield her from Roarke and his men. Roarke understood the lad was really trying to protect her from the agony of her own suffering.

"Come, Melantha," Daniel said, casting an accusing look at Roarke. "We don't need to stay here and listen to the lies of these thieving MacTiers. It's time to go, Matthew and Patrick." He gestured to his younger brothers.

Roarke watched helplessly as the boy took Melantha's hand and led her away, powerless to protect her from what had already happened, or change the fact that he was a kinsmen of her tormentors.

"If you ever do that again, I'll kill you," vowed Eric.

"I don't see why you're so upset," objected Donald, languidly stretching back against his pallet. "I thought she was perfect for you. After all, she had the broad hips and stout legs with which you and Myles are so enamored. I'm quite sure she could birth a brood of little Vikings with no trouble whatsoever."

"She had the face of a sow."

"You never mentioned the face as being important," he protested. "You just went on about strength. There's no denying she was strong—no weak-armed woman could carry six heavy pitchers of ale at once."

"She was a shrew," objected Myles. "And she should have dumped the ale on you, not Eric. You were the one who insulted her by commenting on her girth."

"I was merely trying to let her know that Eric found her attractive," Donald explained innocently. "And she poured the ale on Eric because she likes him. Women always abuse the men they are attracted to—that's how they get their attention."

"I've no desire for her to like me," Eric snapped. "Now my shirt and plaid are sodden with ale and my hair reeks!"

"Lewis offered to bring you a change of clothes and you stubbornly refused," said Donald. "I can't imagine why he keeps trying to see to your comfort. Every time you glare at him he trembles so hard I think he will shatter into a thousand pieces."

"I will not wear the clothes of my enemies."

"I don't know why not, since they're all wearing clothes that have been stolen from others. I'll wager they probably could have found a MacTier plaid and shirt for you to wear."

"How much longer are we staying here?" demanded Eric, turning suddenly to Roarke.

Roarke sighed. It was clear his men were getting restless. "I'm not sure."

"You know we could leave at any time," Eric pointed out, wondering if perhaps Roarke had somehow overlooked this fact. "Since Laird MacKillon ordered that we no longer be kept bound, it would be easy to grab a few swords and fight our way out."

"I doubt it would be as easy as that," objected Donald. "After all, these MacKillons are rather annoyed with our clan. I don't think they would hesitate to shoot us if we tried to escape."

"Then we take a hostage," Myles suggested. "They won't shoot us if they think we're about to cut one of their throats."

"True enough." Donald sat up and briskly rubbed his hands together, filled with sudden energy. "What about it, then, Roarke? Are we leaving, or do we stay and endure the supreme humiliation of MacTier sending out a party of warriors to rescue us?" He laughed.

"We stay."

His men looked at him in astonishment.

"A few days," Roarke elaborated. "No longer. Just enough time to help these MacKillons organize their repairs and work on a defense strategy that will help them fend off an assault."

"You want to help them against our own clan?" asked Donald, confounded.

"I want to help them defend themselves from any clan," Roarke responded. "MacTier will never pay a ransom for us, so they can't hope to buy an alliance. Which means they must learn to protect themselves. Once the preparations for their defense are under way, we will escape and intercept the MacTiers before they arrive." He leaned back against his pallet and wearily closed his eyes. "Then we can go home."

"What about the Falcon?" Eric demanded.

Roarke said nothing.

It was a matter of great pride to him that he had never failed in his duty to Laird MacTier. Not once in over twenty years of dedicated service. If he chose, he could keep that stellar history of achievement unblemished. Laird MacTier had long promised to reward Roarke, his most accomplished and favored warrior, with his own holding when his days as a warrior were finished. It was his payment for a lifetime spent aggressively expanding his clan's power and influence, and enriching MacTier's coffers at the same time. When this reward was first offered, Roarke had been unable to imagine any life beyond the one he had chosen, and had imperiously assured MacTier that he would die in battle with a sword in his hand.

But during these past few years it had become harder to rise each morning from the damp, hard ground and ignore the stiffness and aches plaguing his battered body. The thought of being comfortably ensconced in his own home began to beckon to him. At first Roarke had rejected his musings in disgust, telling himself he had many long years of journeying and battle left in him.

That was before he had been wounded.

He remembered the day with perfect clarity, although already a year had elapsed. It had been a glorious summer morning, and the air was hot and thick with the promise of rain. Roarke preferred cooler days for battle, because the heat made it difficult to maintain a solid grip on the hilt of his sword. He was leading a force of some four hundred men against an insurrection in Moray, in the name of King Alexander. The battle had begun well enough. After disabling or killing at least a dozen men, Roarke found himself surrounded by three warriors on horseback. He disposed of two of them without an inordinate amount of difficulty, enabling him to focus his attention on the third. His remaining opponent was a steely-muscled young warrior with a powerful arm, who looked to be some ten years Roarke's junior. Amazingly, the lad managed to deflect every slice and thrust of Roarke's sword, until finally Roarke's weapon grew heavy and his breathing became labored. The need for absolute concentration to fight this arrogant pup prevented Roarke from sensing the attacker behind him.

The first blow only slit the muscles of his back.

It was the heavy chop of the ax into his right shoulder that rendered him helpless.

As he fell from his horse Roarke knew a moment of perfect, almost dreamy astonishment, unable to believe that he could have failed so completely in this final conflict. That he was about to be disemboweled by his young opponent seemed less disturbing than the incomprehensible fact that he had actually been overcome. The warrior gave him a triumphant smile as he raised his blade, not disdainful or malicious, but merely an acknowledgment that it had been a challenging contest between two able warriors, and he was genuinely pleased to have emerged the victor.

Then the point of Eric's sword burst through the warrior's chest.

It took months for Roarke's back and shoulder to recover adequately enough for him to wield his weapon once again. Even when he impatiently declared himself recovered, he knew in fact he was not. When Roarke finally summoned the humility he needed to speak to MacTier about his long-promised reward, his laird listened to his request with a vaguely disappointed expression, as if he had not actually believed the day would come when Roarke would accept his offer. Ultimately MacTier had said he would honor his word, but first Roarke had to complete one final mission.

He was to seek out the notorious Falcon's band and destroy it, and bring the Falcon himself back to MacTier for execution.

It was unthinkable.

"We never found the Falcon." He regarded his men with steady calm.

"MacTier won't like that," ventured Myles.

"I know."

"You realize that even if we leave her here, MacTier will immediately dispatch another group to find the Falcon," said Donald. "Eventually she will be caught."

"She won't be caught if she stops this foolishness of dressing up like some wandering horseman in a rusty helmet and robbing every stranger who crosses her path."

"Maybe not," allowed Donald. "But I don't think she is about to abandon her pursuits as an outlaw. Despite their weaknesses individually, she and her men are actually quite good at their game, and therefore have no reason to stop."

"The only reason they haven't been caught or killed yet is because they have been extremely lucky," argued Roarke. "And that luck is bound to run out."

Donald shrugged. "You could say the same thing about us."

"We are skilled, deadly warriors," Eric objected. "Luck has nothing to do with our survival."

"If we're so skilled, then why did we stumble blindly into the trap the Falcon set for us?" challenged Donald.

"Because we're accustomed to fighting our battles in the open, against an enemy who is not afraid to show himself," Eric replied, "not old men and children who drop from the trees like acorns."

"It doesn't seem that our clan was being overly conspicuous on the night the MacKillons were attacked," reflected Donald. "Scaling the walls in the dead of night and attacking these people as they slept."

Roarke shifted uneasily on his pallet. Only a few days earlier he and his men had been contemptuous about the Falcon's band attacking a group of MacTiers as they slept, dismissing it as a cowardly way of overcoming one's enemy.

Melantha had only been subjecting the MacTiers to their own methods.

"Attacks on holdings are different," Eric argued. "Surprise is a necessary tactic."

Donald was unconvinced. "So you think the Falcon's band should have given us some kind of warning before they trapped us?"

"They should have let themselves be seen and fought like warriors."

"Then they would have lost."

"It would have been a nobler battle."

"I fail to see what's so noble about the smaller, weaker group being carved to pieces," Donald said. "By using the weapon of surprise and those nets, there was virtually no battle at all. Except for Roarke's swordplay with the Falcon, which resulted in his becoming intimately acquainted with an arrow." He grinned at Roarke. "How is that healing, anyway? Do you need fair Edwina to take a look at it?"

Ignoring his gibe, Roarke rose and began to slowly pace the width of the hall, thinking. The MacKillons needed to be able to defend themselves, but it would take months to complete the repairs to their castle. These repairs were absolutely crucial to fend off an attack.

Unless they tried to repel an assault in a totally unexpected way.

He turned to his men and smiled.

CHAPTER 5

Melantha snapped upright and grabbed the sword at her side.

A hint of flat, gray light was filtering through the windows, telling her the curtain of night had barely lifted. She swiftly appraised the surrounding shadows, hunting for the least flicker of movement, preparing to spring from her bed with her sword raised.

The air was still.

She strained to listen beyond the blood pounding in her ears, but all she heard was the gentle breathing of the forms lying curled upon the floor beside her. Still gripping her weapon, she peered over the edge of her bed and counted.

One. Two.

Panic streaked through her.

A sleepy sigh drifted through the air. Slowly expelling the breath frozen in her chest, she turned and saw a thatch of hair peeping out from a small mound of blankets huddled next to her. She gingerly grasped the edge of the covers and peeled them down, then laid her hand with aching tenderness on the freckled velvet of Patrick's cheek. He nuzzled closer, clutching at the warm plaid that was draped over both of them. Melantha studied the shadows of her chamber once again. Nothing seemed amiss. Gradually permitting herself to believe that all was well for the moment, she eased herself against her pillow, one hand caressing Patrick's tangled hair, the other still clutching the hilt of her sword.

She could not remember what it was like to sleep without fear.

Of course she realized that she had not always been like this. There had been a time when she had floated into slumber with trusting ease, knowing that when she awoke everything in her world would be just as it had been the day before. But she could not recall the innocent sensation of feeling completely safe, of knowing that everyone she loved was near, and that the days stretching out before her would be filled with nothing but wonderful adventures.

Everything had changed when her mother died.

She had never thought of herself as sheltered—if anything she had always fancied herself more daring and experienced than most girls her age, a fact that had made her feel special and even slightly superior. Her father had hoped for a son to be his firstborn, but when Melantha arrived instead, he philosophically decided to make the best of it. He had cradled her on his horse when she was but a few days old, then seated her astride as soon as she could hold herself upright. Her mother would shake her head with gentle exasperation when she described it, saying that it was all she could do to make sure he kept a firm grip on Melantha's waist, so certain was he that his little lass would ride before she could walk.

Melantha didn't know which she could do first, as her father proudly swore she rode first, and her mother assured her she most certainly did not. What her parents did agree upon was the fact that from the moment she could support herself on her wobbly little legs she had traipsed eagerly after her beloved da. He had loved to have his daughter with him, and his daily affairs were of far greater interest to her than the endlessly tedious domestic chores that occupied all of her mother's time. During the nine years it took for Daniel to finally arrive, Melantha's father seemed to decide that if she was to be his only child, then he was going to make sure she learned how to do anything a lad could, and he would make no allowances for the fact that she was a lass. Melantha's mother could scarcely disapprove of her learning to ride well, and she even agreed that fishing was a valuable skill. But the day her da presented his five-year-old daughter with a tiny bow and quiver filled with smooth, slender arrows, her mother seemed less certain. Melantha's father had just laughed and said any daughter of his should know how to hunt and feed herself, and that seemed so reasonable her mother said nothing more.

Melantha had loved the strong, supple feel of that little bow in her hands, loved the sensation of pinning her gaze upon her target, drawing back the string until it nearly shivered with tautness, then ultimately releasing her arrow to soar through the air. At first the arrows did little actual soaring; instead they darted crazily in every direction except the one she had intended. Undaunted, she would pay rapt attention to her da's instructions, and then devote the entire day to practicing. Many hours later her mother would finally come searching for her, telling her it was fine and well to learn to shoot, but she still had to come home and eat occasionally.

Once Melantha had mastered sufficient control over the direction her arrows took, her father began to take her hunting. This meant gloriously long days spent tracking all manner of birds and beasts in the fragrant, thick woods on the MacKillon lands. It was more than two years before Melantha actually managed to shoot anything, but in that time she learned much about moving in liquid silence across the ground, listening to the hundreds of voices chirping and whispering around her, and making herself merge with the ever-changing colors and contours of the forest.

When her father presented her with a tiny wooden sword, her mother really was bewildered. Melantha was all of six, and she was absolutely delighted with her new toy. Her da taught her the most basic skills of swordplay, and since none of the girls her age were permitted to play with swords, she quickly began to challenge the boys, including Colin and Finlay. At first they were near equally matched, but as the boys grew bigger and stronger, Melantha was forced to work harder to maintain her worthiness as an opponent. One day when she was about twelve Colin bested her in every one of their matches, and Melantha went home and angrily tossed her sword into the hearth. That evening she bitterly informed her father that she was never going to play with swords again, because it was unfair that Colin could win simply because he had grown taller and stronger than she. Her father responded with no sympathy whatsoever. Instead he made her another wooden sword, and began to train her in the elements of speed and surprise, which he assured her she could develop as well as any man.

"You can kill a man just as dead with a light sword as a heavy one," he would say, "and the same principle applies to the swordsman. 'Tis skill, sweet Mellie, not size, that is going to win the day."

Of course, he had never believed that Melantha would ever actually need to kill anyone.

She closed her eyes, her fingers tightening protectively on Patrick's thin little shoulder.

Darkness blew into Melantha's life on a swift, cold wind. At least that was how she remembered it, for her mother had never been ill before, and then suddenly it was winter and her mother could barely draw a steady breath, so painful was the cough that plagued her. At first Melantha took little notice. Her mother seemed tired, but still managed to perform the dozens of daily tasks needed to maintain their home and care for her three younger brothers. Of course Melantha was required to help with these chores, but she did so hastily, anxious to flee the drudgery of domestic work and join her father with whatever task he had engaged upon. Her mother did not complain, for she had long understood that Melantha was not a typical lass. As for Melantha's father, he could not be blamed for not recognizing the severity of his wife's condition. Somehow her mother always managed to look stronger in his presence, and if she coughed, she assured him it was nothing.

But one day Melantha and her father returned home to find her mother lying amid a litter of shattered crockery, and they realized something was seriously amiss.

Her illness quickened then, racing through her body like fire devouring an arid twig. Melantha desperately tried to assume all the household tasks her mother normally performed, only to find herself ill equipped and overwhelmed. When her mother died, Melantha experienced a shock and an emptiness she had not imagined possible. All her life she had loved her mother from a distance, never taking the time to be close to her the way she was with her da. Yet once her mother's gentle, reassuring presence was gone, Melantha found herself nearly paralyzed with grief. But there wasn't time to indulge in such weakness, because suddenly she had Daniel, Matthew, Patrick, and her da to care for, and their suffering and needs far outweighed her own.

Gone forever were the days spent innocently practicing swordplay or dreamily wandering the forest. There were five mouths to feed, and clothes to wash, and food to be prepared for today and tomorrow and next month. Never in her life had she imagined how much hard work it was to keep five people clean and fed and clothed, to say nothing of making sure her brothers didn't jump out of a tree and smash their skulls open, or wander down to the loch and drown themselves, or toss pebbles at the cows and end up trampled to death. Life became utterly exhausting and endlessly worrisome, and each night when she collapsed onto her bed she would weep silently into her pillow, tears of weariness and worry and loss. She thought that God had been unspeakably cruel to steal her mother from all of them, leaving a bleeding gash in their lives that would surely never heal.

How could she have known the worst was yet to come?

"Melantha," called Gillian, rapping softly against the door, "are you awake?"

"Aye," said Melantha, keeping her voice low so as not to wake the boys. "Come in."

The heavy wooden door opened slightly and Gillian crept inside. The light from the windows had advanced to a pearly haze, etching her friend's delicate form in ghostly luminosity against the dark stone wall.

"Is everything all right?" asked Melantha.

"Everything is fine," Gillian whispered. "But Laird MacKillon has ordered everyone to gather in the courtyard for an important announcement."

Frowning, Melantha glanced at the window. "It's barely dawn."

"It is peculiar," Gillian agreed. "Obviously whatever he wants to tell us is of great importance."

Melantha tossed back her covers and scrambled out of the bed, taking care not to stumble over the sleeping forms of Daniel and Matthew. If Laird MacKillon was summoning his people at this time of the morning, it could only mean that something terrible had happened. She heard no sounds of battle, so she didn't think they were under attack.

"What else did he say?" she demanded, hastily pulling on her leggings. A dreadful thought occurred to her. "Did the MacTiers escape?"

Gillian shook her head. "I passed through the great hall on my way up here, and they were seated at a table."

"Eating, no doubt," said Melantha contemptuously. She had never seen men consume as much food as those four. Granted, they were huge warriors and there was little in the way of meat to fill their bellies, but even so it made her furious to think of how much they were ingesting. Every morsel in their mouths meant someone else in the clan had to be satisfied with less. She would have to be sure to add the food they ate to the price of their ransom.

"Actually, they were discussing some drawings with Laird MacKillon."

Melantha squeezed her foot into a boot. "What drawings?"

"I'm not sure, but they seemed to have something to do with the defense of the castle. The dark one, Roarke, was saying something about the curtain wall, and the short, brawny one named Myles was shaking his head and arguing that it was impossible. Then the comely one got angry and said that they should just forget all this and go home."

"You mean Donald," supplied Melantha, pulling her leather jerkin over her head. It irritated her enormously that they talked about going home as if it were up to them. When would they understand that they were prisoners there, not guests?

"No," said Gillian, shaking her head. "I meant the Viking."

Melantha looked at her in surprise. "Eric?"

She nodded.

"You think he's comely?" Melantha demanded, her disbelief apparent.

The light was muted, but it was enough for her to see a faint cast of embarrassment rise to Gillian's cheeks. "I don't think he's ... unsightly," she ventured shyly.

"Sweet saints, Gillian, the man hurled your posset all over your gown," Melantha reminded her impatiently. "He glowers at everyone who goes near him and has the manners of an oaf. How could you possibly find him attractive?"

" 'Twas his features I was commenting on, not his manners," Gillian responded, sounding mildly defensive.

Melantha stared in surprise at her friend, unable to comprehend what had come over her. Gillian was so shy she nearly started at the sight of her own shadow. How could she possibly be attracted to that scowling Viking?

"He is a MacTier, Gillian," she reminded her sternly.

"Roarke said he and his men were not part of the raid on our home."

"It doesn't matter if they were or not," Melantha argued, although she had secretly been relieved to learn that they were not. "He is our sworn enemy. You must not let yourself think foolish thoughts about him."

Gillian bit her lip and studied her feet, causing the coppery gold cape of her hair to fall forward. It was a gesture she had adopted as a little girl, and she did it when she felt embarrassed and no longer wanted to participate in a conversation. Melantha instantly regretted her adamant tone. Gillian rarely adopted this defeated stance when the two of them were together. She did not like to think that she had caused her gentle friend any distress.

"Forgive me, Gillian," she said, putting her arm around her. "I did not mean to berate you. It's just that the MacTiers are our prisoners, and as soon as their ransom is paid, they will be returning to their clan. I just want you to remember that."

"I know," Gillian said softly. "And I would never dream of actually speaking to the Viking—he frightens me. But I didn't think there was anything wrong with noticing that he has a strong, handsome face, even if his eyes are always burning with fury."

"Of course there isn't," Melantha conceded.

How could she say there was, when she had often thought the same thing about Roarke? She despised him and everything he and his men represented—of that there was no doubt. Yet each time she found herself in his presence it was more difficult to look upon him and not notice his powerful form and uncommonly fine features. His was the face of a warrior—hard, fearless, and on the day she had battled him in the forest, he had even looked cruel. His bronzed skin told of a life spent outdoors, his body heated by the sun and cleansed by the clean, sweet winds that blew across the Highlands. Deep lines creased his forehead and the corners of his eyes, a testament to his advancing age, and an existence that had exposed him to sights most people only feared in their most hideous dreams. And yet there was an unaffected elegance to him, a straightness of carriage and a calmness of bearing that seemed almost reassuring. His body was granite hard, and she had matched swords with enough men to know that he was every bit as powerful as his size suggested. But there was a gentleness to him as well, and even compassion, although he was loath to let anyone see it. Melantha had felt it the day she had fallen from her horse. He had cradled her head in his lap and called her name, the low timbre of his voice drawing her from the swirling clouds of pain and into the exquisitely rough heat of his kiss.

Shame whipped through her, making her feel small and sullied.

"Are you going to rouse the lads?" asked Gillian.

Melantha fumbled clumsily with her belt, then finally succeeded in strapping on her sword. Her cheeks sufficiently cooled, she lifted her gaze to her three brothers. Part of her wanted to let them sleep, because she knew they were growing and needed their rest. But the possibility that something was wrong dictated that they should be with her. She could not protect them if they were separated from her.

"Wake up, lads," she called softly, kneeling down to stroke Matthew's cheek.

Daniel groaned and pulled the covers over his head. Matthew rubbed his eyes with his knuckles before opening them to smile at her. And little Patrick continued to slumber peacefully in her bed.

"Come, now, 'tis a wonderful new day and we've lots to do." Melantha moved to the bed to rouse Patrick. "After breakfast you can all practice your swordplay, and later you can help the men with the repairs to the keep."

Daniel reluctantly pushed down the covers. "Will you give me a lesson in shooting today?"

"We shall have to see. Right now you must get dressed and come down to the courtyard with me. Laird MacKillon wishes to address the clan, and we have to hurry."

Patrick sat up and smiled at her with sleepy eyes. His hair was a charming mop of red tangles, and Melantha wondered if she had time to take a comb to it. "Why does he want to talk to us so early?" he wondered.

"Have the MacTiers escaped?" demanded Daniel, sitting upright suddenly. His hands balled into angry fists and his rail-thin body tensed for action, as if he meant to spring from his bed and find them.

Melantha tossed Daniel his tattered plaid. "No," she replied, not surprised that his first thought had been the same as hers. She and Daniel had long been alike in countless ways, and as the eldest male in their family, he saw himself as far more of a man than his thirteen years would permit.

"Then what does Laird MacKillon want?" wondered Matthew, his little brow puckering.

"The sooner you're dressed, the sooner we shall find out," said Melantha airily, trying to soothe his fear. She sat beside

Patrick and began to attack the nest of tangles with a comb. "Splash some water on your faces and get your plaids on. Gillian, please help Matthew, he has trouble with his."

A few minutes later the little party stepped into the cool early morning light of the courtyard. Despite Melantha's and Gillian's best efforts, the boys looked rather disheveled. Their plaids were untidily arranged with their shirts rising out of them, and all of their hair had stubbornly resisted the efforts of her comb, until finally Melantha had seriously contemplated taking the scissors to them.

Fortunately, most of the clan had not fared much better in their haste to get dressed at such an untimely hour. Most were yawning and making only perfunctory attempts to improve their appearance—a quick rake of fingers through sleep-tousled hair, a minor adjustment to a loosely draped plaid that threatened to drop to the wearer's ankles at any moment, a smoothing of a gown that had accidentally been donned backward. The entire assemblage looked tired and grumpy, and could probably have done with a little ale and bread to fill the emptiness in their stomachs before being summoned out there.

Laird MacKillon, Hagar, and Thor were seated on a platform at the end of the courtyard, waiting for the MacKillons to assemble. Thor had his sword placed upon his lap and was lovingly running his fingers along its edges, testing its sharpness. Laird MacKillon and Hagar were intently studying a diagram on a piece of paper. They frowned at it for a long moment, then turned it on its side. After some animated discussion, they turned it on its other side. This did not appear to improve matters at all. Finally Laird MacKillon called to Roarke, who was discussing some problem with the curtain wall with his men. At Laird MacKillon's bidding he abandoned his discussion and mounted the platform to study the unintelligible piece of paper. He looked at it barely an instant before turning it upside down. Comprehension crept slowly across the elders' faces. They began to nod their heads and congratulate each other, pleased that they had sorted it out.

Melantha watched as Roarke strode from the platform and resumed his conversation with Eric, Donald, and Myles. His limp was gone, and he walked with easy, confident purpose. Unlike the rest of her clan, he did not appear to be the least bit weary. His saffron shirt and red-and-black plaid were immaculately arranged, and his dark leather jerkin was tightly laced across the solid expanse of his chest. He gazed up at the battlements and pointed out something to Eric, who was adamantly shaking his head. But Roarke did not agree with his warrior. He continued to gesture at the parapet, and then to the towers, until finally Eric seemed to be swayed by whatever argument he was making. Roarke nodded with satisfaction and turned to regard the crowd.

Power emanated from his very core as he surveyed the group, and the lines of his face were set with rigid determination. Melantha stared at him in fascination. She had told herself that Roarke was her prisoner—a dangerous warrior who had been captured in the woods and was now completely at the mercy of her and her clan. But as he stood with his muscled legs braced apart and his powerful arms folded across his chest, she could not imagine him being at anyone's mercy. A faint breeze was blowing through the long black strands of his hair, causing them to brush lightly against the bronzed plane of his freshly shaven jaw. Melantha found herself recalling what it was like to lay her hand against his cheek, how it had felt warm and strong and rough all at once, like a fine layer of sunwashed sand. When Roarke had bent his head and tasted her with his lips, she had longed for the masculine roughness of his skin next to hers, setting her flesh afire as he flushed her senses with heat and pleasure.

"What's the matter with you, Melantha?" asked Daniel, frowning. "You look kind of funny."

"Nothing," she replied, tearing her gaze off Roarke.

Gillian looked at her with concern. "You do look a little flushed. Perhaps you should sit down."

"I'm fine," Melantha insisted, feeling as if her face were in flames.

"You're all red," observed Matthew.

"Do you feel like throwing up?" chirped Patrick, sounding excited by the possibility.

"No—I'm fine," Melantha insisted, wishing they would all just leave her alone. "I probably just need to eat something."

Gillian and the boys looked at her in astonishment. Too late Melantha realized that she had just succeeded in making them more concerned, for she almost never felt hungry anymore.

"Shall I run inside and fetch you something?" asked Gillian, eager to feed her.

"I could go," Patrick offered.

"I can run faster," argued Daniel.

"That's just because you're bigger," Patrick informed him. "It doesn't make him better than me, does it, Melantha?"

"I never said I was better," objected Daniel, "but I can run faster. That's just a fact."

"But I want to go!" insisted Patrick.

"I'm really not hungry," interjected Melantha.

"Oh." Gillian's disappointment was obvious.

"I am," said Patrick, trying to cheer Gillian up.

She put her arm around him. "Then we shall find you something to eat right after Laird MacKillon's announcement."

"When is he going to speak, anyway?" wondered Daniel impatiently. "I have to go practice my swordplay so I'll be able to fight the MacTiers when they come back."

Matthew regarded him with alarm. "The MacTiers are coming back?"

"Of course not," soothed Melantha, casting Daniel a warning look.

"In case they come back," Daniel amended, understanding that Matthew and Patrick were just babies and could not be expected to understand such grown-up matters.

Laird MacKillon rose slowly from his chair to address his people. "I know 'tis a terrible thing to rouse a body at this ungodly hour of the morning—"

" 'Tis still night as far as I'm concerned," grumbled Thor.

"—but it is very important that everyone hears what Roarke has to say."

"Then let's hear it so we can go back to bed!" suggested Ninian.

The clan laughed.

"As you know, the attack by the MacTiers some months ago has left our holding in rather a bad way," continued Laird MacKillon. "And Roarke has brought it to my attention that we might not be able to defend ourselves should we be attacked again."

"Who would want to attack us?" wondered Gelfrid. "We've nothing left since the MacTiers stripped us of everything."

"I've got this worn pair of boots." Mungo raised his foot to wiggle his naked big toe. "Perhaps the greedy filchers will be back for them!"

Laughter rose once again from the clan.

"A vulnerable holding will draw an attacker," Roarke said with flat certitude. "There is always something to be gained, even if it is just a night of revelry and some food."

Uneasy silence fell over the courtyard.

"When the MacTiers attacked you the first time, they could not be sure if there were riches within these walls, or nothing more than a few rusted swords and some barrels of ale," he continued, regarding them seriously. "It didn't matter. Whatever they found was theirs for the taking, and it cost them virtually nothing. By now the tale of your effortless defeat has reached other clans, who one day may decide to ride over here and see what remains for them to acquire."

"You mean steal," corrected Ninian angrily.

Roarke shrugged. "Call it what you will."

"By God, if anyone dares attack us again, they'll feel the cold steel of my sword slit their belly!" shouted Thor. He braced his hand on the back of his chair and struggled to rise while lifting his heavy sword. Ultimately the effort proved too much, and he collapsed into the chair, dropped his sword, and dissolved into a fit of phlegmy coughing. "Ale," he gasped, motioning to young Keith.

The lad obligingly went running to fetch him his drink.

"Better bring a jug of it," Thor advised, thumping himself on his chest. "If this is my time, by God, I shall not go out in need of a drink!"

"If we're in danger of attack, what are we supposed to do about it?" demanded Gelfrid.

"The MacTiers slew some twenty-six of our bravest men, and tried to destroy our homes and reduce our castle to rubble," said Ninian. "We're less able to defend ourselves now than we were when they attacked the first time."

"But we won't be once we get the ransom for these prisoners and secure an alliance with the MacKenzies," Colin reminded them. He looked pointedly at Roarke. "That's why they're here."

"It is good that you plan to make alliances with other clans," said Roarke, ignoring the issue of his ransom. "But it is not enough. No invader is going to send you a missive detailing the day and time of his attack. You must be prepared to fend off an assault yourself, at least until you can get word to your allies and they are able to get here."

"That's a grand idea, laddie," said Magnus, smiling with approval.

"It's impossible," argued Ninian impatiently.

"Once an army gets in, we've no hope of defeating them," added Gelfrid.

"Of course we do!" roared Thor, much restored by the

cup of ale he had just drained. "All we need do is hack off their heads, and toss them in a pile to be ground into bread!"

Laird MacKillon regarded him curiously. "Your pardon, Thor, but have you ever hacked off a man's head before?"

"Dozens of times," Thor boasted, patting his sword.

Laird MacKillon looked skeptical. "Didn't you find it rather a lot of work?"

"Not at all," Thor assured him. "Just like cutting a dumpling."

"You must focus your energies on preventing an attacking force from breaching the wall," continued Roarke, struggling for patience.

"But how?" asked Hagar. "The MacTiers appeared in the middle of the night, and were up the wall and waving their swords in our faces before we even knew what we were about."

"We had some fine, brave men keeping watch," Magnus added, "but it was dark and they couldn't see them until it was too late."

Roarke nodded. "Many clans prefer to attack a stronghold at night, knowing that the inhabitants are sleeping and they can use the cover of darkness to their advantage. What you need to do is establish a warning system, so that you are apprised when an aggressor is near and you can quickly prepare yourselves for defense."

Laird MacKillon looked at him blankly. "A warning system?"

Roarke nodded. "First, you must increase the number of guards you keep posted on the wall head to watch for anything unusual. Every pair of eyes helps. But in the dead of night it is difficult to see what is happening below. That is why you must set traps."

Magnus's brows knitted into a single white pelt. "Ye mean like for an animal?"

"Exactly," replied Roarke. "You will dig a series of pits around the base of the curtain wall. Each pit must be no less than twelve feet deep and ten feet across, with a covering of branches to hold the sod you will place over it. Eventually you should have a pit every twenty paces, but begin by placing one at each corner of the wall, adjacent to the towers. Most attackers will approach a castle wall at the sides rather than attempting to climb straight up the center. As they make their way toward the wall, a number of warriors will step on the covering for the pit and fall in, bellowing in fury as they go."

"And that's our warning!" said Magnus happily.

"It's very clever," Hagar admitted, "as it has the added benefit of reducing their numbers at the same time!"

"Even if we dig ten pits, we can't expect an entire army to fall into them," objected Colin, regarding Roarke with contempt. "That's not going to be enough to win a battle."

"No, it isn't," Roarke agreed, ignoring Colin's hostility. "And since your numbers are limited, you must employ more imaginative methods of retaliation. Methods that the notorious Falcon might use as she preys upon unsuspecting targets in the woods."

Melantha kept her expression contained. Was Roarke actually complimenting her technique?

"The Falcon's band is able to surprise its targets because they are the ones planning the ambush," Mungo pointed out. "It isn't the same as *being* attacked."

"Not the same at all," agreed Ninian.

"The principle of surprise remains the same," Roarke argued, "and that is what you are trying to do—surprise them and reduce their numbers. At worst you are eroding their confidence and shrinking their size. At best, you may cause them to reconsider their assault and retreat."

"The lad's right," said Magnus. "Many's the time the Falcon's band has attacked a group much larger than us. By the time we're through, we've stripped them of their possessions and have them quivering in their skins, wonderin' if we're goin' to let them live to see another day."

"You swore to me that you'd never slain anyone," objected Edwina.

"We haven't," Magnus admitted, "but our victims don't know that."

"I wanted to kill these MacTiers," said Finlay. He gave Roarke and his men a menacing look and spat on the ground.

"Good for you!" burst out Thor.

"Why didn't you?" Hagar wondered.

Finlay looked sheepish. "Melantha wouldn't let me."

The clan laughed.

"And it's a good thing she didn't," interjected Laird MacKillon, "or else we wouldn't have Roarke here today giving us these fine ideas. Tell us, lad, what other tricks did you have in mind?"

"My men and I have learned firsthand about the effectiveness of dropping nets," Roarke continued. "If you place nets above those chambers with easily accessible windows, you will be able to capture your intruders as they steal across the floor—quickly, quietly, and without bloodshed."

"A net is only good for capturing a few men," Mungo objected. "Our time would be better spent practicing our fighting rather than making nets."

"If they are used properly, the nets will do the work of twenty men," argued Roarke. "Lewis, I'm sure, can develop an effective system for quickly raising the net after the prisoners have been removed, so that it can be used again."

Lewis stared at him in shock.

"Does he mean our Lewis?" demanded Thor.

"I have some other ideas on which I would like to confer with Lewis," Roarke continued. "As you all know, he has an exceptionally quick mind when it comes to solving problems."

Lewis looked around uncertainly, as if he expected some-one might laugh.

"I think he's talking about one of his own men," Ninian decided. "Probably that fancy one who keeps staring at the lasses." He pointed to Donald.

"It is essential that everyone be assigned a duty, and that you are thoroughly drilled in performing that duty," contin-ued Roarke. "If you are attacked, each man, woman, and child must know exactly where they have to go and what they are to do. Practice curtails panic. You will be divided into groups, and your groups will rotate between training and other du-ties. One will train, one will work on the castle's defenses, one will produce an ample supply of weapons, and one will pre-pare food in case of a siege. Your battle with the MacTiers only lasted a day, but if your next attackers don't defeat you with similar alacrity, they may decide to linger awhile. You must make sure you have enough arrows and bread to main-tain your defense."

"We'd have a lot more bread if MacKillon here would just let me slay you lot," grumbled Thor.

"I have some suggestions as to who might lead the train-ing sessions," continued Roarke, consulting his notes.

"I'm happy to sharpen the men's skills with a bow," Mag-nus volunteered. "I'm sure I don't need to remind ye that I'm a wee bit more than a fair shot," he added, giving Roarke a sly wink.

"No, of course not." Roarke thought of Magnus's trem-bling hands as they fought to restrain his arrows. "But since you will have a large group to train, perhaps Donald could as-sist you."

"An apprentice, ye say?" Magnus doubtfully scratched his white head. "Very well. If ye keep yer eyes more on me and less on the lasses," he said, regarding Donald sternly, "maybe I'll be able to teach ye a thing or two."

Donald gave him a graceful bow. "I shall forever be in your debt."

"Now, then," continued Roarke, "for the training with swords—"

"All right then, I'll do it," interrupted Thor grumpily, as if he had just relented to Roarke's lengthy beseeching. "But I warn you, I don't tolerate laggards."

Roarke cast an inquiring glance at Eric.

"Never," growled the fair-haired warrior. "I would sooner have my bowels dragged slowly from my body and be left to rot in their hot, stinking—"

"Eric will help you, Thor," said Roarke amiably.

Thor glared ominously at Eric. "If you give me so much as a whit of trouble, Viking, I shall have no choice but to kill you."

"Only if I don't kill myself first," muttered Eric, glowering at Roarke.

"I propose that Lewis be in charge of designing the traps," Roarke continued, "and he should oversee the men as they build them, to ensure that his instructions are carried out accurately."

Lewis shook his head. "I can design them," he said, not sounding terribly confident even on that point, "but I can't supervise the men."

"Of course you can," Roarke insisted.

Lewis shook his head more adamantly.

"The lad's right," said Gelfrid.

"He's too timid to make a crew of men do his bidding," Ninian scoffed.

"Why don't you believe you can, Lewis?" asked Roarke, irritated by the way everyone constantly contributed to the youth's lack of confidence.

Lewis stared at the ground. "Because no one will listen to me." His face was nearly crimson with embarrassment.

"Of course they will listen to you," Roarke objected, "or

they will have to deal with—" He stopped suddenly, realizing he had been about to say himself. But he had no authority here—he was a prisoner, for God's sake.

"They will have to deal with me."

Everyone looked in surprise at Laird MacKillon.

"According to Roarke, our Lewis has a special talent. If this is true, then we should ensure that he is able to put this talent to work for the good of the clan, should we not?"

The clan regarded him in uncomfortable silence.

"Splendid. I'm sure I can count on everyone assigned to implement Lewis's designs to pay close attention, and to carry out his instructions to the best of their abilities."

Mortified at being the center of this discussion, Lewis continued to study his feet.

Roarke swept his gaze over the courtyard. It was clear the MacKillons were unconvinced, but knew better than to contest a direct order from their laird. He sighed inwardly, hoping Lewis would be able to overcome his lack of confidence, thereby earning the respect of the clan.

"Well, I'm happy that's all sorted out," said Laird MacKillon, rising slowly from his chair. "And now, I suggest that everyone go back to bed and get a bit more sleep—there's plenty of time to address all of these things."

"We must begin immediately," Roarke objected.

"Now, lad, I know you're anxious to get things started," Laird MacKillon returned, "but I'm sure you'll find everyone can apply themselves far better once they've had a little more rest."

"There is no time to be wasted," persisted Roarke, watching in frustration as the clan gratefully began to disperse. "We should be dividing the clan into groups—"

"*We* will take care of it," said Colin emphatically. "I must confess, I do find your sudden concern for our welfare somewhat perplexing. Just what, exactly, are you planning?" His gaze bored into Roarke. "Do you believe that if you keep everyone occupied with training and building, you and your warriors will be able to escape unnoticed?"

"No." Roarke was acutely aware that Melantha and her brothers were listening to their discussion.

"Then why are you pretending to want to help us?"

He curled the paper he was holding into his hand. "I have my reasons."

"And no doubt they are eminently noble," drawled Colin. "You are here as a prisoner, and now that you have seen the state we are in, you wish to help us, is that it?"

"Something like that."

"Such valor. Tell me, Roarke, if your clan's army was climbing our walls tonight in a bid to free you and your men, what would you do? Would you grab a weapon and help us fight them off, knowing the devastation we face should they defeat us once again? Or would you slaughter all who got in your way as you fought to reach the gate and let them in?"

Roarke said nothing.

"Don't bother pretending it's a decision over which you would agonize," Colin snarled. "We both know which choice you would make."

Roarke kept his expression impassive, refusing to confirm or deny Colin's allegations. Colin thoroughly despised him, and nothing Roarke said or did could possibly change that.

"Finlay, take these prisoners back into the great hall," commanded Colin, "and don't let them out of your sight."

He went to Melantha, laid his hand at the small of her back, and placed his arm protectively around Daniel, as if he were gathering his family.

Then he shepherded her and the boys back toward the castle, leaving Roarke to stand and wonder at the powerful emotions stabbing his chest.

CHAPTER 6

"Lay down your sword, you scrawny, miserable pup, or I'll run you through like a hare on a spit!"

Patrick obediently dropped his wooden sword.

"You're not supposed to do it, Patrick!" said Daniel in disgust.

Patrick regarded his brother in confusion. "But you told me to."

"It doesn't matter if I tell you to. An attacking warrior says all kinds of horrid things to frighten people into surrendering—it doesn't mean you listen to them."

"But if I didn't obey you, you were going to run me through," objected Patrick.

"Now that you have no weapon, I'm going to run you

through anyway." He thrust his sword alongside Patrick's waist. "There, see? Now you're dead."

Patrick's blue eyes rounded with disbelief. "But that's not fair! I did just as you told me to!"

"Attacking warriors don't care about what's fair," Daniel informed him authoritatively. "All they care about is how many they maim and kill—isn't that right, Magnus?"

"Well, now, I suppose that's mostly true." His eyes squinting against the afternoon light, Magnus nocked his arrow against the string of his bow and took careful aim at a straw-filled wagon in the courtyard below. The string of his weapon grew taut, then began to shiver as his aged hand quickly tired. Unable to restrain it any longer, he released the arrow into the air.

Daniel, Patrick, and Matthew peered over the battlements to watch its voyage. The arrow veered far to the right of the wagon, then burrowed into the earth by the stone well, missing Thor's feet by scarcely a hairsbreadth.

"God's teeth!" Thor roared, raising his sword to defend himself. On seeing Magnus gazing down from the parapet, he grew even more agitated. "What are you trying to do, kill me?"

"Ye were in no danger," Magnus assured him. "The arrow went exactly where I wanted it to go."

"The devil it did!" countered Thor furiously. "Unless you were trying to spear my foot to the ground!"

" 'Twas not your foot I was aiming for," Magnus returned. " 'Twas that scrap of leaf lying on the ground beside it that had caught my attention."

Thor squinted at the grass. "There is no leaf here."

"Not anymore, there isn't," Magnus agreed. "That's because the head of my arrow drove it deep into the ground."

Unconvinced, Thor plucked the shaft from the ground and critically examined its tip. "I don't see any—"

"Thank ye for retrieving my arrow for me," said Magnus,

waving. "Don't trouble yerself by bringin' it up—I shall be down later to collect it."

"Did you really mean to hit the earth so close to Thor's foot?" asked Matthew, impressed.

"Aye."

"I don't see how you could hit a leaf down there," objected Daniel, straining to see something equally small. "It's too little."

" 'Twas nothing," Magnus scoffed, slinging his bow over his arm. "When ye've launched tens of thousands of arrows, as I have, ye learn to sense their flight before ye set them free. 'Tis almost as if we are one."

"Were you one with the arrow that hit Roarke in the bum?" wondered Patrick.

Magnus chuckled. "Now, that was as fine a shot as any a man has ever made. That's why I saved the arrow." He pulled the prized shaft from his quiver so the boys could examine it.

"Why did you aim for Roarke's bum?" wondered Matthew, running his fingers in awe along the shaft.

"Why didn't you aim for his heart?" asked Daniel harshly.

"Well, now, the heart is a very tiny part of a man, and ye need only look at Roarke to see that he's an uncommonly big fellow. There he was, crashing through the woods on his enormous black charger, swinging a great silver sword with the strength of ten men or more, and there was our dear Melantha, bravely meeting him blow for blow. But though the Falcon is quick and able, she could not match Roarke's powerful strikes for long. And so I knew I had to do something and double quick, or else it might be all over for the Falcon and her band. The MacTier's back was to me, so I steadied my arrow and aimed for his heart, knowing I could pierce it straight and true. But then I began to worry that his leather jerkin might be thick enough to resist the impact of my arrow, or perhaps the tip would strike squarely upon a rib and not delve in more than an inch or so, which would only succeed in making him even more fearsome than he already was."

Magnus paused for effect, looking with satisfaction at the three pairs of eyes fixed upon him in rapt fascination.

"What did you do?" demanded Patrick eagerly.

"I set my gaze lower and pierced him where he was far more vulnerable," Magnus finished triumphantly. "The mighty MacTier warrior was off his horse and squalling like a bairn faster than ye could spit!" He slapped his thigh and shook with laughter, causing the boys to giggle as well.

"I don't recall 'squalling,'" objected a low voice.

The three boys instantly stopped and regarded Roarke with varying degrees of fear, fascination, and contempt. Magnus, however, gazed at Roarke with amusement.

"Ye were in far too much pain to be able to recall exactly how ye were," he told him, still chuckling.

"Does your bum still hurt?" asked Patrick sympathetically.

"No," snapped Roarke, wishing to close the topic.

Little Patrick's face fell.

Roarke instantly regretted his tone. "Thank you for asking," he added, feeling somewhere between an ogre and an idiot.

"Have ye come to work on the wall head?" asked Magnus, seeing Lewis and Finlay appear from one of the entrances leading some twenty men. They were burdened with heavy timbers, wooden planks, axes, saws, hammers, and nails.

Roarke nodded. "The pits are coming along well, and Lewis and I have been discussing some ideas for making it more difficult to breach the wall," he explained. "We're going to begin construction on six wooden hoardings to project from the parapet. Each will have openings in the floor through which heavy stones and boiling oil can be dropped on the attackers below. These will give you a better vantage point than just hurling rocks over the battlements."

"We're going to build one right over the gate," added Lewis. "That's going to keep any attackers from ramming it."

"It will make it more difficult," amended Roarke.

"Ye don't say?" said Magnus, clearly intrigued. "But won't that leave the lads perched on the hoarding in danger of being shot?"

"I've designed the hoardings to be almost completely enclosed," said Lewis. He unrolled one of the drawings he was carrying and showed it to Magnus. "There will be walls on all three sides, with cross-shaped openings to allow the men to see," he explained, proudly pointing to these features on his neatly detailed diagram. "They can also see through the openings in the floor."

"An excellent idea!" said Magnus. "Do ye think I could shoot from one of these?"

Lewis frowned, studying his design. "I don't believe there will be enough room for an archer."

"The hoardings will be manned by two men who need room to move and keep a stockpile of rocks," explained Roarke. "There won't be space for an archer as well."

"A pity." Magnus sighed wistfully. "I could make some fine hits from a platform like that."

"You would also have an excellent vantage point if you shot from one of the upper chambers," Roarke suggested. The wall head was a dangerous place during an attack, and he did not particularly relish the idea of Magnus being caught in the thick of it. Beyond that, there was also the distinct possibility of Magnus accidentally planting an arrow into one of his own clan.

"Ye might be right," said Magnus, thoughtfully stroking his beard. "But there's no point in thinkin' about that." He sighed. "Duty requires an old warrior like me to be up here, so I can lead my men to victory."

Roarke wasn't certain which men he was talking about, but he refrained from questioning him on that point. "The entire clan would be better served by your skills as an archer, Magnus," he suggested, wondering just why the thought of the old man being exposed to danger bothered him.

"And you're a great archer!" gushed Patrick enthusiastically. "You should have seen the way he hit the leaf beside Thor's foot," he told Roarke. "It was so close, Thor was actually afraid for his life!"

" 'Twas nothing," said Magnus, thoroughly pleased with himself.

"The arrow went so deep, it made the leaf disappear!" added Patrick.

Roarke raised a skeptical brow. "Really?"

"Now, lads, ye don't want to sound like yer braggin'," admonished Magnus, looking slightly uncomfortable. "Run along and play somewhere."

"I don't play," Daniel informed him stiffly. "I'm training to be a warrior. And I want to stay here and help build these platforms."

"I want to help build platforms too," volunteered Patrick.

"Me too," added Matthew, although he sounded less than certain.

Magnus regarded them dubiously. "Do ye think ye can find somethin' for them to do?" he asked Lewis.

"There are all kinds of things they can do to help," Lewis assured Magnus. "We need every pair of hands."

"Fine, then. Ye can stay up here and help—but make sure ye don't get in anyone's way," instructed Magnus sternly. "Do ye hear?"

The three boys nodded.

"Well, then, I suppose I'll collect that arrow I shot into that leaf before leadin' the men in their archery practice. Ye know how I hate to waste a perfectly good arrow." He cast Roarke an amused look.

Not waiting for Roarke's response, he jauntily slung his bow over his shoulder and disappeared.

"Give me your sword!"

Melantha watched in disbelief as Ninian obediently handed his weapon over to Eric. Her hand instinctively flew to the hilt of her own sword. Did Ninian not realize the danger of allowing this MacTier prisoner to be armed?

"Brace your feet a shoulder width apart, so your stance is solid," Eric instructed, positioning his own feet at the same time. "You are thin, and although Gelfrid here is short and fat, he outmatches you by weight."

"I'm not fat," protested Gelfrid. He lowered his sword so he could mop his sweating brow with his sleeve. "I'll have you know this is sheer muscle." He thumped the generous round of his belly with his pudgy fist.

"More like sheer ale," countered Ninian.

"Whatever it is, the Viking is saying that I have the advantage," said Gelfrid testily.

"No, he's saying I'd best not let you sit on me or I'll be crushed," Ninian retorted.

"Why don't we try it and find out?" snapped Gelfrid, tossing his sword down and stomping toward his friend.

Eric felt the taut thread of his patience snap. *"Enough!"*

Every MacKillon in the yard instantly stopped what they were doing and stared at Eric in bewilderment.

"What's amiss, Viking?" demanded Thor, who was seated comfortably in a chair with a cup of cool ale in his hand. "Is the training over for today?"

"No," said Eric, struggling to rein in his temper. "Everyone continue."

The thirty or so men who were training resumed their exercises.

Eric fixed Gelfrid and Ninian with a steely stare. "Do you wish to learn to fight, or do you prefer to squabble like a pair of old women?"

The two MacKillons exchanged chastised looks.

"We want to learn to fight," said Ninian.

"Like warriors," Gelfrid added.

"Fine. Let us continue." Eric assumed his braced stance once again. "If your opponent is larger than you, you must make it hard for him to knock you off balance. Grip your sword firmly with your right hand, like so, and keep your left arm out, to help maintain your footing. . . ."

Melantha watched Eric in confusion, her hand still gripping the hilt of her sword. The enormous warrior had a weapon in his hand. This was a perfect opportunity for him. Why didn't he just grab either Gelfrid or Ninian and put the blade to their throat, then threaten to slay them if he and his fellow MacTiers weren't released at once?

"He's very strong, isn't he?"

Melantha turned to see Gillian standing beside her. Her faded gray gown was limp and splattered with grease, indicating that she had been working in the kitchen. Despite the shabby condition of her attire, Melantha thought her friend looked remarkably pretty. Her red-gold hair formed a gauzy veil about her pale face, and her eyes were large and shimmering, like a loch glistening with sunlight.

"Look how effortlessly he wields Ninian's sword," Gillian commented, her gaze fixed upon Eric. " 'Tis barely more than a twig to him."

"Aye, he's strong," agreed Melantha. "Strong and well trained and a MacTier warrior. That makes him dangerous, Gillian."

"And yet he has not tried to harm any of us," she reflected softly.

"He has not tried to harm anyone because he is a prisoner," pointed out Melantha, "and knows he would be vastly outnumbered were he to raise so much as his hand."

"Perhaps." Gillian watched as Eric demonstrated several deadly slicing motions with his sword, then handed the weapon back to Ninian so he could practice. "But why is he helping to train the very people who hold him prisoner? Surely it would be better for these MacTiers if we remained weak and defenseless, in case their clan comes to free them."

Melantha did not know the answer to that question. All around her, members of her clan were busily digging pits, making weapons, preparing food, and training. Why had Roarke and his men instigated these projects? It could only have something to do with their plans for escape, she reflected darkly. Roarke was far too proud a warrior to placidly bide his time here and wait for his ransom to be paid. But what, exactly, were they planning?

"Do you know where Roarke is, Gillian?" she asked.

"He is up on the wall walk with Lewis and a group of men. They are constructing some kind of platform from one of Lewis's designs."

"I am going up to see what they are doing. Are you coming?"

"I have to get back to the kitchen," said Gillian, not taking her eyes off Eric.

"Very well." Melantha turned toward the keep, noting that her friend showed absolutely no sign of moving.

The wall head was teeming with activity, and she had to step carefully to avoid tripping over a tool or being hit by one of the dozens of heavy planks being carried to and fro.

"Melantha! Look at what I'm doing!"

Melantha turned to see Patrick standing beside the burly form of Myles.

"We're building a wall for one of the platforms," Patrick informed her, his freckled face beaming with excitement. He eagerly handed Myles a nail.

The MacTier warrior positioned it over one of the boards lying on the ground before him, then drove it in with two powerful swings of his iron mallet. It was a blow that could easily kill a man, Melantha thought. Or crush a child's skull.

"That was a good one," said Myles, inspecting the sunken scrap of iron with approval. "Find me another like that one, Patty—straight and true with a good, sharp tip."

His red brows puckered with concentration, Patrick fished through his black pile of nails. "Here's a good one!" he said triumphantly, extracting a dark pin that looked exactly like the rest.

"Perfect." Myles took it from him and positioned it on the board. Two more powerful raps and the nail had disappeared. "Smooth as a greased dirk."

"Why would you want to put grease on a dirk?" Patrick wondered.

" 'Tis an old trick of mine," Myles explained. "Makes the dirk sink into a man's gut like a blade in warm butter."

"Really?" Patrick's blue eyes widened with childish fascination. "How many men have you killed, Myles?"

"Come here, Patrick," said Melantha suddenly.

Patrick turned to look at her. "Why?"

"I have something I need you to do for me," she replied, giving Myles a disapproving look.

Patrick remained planted beside Myles. "What?" It was clear he was reluctant to abandon his privileged position as an assistant to the forbidding-looking MacTier warrior.

"I need you to—help me find Daniel and Matthew," she improvised.

"They're practicing their swordplay just beyond the west tower," said Patrick. "Look, you can just see them."

Melantha glanced over to see the two boys playfully cracking their wooden swords together.

"Then I need you to help me find Roarke."

"He's right over there."

Melantha followed his grubby little finger and saw Roarke standing at the far end of the wall head, directing the efforts of several men who were inserting a square timber through an opening in the parapet.

"Come with me while I go to speak with him." She extended her hand to him.

"I want to stay here and help Myles," Patrick insisted. "He needs me."

"Maybe you'd best go with your sister, Patty," said Myles, sensing Melantha's displeasure. "I can manage without you."

"But you told me you needed me." Patrick sounded crestfallen. "You said my job was important."

"And so it is," Myles assured him. "But now that we've got this wall well in hand, perhaps there is someone else needing your assistance—like Lewis."

"I don't want to help Lewis," Patrick objected, his expression pleading. "I want to help you."

Myles gave Melantha a helpless look.

Melantha was on the verge of ordering Patrick to come to her side at once. But something in Myles's eyes caused her to hesitate. They reflected warmth and gentle humor as he looked at her, as if he were saying, Well, what are we to do with this lad now?

He was a MacTier warrior, Melantha reminded herself firmly, who had the strength to kill Patrick with one deliberate blow of his mallet. And yet, despite his forbidding countenance, with his shaved head and his thick arms sheathed in battered metal guards, Melantha sensed no danger from Myles as he towered over the small form of her baby brother. If anything he was being extremely sweet with the lad— giving him a simple task to make him feel needed, and complimenting him on his performance. Patrick was only seven years old, but already he had lost both his parents and seen his clan brutalized by attack and near starvation. If he had found a morsel of pleasure standing in the sunlight passing Myles the very best nails, then what harm was there in letting him do so? The wall head was crowded with her people, any one of whom would intervene if they thought for an instant that Patrick was in danger.

"Very well," she relented. "You may stay here and help Myles—but no more talk of dirks, understood?"

"Yes." Patrick's blue eyes danced with delight.

"I am also speaking to you, Myles," Melantha added in a stern voice.

Myles nodded meekly, then gave Patrick a conspiratorial wink.

Melantha turned and made her way to the end of the wall walk, wondering if she should have included swords and other weapons in her directive.

"A little farther out . . . a little more . . . there," Lewis said, finally satisfied with the position of the beam. "Now place the others parallel to this one, and make sure they are well secured before you nail the planks on top."

"Are you sure this thing is going to hold the weight of two men and all those stones?" demanded Mungo skeptically.

"Roarke has seen similar galleries built out from some of the castles he has attacked. He has assured me that if they are constructed correctly, they are extremely secure."

"But how do we know if we're building it correctly?" wondered Finlay. "We've never made one of these contraptions before."

"I have calculated a man's weight against the strength of the design," Lewis explained. "It will hold."

"But how can you know for certain?"

Lewis dropped his gaze to his diagram, uncertain how to convince them.

"Lewis's design is excellent," interjected Roarke. "He has even improved upon the platforms that I have seen by placing an additional cross piece, here, to better distribute the weight," he added, pointing this feature out on Lewis's drawing.

"That may be, but I'll not be the first one out to test the thing!" Mungo chortled, shaking his head. "I've no desire to fall through the air and break both my legs, no matter how pretty Lewis's drawing is!"

"Nor I," added Finlay, laughing.

"You won't fall," protested Lewis in frustration. "The hoarding will hold you."

"So you've said," replied Mungo, "but I'll be keeping my feet on firmer ground, all the same."

"Once the timbers are in place, I will go out and nail the planks down myself. That way you will see the hoarding is secure."

Lewis, Mungo, and Finlay looked at Roarke in astonishment.

"You would do that?" said Lewis.

"Of course," he replied. "Because I have no doubt that your design is sound. Now, if you two are sure enough of what you are doing to carry on, Lewis must check with the men on the other end of the wall—" He stopped suddenly, his thoughts completely arrested by the sight of Melantha.

In the three days since he had addressed her people in the courtyard, Melantha had managed to avoid Roarke completely. He had known she was angry with him for not playing the role of prisoner to her liking, and for convincing her clan to institute some of his ideas. He could only guess what she imagined his motives to be, but he had little doubt that she suspected his assistance was directly entwined with some nefarious plan of escape.

Strangely enough, Roarke had actually missed her glowering presence. At this moment her expression was marginally softer—not precisely welcoming, but not exuding its characteristic scorn and bitterness either. She was garbed in her customary outfit of leggings, high deerskin boots, a loosely fitted tunic of plain brown wool, and a moss green quilted jerkin. Although he would have preferred to see her draped in a richly colored gown of fine silk or soft wool,

Roarke found himself admiring the firm curve of her legs, which these particular leggings did little to obscure. Her dark hair was loosely secured with a frayed length of ribbon, but Roarke suspected this was purely for keeping her hair out of her eyes, rather than any capitulation to female vanity. Despite her utter indifference to her appearance as a woman, he found her completely enchanting as she gazed up at him. A honeyed cast of sunlight warmed the chiseled paleness of her cheeks, softening the sharp lines of deprivation that disturbed him so, and her eyes were large and mysteriously veiled, drawing him deeper into their depths as he tried to discern her mood.

"Good afternoon, milady." He gave her a polite bow.

Melantha frowned, not sure if he was making sport of her or not. She was well aware that her attire made her look anything but a lady. She searched his expression but could find no trace of mockery in it. Instead he regarded her with something akin to warmth, as if he were actually pleased to see her.

"I came to see the progress on the wall," she said, as if her presence in his company required an explanation.

"It's going very well, Melantha," said Lewis enthusiastically. "We have cut openings in the parapet to hold the timbers for four hoardings, and now we're just positioning—"

"*Look out below!*"

Melantha, Roarke, and Lewis peered over the battlements just in time to see a heavy timber sail through the air, effectively scattering the MacKillons working on the ground below before it landed with a heavy crash.

"God's ballocks, Mungo, *are you tryin' to kill someone*?!" shouted Finlay furiously.

"I had to sneeze!" Mungo retorted defensively.

"Well, you might bloody well let me know before you leave all the work to me!" snapped Finlay.

"Did you see that, Matthew?" asked Daniel, climbing

into the crenel between the merlons to get a better look. "The timber sank right into the ground!"

Matthew craned his head to see around his brother. "Where?"

"Climb in that opening over there," directed Daniel, pointing to the next crenel. "You'll be able to see better. Don't be scared," he chided, seeing his brother hesitate. "Just hold on to the merlon and you'll be fine."

"Do you think we can still use that timber?" asked Lewis doubtfully.

"I think it's best not to," Roarke decided. "A fall like that probably cracked it, or created a fault deep within its center. Better to use one we know we can rely on."

"Now, that's a bloody waste." Finlay glared at Mungo.

"It wasn't my fault," Mungo objected. "How was I to know I was going to sneeze?"

Melantha caught sight of Matthew and Daniel precariously balanced in the crenels of the parapet. She was about to order them to get down when suddenly Matthew lost his footing. He clawed wildly at the merlon beside him, his fingers scrabbling over the rough stone.

"Hold on, Matthew!" shouted Roarke, racing toward the boy.

Matthew cried out in terror, his hands grasping for Roarke. And slipped off the battlements.

Melantha screamed, a ragged, agonized sound that hung with deathly finality upon the air.

His heart frozen with dread, Roarke braced his hands on the parapet and forced himself to look down.

Instead of finding Matthew's broken body lying in a crumpled heap upon the ground, he saw the lad's ghostly pale face staring up at him from some ten feet below. Miraculously, the boy had managed to find a hold in an opening between the stones as he fell. He now clung to the wall, trembling.

If he lost his grip, he would die.

"Someone hold my legs!" Roarke commanded.

Every man on the wall head rushed toward him, desperate to help. Myles and Finlay reached him first. The two powerful men each grabbed hold of one of Roarke's legs, then held him fast as they lowered him down the wall.

"Hello, Matthew," Roarke said, affecting a casual tone that completely contradicted the direness of the situation. "I'm going to take hold of your arms, and I want you to lock your hands as best you can around my arms—do you understand?"

"I can't," Matthew whimpered.

"Of course you can," said Roarke, his voice low and reassuring. "You just hold on, and I'm going to take you back up." He stretched his arms out, then cursed silently.

The boy was beyond his reach.

"Don't let me fall!" pleaded Matthew. Tears spilled from his eyes.

"I won't let you fall, Matthew," Roarke insisted gently. "Finlay," he said, his voice utterly calm, "I need to be a little lower."

Finlay and Myles obligingly eased him down a few more inches.

"I don't know about you, Matthew," Roarke said cheerfully as he reached for the boy once more, "but I'm getting hungry. What do you say we go inside and find ourselves something to—"

"I'm slipping!" shrieked Matthew, his face wild with terror.

Roarke surged toward him, straining every inch of his muscle and bone and skin. His hands clamped with brutal strength around Matthew's slim forearms.

"Pull us up!" he commanded.

Using their combined strength, Finlay and Myles hauled the enormous warrior and the terrified boy up the wall.

A deafening cheer exploded from every member of the clan. Roarke stood with his massive arms closed protectively around Matthew's shivering form.

"Easy, now," he murmured, bending to rest his chin atop the lad's head. "You're safe now."

Matthew clung tightly to Roarke, his face buried in the warrior's chest.

"Matthew!" cried Melantha, grabbing him and turning him around to face her.

A purple stain was spreading on his cheek and blood leaked from a gash on his forehead. She knelt and urgently ran her hands along the sides of his face and down his shoulders and arms, which were pink and raw with cuts and scrapes. Once she was absolutely certain there was nothing seriously cut or broken, she wrapped her arms tightly around him and closed her eyes.

Thank you, God.

"Ow—you're hurting me, Melantha," Matthew complained in a muffled voice.

Reluctantly, she released him.

"I'm sorry about that, Matthew." Daniel's fine, pale features were twisted with guilt. "I never should have told you to climb onto the parapet."

"No, you shouldn't have," Melantha agreed, her overwhelming relief making it difficult to feel any genuine anger. "You are Matthew's older brother, Daniel, and I expect you to take care of him, not to encourage him to try such foolish antics."

Daniel hung his head, deeply ashamed.

"You are both forbidden to come up here again—is that clear?"

The two boys nodded glumly.

"Let's get you inside and tend to those cuts," she said, gently tracing her finger over Matthew's scraped cheek. She rose to lead him away. "You come too, Daniel." Her voice was soft, making it more an invitation than an order.

The little trio disappeared into the castle, leaving the rest of the clan to breathe a sigh of relief, before turning to regard Roarke with a newly forged reverence.

"And then we lowered him over the wall, each of us gripping a leg as massive and heavy as a tree trunk," continued Finlay, his face flushed with a generous measure of both pride and ale.

"Dear me, Roarke is a very big chap," fretted Laird Mac-Killon. "Were you not afraid of dropping him?"

"I was only worried that poor old Myles here might not be able to hold up his end," joked Finlay, slapping Myles lustily on the back.

"More like you were praying I would take over your burden as well," grumbled Myles. "We could have boiled a haggis in the sweat dripping from your brow."

"If I had let go, it would have been so I could shade my eyes from the blinding sunlight bouncing off your shiny pate," laughed Finlay, unwilling to be bested by a MacTier.

"Be glad you were blind—you were spared the sight of Roarke's bare arse!" roared Myles, doubling over with drunken amusement.

The entire clan laughed.

"Will you have some more ale?" asked a black-haired girl with a lush bosom and a saucy swing to her hips.

"Ah, sweet Katie, you've the powers of a seer," sighed Finlay, happily lowering his cup so she could fill it.

"And what about you, my fine hero?" she asked, her rosy mouth curved in amusement. "Can you drink some more?"

Myles regarded her with bleary rapture. "I like your arms." He vaguely hoped she would dump the pitcher of ale over his head. Hadn't Donald said that meant a woman liked a man?

"Do you, now?" she said, her brown eyes twinkling. "Now, there's a compliment I've not heard before."

"I like your hips too," Myles added, gazing at them appreciatively. "They're good and broad."

"God's teeth, I think the lad is in love!" laughed Magnus, slapping his thigh.

"Careful now, Katie, you don't want to have your head turned with such flowery talk," joked Gelfrid.

"And why not?" demanded Katie, still smiling at Myles. " 'Tis not every day a lass has a hero fill her head with such sweet words."

"I'm a hero too," protested Finlay.

"Ah, Finlay, I'm thinking 'tis too late to capture fair Katie's heart," commented Mungo, "unless you tell her quick how much you love her big feet!"

The clan roared with laughter.

"Are you going to dump that ale on me?" asked Myles hopefully.

"Of course not," Katie chided. "I know you mean no harm."

Myles watched in disappointment as she filled his cup. "Are you going to dump it on Finlay?"

"Now, there's an idea," Katie mused, smiling. "A little shower might help douse his shameless boasting."

Jealousy pricked Myles's ale-soaked contentment.

"But t'would be a waste of a perfectly fine pitcher of ale," she finished, shrugging her shoulders.

His spirits lifted once more. Obviously this Katie was a thrifty lass. Thriftiness was an admirable quality in a woman, he decided, gazing at her longingly.

"I do believe 'tis time to raise our cups in a toast," said Laird MacKillon, standing. "To our honored prisoner Roarke. But for his strength, courage, and quick thinking, this day could have ended in tragedy, instead of the happiness you see round you tonight."

The great hall filled with cheers.

"What about me and my friend Myles?" demanded Finlay thickly.

"Your pardon, Finlay," said Laird MacKillon. "Of course we are indebted to you and Myles for your actions today as well. Everyone, to Finlay and Myles."

The MacKillons happily drank from their cups again.

"I'm not of a mind to brag, but 'twas my arrow that felled Roarke and brought him here in the first place," pointed out Magnus. "Therefore I had some hand in what happened today."

"To Magnus, for shooting Roarke in the arse!" shouted Gelfrid.

"To Roarke's arse!" rose the drunken toast, giving everyone yet another reason to drink.

"Do you think you will ever be able to live down that injury?" wondered Donald, thoroughly amused by Roarke's disgruntled expression.

"No one beyond these MacKillons will ever hear of it," Roarke said flatly. "Is that understood?"

"An arrow in your backside is nothing," scoffed Thor, thoroughly unimpressed. "A sword in your belly—now, that's an injury worth talking about."

"Forgive me, Thor, but I don't think one could survive a sword in one's belly," pointed out Hagar.

"That's the problem with you striplings—you're too soft!" complained Thor.

"I'm not soft," Eric objected.

"You're the softest one here, Viking!" growled Thor. "You couldn't even swallow a mouthful of Edwina's posset without weeping like a bairn!"

Donald and Myles roared with laughter.

"Enough!" snapped Eric. "Bring me a cup of that damn posset now!"

"Quick, before he changes his mind!" Donald rose to his feet. "Where's Gillian?"

On hearing her name, Gillian tentatively turned to look at the men at Roarke's table.

"Fair Gillian," Donald began, placing his hand over his heart, "my Viking friend here is sorely ashamed for the way he has behaved in your charming company—"

"Stop it," growled Colin. "You're embarrassing her."

"—and to make amends to you," continued Donald blithely, "he has requested you bring him an entire jug of your delectable posset at once, so he may forever vanquish any reservations about its highly unique flavor!"

The entire clan gasped.

"I'm going to kill you, Donald," Eric vowed in a hard voice. "Slowly and with great pain."

Gillian's gaze flitted nervously to Eric. "Do you really want some?"

Her eyes were wide with uncertainty, and her hands were clutched tightly together, as if in anticipation of some terrible outburst from him.

It bothered Eric that he frightened her so. He was not in the habit of terrifying maids—at least not on purpose.

" 'Tis all right, Gillian, lass," Hagar began, "the lads here were just having a wee bit of fun—"

"Yes," said Eric suddenly. "I want some."

"Then I'll get it for you," Beatrice announced, unwilling to permit her daughter to be subjected to any further humiliation. "And you'll not dare throw it at me, or I'll take that wooden platter and break it over your thick Viking head!"

"No, Mother." Gillian's gaze was fixed upon Eric. "I can get it."

Hagar regarded his daughter with concern. "Are you sure, lass?"

She nodded.

"Excellent." Donald rubbed his hands together in anticipation as Gillian went to fetch the drink.

"If you do anything to upset my sister, I swear I'll kill you," Colin vowed.

Eric said nothing.

"I don't see what all the fuss is about," remarked Laird MacKillon, confused. "I think Edwina's posset is quite tasty."

" 'Tis marvelous for cleansing the bowels," added Edwina, pleased that her special brew was receiving so much attention.

"Best to toss it down in one gulp," warned Magnus stealthily as Gillian returned. "Trust me, lad."

Gillian approached Eric with admirable calm, especially given that everyone in the entire clan was now watching her. She bore a small wooden tray on which she had placed a single fresh goblet and a pitcher.

"Would you like me to pour it for you?" Her voice was small and soft in the silence that had descended over the great hall.

Eric shook his head. "Give me the jug."

The clan gasped in horror.

"Are you certain?" Gillian regarded him with concern. " 'Tis a strong brew."

"Did you make this batch?" asked Eric.

She nodded.

"Then I will drink the entire jug."

"That's bravery for certain," muttered Magnus under his breath.

Edwina gave him a chastising look, and Magnus responded by giving her a playful squeeze.

Gillian handed the jug to Eric.

"Thank you," he said, holding the foul-smelling potion as far from his nose as was decently possible.

"All at once, lad," Magnus reminded him.

Eric did not hesitate. Calling upon the harsh resolve of a warrior about to face his most dreaded enemy, he tilted his head back, bravely downed the contents of the jug, then banged the empty pitcher on the table.

The crowd in the great hall cheered wildly.

"By God, that's courage!" marveled Magnus. "I've been drinking the wretched stuff for years, but I never could stomach an entire pitcher!"

"He'll be feeling the benefits of that for days," predicted Edwina with satisfaction.

"No doubt," commented Hagar, looking sympathetic.

"Would you like some ale to wash that down?" asked Donald merrily.

"No," said Eric, his gaze on Gillian. "It isn't necessary."

Gillian gave him a small, shy smile before picking up her tray and disappearing back into the kitchen.

"All this fuss over a pitcher of drink," complained Thor, scowling. "I never saw a more coddled basket of kittens."

"At least the Viking is trying," remarked Magnus, winking at Eric. "It reminds me of when I was a lad, and had to fight a terrible, two-headed beastie with lungs of fire and teeth like a thousand deadly sharp swords. . . ."

Roarke drank deeply from his cup, then filled it again and drank some more. His back, neck, and shoulders were rigid with pain, making it difficult to turn his head. Even lifting his goblet to his lips seemed to require an inordinate amount of effort. He had been painfully aware of the protests of his aging, battered frame while hanging upside down on the battlements. Once he could have hoisted himself over the parapet and plucked Matthew back to safety with graceful ease, then drunk himself into a pleasant stupor to celebrate his victory. That was a younger Roarke than the weary warrior who sat hunched at this table tonight, drinking to numb the pathetic whimpers of his deteriorating flesh. Matthew was safe, and for that he was profoundly grateful. But the incident had taken a grueling toll on his body, reminding him that his days as a warrior were numbered.

". . . and then with one powerful blow I sliced his green beastie head from his massive, stinking body, leaving a steaming river of blood flowing into the ground and staining the dried grasses a horrible black for all time. Ye can still go there and see the spot where he died," Magnus finished cheerfully.

Thor regarded Magnus with frank skepticism. "Really, Magnus, you go too far with these foolish tales." His dark little eyes were all but obscured in the wrinkled folds of his face as he cynically demanded, "Do you really expect me to believe the beastie's blood was black?"

"By the toes of St. Aidan, I swear it was," Magnus vowed. "As black as night, with a terrible stench of rotting corpses on a still summer's day."

"Magnus, people are still eating," chided Edwina disapprovingly.

"Melantha could tell you if she were here," Magnus said, sensing he needed an ally to validate his tale. "I took her father to the very spot where the beastie fell, and he could see the ground was black and stank of death. The lad talked about it for years afterward."

"Where is the lass, anyway?" wondered Laird MacKillon, looking about the hall in confusion. "She never seems to dine with us of late."

"She is in her chamber tending to Matthew," Beatrice replied. "The poor lad was sorely frightened by his fall today, and Melantha wanted to stay by his side and make certain he was all right."

"The lass is wonderful with those boys," Magnus said fondly. "Her mother and father would be proud."

"I don't think either would be pleased to know about their daughter dressing like a man and traipsing about the woods in search of someone to rob," objected Beatrice. "She should stay at home with the lads and leave the business of thievery to you men."

"Why is it that Melantha is permitted to go with you?" asked Roarke curiously.

"Permitted to go with us?" Magnus regarded him with amusement. " 'Tis she that had to be convinced to let us accompany her."

"She was most reluctant about it at first," recalled Laird MacKillon, shaking his head. "She only relented when I absolutely insisted."

"Before that she was going off on her own—hunting, she used to call it." Hagar chuckled.

Roarke stared at them in disbelief. "Are you saying Melantha would go out and rob people all by herself?"

"And she was very good at it," Magnus assured him proudly. "The lass has a real talent for thievery."

"You must understand, she only took to it after her father was killed," explained Edwina, sensing Roarke's disapproval. "Had we not been attacked, I'm sure Melantha would never have considered going out and taking that which did not belong to her."

"She was always a good lass," said Magnus fondly. "And she loved her da. I don't think I've ever seen a girl grieve so at the death of her father."

" 'Twas doubly hard because her mother had died not two years earlier," added Beatrice. "Suddenly Melantha and the boys were alone, and worse, they had absolutely nothing. Their cottage was burned to the ground in the attack, and whatever belongings and food stores they had were either stolen or destroyed."

Roarke could scarcely imagine the awesome burden of loss and responsibility falling without warning upon a young girl's shoulders. "But she was a member of this clan. Surely everyone here would share what they had to help look after them."

"Of course we would," said Colin flatly. "We MacKillons look after our own."

"I insisted that everyone who lost their home in the attack move into the castle," said Laird MacKillon. "You could scarcely walk about at night without tripping over someone curled upon the floor, but everyone had a roof over their head."

"There was little to eat then," continued Hagar, "but there were still a few deer to be killed and fish to be caught."

"And then we suffered the worst winter we had endured in forty years," said Ninian. "Even the beasts in the woods couldn't find anything to eat. Most froze to death while searching."

" 'Twas a terrible time," Gelfrid reflected. "Watching the faces of the children grow thinner each day, knowing there was nothing more to give them."

"Until then Melantha had been completely absorbed in looking after the boys," said Beatrice. "But when wee Patrick fell ill and refused to eat anything we offered, Melantha picked up her bow and arrow and rode into the woods herself, determined to kill something and make a nourishing broth of it."

"That night she came back with a scrawny hare, a new sword, a sharp dirk, and a nice saddle!" said Magnus triumphantly. "And that's when we knew Melantha had a real talent for hunting!"

Everyone laughed.

"And the Falcon's band grew from that," surmised Roarke.

"Since there was no stopping the lass from going into the woods, Colin, Finlay, Lewis, and I decided to go along and help her," explained Magnus. "It took some convincing, but finally we made her see that we could do better as a group than she could on her own."

There was no denying that the Falcon's band had done well, Roarke mused, especially given its small size and the peculiarities of its members. It had certainly created enough of a problem for his own laird to want the band destroyed and its leader brought to him for retribution.

He took a deep swallow of ale, feeling angry and disgusted with both his clan and himself. How he would ever convince Melantha to abandon her exploits as the Falcon, when all she was doing was trying to provide for her family and her people, he had no idea.

Melantha slipped silently along the cool, dark passage, following the oily flicker of the dying torchlights.

The corridor was still, lacking even the low rumble of contented snores that filled the great hall now that the evening's celebration had finally come to an end. Most of her people had managed to make their way to their beds, but a few determined revelers had kept drinking until movement was all but impossible. Thus she had found Finlay sprawled upon a hard bed of greasy platters, looking as content as he might were he stretched upon a feather mattress, and Lewis curled like an exhausted puppy on the cold floor, his half-empty cup still clutched in one hand. A quick perusal had revealed that Roarke and his men were not among those sleeping off their drink.

She had felt a moment of alarm, for she had feared that the MacTiers had cleverly used this opportunity to escape. Then she recalled that their prison had been moved from the great hall to the cleared-out storeroom in the lower level of the castle. Colin was not one to drink to excess on any occasion, and Melantha was certain that he would have made sure the prisoners were safely ensconced before retiring for the night. Colin despised the MacTiers to the depths of his being, and would not permit something like Roarke's remarkably selfless feat of that day to erode his rancor toward them.

She turned the corner and saw Gelfrid slumped in a chair

beside the storeroom door, snoring soundly. His sword and dirk lay discarded upon the ground, and even the heavy key that secured the door he was guarding so carelessly had slipped from his belt. She had planned to ask whoever was watching the prisoners to open the door and bring out Roarke so that she might speak with him. She had thought to thank him for his actions that day quickly, in the corridor, with the comforting propriety of one of her own people standing by. But as she studied the steady rise and fall of Gelfrid's substantial belly, she hesitated. In his ale-sodden state Gelfrid might prove difficult to waken, and if he made a lot of groaning, fumbling noises as she roused him, it would only draw unnecessary attention to her desire to speak with Roarke in the middle of the night. It would be far quicker and more discreet to just open the door and talk to Roarke in his chamber.

She picked up the key and fit it into the lock.

The door made no sound as it crept open, for someone had taken the care to ensure that its aged hinges were well oiled, no doubt out of consideration for the MacTier prisoners. A soft wash of coppery light illuminated the four warriors lying upon their narrow beds, which seemed far too small and confining for men of their uncommon stature. The room was spare and tidily arranged, reflecting the organizational standards of Beatrice, and it smelled of smoke and pine, one scent emanating from the single torch burning low on the wall, the other from the soft carpet of pine branches that had been laid over the packed earth floor to obliterate any hint of dampness. It was a generous space, and arguably as clean and comfortable as any chamber in the castle, excluding the fact that it lacked both a window and a hearth.

Roarke lay on his side with his head resting on his arm. His eyes were closed and his breathing deep, but Melantha approached him warily nonetheless, suspecting that he had long ago perfected his ability to feign slumber when in fact he was preparing to attack. It was only after several long, guarded moments in which she strained to detect the least indication of consciousness that she finally decided he was, indeed, asleep. Releasing a taut breath, she moved a little closer.

The black fall of his hair was carelessly tangled over his massive shoulder, and a few strands lay against the dark shadow of his elegantly chiseled jaw. He was not an unattractive man, she conceded reluctantly, although this was an observation she had fought from the moment she had first swung her sword at him in the woods. His face was pleasingly sculpted, with a hard, rugged beauty in its weathered edges and planes, and an etching of lines that told her he had seen much in his life. His mouth was full and sensually shaped, and although she could not recall it ever softening into a smile, she suspected that when it did the effect would be mesmerizing.

His brow was deeply creased at that moment, not in the irritated scowl she had witnessed so often when he was awake but with something that seemed more reflective of worry, or perhaps even discomfort. She supposed it was difficult for a man of his considerable size to find comfort on a small trestle bed. Then of course there was the wound in his buttock, which should have mostly healed by now, but might still bother him even so. She felt a flash of guilt at the thought that she had let Magnus stitch it closed despite Roarke's objections. She bit her lip, considering her old friend's fading abilities. Magnus's eyes were far from sharp, and with his quivering hands and the challenge of stitching a wound together in virtual darkness, how good a job could he possibly have done? Then of course there was the risk of the flesh festering, a possibility that had completely eluded her interest at the time. But with Roarke's unexpected actions on the wall head that day, Melantha found she could no longer be so cavalier when it came to his welfare. She recalled Edwina demanding that Roarke let her look at his buttock, and his outright refusal. Had anyone assessed its progress since then, she wondered? It seemed unlikely, given Roarke's apparent modesty and the fact that no one in her clan had any reason to care.

She stared at the scarlet-and-black wool draped over the smooth rise of his hip. His plaid was lying high upon the thickly muscled length of his thigh. It would not take more than a small, feathery tug to ease the fabric up and bare his buttock for her examination. His sleep seemed genuinely deep, so surely such a swift, whispering sensation would not rouse him. After all, he had probably imbibed generously of the ale that had flowed that night, thereby dulling his senses. And as a warrior accustomed to sleeping on the hard ground with the wind whipping over him, it seemed unlikely he would be awakened by something so trivial as the slight shifting of his own plaid. Just one quick glance to assure herself that his wound was not festering. Then she would immediately cover him again and he would never know.

She moved in silence behind him, then tentatively grasped a fold of fabric. The wool was heated through by Roarke's body, and felt pleasantly warm against her chilled fingertips. She hesitated a moment, debating the merits of slowly skimming the cloth up as opposed to a swift pull. As she considered this Roarke shifted, inadvertently moving his plaid without any effort from her at all. Encouraged that her task was now even simpler, Melantha eased the plaid up, slowly unveiling the hard, sinewy curves of Roarke's backside.

"Good evening, milady. Was there something you wanted?"

She gasped with horror and whipped his plaid down.

"Thank you," said Roarke. "It was getting drafty in here."

"I only wanted to see your wound!" Melantha blurted out, stepping guiltily away from him.

He raised a skeptical brow.

"I wanted to be sure it wasn't festering," she explained.

He said nothing, but regarded her with an infuriatingly amused look.

"It seems to be—healing well," she finished helplessly. Her cheeks scalding with mortification, she hurried toward the door.

"Was that the only reason for your visit, milady?" enquired Roarke mildly.

Her hand gripping the latch, Melantha hesitated. It was not possible to stay and thank him for saving Matthew—not when he had caught her in the act of looking up his plaid. But it was far worse to flee and have him think she had slipped into his prison for the sole purpose of clandestinely examining his buttocks.

"I wanted to speak with you," she admitted, trying to piece together the tatters of her dignity.

Myles sleepily cracked open an eye. "What's happening?"

"Melantha has come down to visit us," explained Roarke cheerfully.

"At this hour?" muttered Donald, not bothering to lift his lids.

Eric groaned and forced himself to raise his head. "Is something amiss?"

Melantha cast Roarke a pleading look. If he told his men he had caught her lifting his plaid, she would surely die.

"Everything is fine," Roarke assured them. "Go back to sleep."

Their heads still pounding from the effects of too much drink, they happily complied.

"Now, then, milady," said Roarke, propping himself up comfortably on his elbow, "what was it you wanted to discuss?"

Again, she hesitated. She could not thank him here, not with his men half listening and him lounging on his bed. The chamber suddenly seemed insufferably small, the atmosphere taut and unnaturally silent.

"I would prefer to speak to you in private," she said, attempting to assert a modicum of control over the situation. Not waiting for his response, she quit the chamber.

"You should speak to Gelfrid about sleeping on his watch," advised Roarke, studying his snoring guard as he entered the hallway.

Melantha locked the door to his cell and slipped the key into her boot. "Everyone is unusually tired this evening," she murmured. "We will move farther down the passage, so we do not waken him."

She moved swiftly along the dimly lit corridor, then rounded a corner, leading him deeper into the cool silence of the lower level. She walked with her back to him and her weapons sheathed, acutely aware that he could overpower her at any moment and steal the key to the storeroom, and absolutely certain that he would not.

When they reached a final sputtering torch, she stopped.

Roarke regarded her with curiosity. There was no mockery to his expression now, perhaps because he sensed her unease and had no desire to intensify it. His manner was admirably relaxed, as if there were nothing peculiar about her rousing him in the middle of the night and leading him into the very bowels of the castle.

Melantha dropped her gaze to the earthen floor, suddenly uncertain. All day and into the evening she had thanked God for saving Matthew. Over and over she had silently prayed as she bathed her brother's cuts and soothed them with healing ointment. She had thanked God for saving Matthew as her brother lay staring at her with huge, frightened eyes, and she had thanked God even more when the lad finally fell asleep, his hands clutching his blankets as if he feared falling from his pallet. She had refused to leave him even for a moment, telling herself he might waken and need her, but knowing deep within her soul that she also needed to be with him. She needed to skim her fingers soothingly over his bruised brow and cheek, to clasp his small, scraped hand tight within hers, to adjust the thin plaid covering his too-slender frame for the hundredth time. And when her three brothers lay peacefully slumbering, their smooth faces as innocent and serene as angels, she had thanked God again, for bringing her brothers into her life, and for always keeping them safe.

Her life had not been long, but she had already learned the harsh lessons of loss. If not for Daniel, Matthew, and Patrick, she did not think she would have been able to survive. Children had a way of piling layers over even the most excruciating anguish, she reflected with tender sadness. There were those endlessly exhausting layers of constant need, for food and clothing and beds and attention. And there were layers of wonderfully simple pleasures, like lying together on the sun-warmed grass watching the sky drift by, or seeing who could hold their breath the longest, or turning over a rock and watching the scurrying village of bugs beneath. And then there were those exquisite layers of pure, overwhelming love, which arose every time she watched her brothers sleeping, or heard them laugh, or dried their tears.

As she had guarded them tonight, feeling her love wrap protectively around her small charges, she had realized that if not for Roarke, the very foundation of her deeply injured life might well have been destroyed that day. She was a strong woman and capable of enduring much, but the limits of her fortitude did not extend to her brothers. They were her strength, her happiness, her life. And that life could not suffer any more losses.

If Matthew had died, she would not have been able to bear it.

"Melantha?"

Roarke's voice was low and rough with concern, as if he

could feel her despair. She swallowed thickly and blinked, fighting the hot tears threatening to spill from her eyes. This was not how she wanted to appear before him.

"What's wrong?" he demanded softly, resisting the impulse to reach out and caress her pale cheek with the back of his fingers.

"Nothing is wrong." She inhaled a ragged breath, steadying her emotions. "Matthew is a little scraped and frightened, but he sleeps soundly now and will be fine."

He waited.

"He could have died today," she finally murmured, the words small and strained. "He could have slipped from the parapet and been broken on the ground below in but a few seconds. It happens, you know," she insisted, as if she thought he were about to argue the point. "Children fall all the time. They climb trees, or scramble up rocks, or foolishly balance themselves atop a wall. And most of the time they get down and they are perfectly fine, and their parents don't ever know about it. But sometimes they fall and are killed. And their parents are left to suffer in hell for the rest of their lives, thinking they will go mad from the agony of it."

She wrapped her arms around herself, suddenly cold.

"He didn't fall, Melantha."

"No, he didn't," she agreed, her voice quivering. "Or at least he didn't fall far. Because you were there to grab him. A MacTier." She shook her head in bewilderment, unable to comprehend the irony of it. "You were there to fling yourself over the parapet and bring him back to safety. You risked yourself to save his life. Why?" she whispered, raising her gaze to his. "What was one more life, when your clan has already destroyed so many?"

"That was battle, Melantha," he told her simply. "A battle in which I was not a participant." It seemed important to remind her of that, even though she had already told him his absence didn't matter. Perhaps he also needed to remind himself. "And even if I had been, it would not have changed what I did today."

"You are an enemy here," she protested, desperate to keep the lines between them clean and deeply cut. "A MacTier."

"That is true," he agreed, moving toward her.

"You came to crush my band, and if you'd been able, you would have killed me that day we fought in the woods," she continued, backing away from him. The cool stones of the wall pressed into her, arresting her retreat.

"You were every bit as determined to kill me." He reached out and gently brushed a dark strand of her hair away from her face. "Remember?"

His fingers were warm against her skin, warm and filled with gentle strength. It was wrong to stand there and endure his touch, and yet she found she couldn't move, could scarcely even draw a breath as he held her steady with nothing more than the raw desire emanating from him.

"Why?" she whispered. A single, anguished tear trickled down the pale softness of her cheek. "Why did you save my brother, knowing you might die yourself?"

He captured the tear with his thumb, then brushed a tender kiss on her cheek where he had found it. "I did it for Matthew," he murmured, his voice rough. "And I did it for you," he added, grazing his lips across her other tearstained cheek. "And believe it or not, Melantha, I did it for me. Because somewhere deep inside this weary warrior's soul of mine, I like to believe I still know the difference between right and wrong." He held her by her shoulders and searched the glimmering depths of her eyes, knowing he had exposed a fragment of his soul to her, yet wanting to have this moment of honesty between them. "Do you find that so impossible to believe?"

His gaze was pleading, even tormented. The air hung frozen between them as he waited for her response. Yesterday it would have been easy for her to answer his question, for she had believed she knew exactly who and what he was. But that was before he had bravely dangled fifty feet above the ground, his body straining as he lunged toward the earth and pulled her beloved brother from certain death. In that moment he had shown himself for what he really was. A warrior who would risk everything for a child he barely knew.

Because he had a compassionate heart.

Her tears began to fall in hot, pain-filled streams. She bowed her head, vainly trying to hide her anguish from him.

Her distress cut him to the bone. He could only imagine the depths of her suffering, although he knew what it was to lose those one loved. But he had tried to escape the ruins of his domestic life, while Melantha had been forced to stay and assume responsibility for those left behind. Not only for her brothers but for everyone in her clan, whom she desperately tried to feed and clothe with every scrap of cloth and morsel of food she procured as the Falcon. It was an awesome, daunting task, and one that she performed with steely courage and uncomplaining resolve. He was suddenly filled with a desire to tell her how fine she was, how brave and strong and rare. But he feared the words would sound meager and hollow coming from him. After all, he was a MacTier. If not for the actions of his clan, she would never have suffered the atrocities she and her people had endured. But for his people, her father would still be alive, her clan would be well fed and well clothed, and she would not bear the jagged scars of fear and deprivation and hatred. He had not been part of that fateful raid on her clan, but it did not matter, he realized harshly. He had lived his life as a warrior, and had raided and ruined countless lives as his legacy.

Self-loathing poured through him, making him feel sick.

"I'm sorry, Melantha," he murmured, releasing his hands from her shoulders. "Forgive me." He began to turn away.

Melantha thought she was falling, so acute was the sudden void swirling around her. She did not understand the emotions gripping her, except that she suddenly felt tiny and fragile and alone, and she couldn't bear it. She threw her arms around the solid expanse of Roarke's shoulders and buried her face into his chest, letting a sob escape her throat. *Stay,* she pleaded silently, feeling as if she were being crushed from within. *Please stay.*

Roarke froze, uncertain.

And then he closed his arms around her and ground his lips savagely against hers.

She did not fight him, but pushed herself even farther into his embrace, as if she wanted to be completely enveloped by his heat and strength. Roarke groaned and deepened his kiss, tasting the honey-sweet darkness of her mouth, inhaling the clean, sun-washed scent of her skin, feeling the willowy lean softness of her pressing against him. He tore his lips away to rain a trail of kisses upon her silky cheek, the delicate curve of her jaw, the cool column of her pale neck. His fingers found the laces at the top of her linen shirt and swiftly bared the creamy skin of her throat. A slender silver chain lay draped around her neck, bearing a small silver orb with a shimmering stone of deepest emerald. It surprised him to see that she secretly wore a pendant of such beauty, for it was not like Melantha to indulge in something so frivolous. He nuzzled his way beneath it, thinking it could not be of any value, for if it had she would certainly have sold it for food or blankets or weapons. His tongue drew hot, wet circles across the smooth silk of her while he opened her shirt even farther, until finally the pale swells of her breasts were released into his hands. He grazed his rough jaw against their incredibly fine softness, reveling in the feel of something so lush against his weathered skin. Taking one coral-tipped bud into his mouth, he began to suckle.

Pleasure shot through Melantha in a fiery streak. She plunged her fingers into Roarke's black hair, holding him at her breast as liquid heat poured through her. He worshipped the taut peak of her breast with hungry reverence, then shifted his attention to the other, drawing it deep into the hot recesses of his mouth and sucking long and hard, until she felt she would melt from the exquisite sensations radiating through her. She was vaguely aware of Roarke freeing her shirt from her leggings as he continued to taste her, and then the rumpled fabric was skimming over her head and she was naked to the waist, with the dark fall of her hair caressing her bare skin in a silky veil. A long, pink scar snaked down her left arm from her shoulder to her elbow. Roarke paused to trace his finger along its ragged trail, feeling anger surge through him at the thought of anyone attempting to harm her. The injury was not old, perhaps two months at best, and had probably been inflicted during one of her raids as the Falcon. He dared not ask about it, for fear of shattering the bond between them, and so he simply caressed it, his manner void of judgment or pity. He had seen thousands of scars in his life, for no warrior could live for long without acquiring at least a few, but he was unaccustomed to seeing them on a woman. Dismissing this intrusive reminder of her life as an outlaw, Roarke cupped his hands around her breasts and pressed his face between them, inhaling deeply of her, and then he began to kiss the cool flesh beneath. His hands abandoned her breasts to learn the contours of her waist, her hips, her thighs, his touch insistent and possessive as his palms roamed over her. He fell to his knees so he could better revere the flat plane of her belly, grazing his lips across the milky skin, and then the soft wool of her leggings was peeled away and his face was pressed into the dark triangle between her thighs. Melantha gasped in horror and tried to push him away, but Roarke shackled her wrists in the powerful grip of his hands and bound them to her sides, pinning her helplessly against the wall as his tongue slid into her most intimate place.

Pure pleasure ignited inside Melantha, forbidden and frightening and wonderful, rendering her silent and still.

Roarke tasted her lightly at first, his tongue flitting into the honeyed wetness of her in a teasing, rhythmic cadence. Melantha stood unmoving, no longer fighting him, but unable to release her breath or ease the rigid set of her body. And then Roarke drove his tongue into her with a searching stroke, and she cried out and fought to free her wrists. Roarke responded by tasting her deeply once more, gradually releasing his grip on her as he continued to lap at her slick heat. A low groan of masculine arousal rose from his chest as he felt her fingers thread urgently into his hair. In and out his tongue swirled, learning every intimate fold of her, tasting her and caressing her and exploring her. Melantha could not bear it an instant longer, she was certain of it, and yet she stood there and endured his shamefully exquisite caresses, feeling a dark excitement at the sight of him kneeling before her, pleasuring her with such carnal abandon.

A tight bud of intense sensation began to bloom within her, making her breaths come in shallow little pants and her flesh feel as if it were afire. Any inhibitions she might have had were overwhelmed by the swell of pleasure now pulsing within her. Roarke cupped her breast as he continued to devour her, holding her steady before him with nothing but the silvery web of throbbing need he had woven over her. Melantha opened her thighs slightly and held his head at her wet womanly heat, knowing he would surely think her wanton, and not caring, finding herself unable to care about anything except the sweet prison of rough, cool stones at her back and Roarke's mouth on her heated body and the silky feel of his hair in her hands as he forced her to breathe faster, shallower, harder, leaning into him and over him and focusing with fervent concentration on the exquisite sensations mounting throughout every fiber of her body. A dull ache was stretching within her, a previously unknown void buried deep inside, and a moan spilled from her lips. Roarke's finger eased into her as he continued to stroke her with his tongue, filling the aching hollow, stretching her and caressing her until she felt she would surely go mad from such magnificent torment. Her hands gripped his granite-hard shoulders, needing to hold on to him for support now, and small, desperate gasps escaped her throat. Suddenly the sensations within her melded into one, keen and shimmering and white hot, and Roarke tasted her with swift, hard caresses as he buried his finger inside her, until it was more than she could bear, and she felt herself begin to shatter in a golden burst of liquid fire. She strained against him, every muscle and bone in her body taut, and then she cried out and collapsed, her arms wrapped around his shoulders and her head buried against the hard pounding of his chest.

Cradling her with one arm, Roarke swiftly unwrapped his plaid and dropped it in a rumpled pool upon the floor, then eased Melantha back against its warmth. An amber spill from the torch bathed her skin in apricot light, illuminating her pale beauty in velvety shadows. He stripped away her boots and fallen breeches and rapidly removed his own shirt and boots. Then he spread himself over her, his body hard and aching with need. Her creamy skin was like silk against him, still warm and flushed with desire. He wanted to bury himself within her, to lose himself to her softness and heat, but he knew she was inexperienced and would require gentle care. He inhaled a steadying breath, forcing himself to gain control. Melantha stared up at him, passion still smoldering in the luminous depths of her eyes, smoky and profoundly stirring. He bent his head and kissed her with rough tenderness, wanting her to the point of madness. If he were able he would wash away the pain she had endured, would cleanse her mind of all she had witnessed that terrible night her beloved father had been slain, and all the suffering that had followed. But all he could offer her was the refuge of his touch, with the warmth of his plaid and the heat of his desire shielding her from the coolness of the torchlit passage, and the unforgiving world that awaited them in the morning.

He kissed her deeply as his hands skimmed over her, rousing her sated flesh once more. She wrapped her arms around him and pulled him closer, then set her hands free to explore the marble contours of his chest and shoulders and back, lingering at the thick cord of scarred tissue upon his shoulder, and the ragged scar that had severed the muscles of his back. Her fingers felt soft against his ravaged body, but any soothing effect they might have had was eradicated by the incredibly erotic effect of her tentative touch. Roarke plundered her mouth as his fingers slipped into the hot slickness between her thighs, stroking and probing until she was rising against his caresses once more. Knowing she was ready he positioned himself between the slender columns of her legs and entered her, just a little, shackling his need to a wall of self-control, so determined was he not to hurt her. He kissed the wine-stained tip of her breast as her body adjusted to him, distracting her with his suckling, and when she sighed and arched her back he entered her farther, slowly, carefully, giving her the time she needed to open herself to him. It was agonizing to hold himself over her so, caught between ecstasy and torture, every muscle in his body straining for release. He turned his attention to her other breast, vaguely wondering if he were trying to divert himself more than her, feeling the taut thread of his control stretched to its limit as Melantha shifted restlessly against him, her hands still roving the sinewy contours of his shoulders and back. He withdrew slightly, fighting to regain his control. Melantha murmured a ragged protest and grabbed hold of his buttocks, suddenly pulling him into her as she raised herself up to him, enveloping him in the hot, tight clasp of her magnificent body.

Roarke groaned, struggling with the incredible sensations surging through him. After a moment he raised his eyes to look at her. She seemed more startled than frightened, but her body had gone utterly rigid.

"Easy, Melantha," he murmured hoarsely. "The discomfort will pass—I promise."

He bent his head and began to kiss the silky skin of her throat as his hand moved down to where they were now joined. He caressed her lightly while his lips found hers and tasted the ripe sweetness of her mouth. She sighed and opened her legs a little wider, releasing the tension that had gripped her a moment earlier. He began to move within her, slowly, gently, stroking her and kissing her as he made her his, whispering gentle words of praise and reassurance as she began to pulse in rhythm with him. Over and over he sank himself into her, losing a little of himself with each aching thrust, trying to bind her to him as he filled her and covered her and worshipped her, and knowing it was futile. Melantha was strong and courageous and untamed, and she would never belong to anyone.

He kissed her fiercely, almost angrily, searching out the deepest secrets of her mouth, her silky cheek, the elegant curve of her neck, all the while burying himself into her again and again, holding her and tasting her and stroking her, wanting her to be his, not just in this passion-filled moment but always. It was madness, he realized that, for there was no escaping who and what he was, and she would never forgive him for it. Deeper and deeper he drove into her, pleasure and despondency melding into one as her arms wrapped tightly around him and she rose to meet every stroke, soft little moans unfurling in her throat, her body holding him in its hot, wet embrace, until he no longer knew where he ended and she began. He wanted it never to end, wanted never to be separated from her, wanted never to leave the shadowed confines of this torchlit passage. And suddenly he could feel himself slipping over the precipice of ecstasy, and he cried out, a cry of pleasure mingled with unbearable regret. He pushed himself into her as far as he could and kissed her fervently, spilling himself into her, losing the last vestiges of himself to the incredible beauty and heat of her, and feeling as if he were suddenly, irretrievably lost.

They lay together a long moment, their hearts pounding in frantic unison, their bodies still intimately joined. Melantha clung to Roarke tightly, unable to comprehend the vortex of emotions churning within her. She wanted Roarke to hold her and keep her safe, to whisper gentle, calming words into her ear and keep her warm beneath the muscled cover of his body. But shame was already gnawing at the pit of her, dousing her desire and rendering her cold. He was a MacTier warrior, part of the clan that had so brutally attacked her people and murdered her father. The fact that he might not have been part of that raid scarcely mattered—had he been ordered to be there, he would have enthusiastically taken part. And more, he had been sent by Laird MacTier to kill her band and capture her so that she could be executed before his people. For all she knew he still intended to do so, given the opportunity. She shifted and pushed against him, wanting his unbearable weight off her before she was crushed.

Roarke sensed the change in her instantly, even before her once-gentle hands shoved against his shoulders. Profound sadness seeped into him, stripping away the last of his desire. He wanted to talk to her, to somehow convince her that what had passed between them was not wrong, or something she should regret. But it was already too late, he could see it in the dull glint of loathing in her eyes, could feel it in the angry stiffening of her body and the cooling of her flesh. Whatever madness had burned so brightly between them was now extinguished.

Feeling hollow and alone, he rolled off her and began to dress.

Melantha clumsily donned her shirt, leggings, and boots. Shame gripped her in a suffocating wave, eradicating the pleasure she had felt in Roarke's arms. She could not begin to imagine what darkness had possessed her to behave in such a thoroughly wanton manner. She had not only disgraced herself but she had dishonored the memory of her darling da, and all those other brave, fine men who had died while fighting Roarke's clan. She had vowed to spend the rest of her life hating all MacTiers to the depths of her being, and to doing whatever she could to punish them for destroying her life. This was what sustained her, this and her overwhelming devotion to her brothers and her people. By giving herself willingly to Roarke, she had shaken the foundation of hatred that nourished her. Appalled by her conduct, she forced herself to adopt an air of cool indifference in a desperate bid to restore some shred of formality between them.

Sorrow tore through Roarke as he watched Melantha struggle with her emotions.

"I presume you wish to escort me back to my dungeon?" he asked, his tone flat.

She nodded warily, uncertain what he intended to do next.

"Very well."

They walked together in awkward silence through the dim passage, which suddenly seemed frigid and bleak. Gelfrid still snored comfortably by the door to the storeroom, blissfully unaware that one of his prisoners was missing. Melantha produced the key and nervously opened the door. Roarke did not know if their passion had made her uneasy, or the very real possibility that he might suddenly take her prisoner and free his men, using her as a hostage to escape the confines of this castle. For a moment he seriously entertained the thought, feeling weary and longing for nothing other than to be home. But there were still a few more days of work to oversee, and although the MacKillons were making progress with their training, they were not ready to meet an invading force. Guilt and an innate sense of responsibility forced him to enter his chamber. He turned to face her before she could close the door.

"Melantha."

She raised her eyes to his. Uncertainty shimmered in their depths, uncertainty and confusion. And shame. She was fighting desperately to hide it from him, but he could see it, as clearly as if it were branded across the milky skin of her forehead. He longed to reach out to her, to brush the dark silk of her hair that had fallen against her cheek, to enfold her trembling form in his arms and draw her close, protecting her from the MacTiers and her memories and the torment that was punishing her so cruelly. Instead he remained where he was, knowing the wall between them had risen once again, and not having any idea how to scale it.

She did not belong to him, he reminded himself harshly. For one brief, magnificent moment she had, but now it was passed. It had not been anything but a sweet, stolen illusion, as magnificent and ethereal as a wisp of snow that is hopelessly destined to melt against the ground, or else be crushed beneath the weight of the storm that follows.

"I'm sorry," he said helplessly, knowing it could not begin to ease her anguish.

She looked at him in surprise, as if she had expected him to say anything but that.

And then she bit her trembling lip and quickly closed the door, sealing the wall between them.

CHAPTER 7

"A quick release and my arrow drove clean into the target, showing that with a sharp eye and uncommon skill, 'twas a shot that could be made," boasted Magnus proudly.

"Excellent work, Magnus," praised Laird MacKillon.

Hagar bobbed his balding head in agreement. "No wonder Melantha insists you be part of her band."

"A pity you were aiming for the bale of hay far to the left of the bucket at the time," muttered Thor sourly.

Magnus's white brow shot up in indignation. "I most certainly was not!"

"Then why had you told your men that was the target?" challenged Thor.

"That was *their* target," Magnus qualified. "But when

ye've such keenly honed skills as mine, ye must challenge yer-self, or else ye lose yer touch."

"And I suppose you were challenging yourself that day you nearly speared my foot to the ground?" Thor's voice was quivering with anger.

"Now, Thor, I've told ye time and again ye were in no danger," said Magnus. "I was aiming for a wee stone beside ye, and that's what I hit."

Thor gasped in outrage. "You said it was a leaf!"

Magnus shrugged. "The details aren't important."

"You can't remember because there was no leaf!" roared Thor. "And no one in their right mind would want to *put a hole in a slops bucket!*"

"Bea did complain about the mess it made," reflected Hagar.

"If Magnus says he was aiming for the slops bucket, then I'm sure he was," intervened Laird MacKillon. "After all, his exemplary skills as an archer have been proven time and again during his raids with the Falcon."

"In case ye've forgotten, I was the one who felled Roarke just as he was about to slay Melantha," Magnus reminded Thor. "Now, there's a shot to make ye choke on yer unsavory accusations!"

"Who in their right mind aims for a man's backside?" scoffed Thor. "You should have shot him through his greedy, shriveled MacTier heart, then plunged your dirk deep into his gut and hacked out his stinking bowels—"

"It worked, didn't it?" Magnus challenged.

"It certainly did," agreed Laird MacKillon, "and Roarke seems to be none the worse for it. Thor, why don't you tell us how your training is going with the MacTier Viking?" he suggested, changing the subject.

"I never met a more objectionable, impatient, arrogant know-it-all in my entire life," huffed Thor irritably.

"I have," Magnus muttered.

Thor's dark little eyes bulged in fury as he reached for his sword. "By God, Magnus, if it's a fight you're wanting—"

"Your pardon, gentlemen, but we've no time for this," objected Laird MacKillon. "We still haven't heard from Laird MacTier regarding our ransom demands, and the MacKenzies have refused to agree to an alliance until they receive payment in gold. As we don't know what the MacTiers plan to do next, it is essential that we be prepared for an attack. Are we?"

"Almost," said Magnus evasively.

"Shouldn't be much longer," added Thor.

Hagar looked at them in confusion. "How much longer?"

Magnus scratched his snowy head, considering. "A week," he decided. "Two at the very most."

"Two weeks may be fine for teaching a lad to pitch an arrow at a slops bucket," snorted Thor, "but to train him to wield a sword takes longer."

"Any bumbling lout with an arm can wield a sword," Magnus challenged heatedly, "but to shoot well ye must learn to be one with the arrow—"

"And of course you were one with the arrow that nearly broke my bloody foot—"

"How much longer?" interrupted Laird MacKillon.

Thor thought for a moment, stroking the hilt of his weapon. "It takes a lifetime," he finally decided.

"I'm afraid we don't have that much time," fretted Hagar.

"Strange Laird MacTier hasn't answered our ransom message yet," mused Magnus. "Ye'd think he would have arranged to pay for the lads' return by now."

Hagar regarded him worriedly. "Do you think it's possible he doesn't want them back?"

"Of course he wants them back!" barked Thor. "Do you think great big chaps like that are easy to come by? Why, he must have spent a fortune just growing them to that size!"

"Then why doesn't he send a message saying he plans to pay the ransom?" wondered Laird MacKillon.

"Could be he's not botherin' with any missives, but is just sending the ransom to us directly," suggested Magnus.

"It would take time to organize all that food and clothing," reflected Hagar. "And don't forget, there are livestock and weapons involved as well, not to mention the gold."

"That would take some effort to arrange," agreed Laird MacKillon, steepling his aged fingers together. His wrinkled brow furrowed with concern. "But what if he decides he simply doesn't want the lads back?"

"Then we hack them to pieces where they stand!" declared Thor happily. "We take those mangled pieces and chop them into wee bits, and boil them over a fire to make a nice, thick stew!"

Hagar looked somewhat sickened by the prospect. "I really don't think I'm up to eating them."

"We can't kill them," protested Magnus.

"Why not?" demanded Thor.

"For one thing, it would start a war between us and the MacTiers, and that's a battle we've no chance of winning," Magnus pointed out.

"Of course we could!" Thor argued. "A few more weeks of training and our lads will be able to face any army in Scotland!"

Laird MacKillon's eyes widened in astonishment. "Really?"

"No," returned Magnus flatly.

"You're forgetting about our secret weapons," Thor said.

Hagar regarded him curiously. "What secret weapons?"

"The traps! Those MacTier chaps and Lewis have come up with some dandy ones!"

"The traps won't hold off an entire army," protested Magnus.

"Maybe not, but they can whittle it down to a size we can easily slay," Thor argued.

"It would have to be a very small army," retorted Magnus.

"But what if no one comes at all?" Hagar wondered. "Then what do we do with our prisoners?"

Thor huffed with impatience. "Are you not hearing well these days, Hagar? We've already agreed to make them into stew!"

"Your pardon, Thor, but we cannot kill them," said Laird MacKillon. "Not after they have been such pleasant, helpful company."

"I don't find that Viking pleasant at all," Thor objected.

"He didn't seem agreeable at first," allowed Hagar. "But I must say, after watching the poor fellow bravely down an entire jug of my daughter's posset without so much as wincing, I find I have had to reconsider my opinion of him."

Magnus slapped his thigh. "Now, that was a feat, to be sure," he said, chuckling. "Over the years I've developed a belly that can withstand the stuff, but I'd never want to drain an entire jug!"

"If we can't chop them up for stewing meat, then what are we to do with them?" demanded Thor.

Laird MacKillon sighed. "I suppose we would have to let them go."

"But we can't," objected Hagar. "They know who the Falcon is and where she and her band of outlaws hide. If we let them go they could lead an army back here and kill them."

"Roarke and his men seem like good, decent fellows, even though they are MacTier warriors," said Laird MacKillon. "I cannot believe they would ever do anything so cowardly."

"Perhaps not willingly," Hagar allowed. "But every man must obey the orders of his laird. If MacTier told them to return here, what choice would they have?"

"Hagar makes a good point," Magnus reluctantly conceded.

Laird MacKillon considered this a moment. "Then there is only one thing to do," he finally said.

The other council members regarded him expectantly.

"If the Laird MacTier does not fulfill the demands of our ransom, then we must keep the prisoners here."

"Forever?" asked Magnus.

He nodded.

"It would be a lot easier just to carve them up and make a stew out of them," Thor grumbled. "Do you have any idea how much those brutes will eat over the years?"

"I don't believe it will come to that," said Magnus. "As ye've already pointed out, these are four fine big lads, and I'm willin' to wager MacTier is not about to just let his warriors go. He'll either pay the ransom and be done with it, or he'll come for a visit and try to take them back by force."

"Then let's hope he chooses to simply pay the ransom," Laird MacKillon responded, "and save us the trouble of having to put Lewis's contraptions to the test."

Eric watched with swiftly eroding patience as Mungo clumsily ascended the stone stairs backward.

"Stop looking behind you," he commanded, the rusted steel of the dull sword he had been allocated for training cracking hard against Mungo's only marginally sharper blade. "I could have killed you ten times by now, with all your stumbling and looking over your shoulder. The steps are there—now forget about them and concentrate on killing me."

"But I could fall," protested Mungo, stealing an anxious glance behind him at the stairs leading from the courtyard to the second level of the castle.

"You won't fall because your opponent will have his sword buried in your belly long before you make it up the first step," complained Eric. "If you fear falling so much, then use it to drive me back—don't let me make you retreat."

Mungo dutifully jabbed at the warrior, only to have his blow squarely deflected by Eric's pitiful weapon.

"Again!" commanded Eric, still forcing Mungo up the stairs. "Don't just stand there—thrust at me again!"

Mungo flailed his sword once more, and the blow was promptly countered.

"Faster!" ordered Eric, advancing yet another step. "I could slay an army in the time it takes you to return a thrust! Keep your blade moving!"

Once again Mungo stabbed at Eric, and once again his weapon was deflected as Mungo glanced over his shoulder and nervously ascended yet another step.

"You are leading your opponent right into the castle," observed Eric in disgust. "Why don't you just step aside and invite me in?"

"I'm trying to keep you out!" protested Mungo.

"Then keep your eyes locked on mine," Eric instructed, engaging him with his sword once more. "Drive me back with the sheer force of your hatred, and whatever you do, don't look behind for so much as—*look out*!!"

Mungo gasped in surprise as his body collided with another. He threw his arms up in the air in a frantic attempt to regain his balance, and might have succeeded had Eric not shoved him out of the way in his race to catch Gillian.

"Help!" cried Mungo as he toppled awkwardly over the side of the stairs and landed solidly on the grass below.

"Are you all right?" Eric demanded.

"I think I bruised myself," replied Mungo, rubbing his backside.

"Not you!" snapped Eric. Realizing she might find his harsh tone unsettling, he lowered his voice as he asked Gillian, "Are you hurt?"

Shocked to find herself suddenly caught in the hard crush of Eric's arms, Gillian shook her head. "I—I'm fine," she stammered, mortified by the thought that he could probably feel the pounding of her heart against his chest. "I'm just finding it a little difficult to breathe."

Eric instantly eased his hold on her, but he kept one arm wrapped protectively around her shoulders, as if he feared she might stumble again. "You're certain?"

Gillian tilted her head up. His face was a forbidding mask of hard lines and unforgiving angles, but it was his eyes that drew her attention. Their icy blue gaze was far too intense to be characterized as gentle, but there was a ray of concern within them that touched her nonetheless.

"I'm certain," she assured him softly.

"I'm sorry I bumped into you, Gillian," apologized Mungo, ruefully rubbing his posterior. "I didn't know you were there."

Gillian smiled. " 'Twas my fault entirely, Mungo."

"It was both your faults," Eric informed them brusquely as he escorted Gillian down the staircase. "You must learn to sense what is around you and react swiftly to it," he informed Mungo. "And you must learn to watch where you are going," he admonished Gillian. Satisfied that she was not injured, he directed his attention to the men he was training. "Divide yourselves into groups and line up at the bottom of the exterior staircases. Each of you will ascend and descend the stairs twenty times—backwards."

"That will take us until nightfall!" protested Gelfrid, leaning against his sword as he mopped his sweating brow.

"By the end of the day you will have either overcome your fear of stepping back, or you will be too exhausted to worry about it," Eric predicted. "Either way, you will learn to fight on the steps without stopping long enough to be split open every time you shift your feet."

"By all the saints, I swear he's going to kill us," muttered Mungo, dragging his damp sleeve across his face. "He's going to train us to bloody death."

"I'm thinking he'll just exhaust us so that we haven't the

strength to lift so much as a finger in the event of an attack," Ninian complained grumpily. "Then the MacTiers will come and finish us off where we lie."

"I wish they'd come soon," said Gelfrid. "I'd like to be dead before I have to climb up and down those bloody stairs twenty times."

Reluctantly they began to assemble themselves.

"I must be going," said Gillian, suddenly feeling shy in Eric's presence.

"No," he snapped.

Her eyes widened with startled apprehension.

Frustration swept through Eric. Why was it that every sentence that escaped his mouth sounded so harsh? He raked his hand through his blond hair, struggling to find the right thing to say next.

"You will stay a moment," he elaborated, then realized it still sounded as though he were giving her an order. "If it pleases you," he finished awkwardly.

Gillian hesitated. "Are you inviting me to stay with you?"

He frowned. He was accustomed to commanding, not inviting. But as Donald had frequently pointed out, his behavior around women often had the effect of frightening them away, and he didn't want to frighten Gillian. If she would prefer to think he was inviting her, so be it.

"Yes," he decided, nodding. "I'm inviting you to stay."

"Very well." She stood there a moment, waiting for him to say something more. When he didn't, she screwed up her courage and meekly inquired, "Are you angry with me?"

He looked at her in confusion. "Why do you say that?"

"It's just . . . the way you are looking at me," she explained hesitantly.

Her comment completely baffled him. "What do you mean?"

"You look like you are displeased with me."

"I am looking at you the same way I look at everyone."

But that wasn't quite true, he realized. Not everyone had hair like a roaring fire, and skin that glowed like fresh cream tinged with berry juices.

"Oh," said Gillian, clearly relieved. "Then I imagine that scowl of yours comes in very handy during battle. 'Tis truly fearsome."

Eric raised his brow. "I'm scowling?"

"It doesn't make your face unpleasant to look at," she assured him.

"It doesn't?"

"Of course not. It just makes you look rather severe."

Eric stared at her in disbelief. His experience with women was extremely limited, but he was almost certain she was complimenting him. He hesitated, wondering if he was supposed to pay her some sort of tribute in return. He tried to recall his conversations with Donald, but no suitable comment came to mind. Besides, Gillian did not have any of the attributes he had thought he desired in a woman. Her arms did not look like they could carry a heavy load of wood, but with their slender grace they should not have to manage anything more cumbersome than a basket of flowers. As for her hips, they were narrow and sweetly shaped, not the kind that would bear a brood of children with sturdy indifference, but the type that would drive a man to the edge of madness as he cupped them in his hands and pulled her tight against him.

Heat stirred his loins.

Gillian regarded him uncertainly, unable to comprehend the strained silence that had fallen between them. "Forgive me—I meant no insult," she apologized, thinking she had offended him. "I should be going."

"No." Even as he said it, he knew it wasn't the right thing to say.

She paused, wondering why he wanted her to stay when he wasn't saying anything to her. She was usually the one who had trouble making conversation with people, yet here it was the Viking who seemed to be painfully ill at ease. "Was there something you wanted to tell me?" she ventured shyly.

There was much he suddenly wanted to tell her, but he knew he would never find the right words to express himself. Should he tell her that her eyes were like sapphires? he wondered. But that was wrong—sapphires were dark, and Gillian's eyes were the deep, clear blue of a winter sky, or a clean strip of ocean seen from atop a mountain on a crisp day. Would she understand if he described them as such? Or would she laugh and think his words were ridiculous? Feeling desperate, he tried to think of something else. The groans and shouts of the MacKillons stumbling up and down the stairs permeated the air, distracting him. What else had Donald said women liked to hear? They didn't want to be told about their hips—he'd had a pitcher of ale poured over him to illustrate that point. What about their hair, he wondered? If he told her it was like a fire, would she think that was good? Or would she think that fires were smoky and filled with ashes, and be offended?

"I like your gown," he said, deciding apparel was a safer subject.

Gillian looked down in complete bemusement at the shapeless, faded, generously stained gown she wore. She had soaked it and scrubbed it to a point where the fabric could scarcely endure another washing, and although she knew the cloth was clean, many of the stains had resisted her efforts—including the dark splash of posset this warrior had thrown at her feet.

Eric could see he had made a mistake, it was etched all over the confused expression on her face. He had absolutely no knowledge of women's gowns, but even he had the wit to recognize that what Gillian wore was little better than a rag. Did she think he was mocking her? he wondered miserably. Anxious to make amends, he quickly added, "What I mean is, I like it on you."

A hesitant smile crept across her face. "Thank you."

Her smile eased his agitation considerably.

"I'm afraid I never did quite get your posset out of it." She tossed him a teasing look.

Her ability to make light of that terrible moment surprised him. And pleased him immensely. "I'm sorry," he said simply.

"I know you didn't mean to throw it on me. In truth, I don't know how anyone stomachs the taste of that wretched stuff."

Surprise chipped away some of his discomfiture. "You don't like it?"

"I think it's absolutely vile," she confessed. "The only reason I make it is because Edwina has decided that I must be the guardian of her recipe. But I never sample it as I make it, which is probably why that batch you had when you first arrived was so strong."

"It had a rather powerful effect on me," he conceded. "The posset I drank the other night in the great hall was better."

Gillian nodded. "That's because it was just fresh milk and ale—I didn't put in any of Edwina's other foul ingredients."

"Why not?"

She lifted her shoulders in a dainty shrug. "I didn't want you to suffer as you drank it. Not with the entire clan watching."

He didn't know what to make of that. Why should she care if he suffered?

"I really should be going."

He wanted to tell her to stay, but he could hear the MacKillons loudly complaining about their weariness and their broken bones, and how his training was going to kill them long before anyone else could. He sighed inwardly. He supposed he should resume leading them in training. "Very well."

She smiled at him, a small, hesitant lifting of her perfect lips, and he felt as if he had been warmed by a sudden burst of sunlight.

Then she turned and hurried away, leaving him alone with the griping MacKillons.

Roarke paced the length of his cell like a caged beast, unable to quell the unease gnawing deep with him.

Nothing had been the same since that magnificent night he had lost himself to Melantha. He had not seen her since then, although he had walked nearly every inch of this castle as he inspected the progress on its fortifications. She made no appearances in the great hall, nor did she cross his path in the courtyard, or on the wall head, or in any of the castle's chambers or passages. At first he had wondered if she had gone with her men to procure goods for her clan, but Magnus assured him that Melantha was around somewhere, although the old warrior could not precisely recall the last time he had seen her. It was clear to Roarke that she was profoundly disturbed by what had happened between them, and could not bear to face him.

He tried to focus his thoughts on the far simpler subject of battle. It had been nearly a week since the MacKillons had delivered their demands to his clan, and according to the elders, they still had received no reply. Roarke knew MacTier well enough to know that his laird would never ignore such a humiliating affront. To have four of his finest warriors taken prisoner by a clan as insignificant as the MacKillons was an offense MacTier would not endure lightly. If MacTier had not yet sent a missive telling the MacKillons to go to hell, it could only mean one thing.

An army was on its way to deliver the message in person.

"We're leaving," he announced suddenly.

Donald groaned and barely opened a sleepy eye. "Now?"

"Now," said Roarke. He adjusted his belt, cursing silently as his hand reached out of habit for the dirk that wasn't there. No matter. He would take Gelfrid's dirk and sword after they lured him in here.

"It's the middle of the night," protested Myles, his words slurred by the quantity of the ale he had consumed at dinner. "Couldn't we leave tomorrow?"

"We leave now," said Roarke.

Eric sat up, but looked decidedly reluctant to move. "We haven't finished our work here," he pointed out. "I still have much training to do with these MacKillons."

"You could train them for the next twenty years and they still wouldn't be ready to face an army of MacTiers," Roarke retorted. "If MacTier has not answered their missive by now, it means they are on their way. We must intercept them before they attack."

The threat of the MacKillons being attacked had them off their beds and ready for action in barely a second. The irony was not lost on Roarke. Any animosity they might once have felt for their captors had long since disintegrated. All that was left was this nagging sense of responsibility for their plight and a genuine desire to help them.

"Gelfrid," called Roarke, rapping on the storeroom door.

Deep, contented snoring filtered through the heavy wood.

"Gelfrid!" barked Roarke, banging harder. "Open this door at once!"

There was much snuffling and coughing before Gelfrid sleepily demanded, "What is it?"

"There is an enormous rat in here," Roarke told him. "We need you to come in and kill it."

"A rat?" Gelfrid sounded thoroughly unnerved. "Why don't you just kill it yourselves?"

"We haven't any weapons," explained Donald.

The door to their cell remained stubbornly closed. "I don't know anything about killing rats," Gelfrid objected, sounding rather overwhelmed by the idea. "Maybe I should go and fetch Mungo and Ninian."

"By the time you wake them and drag them down here, this foul rodent will have bitten us all," argued Roarke, not relishing the idea of having to overcome more MacKillons than necessary. "All we have to do is capture it in a blanket, and then you can dispose of it as you see fit."

There was another long pause. "You'll help me to catch it?"

"Of course."

The lock turned.

"Where is it?" Gelfrid demanded, peering cautiously around the door.

Roarke pointed into the shadows. "In that corner."

Gelfrid stepped into the chamber with his sword drawn, but remained steadfastly by the door. "I don't see it."

"Of course you can't see it from over there," said Roarke, "you've got to move in closer." He put his hand on Gelfrid's shoulder and guided him across the room. "There, now—do you see it?"

Gelfrid hunched a little lower as he squinted into the darkness. "I think so—what in the name of St.—"

Whichever saint Gelfrid chose to call upon was lost in the rag Donald used to bind his mouth, while Eric and Myles made short work of immobilizing his wrists and ankles. Once he was adequately trussed and stripped of both his sword and dirk, he was laid upon one of the trestle beds and a blanket was draped over him.

"Forgive us, Gelfrid, but we find ourselves unable to enjoy your clan's hospitality any longer," apologized Roarke. "Tell Laird MacKillon we have enjoyed our stay, and will do what we can to keep any other MacTiers from visiting." He went to the door to check the corridor, followed by Myles and Donald.

Eric lingered a moment. "I would ask a favor, Gelfrid," he

began hesitantly. He paused, desperately searching for the right words. "When you see Gillian, tell her I said . . . thank you." It wasn't right, that wasn't at all what he wanted to say, but he couldn't think of anything else except good-bye, and somehow he couldn't bring himself to leave that as his final message to her. "Will you tell her?" he demanded.

His eyes wide with fear, Gelfrid nodded.

Eric went to leave, wondering why Gelfrid seemed so anxious. Surely he must realize they had no intention of harming him? He was all but through the door when he suddenly understood the source of his alarm.

"There is no rat, Gelfrid."

The light was dim, but Eric could see relief pour over Gelfrid's face. Satisfied that he wasn't going to die of fright, Eric closed the door.

They moved silently through the castle, pausing only to relieve the sleeping forms of Mungo and Finlay of their weapons before making their way to the door leading off the kitchen. The moon was buried beneath a thick mantle of charcoal cloud, effectively dousing any light that might have revealed their forms to those posted to watch on the wall head.

"Here," said Roarke, passing his sword to Eric. "You and Myles open the gate while Donald and I fetch our horses."

Eric nodded and moved toward the iron portcullis with Myles.

The stables were dark and quiet but for the shifting of hooves and the gentle snorting of the horses. During his inspection of the castle Roarke had made a point of finding out exactly where his and his men's mounts were kept. He moved through the blackness with his dirk gripped firmly in his palm, while Donald followed with his sword drawn. Neither had any intention of actually using their weapons on any MacKillon they might encounter, but both knew it was vital to appear prepared to employ deadly force if necessary.

Roarke's horse sensed his presence long before he could see his master's shadow. The beast whickered loudly and tossed his head.

"Hello, my friend," whispered Roarke, running his hand gently over the animal's neck. "Feel like going for a ride?"

His horse pressed his nose roughly into Roarke's side, then snorted impatiently. Roarke turned to fetch the bridle hanging on a nail on the wall.

And froze.

Melantha's face was a pale oval against the shadowy darkness, her skin so luminous he could make out every bitter line in her taut expression.

"Drop your dirk," she ordered in a hard voice.

Roarke stood utterly still, his dirk firmly encased in his hand. He had not wanted it to be like this, he reflected desperately.

Every night for the past four days he had tormented himself by lying awake thinking about her. He had recreated every glorious detail of her in his mind: her sunwashed scent, her silky softness, the hot, lush feel of her lying beneath him as he buried himself deep inside her and lost himself to her exquisite sensuality. And he had indulged in the most ridiculous of fantasies by trying to imagine how it would be when they saw each other again; how she would look at him with shy tenderness, what impossibly clever and charming things he would say to her to make her laugh and put her at ease. Of course he had known that in reality it would be awkward, possibly even painful. But never in his most haunted reflections had he ever imagined her looking so utterly betrayed. Her body was rigid as she stood facing him, her sword raised and ready to drive through him on the least provocation, but it was her eyes that commanded his complete attention. They were shimmering with a terrible anger and an agonizing sorrow, and the combination was so appalling he very nearly dropped his dirk and begged her to forgive him for hurting her so.

Then he remembered that if she or her beloved clan had any hope of surviving, he must leave immediately and stop the MacTiers from attacking.

"I am leaving, Melantha," he informed her, his voice betraying none of the emotions churning within him.

"What did you do to Gelfrid?" she demanded.

He nearly smiled. Even in a moment like this, her first thought was not for herself or her own safety but only for the welfare of another of her clan.

"Gelfrid is unharmed," he assured her. "He is merely resting in the storage room."

If she experienced any relief from this knowledge, she refused to show it. "Where are the others?"

"Listen to me, Melantha," he said, his voice achingly gentle. "We cannot stay any longer, because our very presence here is putting you and your people at risk. Do you understand? MacTier has not answered your people's ransom missive, and that is because an army is on its way here to collect us. But they won't be coming just to free us. They will be under orders to make you pay for attempting to ransom us, and to ensure that you never try anything so foolish again."

"Then we will fight them," Melantha informed him coolly, raising her sword.

"Your people tried to fight the MacTiers once before, and you were hopelessly defeated."

"We have been working on the castle's defenses, and our men are now better trained," she pointed out.

"You are more prepared than you were before," he acknowledged. "Even so, you cannot possibly hold off an army of MacTiers."

Her gaze was contemptuous. "You're just saying that so I'll let you go free."

"No, Melantha. I'm saying it because I don't want to see either you or any of your people hurt."

Melantha kept her sword pointed at Roarke's chest, contemplating what he was telling her. She wanted to believe that he was wrong, that if an army of the clan she most despised were coming, she and her people had the power to fight it. After all, she, Magnus, Colin, Finlay, and Lewis had been waging their own private war on small groups of MacTiers for months, and they had always emerged victorious. But that was in the protected arbor of the woods, where they were the aggressors, not the defenders. They always had the element of surprise in their favor, their extensive knowledge of the forest, and their ability to lure their prey into carefully laid traps. Fending off an assault on their home was not the same. An attacking army could lay siege to their holding for days or even months, slowly eroding their resistance until finally they were too weak to continue to defend themselves. Of course Melantha had always known this—that was why she had proposed ransoming Roarke and his men in the first place. She had wanted to strike back at the MacTiers by bleeding their coffers, but she had also hoped to restore her holding and buy the alliance of the MacKenzies so that her people could better defend themselves in the future.

She had not anticipated that Laird MacTier would care so little about his own warriors that he would rather risk their lives than pay their ransom.

"There's a problem," said Eric, appearing suddenly at the entrance to the stables with Myles.

"What is it?" Roarke demanded.

"A force of about two hundred MacTiers has positioned itself outside the castle wall. They are preparing to attack."

"Sweet Jesus," swore Roarke. "Is the gate open?"

"No."

"Who is leading them?"

"I don't know—'tis too dark to see clearly."

Donald emerged through the black. "What are we going to do?"

Roarke hesitated. Even if he and his men rode out of here unharmed, it was going to be bloody difficult to convince an army of MacTiers poised to attack that they should simply turn around and go home—especially if they had been given orders by their laird to crush the MacKillons.

"We'll go up to the wall head and show them we haven't been harmed, then make it seem like we're being released in exchange for them holding off their assault," he decided quickly.

"You're not going anywhere except back to your cell," Melantha informed him. "My clan will handle this matter."

"Rouse everyone in the castle and see that they are armed and put into their positions," Roarke instructed his men, ignoring her. "We must be ready in case whoever is leading this force is not prepared to listen to reason. See that the women and children are taken to the lower level of the castle, and assign four men to guard them. Once you are certain all areas are manned, join me on the wall head."

"Wait!" cried Melantha as Donald, Eric, and Myles hastily departed.

"What is it?" Roarke demanded.

"You and your men cannot participate in this battle."

"What would you have me do, Melantha? Do you think I should just stand by and watch while your people are destroyed?"

Shouts could be heard coming from the wall head, and people were rushing to and fro outside. She swallowed thickly, fighting the fear rising in her chest as she desperately tried to comprehend Roarke's motives.

"It is your clan waiting outside our walls and they have come to rescue you. How can I believe you will not undermine our efforts to fight them?"

Her eyes were shimmering against the paleness of her

face. He could see she was frightened, and well she should be, given the brutality his clan had inflicted upon her people once before. Her father had been killed in that battle, along with many other friends and loved ones, and her people had been left virtually destitute. It agonized him to think how much she had suffered, and how much she was suffering in this moment. Had there been time, he would have taken her into the comfort of his arms and soothed her with soft words, making gentle assurances to ease her fear. But there was no time. Every second he wasted here was keeping him from getting on the wall head and ending this battle before it began.

"Listen to me, Melantha. Regardless of who or what I am, I swear to you that I would never do anything to hurt either you or your people. You can trust me in this, or take that sword and run me through. The choice is yours."

Melantha stared up at him, completely and utterly torn. "I can never trust you." Her voice was ragged with despair.

"You can tonight," he insisted. "That is all I ask."

She hesitated a long moment, the silver blade of her sword flashing in the dark abyss between them.

And then she lowered her eyes and let the weapon fall, knowing that when she looked up again he would be gone.

CHAPTER 8

"And so we thank you for coming here to put past wrongs to right by reimbursing us for our losses, in return for which we are delighted to return your great and valiant warriors," finished Laird MacKillon, squinting as he struggled to read his speech by the flickering torchlight.

The MacTier warriors stared up at the wall head, apparently speechless.

"They certainly are a polite lot," commented Hagar. "Not so much as a peep out of any of them."

"Much better behaved than the last group," Magnus agreed. "Perhaps there's hope for these MacTiers after all."

"And now," continued Laird MacKillon, "we shall mark this momentous occasion in our history with a wee tune upon the pipes." He gestured toward Thor, who was struggling to hoist his unwieldy instrument into his arms.

"I came up here to slay MacTiers, not to play music to them," Thor grumbled irritably.

"I really don't see how we can slay them when they are being so agreeable," remarked Laird MacKillon. "It wouldn't be courteous."

"After listening to Thor play they'll wish we had slain them," Magnus predicted.

Thor glowered at him, then inhaled a deep, rasping breath and proceeded to play with murderous conviction.

The deafening drone that choked the air caused some MacKillons to press their hands to their ears, while the MacTier warriors looked on in complete bafflement. By the time Thor finished his first piece he appeared to have forgotten who his audience was, and he enthusiastically embarked upon another equally torturous strain.

At that point the MacTiers had heard enough and sent a volley of arrows flying over the battlements.

"God's teeth!" swore Thor, looking down at the arrow protruding from the bag of his deflated instrument. "Those scoundrels have ruined my pipes!"

"Here, now, lads," Laird MacKillon chided, wagging his finger at the warriors below, "that's no way to behave on such a momentous occasion as—"

His words were cut short as he ducked to avoid the second volley of arrows.

" 'Tis war, then, by God!" roared Thor, casting aside his murdered pipes and reaching for his beloved sword.

Roarke arrived just in time to see the wall head erupt in complete chaos.

"Take that, ye foul wretches!" Magnus bellowed, releasing an arrow into the darkness below. "There'll be shafts buried in every one of ye before I'm through!"

"You can't be here, Finlay," objected Ninian as he blocked

Finlay's access to one of the hoardings. "I told Gelfrid I would only work with him."

"Gelfrid isn't here," Finlay protested.

"Well, I'm sure he'll be along in just a moment," countered Ninian, "and when he gets here I don't want to listen to him whine about how I let you take his place. You know how he goes on about things—"

"Ninian!" shouted Roarke, "stand aside and let Finlay start hurling those rocks over *now*!!"

"But I promised Gelfrid—"

"*Now, Ninian!*"

"There's no need to shout," Ninian grumbled, reluctantly moving aside.

"Here, now, Roarke, what the devil is the matter with these clansmen of yours?" demanded Laird MacKillon, his white brows furrowed in agitation. "One minute we're all getting along and enjoying a pleasant bit of pipes, and the next they're shooting arrows at us and trying to scale the wall."

"Perhaps they didn't like Thor's playing," Magnus joked, releasing another arrow. "Did I kill anybody?" he asked Lewis, who was standing beside him.

"No, but with every shot you're getting closer," Lewis assured him encouragingly.

"Takes me a few minutes to get going," Magnus said, undaunted. "Watch me, lad, and see how I become one with the arrow." He sent another shaft sailing into the air, which landed a good three yards from the nearest MacTier. "That's got them worried!" cackled Magnus cheerfully.

"They're preparing to scale the wall!" Laird MacKillon fretted as a tightly formed line of MacTiers moved forward bearing ladders.

"I'll take care of them!" announced Mungo. He heaved two enormous stones off the hoarding on which he was perched. The rocks dropped heavily to the ground, cleanly missing any MacTiers.

"Hold back!" Roarke shouted.

Laird MacKillon looked at him in bewilderment. "Your pardon, Roarke, but we're at war here. 'Tis hardly the time for exercising restraint."

Colin raised his sword to Roarke's chest. "Do you really believe we are such fools that we will listen to you?"

"You are wasting precious arrows and rocks by releasing them too early," explained Roarke quickly. "Let the MacTiers advance into the pits, which will reduce their numbers and create confusion. Then shower them with everything you have."

"That's a sensible suggestion," remarked Hagar.

Colin regarded Roarke suspiciously. "Why would you act against the interests of your own clan?" he demanded, his sword still trained upon him.

"I don't want to see any MacKillons harmed."

Colin gave a scornful laugh. "Do you expect me to believe that?"

"I don't give a damn what you believe, Colin," Roarke snapped. "But if you let your people exhaust their weaponry before the MacTiers are close enough to be damaged by it, how will you fight them?"

Colin considered this barely an instant before shouting, "Hold back!"

"Look how nice and neat they keep their line as they approach," marveled Hagar, scratching his shiny head with the tip of an arrow. "It looks almost like a dance."

"Each man has been given a position and must maintain it until the ladders are up and the warriors are climbing," Roarke explained, watching as the MacTiers performed their familiar maneuver. "They are trained to approach even in the most heated of battles, because it is vital to get the walls scaled."

"Hello, there, lads," called Magnus, waving amiably to them. "Just a few more steps and we'll begin again."

The ladder-bearing MacTiers looked up in confusion as they marched, unaccustomed to approaching a castle without being fired upon.

And then the line disintegrated as over two dozen of them suddenly dropped into the pits.

"Now, that was simply splendid!" burst out Laird Mac-Killon, watching as the remaining MacTiers froze in their tracks, wondering what other surprises were in store for them. "Why, we must have captured at least thirty men in those pits—maybe more!"

"Shoot at the rest of them!" Roarke commanded. "Now!"

The MacKillons obligingly pelted the remaining Mac-Tiers with stones and arrows.

"Take that, ye great, ugly brute!" shouted Finlay, dropping an enormous stone off his platform.

He peered over the edge and watched as it landed squarely in the arms of a powerfully built MacTier who had managed to ascend much of a ladder. Laughing triumphantly, the mighty warrior hoisted the rock over his head and showed it to Finlay.

"Aye, you're a strong one," Finlay agreed, nodding. "But shouldn't you be holding on to the ladder?"

The warrior's expression dissolved. He waggled back and forth for one desperate moment, then fell backward, taking the rock and the two warriors on the rungs below with him.

"Three MacTiers downed with just one stone!" marveled Magnus, impressed. "Let's see if anyone can top that!"

"Let a few of them get up here so I can chop them into wee bits with my sword," ordered Thor, struggling to raise his weapon. "I want to make those villains pay for ruining my pipes!"

"Keep them down for as long as possible!" Roarke countered firmly. "The whole idea is to stop them from climbing the wall!" He looked down to see a group of MacTiers preparing to ram the gate with a heavy timber. "Get ready to pour boiling oil on those men at the gate!"

The men standing by the enormous black cauldron positioned over the gate obligingly began to ease it onto its side.

"Wait for my order!" commanded Roarke, pausing until the rammers were in the optimum position to be hit by the scalding oil. "*Now!!*"

A torrent of liquid cascaded over the wall, drenching the startled MacTiers below, who instantly dropped their timber and began to beat wildly at their sodden clothes.

After a moment they stopped their frenzied palpitations and looked at each other in confusion.

"Bloody hell, I'm soaked to the bone!" complained one.

"Lewis, what the hell was in that cauldron?" demanded Roarke, watching as the dripping wet MacTiers gamely picked up their battering ram once more.

"We didn't have that much oil to spare, so we had to use plain water," Lewis explained apologetically.

"And just exactly how hot was it?" demanded Roarke.

"Actually, it was cold," Lewis admitted. "We didn't want to waste too much wood keeping it hot, so the fires were only lit a short while ago."

Roarke struggled for patience as the MacTiers began to pound the gate. "Myles, Eric, start dropping stones on the rammers!" he shouted, seeing his men appear on the wall head. "Donald, make sure the archers are actually aiming for MacTiers and not just shooting arrows into the darkness!"

"Who is leading them?" asked Eric, scanning the attacking warriors below as he hoisted up an enormous rock.

"No one we know, otherwise I would have tried to talk to him," Roarke answered. "That big blond warrior off to the right is giving the orders."

Donald regarded him seriously. "What are we going to do?"

"For the moment we have little choice but to try to hold

them off," said Roarke. "If I try to talk to them, I'm more likely to get shot than command their polite attention."

"But how long can the MacKillons withstand an attack like this?" wondered Myles, watching with satisfaction as his stone struck one of the rammers below.

"Long enough to let the MacTiers know this is not the same pathetically unprepared holding they attacked last year," Roarke replied. "Their numbers have already been reduced by the pits, and we'll hope that if any make their way into the castle they will be caught in the nets. Once they realize this holding is not going to be easy to capture, they will stop and listen to reason."

Eric hoisted another rock over the battlements. "And then what?"

"And then the MacKillons can tell them that we will be released in exchange for their withdrawal," Roarke answered. "That will give the MacTiers the sense that they have won a victory without having to completely destroy—*Colin, get down*!!"

Colin dropped to the ground just as the MacTier warrior who had scaled the wall behind him delivered a deadly blow with his sword.

Roarke hurled his dirk at the MacTier, burying the blade deep into the assailant's shoulder. The man's weapon clattered to the ground as he was grabbed by Myles and Finlay.

"Bloody hell, that was a wee bit close!" swore Magnus.

"Are you all right?" Roarke asked Colin.

Colin nodded, but Roarke could see the muscles of his jaw contract as he rose to his feet.

"Now, that's as fine a cut as any man could hope to have and live to tell about it," said Magnus, admiring Colin's back. "It goes clean from one side of yer ribs to the other. I'd be happy to stitch it for ye later, lad, if ye think ye can wait until I'm finished dealin' with these MacTier rascals."

Hagar's face blanched at the crimson stain quickly

spreading on his son's shirt. "Perhaps you should go in and have your mother look at your wound, lad," he suggested, refraining from actually inspecting the injury himself. "She'll know what to do."

"It's nothing," said Colin.

"Of course it's nothing," scoffed Thor, barely glancing at it. "Why, I have scars all over my body that go twice as deep as that, and you don't see me running in to my mother."

"A good thing, since yer poor mother's been buried for well over fifty years," observed Magnus. "And the only scars I've ever seen on ye are the ones ye got the day those bees chased ye into a bramble bush, and ye were cryin' for yer ma so loud I was tempted to stuff a rag in yer mouth—"

"Are you certain you're all right, Colin?" demanded Roarke, ignoring the elders' bickering.

"It's just a scratch," Colin assured him brusquely. "I'm fine."

Roarke tilted his head in acknowledgment and began to turn away.

"Roarke."

He paused.

"Thank you."

Roarke nodded, knowing full well how much it had cost Colin to say those words.

Melantha appeared on the wall head just in time to see a volley of burning arrows rain down upon her people.

"Great God in heaven, it's raining fire!" said Laird MacKillon, looking about in awe.

Magnus promptly picked up one of the burning arrows and sent it flying right back at the MacTiers. "Take that, ye foul wretches!" he shouted gleefully. "Ye can't burn good Scottish stone, so all ye're doin' is helpin' us to see ye better in the dark, ye stinkin' clods of cow dung—"

"Magnus, your plaid's afire!" shouted Melantha.

Magnus yelped in surprise and began to dance wildly

about, unraveling his plaid as he struggled to stamp out the flames consuming the ragged wool.

Thinking fast, Lewis dipped a wooden bucket into one of the cauldrons and hurled its contents onto Magnus.

"God's ballocks, that water's freezing!" shouted Magnus, instantly forgetting his previous problem.

"Sorry," Lewis apologized.

"That's all right, lad, ye couldn't have known. Where have ye been, Melantha?" Magnus asked, adjusting his sodden plaid as best he could before picking up his bow once more.

"I was in the castle helping with one of the nets," Melantha replied, moving over to the parapet so she could see what was happening below.

"Was it working well?" asked Lewis hopefully.

"Your design was brilliant, Lewis," Melantha told him. "It comes down with barely a whisper, and can be hoisted again so fast it's ready for the next intruders within minutes. Already we've captured over fifteen men."

"What are ye doin' with the prisoners?" wondered Magnus.

"Gelfrid is locking them up in the storeroom," Melantha replied. "And then he's scaring them with some tale about a big rat."

"A pity we can't just drop a giant net on the lot of them," observed Magnus, firing another arrow into the air. He sighed as his shaft landed several feet to the right of the warrior he had intended to hit. "That would put an end to all of this."

"Magnus, aim to the left of your target," suggested Donald.

"Now, why would I want to do a foolish thing like that?" wondered Magnus. " 'Tis hard enough to hit these MacTier curs in the dark as it is, without purposely aimin' away from them. An' if yer thinkin' to comment on my bein' a wee bit off tonight, well, I'm sure I don't need to remind ye about that time I hit yer fearless leader right square in the—"

"Just try it," interrupted Donald. "Once."

"Most idiotic thing I ever heard," grumbled Magnus, nocking another arrow against the string of his bow. "Fine, then, I'm aimin' to hit that big beast of a MacTier standing by the well, the one who is about to shoot another one of those bloody flaming shafts at me."

"Aim to the left of him, Magnus," Donald instructed, moving beside him. "By about one yard."

"Pure idiocy," muttered Magnus, reluctantly adjusting his aim, "as if I can't see clear enough to know which way the bloody arrow is going to fly—"

"You got him, Magnus!" burst out Lewis in amazement. "Right in the thigh!"

"That'll teach ye to try to shoot yer elders!" Magnus shouted, shaking his fist in triumph. "Now, drop yer weapon and run on home, before I fix it so that ye're the last of yer line!"

The terrified MacTier instantly threw down his bow and scurried away as fast as his injury would permit.

"Your pardon, Roarke, but are we winning?" asked Laird MacKillon, clearly confused by the progress of the battle. "With all these flaming arrows and rocks flying about, 'tis rather difficult to tell what's what."

Roarke watched in frustration as the MacTier rammers continued to methodically bash at the wooden gate with their timber. Several of them had been knocked out by the falling stones, but these men were simply dragged out of the way and replaced by others. The gate was solid and was reinforced by a heavy bar, and if they broke through they would still have to haul up the iron portcullis. Even so, no castle was impenetrable. If the MacTiers didn't succeed in forcing their way through the entrance, they would eventually find another way in.

He had to orchestrate a bargain with them before that happened.

"All we're doing for the moment is holding our own," he told Laird MacKillon.

"I'd say we're doin a wee bit more than that, laddie," countered Magnus. "Looks to me like these filchers are goin' to pay yer ransom—they're bringin' forth an enormous cart piled high with goods!"

Roarke glanced down to see two horses pulling a heavy wagon that was draped in rough blankets.

Uneasiness seeped through him.

" 'Twould appear these MacTiers are wise enough to accept that they cannot win," declared Laird MacKillon approvingly. "And a good thing, too—we've almost completely exhausted our store of rocks." He clapped his hands to capture his clan's attention. "We will release our prisoners in exchange for this ransom, and that will put an end to any further unpleasantness."

"They had better have another set of pipes in there for me," grumbled Thor, "or else I shall be forced to demand the life of one of them as payment!"

"They couldn't possibly have packed everything we demanded into one wagon," reflected Melantha, straining to see if there was another cart hidden somewhere in the shadows. "Where is all the livestock they were supposed to replace?"

"Perhaps it will be delivered at a later time," Hagar suggested.

"I'm sure they've at least got some fowl in cages on that wagon," mused Mungo. "Just look at how high it is stacked."

"That leader of theirs really ought to tell those chaps to stop banging on the bloody gate," complained Ninian. "In another minute they're going to crack the wood!"

"Look, they're taking off the blankets!" Lewis said excitedly.

The entire clan watched in rapt silence as the MacTier warriors severed the ropes holding the shroud of blankets in place.

"That's not what we asked for," protested Laird MacKillon

in confusion. "What in the name of St. Columba are we supposed to do with a contraption like that?"

"Here, they're going to demonstrate how it works for us," said Hagar.

"*Get down!!*" roared Roarke, raising his arms to attract the attention of all the MacKillons who had lined up in a fascinated row on the wall head. "*Everyone get down, now!!*"

Before he could issue any further warning Melantha plowed into him, knocking him to the ground with such force he could almost feel his ribs crack.

"What the hell is the matter with you?" he demanded, roughly shoving her aside. "Your people are in danger and I have to let them—"

His words died in his throat.

Melantha stared at him in ashen silence. She was shivering slightly, but that was the only concession she made to the arrow buried deep within her arm.

"Oh, God, Melantha, I'm sorry—"

At that point the first boulder was vaulted from the stone-throwing machine below. It crashed heavily into the battlements, shattering one of the merlons before smashing with brutal power against the floor.

"Great God in heaven, they're going to destroy the castle!" Laird MacKillon realized, appalled.

Every MacKillon on the wall head immediately retreated a step, fearful of being crushed by the next missile.

"Bring the men in from the hoardings!" shouted Lewis, helping Finlay scramble onto the wall head from his precarious little platform. "They aren't designed to withstand this kind of assault!"

Just then a huge boulder crashed into the small wooden gallery, tearing away its wall and more than half of its flooring. The powerful impact knocked Ninian down, leaving him dangling helplessly from one of the few remaining timbers.

"Help!" he cried, desperately trying to hold on as a flurry of arrows sailed toward him.

"Stand aside, Lewis!" roared Eric, racing forward. Ignoring the shafts flying all around him, the Viking warrior squeezed through the crenel, grabbed Ninian by both his shoulders, and hauled him to the relative safety of the wall head.

"Did you see what they did?" demanded Ninian incredulously. "They blasted away the very floor I was standing on! I could have been killed! Killed, I tell you!"

At that point another boulder crashed into the parapet close to Ninian's head, shattering yet another of the merlons.

"I don't think we can fight this kind of attack," said Laird MacKillon, his aged frame stooped with defeat. "I believe we must surrender."

"We will never surrender!" shouted Thor fiercely over the wall. "We would rather be smashed to pieces and die mangled and bleeding, but with honor—do you hear, you vile, filthy MacTier scum!"

"They won't withdraw even if we release you, will they?" Melantha asked, her gaze upon Roarke intense. "That's why they brought that machine. They intend to destroy us completely, regardless of what we do or say."

Roarke knotted the rag he had wrapped around her upper arm above the arrow, his expression grim. The MacTier warriors were merely following the orders of their laird, just as he had done for so many years. The fact that they had taken the trouble to haul this deadly machine all these miles meant that they had been instructed to put it to use, regardless of whether or not it was actually necessary. The rescue of Roarke and his men was secondary to this mission, he realized furiously.

The MacKillons had dared to lash back at their oppressors. For that, they would be destroyed.

"Stay down," he ordered tautly.

Melantha immediately rose to her feet, ignoring the pain gripping her left arm. "What are you going to do?"

He did not waste time answering her, but strode purposefully over to Colin. "Grab hold of me and put your sword to my throat," he ordered. "Finlay, you take Myles, Lewis take Eric, and Magnus take Donald. Tell these bastards you will slay us before their eyes if they don't retreat at once. Do it *now!*" he snarled, seeing the MacKillons hesitate in confusion.

Colin immediately grabbed Roarke and pressed the blade of his sword against his throat.

"Cease your attack or this MacTier is dead!" he bellowed, moving closer to a torch so he and Roarke could be seen by the MacTiers below.

"*Halt!*" commanded the golden-haired leader, raising his hand into the air.

The MacTier warriors froze. The stone-throwing machine was poised to launch another boulder, the battering ram was inches from the gate, arrows were positioned against quivering bows, and men were dangerously exposed upon the ladders, yet no one dared move without the permission of their commanding warrior.

"Tell them they must withdraw if they hope to keep us alive," Roarke directed Laird MacKillon in a low voice. "Tell them if they return to their lands at once, you give them your word that we will be released unharmed in three days' time."

Laird MacKillon nodded and moved to the parapet to address the MacTiers below. "I'm afraid this is a most unfortunate situation," he began apologetically.

"For God's sake, try to sound angry!" hissed Roarke.

Laird MacKillon looked a bit startled by Roarke's curt directive, but then he nodded, apparently understanding that this was not the time for civilized deliberation.

"Return to your lands at once or we will slay the hostages," he said briskly.

The fair-haired warrior urged his horse forward. "We cannot leave without our fellow clansmen," he informed him. "We have been ordered to bring them home with us."

"And I suppose you were also ordered to ravage our castle and butcher every last one of us, weren't you, you depraved demons from hell!" railed Thor, angrily shaking his gnarled fist at them. "One more arrow from any of you, and that big Viking chap of yours will be chopped up and ground into bread!" His wrinkled face was twisted with fury and his white hair was blowing crazily around his head, making him look truly macabre in the flickering torchlight.

"Tell them three days," Roarke prompted Laird MacKillon.

"If you leave at once, we will release these hostages in three days," Laird MacKillon told the MacTiers.

"But if you don't, we shall begin hacking off their heads and tossing them over the wall!" shrieked Thor, who was obviously enjoying the attention he was commanding.

The MacTier leader hesitated, reluctant to retreat from a battle without the prize he had been ordered to procure.

"Tell him to withdraw immediately, or you'll slay one of us just to help him make up his mind," said Roarke, not wanting to give the commanding warrior too much time to consider his situation.

"Leave now, or the Viking loses his head!" shouted Thor gleefully, not caring that it was Laird MacKillon who was supposed to be handling the matter. He raised his sword and lovingly caressed its shimmering edge, effectively giving the impression that he was more than a little mad, and capable of the most hideous acts.

Apparently he made an impression upon the leader. "Will you also release the prisoners you have captured tonight?" he demanded.

"Aye," said Laird MacKillon. "In three days."

"Very well." Believing he had little choice, the warrior turned his horse and motioned for his men to withdraw.

A deafening cheer rose from the wall head.

"Stay here and keep enough men guarding the wall to make certain they don't return," directed Roarke to Eric. "Donald, go with Lewis and assess the damage sustained by the castle. Post guards anywhere that looks vulnerable. Myles, organize a group of men to guard the prisoners caught by the nets in the castle. The ones in the pits can stay where they are for the night."

"Does this mean I can't carve up any MacTiers?" demanded Thor.

"I'm afraid we agreed to release them unharmed," Laird MacKillon said apologetically.

"That's outrageous!" blazed Thor. "Just look what those wretches have done to my pipes!" He pointed a bent finger at the ruined instrument lying in a heap upon the ground.

"Why don't you go with Myles and threaten some of the prisoners?" Roarke suggested. "Tell them all about how you're going to grind them up for haggis."

"It won't be the same as actually doing it," he grumbled.

"Now, Thor, I'm sure you can make those MacTiers quiver in their skins so hard it will be better than actually chopping them up," said Donald, trying to console him. "I know you had me worried when I first came here."

Thor's expression brightened. "Really?"

"Absolutely," Donald assured him. "Poor Eric couldn't sleep for days, he was so afraid you might hack him to pieces where he lay and turn him into a batch of bannocks."

"I might still do it." Thor gave Eric a menacing look.

"Ye should let my Edwina take a look at that arm of yours, lass," said Magnus, moving over to Melantha. "I'd take the shaft out myself, but I'm thinkin' she'd probably do a fairer job of it."

"I want to see my brothers," protested Melantha.

"Of course ye do," said Magnus soothingly. "Let's just

take care of this wee arrow first, and then they can visit ye in yer chamber."

Melantha shook her head. "I need to see them now. I have to make certain they are safe."

"I'm sure they're fine, Melantha," Colin assured her.

"How can they possibly be fine?" Melantha challenged, her voice ragged with despair. "Their father has just been murdered."

Thor frowned. "What's she talking about?"

Roarke moved toward her. "All is well, Melantha." His tone was low and soothing. "You have nothing to fear."

Melantha stared at him a moment, her eyes wide and haunted. "No," she whispered, the word barely audible amid the orders being shouted to the remaining men on the wall head. "No."

Roarke reached out, capturing her in the protective cradle of his arms just as a sea of black obliterated her anguish.

Voices were floating around her, wisps of sound on the cool night air. She struggled to make them out, but they were low and hushed, swirling around her in languid circles, just escaping her grasp. It didn't matter anyway. Nothing mattered anymore. There was a terrible emptiness inside her, a tattered, aching hole that had torn her apart, and although she couldn't recall what was causing her such unbearable grief, she was certain it could never be overcome. She sank further into the warm folds of darkness, vaguely wondering if she were dying. She hoped that she was. Surely in death there would be respite from this suffocating sorrow.

A soft whimper escaped her throat, stripping away some of the layers of blackness. She shook her head, fighting her ascent to wakefulness. But a slow, sure awareness crept cruelly through her flesh, causing her to feel the throbbing in her arm, the rising of her chest, the softness of the plaid lying over her like a fragile shield against the world. *I am not dying,* she realized, and she was overcome with disappointment. In death she might have shared a fleeting moment with her father. In life, she would have to go on without him.

She opened her eyes, feeling utterly lost.

The chamber was washed in honeyed light, which emanated from a small cluster of dripping candles on the table beside her bed. The windows were open to the silky night air, filling the room with the sweet scent of pine, grass, and the acrid tinge of the torches still burning on the wall head and in the courtyard below. Melantha shifted slightly and was surprised by the lash of pain that whipped up her arm. She studied the neatly arranged bandage on her upper arm with complete detachment, as if it were someone else's limb affixed to her body. After a moment she turned her gaze to the other side of the chamber, searching for the sleeping forms of her brothers.

Instead she found Roarke stretched out in a chair beside her bed, sound asleep.

He did not look as though he could be overly comfortable, for his massive frame made the chair appear almost ridiculously small. Nevertheless he was slumbering deeply, which told Melantha he must have been exhausted. She studied him through the soft haze of candlelight, noting the deep lines etched across his forehead, the taut set of his jaw, the dark growth of beard shadowing his handsomely sculpted cheeks. He looked older to her in that moment, older and far wearier, revealing a vulnerability she had never imagined to see in him.

She had always known he was not a young man, for the lines of his face betrayed the experiences of a life lived close to forty years. And yet she had never sensed the slightest hint of weakness in him, either in spirit or in his physical abilities. Of course he had demonstrated some discomfort during their journey here, but she had attributed that to the fresh wound in his backside, and given it no further thought. She thought of him on the wall head earlier that evening, racing back and forth as he directed the battle from every angle, anticipating each move of his opponents, and shouting orders to men who had no reason to obey him. And yet her clan had obeyed him, willingly and completely, despite the fact that he was their enemy, and the warriors they fought were his own.

Roarke had done everything within his power that night to protect her people from the very men who had come to grant him his freedom, risking his own life in the process.

It was this that had caused her to throw herself at him when she saw one of the MacTier warriors training an arrow upon his chest. She had tried to tell herself that she hated him, for he was a MacTier warrior, and represented greed and brutality and savage force. But somehow Roarke had chiseled away at her loathing, until finally it was but a thin veneer of the dark, cold force that had sustained her so well these past ten months.

She swallowed the sob threatening to escape from her throat.

Roarke's eyes flew open as his hand shot to the dirk at his waist. He swiftly scanned the dimly lit room before finally studying Melantha.

"You're supposed to be asleep," he told her, releasing the hilt of his weapon. He rose and went to the table to pour her a cup of ale.

"I'm not tired."

He raised a skeptical brow as he handed her the wooden goblet. "All is quiet now, Melantha," he assured her. "The MacTier army has retreated, and the wall is heavily guarded to alert us should they return. Your brothers are safe, and are spending the night under Beatrice's care. As for your clan, there were a few injuries, but they were relatively minor, and they have been treated. Everyone who is able to is sleeping, including the MacTier prisoners. Except," he qualified, "for those who are too frightened to close their eyes after Thor's ranting about turning them into meals for the next year, and Gelfrid's talk of giant rats lurking in the shadows."

"I must see for myself," she murmured, although she made no effort to move. Just holding the goblet steady in her hand seemed to require an enormous amount of energy. She could not imagine where she would find the strength to actually rise from her bed.

Roarke regarded her sternly. "You have been injured, Melantha, and although the wound is not serious, you did lose a fair amount of blood before Gillian managed to stitch you closed. It is essential that you rest, or you will be of absolutely no use to anyone tomorrow."

Her eyes widened in surprise. "Gillian took the arrow out?" She could not imagine her gentle friend accomplishing such a feat without dissolving into a fit of weeping.

"I removed the arrow," Roarke told her. "I have had more experience in these matters than Gillian, and I believe she was very relieved when I offered to do it. Fortunately for you," he added dryly as he took the cup away from her, "Magnus was not available."

She leaned back against her pillow, feeling immeasurably tired. She was dressed in a simple linen chemise, which left her arms bare but for the bandage, and the pale skin of her chest naked except for the slender silver chain and pendant she always wore. She frowned, thinking the green stone looked far paler than it had before. Telling herself it was just the light, she lifted it to shimmer in the amber glow of the candles. The orb was unusually warm against her fingertips, almost as if it were radiating its own heat.

" 'Tis a pretty piece," Roarke commented. "Was it your mother's?"

She shook her head. "The only jewelry my mother ever owned was a plain silver ring my father gave to her when they were wed. When the MacTiers came, they made everyone bring their valuables into the courtyard and drop them into a pile. I hid the ring in my shoe. But then they made us take off our shoes and boots and place them in another pile, and one of the warriors found the ring before I could hide it." Her tone was flat as she recited the story, but her fingers had tightened around the pendant, bleaching the skin of her knuckles.

Roarke cursed silently. It was obvious Melantha's ring had meant a great deal to her, and it filled him with rage to know his own clan had stolen it from her. "Was this pendant something you took during one of your raids?"

She nodded. "One day we captured a coach that was traveling to your holding. Inside we found a half dozen crates bearing silver chalices, crosses, and trays, and one well-fed priest who seemed a little too eager to hand over everything to us. I thought it odd the way he kept patting at the bloat of his waist, and ordered Magnus to search him. A small box was belted to his girth, and in it lay this pendant." She released her grip to let it glitter once again in the candlelight. "I wanted to sell it with everything else, but Magnus said 'twas by luck that we had found it, and so it would bring us further luck if I wore it." She dropped the orb against her skin. "I think he just liked the idea of me having something from the MacTiers, even though he knew it could never replace my mother's ring."

No, thought Roarke, not even the rarest of jewels could hope to ease the loss of that simple, worn band.

"Do you believe they will return?" she asked quietly.

"They will not return tonight," he assured her, lowering himself into the chair. "Thor did a fine job of making them believe that my men and I would be slain if they did, and that is not what they want. Although they have been ordered to subdue your people, it cannot be at the cost of my life or the lives of my men. That would not be a good victory."

"I see." Her tone was flagrantly bitter.

"This was not my doing, Melantha," Roarke reminded

her. "You knew the risk of attack when you decided to take me and my men prisoner. I tried to warn you, but you refused to listen."

"You were coming to crush my band and capture me," she retorted coldly. "If I had let you go, would you and your men have simply walked home and left us alone?"

Roarke hesitated. "No." He wished he could have said otherwise.

"And if you had managed to capture us, what would our fate have been?"

He shook his head impatiently. "It doesn't matter—"

"It does matter, Roarke," she interrupted fiercely. "You had been given orders by your laird, and it was your duty to carry them out or face the consequences of failure. What would you have done to me and my men?"

He stared at her in frustration. "We had orders to crush the Falcon's band and return with the Falcon himself as our prisoner."

"And that is what you would have done, isn't it? You would have butchered Colin, and Magnus, and Finlay, and Lewis. And you would have captured me and dragged me back to your holding, where I would have been tried before your laird and executed."

"I would never have allowed anything to happen to you, Melantha."

"You nearly cut my head off the first time you saw me."

"Only because you were trying to kill me."

"I was trying to kill you because you were going to slay my men!"

Roarke closed his eyes, suddenly weary. He did not want to talk about killing and duty any more. A sharp blade of guilt was twisting in his gut, making him feel tense and defeated. He had betrayed his own clan tonight, he realized bleakly. Those men down there were his own people, linked to him by history, loyalty, and blood. Some of them he had recognized, although he did not believe any of them were men who had ever fought under his command.

Even so, the magnitude of his treachery was appalling.

Never, in over twenty years of service, had he ever acted against the welfare of his laird or his people. His life had been far from perfect—the lonely deaths of his wife and daughter were an agonizing testament on that point—but he had prided himself on his clear, unquestioning loyalty to his clan. He had always carried out his duties with single-minded purpose, leaving no room for contemplating the devastating effect his actions might have had on others. It had been his lifelong mission to strengthen his clan, to expand its borders, and to constantly enrich its coffers by bringing home the bounty of war. This was not some barbaric doctrine of oppression; it was merely a fact of life in the Highlands. Those holdings he captured then fell under the MacTier influence. He had abated any guilt by assuring himself that the conquered clans were now better off, because they would be protected from others who might dare to attack them.

The MacKillons had made him realize that his perception of his clan's aggression was horribly distorted. An assault on a people exacted a terrible price, and forcing a clan to bend to another could only breed loathing and discord.

He swallowed thickly, wondering if his entire life as a warrior had been nothing but an infliction of misery on others.

"Why did you do it?" queried Melantha softly.

He opened his eyes and regarded her in confusion.

"Your clan was here to rescue you," she elaborated. "All you had to do was go out and join them, and you would have been free." She shook her head, struggling to comprehend his actions. "Why did you choose to stay with us and fight your own people?"

"Why did you threaten to kill me this evening, and then fly through the air to shield me with your body?"

"I don't know," she whispered, but even as she said it she knew it was a lie.

Roarke raised his hand to gently trace his finger along the white fabric of her bandage. Had she moved a second earlier or later, had she twisted her body slightly or stumbled, the arrow would have burrowed into her chest and she would have been killed. He could not imagine what had inspired such an act of selflessness. He had come here seeking to capture the Falcon, and yes, loath as he was to admit it, to escort the outlaw to his death.

Instead, the Falcon had thrown herself in front of an arrow meant for Roarke.

He took her palm and kissed it gently before pressing it hard against his chest.

"There are no absolutes for us anymore, Melantha," he said, his voice low and rough. "No absolute hatred, no absolute loyalty or trust. We can only go moment to moment, making our choices from the deepest part of our soul, instead of letting others make them for us."

"I never let anyone make my choices for me," Melantha whispered, lost in the silvery depths of his eyes as she felt the steady beat of his heart beneath her trembling hand.

"I know," he said solemnly.

He leaned forward and lowered his head until his lips were almost touching hers, still holding her palm against his heart. She had saved his life tonight, just as he had tried to save the lives of her people. They were both trapped in the vortex of a battle that neither wanted to fight, and that was something in which neither of them had any choice whatsoever. Tomorrow he would leave her to return to his clan and convince his laird to abandon his campaign against the MacKillons. After that he would retire to the holding he had been promised, and try to make some kind of life for himself that went beyond the constant infliction of misery and death. It was what he wanted, he told himself fiercely.

And so after tonight Melantha would be lost to him forever.

He groaned and captured her lips with his, crushing her against him with bruising force. A cry escaped her throat as she desperately returned his kiss, her tongue sweeping into his mouth as she wrapped her arms around his shoulders and pulled him down against her. Roarke tasted her deeply as his hands roamed over her, tearing away the light woolen blanket so he could feel the contours of her body through the maddeningly thin veil of her linen chemise. Melantha pulled in frustration at his plaid and jerkin, and Roarke appeased her by rising quickly to shed the offending garments.

Melantha stared in fascination at the naked warrior standing before her, his bronzed body chiseled into a thousand hard angles and sinewy curves illuminated by the flickering candlelight. There were scars etched across the powerful planes of his chest and stomach and arms, each one a testament to a life spent in battle. How many times had he faced death, and somehow managed to elude its grasp? It was impossible to think that his injuries had not affected him, or that his advancing age had not begun to stiffen muscles that were once fluid with youth. And yet he exuded a commanding power she had never known in any other man. The light of the candles was soft, but in that moment she could see him with absolute clarity, every weakness, and every strength.

And she wanted him with an intensity that was terrifying.

She kept her gaze locked upon his as she slowly skimmed the gossamer veil of her chemise up the paleness of her body, enjoying a dark pleasure as his eyes smoldered with desire. The gauzy fabric whispered over her head before she tossed it onto the cool stone floor in a crumpled pool. For an instant she was suddenly shy, but Roarke's searing study of her kept her from crossing her arms over her breasts with maidenly

modesty. She had known him once before, had felt the hard
pressure of his body wrapped around her own and the exquisite glory of holding him deep within herself as he caressed her to the brink of madness. She wanted that again,
that feeling of him moving against her, and with her, and the
sublime knowledge that for one ethereal moment, he be-
longed to her alone.

She held out her arms.

Roarke stretched out over her, plundering her mouth
with his tongue as he reveled in the feel of her slender form
pressing against his hard body. He wanted her with a need
that was staggering, a hunger so consuming he was certain it
could never be abated. And so he tore away his mouth to ravenously kiss the softness of her cheek, the fine hollow at the
base of her throat, the sweet pink shell of her ear. He did not
linger long anywhere, but continued his journey along the
delicate structure of her shoulder while his hands captured
the lush mounds of her breasts. He buried his face into their
softness before taking a claret peak into his mouth, and then
he suckled hard and long, groaning with pleasure as Melantha plunged her hands into the thickness of his hair and held
him tight against her.

Quickly he moved down the creamy flat of her stomach,
until finally he came to the silky darkness between her thighs.
He drew his tongue lightly up the downy cleft, barely grazing
the hidden petals beneath, and felt a hot stab of masculine
pleasure as a small, carnal moan escaped Melantha's throat.
He continued to flicker his tongue over her, tormenting her
with the veiled promise of more, until finally she opened her
legs wider in wanton desperation. He stroked her fully then,
tasting the hot, wet folds of her with slow, sure laps, up and
down, in and out, teasing her and torturing her as he flicked
at every little hidden pleat. He burrowed his tongue deep inside her as his hands moved possessively over her legs and
thighs and hips, drinking in the scent and taste and touch of

her, and then he was swirling against the rosy slickness of her once again, until shallow little pants began to rise from her throat and her body grew restless with need.

Melantha felt as if she were being consumed by fire, so intense were the sensations pouring through her. Her body was all liquid heat and softness, while at the same time she felt as if every muscle and bone were locked so tight she would surely shatter. She opened herself farther to Roarke's exquisite caresses and watched him as he lapped at her, feeling a dark, forbidden thrill at the sight of him devouring her so ravenously. An aching hollow was building within her, and she moaned in frustration, then sank back against the pillow as she felt him press his finger deep into her, filling her as he continued his hot, wet kisses. In and out his finger slid as his lips and tongue licked and suckled at her, igniting every fiber of her being into a raging fire, making her writhe and stretch against the cool linen sheets as her body burned for more. She could not bear this exquisite torment a moment longer, she was certain of it, but instead of stopping him she raised herself against him, taking quick, desperate little sips of air as her body grew rigid and her blood began to pound through her veins. And then suddenly everything stopped, and she was unable to move or think or breathe; all she could do was reach and reach for the incredible ecstasy dangling before her, and when she grasped it she cried out, a cry of wonder and utter joy. Roarke instantly rose up and buried himself deep inside her, filling her emptiness and covering her with the warm, hard shield of his powerful body, holding her safe as she exploded into a glorious shower of stars.

Roarke kissed Melantha tenderly as she locked her body to his, holding him tight within the deepest recesses of her as her fingers bit into the muscles of his back. And then she sighed into his mouth and eased her hold on him, the stiffness of her body flowing away like warm sand. A low growl unfurled from his chest as he began to move within her. He wanted her to the point of madness, and now that he was inside her he only wanted her more. In and out he thrust, feeling as if he were dying with each aching penetration, a slow, glorious death in which he ceased to be whoever the hell he had wasted most of his life being and instead became a part of her. She twined her legs with his and drew him deeper while her hands roamed the rigid planes of his shoulders and back and buttocks, scorching his flesh with her hungry touch, binding him to her body and heart and soul, until he thought he would weep from the impossible magnificence of it. He wanted to be lost within her forever, to feel her softness wrapped around him, the whisper of her breath gusting against his neck, and the sweet, clean scent of sunlit forests forever permeating the air. She was his, but only for this brief, stolen moment, and the knowledge was so agonizing his heart began to break. In and out he moved, desperately fighting his intensifying pleasure as he fought to chain her to him, feeling if he could just hold her longer, touch her more, bury himself ever deeper inside her, then surely he could cleave her to his soul. But there was no more time, for suddenly his body began to thrust faster and harder despite his efforts to restrain it. And then he was shattering, pouring himself into her as he called her name, filling her with his strength and his need as he covered her mouth with his and kissed her savagely.

They lay together a long while, their bodies still joined, their flesh burning between them. But the night air swirled around them in cool currents, eventually chilling their skin. Roarke gathered Melantha into his arms and held her close as he pulled the sheet and plaid over them, unwilling to accept that their time together was almost at an end. They clasped each other in uneasy silence, each unwilling to speak and break the fragile bonds that were already disintegrating between them.

After a while warm droplets began to fall against Roarke's

chest. Grasping Melantha's chin, he tilted her head up and regarded her with concern.

"What is it, Melantha?"

Her eyes were glittering with anguish. "Nothing," she whispered.

"Tell me," he urged, brushing a damp lock of hair off her forehead.

She swallowed thickly and stared at him, obviously torn. And then she inhaled a ragged breath and whispered in a voice so faint he could barely make out the words, "I was thinking of my father."

He drew her closer and began to stroke her hair, caressing her with a soothing touch as he held her even tighter against him.

She lay against him in silence, afraid. She did not know why she had even admitted that much to him. The memory of her father was as precious as it was painful, and not something she chose to share with anyone. Instead she kept it locked within her, buried deep within the ice-cold depths of anguish and remorse.

"When the battle was over this evening, you thought your father had just been killed," Roarke ventured, wondering if she were still in a kind of shock instigated by what she had seen. "You realize that he was actually killed months ago, don't you, Melantha?" he enquired gently.

She laid her cheek against the granite heat of his chest and nodded.

"But the assault tonight caused you to think about him?"

"Yes."

He hesitated a long moment, debating whether or not to ask her more. The silvery drip of tears continued to wet his skin, until finally he decided that there was something she needed to tell him, whether she understood it completely or not. Keeping her cradled against him, he laid his hand against the hot stream trailing down her cheek and quietly asked, "How did he die, Melantha?"

She remained silent, fighting for the courage to speak. And just when he thought she would not open this painful memory to him, the words slowly began to come.

"I was asleep when the MacTiers attacked the first time," she murmured, her voice strangely hollow. "The night was cool and there was a heavy cover of clouds blocking the light of the moon, making it difficult to see anything. When he realized we were under attack, my father told me to take my brothers to the lower level of the castle and hide with them. But I did not want to hide. My father had trained me from the time I was five in archery and swordplay, and I saw no reason why I should not help protect our home. And so I disobeyed him. I left Daniel, Matthew, and Patrick hiding with the other women and children, and I fetched my weapons and ran into the courtyard to fight the invaders."

She paused.

Roarke's voice was gentle as he softly prodded, "What happened, Melantha?"

"The MacTiers were everywhere," she whispered helplessly. "Our men were doing their best to fight them, but they were no match for such highly trained savagery. I couldn't see my father anywhere, and I was glad, because I knew if he saw me he would order me to return to my brothers. I climbed up the outer stairs leading to the second level of the castle, thinking I could kill more MacTiers with my bow than I could with my sword, and I began to shoot."

She stopped again.

"Did you kill anyone?"

"I hit five of them, but I only managed to wound them," she reported, her voice steeped in bitterness. "And then one of the MacTiers shouted an order to shoot the woman with the bow on the stairs. And that's when my father discovered I had defied him."

"He saw you?"

"He was fighting with a warrior down by the well. But when he heard about a woman archer, he was distracted."

A terrible dread began to seep through Roarke.

"He—he only turned his head for an instant," Melantha said, forcing herself to continue. "Just long enough to see me, and to call out my name." She swallowed, fighting the sob rising in her throat. "That was all the warrior he was battling needed to plunge his sword deep into his belly."

"Oh, God," murmured Roarke, feeling her anguish as surely as if it were his own.

"His eyes never left mine as he sank to his knees," she whispered, the words raw and halting. "He looked absolutely terrified. But not for himself," she qualified. "His gaze stayed upon me, and all I could see was this awful fear—for what the MacTiers were going to do to me." A ragged sob began to choke her.

Roarke drew her even tighter into his arms, trying to absorb some of her pain.

"Two warriors grabbed me then, and instead of killing me they decided to just drag me away from the battle. I screamed and struggled against them—not because I cared what they were going to do to me, but because I could see my da was dying and—" She inhaled a shuddering breath. "I wanted to be with him. I pleaded with them to let me go to him, so I could hold him ... be with him ... I didn't want him to be alone." Her words were drowning in tears. "But they just laughed and took me away. And my beautiful, brave da was left to bleed to death on the ground, watching his only daughter be dragged off by two warriors. And he was in agony, because he was terrified of what they were going to do to me and—he was helpless to stop them."

She ground her face against Roarke's chest. Deep, racking sobs shook her body while her breath came in shallow, desperate gasps. Roarke did not know what to do except to hold her. His embrace was so tight he thought he might bruise her tender flesh or even crush a bone, but he did not ease his grip.

He thought about the excruciating burden of guilt, and how it could eat away at a soul until there was nothing but a frail shell left where once there had been a whole person. It was an affliction he knew well, for he believed that if he had only been at Muriel's side to help her endure the shocking pain of their daughter's death, he would have helped his gentle wife to find the strength to go on. Melantha was weeping for the loss of her father, but that was not what was destroying her soul.

What was truly torturous was the belief that she had caused his horrible death.

"It wasn't your fault, Melantha," he told her firmly, pulling her up so he could look into her eyes.

"I killed him," she protested brokenly. "I defied his orders, and distracted him when he was fighting for his very life. Had I obeyed him and stayed with my brothers, he never would have been killed."

"Your clan was under attack, Melantha," Roarke pointed out. "Your father could have been killed at any moment—if not by that warrior, then by the next one who challenged him. And if he had been slain while you hid with your brothers, you would be punishing yourself now for not having fought at his side."

She stared at him uncertainly, weighing the validity of his argument. And then she shook her head, dismissing it. "He died believing I was about to be beaten and raped," she whispered. "I wasn't, but that was his last thought as his life drained into the ground."

"Perhaps," Roarke allowed, tracing the shimmering path of her tears with his fingers. "But do you truly believe that was all that filled his mind in those last moments, Melantha?" he asked, his voice low and gentle. "Your father was not a man who made war, but he understood the importance of knowing how to defend those he loved. That is why he trained you from a tender age in the art of using a bow and a sword. And in those last moments, he was filled with an overwhelming love and pride at the sight of his beautiful daughter standing on the stairs above him, bravely helping her clan to ward off its enemies."

She bit her quivering lip, considering his words.

" 'Tis clear to me your father knew from the time you were a bairn that you were no ordinary lass, and he was determined to see that you were trained to realize the best of your abilities," Roarke continued, his hand caressing the dark silk of her hair. "Imagine the pride he must have felt seeing you shooting arrows into the enemy, showing not the slightest hint of fear as you fought to protect your home. In his last moments he was overwhelmed with the vision of your courage and your love. It is never easy to die, Melantha, but that is as fine an image as any man could hope to take with him as he leaves his mortal body."

Melantha regarded him with anxious uncertainty, wanting to believe him, but reluctant to release the guilt she had so painfully endured for so long. "Do you really think so?"

Her tears had stopped, but her eyes were still glittering, making them large and hauntingly luminous. She was unfathomably beautiful to him in that moment, as all the elements of her melded into one gloriously courageous yet achingly vulnerable woman. She was not his and she never would be, and the knowledge filled him with unbearable loss. But in this hushed moment, as she lay cradled against him studying him hopefully, she was as close to being his as she ever would be.

"Yes, Melantha," he whispered, turning her onto her back and stretching his hard body over her exquisite softness once more.

She rose to meet his kiss, wrapping her slender arms

around the chiseled marble of his shoulders. He buried himself inside her and began to move, kissing her tenderly as he quickly roused her once again. He sought to wash away the last vestiges of her guilt, to free her from the torment that slashed at her heart, and in doing so, perhaps assuage some of his own guilt as well.

And so they pulsed together in the flickering candlelight, lost to the splendid fire burning within them, and the aching need that bound their souls into one.

CHAPTER 9

Melantha sighed and burrowed deeper beneath the warm haven of her covers.

Only the barest hint of light filtered through her leaden eyelids, so she was certain it could not be not much past dawn. Just another hour, she told herself sleepily, nuzzling the feathery depths of her pillow. No one could possibly have risen yet anyway. Another hour, and she would still be among the first to stir within the castle.

A hideous drone shattered the morning stillness, rousing her as effectively as a stake being driven into her ear. Unable to imagine what Thor could be thinking playing his pipes at such an ungodly hour, she heaved back the covers and stalked angrily to the window.

Roarke, his men, and the MacTier prisoners were assembled in the courtyard below, listening with admirable grace as Thor blasted away on his hopelessly damaged bagpipes. Roarke and his warriors were fully armed and their horses were saddled. The other prisoners were not armed and did not have mounts, but it was clear they were also leaving. Daniel, Matthew, and Patrick were at the forefront of the large group of MacKillons who had assembled to bid them good-bye. Melantha watched in surprise as Matthew stepped forward and tentatively offered a folded square of paper to Roarke. The enormous warrior opened it, then lowered himself onto one knee and gently ruffled Matthew's hair.

A terrible chill swept through her. Whirling about, she snatched up the plaid from her bed and wrapped it around her shoulders, then raced down the corridor, her bare feet flying against the frigid stone floor.

*"... and when you look at it, you'll always remember," finished Matthew, his earnest little face regarding Roarke with something akin to worship.

Roarke nodded gravely, studying the drawings he held in his hands. Matthew's artistry was surprisingly skilled for a mere lad of ten. The first sketch showed Roarke being held upside down by Finlay and Myles as he reached for Matthew and dragged him back to safety. In the interest of modesty, Roarke's plaid stiffly defied the forces of nature and remained squarely covering his backside. But it was the second drawing that moved Roarke beyond the possibility of speech. In it Matthew was standing with his arms wrapped around Roarke, and above it, in simple, childish letters, he had printed a single word.

'*Friends.*'

"Do you like it?" prodded Matthew, uncertain of Roarke's silence.

"Yes," said Roarke, fearing if he said more his emotions would betray him. He cleared his throat. "Thank you."

"When I get to be older, will you come back and teach me how to fight?" asked Patrick hopefully.

"He's not coming back," interjected Daniel.

"Why not?" asked Patrick.

"Because he's a MacTier," explained Daniel. His eyes were intense as he studied Roarke, but they did not seem to harbor the same anger they had reflected from the moment he and his men had arrived. "You're not coming back, are you?"

Roarke hesitated, uncertain how to respond.

"I packed you some extra food for your journey," said Gillian, shyly stepping forward to hand Eric a cloth-wrapped bundle. "I thought you might get hungry."

Eric regarded the carefully arranged package in surprise.

"You didn't by chance pack us some of your splendid posset, did you?" teased Donald.

"No," said Gillian, her gaze fast upon Eric. "But I shall always keep some ready—in case you ever return."

Her blue eyes were glittering like a sun-dappled loch, so beautiful and so filled with regret that it made Eric's heart ache to look upon her. He wanted to pull her into his arms and hold her close, to tell her not to be sad, that if she wanted him to stay he gladly would, if only she would say the words. But duty required him to follow Roarke, and an unfamiliar sense of propriety told him it was not fitting to drag a maid into his arms before her entire clan, especially when he had no formal claim upon her. And so he simply held her gaze, feeling not at all like a fearsome Viking warrior, but strangely powerless and wholly inadequate.

"Well, then, my brave hero, it seems this is farewell," said Katie, walking boldly up to Myles. "Now, I'll have your word that you'll not be turning any other lasses' heads with your flowery talk about hips and arms," she scolded with mock severity.

"I'll not be speaking to any other lasses at all," Myles swore.

Katie laughed. "That's just what I wanted to hear, never mind that you won't be able to keep your word beyond the first lass who smiles your way after me!"

"Lasses never smile at me," replied Myles. "Only you do."

She was about to laugh again, but was stopped by the earnestness of his expression. "Well, then, they're fools," she said softly. She leaned into him and kissed him soundly upon his cheek.

"Good Lord, what the devil has possessed Melantha?" demanded Magnus in astonishment.

She was hurrying across the grass in her bare feet, her slender form barely covered by the thin chemise floating about her, the plaid under which she and Roarke had lain together clutched hastily around her shoulders. Her hair was a loose tangle of mahogany, and Roarke found himself longing to reach out and touch it, to run his fingers through its impossible softness and gently brush it off her face.

Instead he forced his hands to his sides and regarded her with deliberate calm, giving no intimation of the passion that had raged between them the previous night.

"Here, now, lass, what in the name of St. Cuthbert do ye think ye're doin' flyin' about half-naked when ye should be lyin' in yer bed restin'?" demanded Magnus sternly.

"I—I came to say good-bye," stammered Melantha, staring at Roarke.

"Of course you did, dear," said Beatrice, "and now that you've done so, let's get you back inside where it's warm."

"Let her stay," objected Thor, wrestling his pipes back up onto his bony shoulder. "I've another tune to play."

"Your pardon, Thor, but unfortunately there's no time for another of your tunes," Laird MacKillon said apologetically. "I do believe the weather is about to turn, and these lads must be on their way."

The early morning sky was choked with clouds and a sharp wind was rising, whipping Melantha's hair against her cheek as she clutched her makeshift cloak even tighter.

"I thought you told your clan three days," she said to Roarke, wondering if she sounded nearly as desperate as she felt.

" 'Tis best we go now," Roarke told her. "The longer we wait, the more time my clan has to grow angry and demand vengeance. The moment I return I will speak to Laird Mac-Tier and stop him from sending any further forces."

It was a perfectly reasonable explanation. He was leaving to protect the welfare of her people.

Why then did she feel as if he were abandoning her?

"You are not safe until my men and I are gone, Melantha," Roarke added gently, sensing her distress. "You know that."

She inhaled a steadying breath, fighting to maintain some semblance of control as she stood before him. "You were supposed to deliver the Falcon to your laird," she pointed out. "How will you explain your failure to do so?"

Roarke shrugged. "Unfortunately, I never found him." He lowered his voice so that the MacTier prisoners could not hear him. "My people only know that the MacKillons captured us—they have no idea that the Falcon is one of them. I don't intend to enlighten them."

"But what if your laird sends you out once again to capture the Falcon?" she persisted.

"My days of leading such missions are over," he replied. "I intend to retire to the holding I have been promised as payment for a lifetime of service."

She could not contain her surprise. "Laird MacTier has built you a holding of your own?"

"He has not built it," Roarke corrected. "He has a number of properties subject to his control which require someone to protect and manage them. I am to be granted one of those estates."

Her expression hardened. "You mean homes that have been taken by force."

"It isn't what you think," Roarke countered. "These holdings have been acquired over many years, and they are stronger and more bountiful for being in our possession. The people who live there go about their lives just as they did before, secure in the knowledge that they are now protected by the entire force of the MacTier army."

"How very comforting," observed Melantha, her voice dripping scorn. "To be guarded by those who attacked you and stripped you of your freedom and possessions. I suppose the only reason your benevolent clan did not see fit to make such an arrangement with us was because they believed there was nothing of value left to protect."

"I cannot change what my clan did to your people, Melantha," he said, knowing it was beyond her ability to ever forgive him for that. "However, I am going to try to convince Laird MacTier to send your clan aid, to help replace that which you have lost."

A bitter laugh erupted from her chest. "Why would he want to help us?"

"Because I will tell him he should," Roarke replied. "If he refuses, then I give you my word that once I am settled, I will send your people provisions myself. All I ask of you is that you cease your raids on the MacTiers and their allies."

"Can you possibly believe that I will accept stolen provisions from an oppressed people?" she demanded, incredulous.

"Any estate I oversee will not be oppressed," Roarke said impatiently.

"They will have been terrorized into submission long before your arrival," she countered. "You will just continue to hold a sword over their heads, forcing them to obey you out of fear."

"Your pardon, Melantha, but are you almost finished bidding our guests farewell?" wondered Laird MacKillon. "I do believe the weather is about to turn for the worse."

Heavy drops of rain began to splat against them.

"Make way for my pipes!" shouted Thor, cuddling his beloved instrument in his arms as he headed back toward the castle. "Stand aside, I say!"

"I am trying to help your people, Melantha," persisted Roarke, disliking the way things were ending between them. "Why can you not accept that?"

"I don't want provisions that have been stolen from others," Melantha informed him coldly. "If my people are in need, then we will take directly from those who have stolen from us—not from their victims."

The rain was falling harder now, soaking her hair and chemise. She pulled her plaid tighter and continued to face him, like some magnificent forest creature who was accustomed to the elements and wholly untroubled by the storm rising around her.

"If you don't mind, lads, I'll be saying farewell now," said Laird MacKillon, waving as he shuffled toward the keep. "Safe journey."

"It is gettin' a wee bit damp," Magnus agreed. "Are ye lads sure ye don't want to wait until the rain is past?"

As he stared down at Melantha, Roarke was sorely tempted to use the rain as an excuse to stay. He had silently bid her farewell when he stole from her chamber early that morning—knowing as he did that if he lingered even a moment longer, he would take her into his arms and never leave her side again. He had hoped she would not waken until after he was gone. Yet he would not have relinquished for anything this moment of seeing her standing before him, rain drenched, angry, and filled with fire.

"We must leave now," he said.

"Well, then, I wish ye a fine journey," said Magnus. His blue eyes were twinkling with merriment as he warned, "Keep a sharp eye for outlaws—I hear the forest is filled with them!"

The rest of the clan quickly followed his example, waving at Roarke and his men as they hurriedly escaped the torrent now lashing against them.

"I cannot tell you what to do, Melantha," said Roarke quietly. "But remember this—if you continue to wage war against the MacTiers, you will only be punished in return."

"What would you have me do?" she demanded. "Do you believe I should stand by and watch my people starve?"

"All I ask is that you give me a little time, Melantha. Whatever happens, I swear to you, I will not let you or your people suffer anymore."

He regarded her with piercing intensity, as if he were trying to reach into her soul, to delve beneath the protective layers she had so carefully forged around herself and etch his vow on her heart. In that moment she almost believed he could protect her from suffering, so strong and sure did he seem as he stood before her in the rain. Crystal drops were falling off his black hair, and his shirt and plaid were clinging to his muscular frame, emphasizing his powerful masculine beauty. She remembered lying within his embrace, wrapped within his heat and his strength, feeling almost safe. But she was not safe, she reminded herself fiercely. Her holding was still vulnerable, there was insufficient food and clothing to sustain her people through the coming winter, and even if Roarke refused to hunt down the Falcon himself, it was unlikely that Laird MacTier would abandon his pursuit of her. As for his offer to send aid, she did not believe MacTier could be persuaded to help his enemies, and she would never accept anything from Roarke's conquered holding.

"I do not believe your laird will help us," she told him. "And I will do whatever is necessary to ensure that my people have enough for the coming winter. It is no less than what you would do, Roarke, if it were your people who were threatened with starvation and cold because of the savagery and greed of another."

Her expression was resigned, as if she took no pleasure from her pronouncement. She looked at him a final long moment, her pale face glistening with rain, her hands gripping the soaking wet plaid that could no longer offer her even the slightest protection.

Then she turned and disappeared into the castle.

"... and so I managed to convince Laird MacKillon to release us the next day, rather than keeping us for the three days he had originally proposed," Roarke finished.

Laird MacTier stared out the window, considering in pensive silence the explanation Roarke had offered him. He was not a man accustomed to defeat. Over the course of his thirty-two years as chief of the MacTiers he had learned a few basic rules of war, and he adhered to these with near religious fervor. He never attacked an enemy unless he was absolutely sure he had dispatched the power and the resources to vanquish it completely. Therefore he was having difficulty understanding why an army of over two hundred of his best warriors, equipped with the very latest design of siege machine, had been bested by the ragged remains of a clan he had all but annihilated some months earlier.

What was even more mystifying was the inconceivable assertion by his most favored and accomplished warrior that he should not bother to retaliate.

"Am I to understand that you do not seek vengeance for your own abduction?" demanded Laird MacTier, turning from the window.

"None of us were harmed," Roarke explained. "In fact, we were treated well."

"Until they put dirks to your throats and threatened to

cut your heads off rather than release you," countered Laird MacTier dryly.

"Laird MacKillon was trying to stop your forces from using their siege machine."

Laird MacTier arched a querying brow. "My forces?"

"Our forces," Roarke quickly corrected.

"You cannot suggest that I should ignore the fact that four of my warriors were taken hostage by this ridiculous little clan. They chose to attempt to extract a ransom from me. They must be taught that I do not take such matters lightly."

"But ultimately no ransom was paid, therefore you did not lose anything," argued Roarke. "My men and I are well, and all of the prisoners taken on the eve of the attack have been returned to you. It seems to me the matter has been resolved—what more is there to be gained by attacking the MacKillons once again?"

Laird MacTier frowned, unable to believe that Roarke could not see what was patently obvious. "I cannot tolerate having members of my clan taken hostage. To do so only invites further abductions."

"You refused to meet their demands. That made it clear that the MacTiers will not yield to those who attempt to extort from them. And you sent your army, demonstrating that you are willing to use force if necessary."

"I am willing to use force," Laird MacTier agreed. "And that is why I intend to crush those damn MacKillons. 'Tis bad enough I have the Falcon's band stealing from me and sending my men home stark naked. No doubt that is what made the MacKillons think you were easy prey. I must make an example of them, to dissuade others from attempting further attacks."

"The MacKillons never would have ransomed us if they hadn't been in desperate need of the items they requested."

"I cannot think of any clan that isn't in desperate need of gold," retorted Laird MacTier.

"The gold was of far less import to them than their requests for food and clothing," Roarke objected. "After our assault upon them, they were left nearly destitute. Their stores for winter were stolen, and every one of their animals was either dragged off or slain and left to rot."

"They had an entire forest of food waiting for them," said Laird MacTier dismissively. "All they had to do was go out and hunt for it."

"That might have been true if they had been attacked in the spring," conceded Roarke. "But they were raided in the autumn and then they suffered one of the worst winters in their clan's history. Most of the animals either starved to death or left the woods in search of food themselves. There was not nearly enough meat to sustain the clan, and scarcely any grains or vegetables left to make up the difference."

Laird MacTier looked at Roarke in astonishment. "What the devil is the matter with you, Roarke? You've raided scores of clans just like the MacKillons, and not once have you ever expressed any concern about their welfare."

He was right, Roarke realized, taking no pride in the observation.

"I never spent any time with any of the clans I raided. With the MacKillons I was forced to witness the consequences of our assault."

"That is the nature of war," said Laird MacTier impatiently, unmoved by Roarke's apparent enlightenment. "There is a victor, and there are the vanquished. We must constantly work to increase our strength and resources, and that comes at a cost to others. Ultimately, all that matters is that we have fortified the power of our own clan. We are not responsible for the vulnerability of those who cannot defend themselves against us."

"We may not be responsible for their inability to defeat us," conceded Roarke, "but we are certainly responsible if we reduce them to a state in which they are left to starve."

Laird MacTier regarded him with irritation. "You cannot make me believe that every last one of them would starve. Somehow, a few strong members of the clan would find a way to survive. These ones might even try to help the others."

"You're right," agreed Roarke. "And if surviving meant ransoming a few MacTier warriors in exchange for food and clothing, how can you fault them for that?"

"Your capacity for absolution in this matter is most unlike you, Roarke," Laird MacTier observed.

"I would like to believe that I am not so hardened a warrior that I cannot learn to empathize with the plight of others. All I'm asking is that you consider the circumstances which forced the MacKillons to ransom us—circumstances which we inflicted upon them. All the MacTier prisoners were treated well and released unharmed. I cannot see the merit in punishing the MacKillons further."

"Perhaps you are right," Laird MacTier allowed. "What of your hunt for the Falcon?" he asked, changing the subject. "Did you find anything that might prove valuable in leading us to him?"

"Unfortunately, no."

Laird MacTier's disappointment was obvious. "I suppose you were abducted early in your search. I have every faith that you will deliver this miserable outlaw to me shortly."

Roarke did not respond.

"You do intend to complete your mission?" It was a statement, not a question.

"I will resume my hunt for the Falcon if you wish it. However, I am not certain that I am the best warrior to find this elusive thief."

Laird MacTier regarded him in surprise. "Why not?"

"It is difficult for any warrior to recognize, much less admit, that he is reaching the end of his days as a fighter," he began, choosing his words carefully. "But when he lies upon the ground and dreams only of a soft bed beneath him and a solid roof over his head, he begins to realize that he is not the young man he used to be."

Laird MacTier raised his hand, stopping him. "You need explain no further, my friend. When you first returned from your long years away I told you that you would soon be rewarded for your outstanding loyalty. I am well aware that you have devoted your entire life to expanding the wealth and influence of this clan. Your countless successes over the years have been unmatched by any of my other warriors—yet your remarkable talents and devotion have denied you the comfort of a wife and a home."

"I had Muriel and Clementina," Roarke reminded him, unwilling to let their memory be so casually discarded.

"Of course," Laird MacTier hastily agreed. "And I know it was most painful for you to lose them while you were away fighting for your clan. At the time there was nothing I could do except send you off to fight again, in the hopes that the demands of battle and the glory of conquest would somehow ease the burden of their loss."

Roarke stiffened at his analysis. Laird MacTier made it sound as though inflicting misery and death on others had been a balm for his own suffering.

"There is a handsome estate about two days' ride from here that I recently acquired," Laird MacTier continued, seating himself at his ornately carved desk. "The lands are not extensive, but they are comely and fertile, and the people there should prove easily manageable under the right master. I am sure you will find it most agreeable. You may leave tomorrow."

A streak of trepidation shot through Roarke. He had assumed he would be given an established holding that had long been under MacTier influence. A newly won estate would still be recovering from its invasion, and its inhabitants would be both fearful and contemptuous of any MacTier who came to rule them.

"You don't seem very pleased," observed Laird MacTier, frowning.

"Forgive me," said Roarke, realizing he had already worn his relationship with his laird dangerously thin. "It is a fine bequest, MacTier. Thank you."

"You may take Eric, Donald, and Myles with you if you wish," Laird MacTier offered. "And whatever supplies you deem necessary. If after your arrival you find that you need more men, just get word to me and I will send them to you. I shall see you before you depart tomorrow." He lowered his gaze to his papers, indicating that their meeting was at an end.

"Thank you." Roarke gave his laird a small bow and quit the chamber.

He had just been given everything he had wanted.

But any pleasure he might have felt was obliterated by the gnawing realization that his laird had not unequivocally agreed to spare the MacKillons any further harassment.

"Enter."

The heavy door swung open and a powerfully built, keen-eyed warrior stepped into the laird's solar. His manner bore the easy arrogance of youth, for at five-and-twenty years he was entering the zenith of his physical abilities, and he had not yet suffered sufficient defeats to temper his conviction of his own invincibility. He wisely affected an appropriate contriteness as he met his laird's hard gaze. MacTier's mood was dark, and his own latest failure was the most likely cause.

"You disappoint me, Derek."

The young warrior said nothing, believing silence would be better received than a bevy of weak excuses.

"You were given a simple task," continued Laird MacTier, drumming his fingers upon his desk. "You were to crush the MacKillons and ensure the safe return of four MacTier warriors. Instead, you permit nearly one-third of your army to be captured, and allow the remainder to be chased away with hollow threats and posturing."

"You wanted Roarke and his men returned alive," Derek pointed out. "I could not secure their safe release if I proceeded with my attack on the MacKillon holding."

Laird MacTier slammed his fist upon the oiled wood of his desk. "You should have penetrated their pitiful defenses within minutes, leaving them no time to retrieve their hostages and use them for bargaining! The force that attacked them previously was inside and opening the gate before the MacKillons had stumbled drunkenly from their beds!"

"Their defenses have been improved upon since then," Derek replied stiffly. "They were able to hold us off longer than we had anticipated."

"Keep your sniveling excuses to yourself," snapped Laird MacTier. "They are of no interest to me." He rose from his desk and went to the window, pondering his next move. "I should have you relegated to shoveling filth for the next year. Instead I am going to give you the opportunity to redeem yourself from your pathetic failure." He paused, studying the magnificent expanse of land stretching before him. "I am most displeased by the fact that the Falcon continues to prey upon both my people and my possessions. As I have just assigned new duties to Roarke, I find I am in need of a warrior who will be able to swiftly find this troublesome outlaw and bring him to me for reckoning." He turned to face him. "Do you think you can manage that?"

"Yes," said Derek without hesitation.

"We shall see," said Laird MacTier, unimpressed by his assurance. "As my patience has grown severely strained in this matter, I expect you to use whatever means necessary to capture this thief. Do you have any ideas?"

"I will set a trap for him."

"How?"

"Several of my men who were taken prisoner by the

MacKillons noticed something strange about their captors," explained Derek. "It seems a number of the MacKillons were wearing plaids of MacTier colors. There were others who swore that they recognized a particular sword or dirk. And all thought it strange that amongst the ragged attire of the clan, one could find an occasional gown or shirt of exceptional quality and workmanship."

"What are you saying?" demanded Laird MacTier impatiently. "That the Falcon is a MacKillon?"

"Perhaps," allowed Derek. "Or it's possible that the Falcon is giving away what he steals to struggling clans like the MacKillons."

Laird MacTier's eyes widened in dismay. "You think he gives it away?"

"He could also be selling it to them. But it couldn't be for much, given how little the MacKillons retained after our previous assault. Whichever it is, it appears the Falcon is concerned about the plight of the less fortunate. That will prove to be his undoing. I will harass the MacKillons until one of them reveals the identity of the Falcon, or the Falcon delivers himself to me in the name of protecting those he apparently cares for."

"You had best be right," warned Laird MacTier ominously, "or you will be up to your knees in excrement for the next year. Is that understood?"

"I will deliver the Falcon to you," Derek vowed.

"See that you do. Now get the hell out."

Laird MacTier watched with impatience as the conceited young warrior left his chamber. When he was alone, he rose from his desk and went to the window to study the meadows and woods spilling out beyond the walls of his castle in a glorious tapestry of texture and color.

When he first inherited the title of laird from his father, the MacTiers had been a sizable clan, but its lands had not nearly matched the needs of its people. He had set out to extend its borders, enabling his people to build homes and hunt and fish in woods and streams far beyond their traditional boundaries. The clan grew as conquered people were absorbed into its fold, and therefore the need for land continued unabated.

He had not initiated this campaign of expanding his borders with anything in mind other than providing for those who depended upon him, but over the years it had gradually evolved into more than that. He had discovered there was an intense, almost sexual pleasure to be found in conquest. Although his clan's holdings and riches now far exceeded his youthful expectations, he found he constantly hungered for more. Roarke had been crucial in establishing the MacTiers as a powerful and feared clan, and MacTier prided himself on having cultivated the warrior's extraordinary abilities from the time he was a mere lad. But it seemed Roarke had lost his zest for battle, and the callow young idiots who surrounded him now were good for little more than ramming or charging—there was not a decent military leader among them. If the expansion and prosperity of the MacTiers were to continue, he would have to assume control of the military campaigns himself.

And for that, he needed the amulet.

Fury streaked through him at the thought of the precious relic having fallen so easily into the Falcon's grasp. The fool priest who had been delivering it to him had blathered on incessantly about how he had very nearly been disemboweled in his attempts to guard it from the Falcon. MacTier had coldly informed him that having his guts smeared upon the ground would have been preferable to the fate that now awaited him. Ultimately, however, his threats had proven hollow. He was a pragmatic man, and had no desire to risk God's wrath by hacking open one of His precious servants unnecessarily. Instead he had given the priest ample time to consider his failure in one of the dark pits below the west tower.

He frowned, wondering if he had ever given anyone the order to release him.

No matter.

All that was of import now was capturing the Falcon and forcing him to return the amulet. Within its silver sphere lay a fragment of bone from St. Columba himself, the shrewdly powerful abbot who had established a monastery on the isle of Iona some six hundred years earlier. Columba had been a man of remarkable foresight and abilities. Not only had he helped to replace the pitifully weak heir to the throne with Aidan the False, a bold monarch who led the Scots to countless victories against the Picts, Columba had also single-handedly vanquished a hideous monster on the shores of Loch Ness. The emerald at the center of the amulet was said to have been found upon the shore by the saint just before that extraordinary altercation. In the centuries since, there were countless tales of how the amulet had faithfully protected its wearer from sudden death in battle.

With that precious relic hanging round his neck, there were no limits to what he could achieve.

He chafed at suggestions that he was growing old. Although he could not wield a sword with the supple ease of his youth, he could still direct the movements of a battle with more wit and skill than any of the dung-brained clods surrounding him. Nevertheless, it was only judicious to secure for himself the finest protection possible. His wife had finally managed to produce a son for him, but the lad was barely ten and worse, he struck MacTier as a weak and cowering brat, who needed many years of rigorous training and education to prepare him for the role to which he had been born. Mac-Tier could not permit himself to be killed, or the clan would select another to assume his lairdship until his son was deemed of age to take his place. In the meantime, a lifetime of brilliant work could be destroyed. No, he could not go into battle without the protection of the amulet. He didn't give a damn if he had to slaughter every last bloody MacKillon in his quest to force the Falcon to bring it to him.

As for the elusive Falcon, the outlaw would pay dearly for daring to steal from him, and for interfering with his rightful destiny.

CHAPTER 10

〜〜 "Blast it, Gelfrid! You nearly crushed my hand!"

"I thought you were finished spreading the mortar," apologized Gelfrid sheepishly.

"You might have taken the time to ask me before you dropped that bloody stone on it!" Ninian complained. "I'll be lucky if it isn't broken!"

"Try to move your fingers," suggested Gelfrid helpfully.

"Just get away from me!" Ninian snapped, cradling his hand against his chest. "I've had enough of your clumsiness for one day!"

Gelfrid's face grew crimson with insult. "Clumsy, is it? Very well—let's see how quickly you build that merlon by yourself!"

"It may take longer," Ninian allowed, "but at least I'll do it without crushing any *bloody bones*!"

"Here, now, what's all this commotion about?" asked Magnus.

"Gelfrid nearly broke my hand," reported Ninian furiously.

" 'Twould never have happened if you weren't so bloody slow!" Gelfrid snapped.

"Come, now, lads," interjected Magnus, "we've got to work together if we're going to fix this damage."

"What difference does it make if we fix it or not?" Mungo demanded sourly. "The MacTiers are just likely to come back and destroy something else."

"Roarke said we must make our repairs immediately," said Lewis hesitantly, afraid of being barked at yet again. So far his gentle attempts to organize the men had failed miserably.

"And that is exactly what we should do," added Melantha, looking up from the arrow she was fletching. "Otherwise it is clear to everyone that we are vulnerable." She added the finished shaft to the pile of arrows she had already completed.

"We weren't so vulnerable when we sent those bloody MacTiers scampering home with their tails between their legs, by God," swore Thor, who was sitting on a chair lovingly polishing his pipes. "Now, there's a tale you pups will be able to tell your bairns!"

"Your pardon, Thor, but if memory serves I do believe 'twas Roarke and his men who in fact helped us to win the day," pointed out Laird MacKillon. "As you may recall, he told our men to put dirks to their throats and pretend we were going to kill them."

Thor blinked in confusion. "What do you mean, 'pretend'?"

"*Look out below!*" Hagar peered over the battlements to watch one of the timbers from the crumbling hoarding hurtle toward the ground, barely missing Colin. "Are you all right, son?"

"Yes," said Colin tautly, wincing at the pain the sudden movement had cost his heavily stitched back. "Do you want me to come up there and help you?"

"No need," Hagar informed him cheerily. "Everything is under control. You just stay down there and rest like your mother told you."

"Fine," muttered Colin, resuming his restless pacing of the courtyard.

"What are you lads doing up here?" asked Melantha as her three brothers appeared.

"We want to help," Daniel informed her seriously.

"To repair the castle," added Matthew.

"We're not babies," Patrick chirped, in case there was any misunderstanding on that point. "I helped Myles build one of the platforms."

"You may help in another area of the castle," Melantha informed them. "Not up here."

"Nothing is going to happen, Melantha," Daniel assured her, his voice edged with defiance. "We'll be very careful."

"I said no, Daniel," Melantha repeated firmly. "If you really want to help, then go and ask Beatrice or Edwina if they need any assistance preparing dinner."

Daniel snorted in disgust. "I don't want to do kitchen work."

"I do," sang out Patrick.

"Isn't there something else for us to do?" pleaded Matthew, who in fact wouldn't have minded working in the kitchen, but wanted to ally with his older brother.

"Fine," said Melantha, feeling totally exasperated. "Take these arrows and vanes and go ask Colin to show you how to fletch them," she instructed, deciding that Colin needed a task to keep him occupied as well. "Once you've finished the lot to Colin's satisfaction, place them in a neat pile by the arrow slit in the south tower."

"That's a good job, Daniel," Matthew said, trying to assess his brother's reaction. "We'll be making weapons."

Daniel scowled.

"Look at all these pretty feathers," marveled Patrick, happily gathering a bouquet into his hands.

"Be careful not to break them," said Melantha. She helped to pile the shafts into Daniel and Matthew's arms, then watched as they went off to find Colin. Then she began to restlessly walk along the wall head, wondering what to do next.

"I'm thinking it's been a while since we went hunting," said Magnus offhandedly. "For meat," he added, lest she think he was suggesting a robbery.

A burst of renewed energy coursed through her.

Matthew tossed his feather into the air and watched as it drifted toward the ground. "You're sure Melantha won't be mad?"

"Why would she be mad?" asked Daniel, trudging ahead of him. "She just said we couldn't go up to the wall head—she never said anything about going into the woods."

"But we're not allowed to play with a bow and arrows."

"We're not playing," Daniel assured him. "We're hunting."

Matthew looked doubtful. "I don't think we're allowed to go hunting, either."

"Why not? Melantha always used to talk about how Da would take her hunting from the time she was scarcely more than a baby. I'm thirteen and you're almost eleven—that's more than old enough."

"But what if something happens?" fretted Matthew. He stooped to pick up his feather. "Then Melantha will be angry with us."

"The only thing that's going to happen is we're going to shoot some nice, fat rabbits and bring them home and have everyone crowd around us and tell us what fine hunters we are," predicted Daniel. "And Beatrice will take them to the kitchen and prepare them for supper, and everyone will cheer us for helping to feed the clan."

"Really?"

"Absolutely. Then Melantha will see that we're practically men, and she'll tell us we can always go hunting with her from now on."

Matthew's eyes shone with pleasure as he considered this possibility. He tossed his feather high into the air and watched again as it gently landed on the pine-strewn earth.

And then the feather began to tremble.

The acrid scent stung Melantha's nostrils long before she and her men burst from the woods.

Thick plumes of black smoke were rising from a half dozen cottages upon the hill, and a series of blazes dotted the dry, scrubby grasses of the fields. Her people were racing in every direction; frantically tossing buckets of water and shovelfuls of sand and earth at the flames in a desperate effort to contain the grass fires and perhaps salvage some part of their homes. Melantha galloped toward the castle, her chest tight with fear. She had to find her brothers. She had to see that they were safe, had to kneel down and wrap her arms around them and feel their lean bodies shift restlessly within her embrace.

Then, and only then, could she focus on what had happened.

She thundered through the gate with Magnus, Lewis, and Finlay following close behind her. Throwing herself off her horse, she flew through the door and into the great hall.

Laird MacKillon, Thor, and Hagar were seated at a table, while Colin paced anxiously before them. On seeing Melantha their expressions, already grave, crumpled.

And she knew something terrible had happened to one of her brothers.

"Tell me," she pleaded, the words small and choked.

"It's Daniel and Matthew," said Colin. "The MacTiers have taken them."

A sickening dizziness swept over her, making her feel hot and cold all at once. *No,* she thought, struggling to make sense of what Colin had just said. She pressed the heels of her hands to her eyes, fighting the shifting and turning of the hall. *Please God, no—*

" 'Tis all right, lass," said Magnus, wrapping his arm around her shoulder and pulling her tight against him. "Just lean against me and take a breath. There ye are. 'Tis no time for panic, do ye understand?" he demanded sternly.

She did not speak but leaned against Magnus, taking comfort in the strong, solid feel of him as he held her steady.

"We're going to get them back, Melantha," Colin vowed fiercely. "I promise you that."

"Aye," agreed Finlay, moving protectively to her other side. "Even if we have to kill every last bloody MacTier to do so."

Lewis also moved closer, saying nothing, but closing the comforting circle of strength and determination around her.

Melantha inhaled a shallow breath, fighting the terror that was pulling her toward hysteria. She could not give in to it, for if she began to rant and weep she would lose precious moments.

"What happened?" she asked, forcing herself to push her emotions aside.

"Daniel and Matthew had gone off to play in the woods," explained Colin. "The MacTiers captured them before we even knew they were near." His gaze was agonized, as if he felt he should have been able to prevent it. "I'm sorry, Melantha."

"It wasn't your fault, Colin." *It is my fault,* she reflected in anguish. *My fault for bringing Roarke and his men here and daring to ransom them. My fault for raising the ire of the MacTiers.*

"After they took the lads, the MacTiers set fire to the cottages and fields," continued Laird MacKillon.

"Was anyone hurt?" asked Magnus.

Hagar shook his head. "Everyone is fine. The MacTiers never even tried to breach the wall. They just thundered about terrorizing everyone and setting things ablaze."

"Filthy, depraved demons!" stormed Thor. "If only I'd had my sword, I'd have chopped them up for stewing meat!"

A terrible question uncoiled in Melantha's mind. Her voice was hollow as she asked, "Were Roarke and his men among them?"

"Dear me, no," said Laird MacKillon, sounding shocked by the possibility. "Absolutely not. Roarke and his men would never behave in such a cowardly manner."

"They were led by that fair-haired chap who tried to collect them the other night," Hagar added. "Derek, I heard his men calling him. And I must tell you, he was most unpleasant."

"What did he say?" asked Lewis. "Was this our punishment for taking Roarke and his men prisoner?"

An uneasy silence fell over the hall.

"Come on, then, out with it," Magnus urged impatiently. "If we're to get the lads back, we need to know what the MacTiers want."

Laird MacKillon sighed. "I'm afraid they wanted to know the identity of the Falcon."

"Of course, everyone denied any knowledge of the Falcon," Hagar quickly assured them. "But I don't believe they were convinced."

"Despicable, cowardly scum!" raged Thor. "In my day, we didn't resort to using helpless lads in warfare!"

"They already know who the Falcon is," Melantha decided, her mind roiling as she tried to make sense of what had happened. "Roarke and his men must have told MacTier—otherwise, why would they have taken Daniel and Matthew?"

"I don't believe they do know, Melantha," countered Colin. "They kept referring to the Falcon as a man, and they didn't expect to find him here—they were trying to intimidate us into revealing his identity."

"I think they took the lads because they were alone and easy to capture," added Hagar. "That Derek chap never implied that he thought they were in any way related to the Falcon."

"But 'twas clear he knew the Falcon has some relationship with this clan," said Laird MacKillon. "That's why he believed the Falcon would hear of what happened and want to do something about it."

"So what did they tell ye to do?" asked Magnus.

Hagar regarded him worriedly. "They said if we wanted to see the lads alive again, we had best make sure the Falcon delivers himself and his men to Laird MacTier within four days. Then the lads will be brought back to us."

Stay calm, Melantha ordered silently, struggling to gain control of her fear. If she permitted herself to panic, she would not be able to formulate a plan. Four days. It took three days to travel to the MacTier holding from here. Clearly Laird MacTier was counting on the MacKillons being able to relay his message to the Falcon quickly, but was giving them a day to find him. Her mind began to race as she considered the possibilities.

"Colin, has your back healed sufficiently that you are fit to ride?"

"Yes," he assured her without hesitation.

"Surely you can't be thinking of going there, Melantha," objected Laird MacKillon, appalled by the possibility. "Once MacTier has you and your men, he'll more than likely kill all of you as well as the lads. I cannot allow that."

"I'll slay the scoundrel before he has the chance!" Thor

vowed. "I'll dice him up so fine they'll have to use a ladle to scoop him off the floor!"

"You're going?" said Laird MacKillon, astonished.

"Of course. 'Tis time I taught these MacTier villains a lesson they'll never forget!"

"Laird MacKillon is right, lass," said Magnus, ignoring Thor. "Ye can't be thinkin' of just walkin' in there and offering yerself in exchange for the lads—'tis certain he'll slay the lot of us and be done with it."

"He'll only slay us if he finds out who we are," pointed out Melantha.

" 'Tis disguises, then, is it?" said Thor, his excitement mounting. He caught a glimpse of his snowy mane and frowned. "Perhaps I should add a hint of color to my hair."

"You're forgetting that Roarke and his men will be there, Melantha," said Hagar. "Disguised or not, 'tis almost certain that if he sees you he will recognize you."

"His duty to his clan will force him to reveal your true identity," Laird MacKillon added soberly. "Even if he is loath to do it."

"I don't believe Roarke will be there," countered Melantha, feigning more assurance than she actually felt. "He told me that his days of battle were over and that he planned to retire to a holding Laird MacTier had promised to give him as a reward for his many years of service. He seemed most anxious to depart for his new home."

Thor was unable to conceal his disappointment. "Was he taking the Viking with him? I wanted to chop him up."

"We had best hope that they are all gone," Magnus reflected. "Otherwise things could get a wee bit tricky."

"I'll take care of any trickiness!" Thor promised.

"Your pardon, Thor, but I do believe it would be better for the clan if you remained here," said Laird MacKillon, seeing Melantha's concerned look. "After all, we need someone with your considerable fighting abilities to help protect the clan should we suffer another attack."

Thor puffed up his chest, pleased by the compliment. "Well, of course, if you really need me—"

"Lewis, run and find Gillian and Beatrice and ask them to meet me in my chamber," said Melantha. "Tell them to bring every gown they can find that isn't worn or stained. I need something beautiful to wear."

Everyone in the great hall stared at her in shock.

CHAPTER 11

Laird MacTier cursed aloud as he furiously scanned the hundreds of losses scrawled in his ledger.

Their sum was staggering, especially if one considered that the Falcon and his band not only attacked MacTiers but had also made a sport of raiding clans who were allies and whose welfare was directly linked to his own. If the Falcon attacked clans other than those with an affiliation to the MacTiers, he had not heard about it. He considered this a moment, but ultimately decided it was less peculiar than it first appeared to be. After all, his was the wealthiest and most powerful clan for nearly a hundred miles in any direction. It was easy to understand why a thief would choose to glean from it.

What was unfathomable was the fact that he had not yet been able to capture this infuriating outlaw.

The possibility that the amulet was protecting the Falcon filled him with rage. The powers of the relic were mysterious, and that idiot priest had not been able to tell him whether it was capable of protecting its bearer only from violent death, or if it also shielded him from other threats such as capture. Clearly it could not guard its wearer from simple theft, otherwise the Falcon would not have been able to steal it so easily from the priest. The bumbling fool assured him that the Falcon had no inkling of the powers of the charm, but obviously he could see that it was silver and bore a stone of some value. MacTier drummed his fingers thoughtfully against his desk. Better to have the Falcon under the protection of the charm than not, he decided reluctantly. At least then the outlaw would have the amulet on his person, as opposed to having sold it or given it away. All MacTier had to do was remove it from his neck when the Falcon appeared and the thief would be mortally vulnerable once again.

He was not troubled in the least by the fact that Derek had taken two MacKillon lads hostage. The MacKillons needed to be punished for daring to ransom his warriors; that they also knew the identity of the Falcon only gave him further reason to strike at them. If Roarke had hoped to arouse his sympathy by describing their current struggles, he had failed completely. MacTier had dedicated his life to the accumulation of wealth and power, which inevitably came at a cost to others. Fortunately, he was not inclined to concern himself with how his victories affected others. That was what had made him a great laird, just as it had once made Roarke a great warrior.

He sighed and reached for his goblet, wondering what had happened to leech the warring spirit out of his greatest fighter. He prayed to God it never happened to him.

A heavy rap upon the door startled him, causing him

to overturn his cup. Wine bled across his precious ledger, staining the yellowed pages scarlet. Cursing viciously, he picked the heavy manuscript up, letting the liquid drip upon his desk.

"Come in," he snarled.

The door opened hesitantly, revealing the towering form of Neill.

"Forgive me for disturbing you, Laird MacTier," apologized the warrior. "I wanted to inform you of the safe arrival of Laird Ross's niece."

"What?" said Laird MacTier, distracted by his efforts to mop up his spilled wine with some paper.

"Laird Ross's niece," repeated Neill. "She has just arrived with an escort of four men, and requested that I inform you directly of her safe journey. She said she knew you would be worried because of the danger of outlaws in the woods, and was most adamant that your mind be put to ease directly."

"Laird Ross's niece?" said MacTier blankly.

"Her name is Laureen," said Neill, trying to be helpful. "She is on her way to visit her cousin, who is wed to the son of Laird Grant's sister. She said to extend her deepest gratitude to you for permitting her and her men to stop here for the night, and said that her uncle was most appreciative of your generous offer to make them welcome."

Laird MacTier briefly searched his memory, vainly trying to recall Laird Ross sending him a missive in which he requested hospitality for his niece. Nothing came to mind, but with so much happening lately it was entirely possible he had read the message and then instantly forgotten about it. There was nothing unusual about members of allied clans stopping there for a night or two before continuing on their journey. He dropped his sodden ledger on his desk, feeling tired and irritated. He was in no mood for playing doting host to some spoiled chit who, if she had even a drop of Ross blood in her veins, was more than likely to have both the body and face of a sow.

"See to it that they are given whatever they need," he instructed indifferently, walking over to the window. "And tell Laird Ross's niece that I extend my welcome, but unfortunately, pressing matters preclude me from being in attendance this evening in the great—" He stopped suddenly, taking in the vision of the exquisite woman who stood in the courtyard below.

Her tall, graceful body was draped in a gown of dove-colored wool trimmed with gold, over which she had pinned a narrow sash of her clan's tartan. A shimmering fall of sable hair had been elegantly arranged in a series of loose braids that were interwoven with creamy strips of ribbon, and a fine coronet of pearls was pinned to the crown of her head. Her features were fine and delicate, but her bearing evoked the confidence of a young lady who had been trained to understand that her place was well above most people she would ever meet. At that moment she was issuing directives to her four men, who were dressed in the Ross tartan and carried shields bearing their clan's insignia. Her escort consisted of a couple of young warriors who looked as if they could handle a sword with decent ability, a flame-haired youth who seemed afraid of his own shadow, and an old man with shocking white hair who could be of no practical use whatsoever, except perhaps to guard her maidenly virtue from the other three.

A powerful heat stirred MacTier's loins.

"Tell her that I am delighted by her presence, and hope she will be able to share our hospitality for longer than one night," he said, suddenly feeling far less weary than he had a moment earlier. His wife had ceased to amuse him in bed long ago, and after she had finally given him his long-awaited son, he had sought his pleasures elsewhere. While he knew better than to force himself upon the tender niece of one of his neighboring allies, what harm could there be in spending an amusing evening with her? It had been some time since he had entertained guests. Now that he could see how young and lovely she was, the prospect of sharing a few cups of wine seemed infinitely more appealing than morosely pondering the current fate of his precious amulet in solitude.

"Inform our guest that my wife and I would be honored if she would share supper with us in my private apartments this evening," he added. He had absolutely no intention of inviting his wife to dine with them, but recognized that propriety dictated that the young woman must believe she was not dining alone with him. "I shall look forward to seeing her then."

The warrior gave his laird a small bow before quitting the chamber.

Laird MacTier stroked his chin as he watched the spirited beauty ordering her men about in the courtyard below. The fire in his loins intensified, until his body was hard and hungry for release. He sighed, reminding himself that he could not have her, which only had the effect of making her appear even more tantalizing.

At least her sparkling presence would help to pass the relentlessly tedious hours before the Falcon finally presented himself for his execution.

"You will take care of the horses first, being sure to rub them down well and see that they have ample food and water," instructed Melantha, affecting an imperious tone for the benefit of the MacTiers who were watching her. "Then you will bring me my bags," she added, looking at Lewis. "All of you may spend the evening as you wish, but you are not to drink to excess, is that clear?" Her forbidding countenance indicated to their audience that this was a weakness to which they were customarily prone. She lowered her voice to a harsh whisper, just loud enough for the others to overhear her as she continued, "I've no desire to waken tomorrow and discover that you have lost all of your compensation to drunken wagering. Don't dare come weeping to me about your misfortunes if you find you cannot control your thirst for ale. Now, go and see to your duties."

With that she turned to gift Neill with a magnificently feminine smile. "Was Laird MacTier pleased to hear of my arrival?"

"Indeed he was, milady," the warrior assured her. "He said to tell you that you and your men are welcome to stay as long as you wish, and we shall do everything possible to see to your comfort. Laird MacTier has also invited you to join him and his wife in their private apartments this evening for a meal. Until then, I would be pleased to escort you to your chamber so you may refresh yourself and rest."

"How very kind." Melantha laid her hand delicately upon his proffered arm. "I'm afraid I find riding about the countryside absolutely wilting—I can only imagine what I must look like."

The warrior looked at her with boyish reverence. "You look beautiful."

Melantha smiled and leaned into him a little more. "How very sweet of you."

She chatted with him gaily as he led her into the castle, affecting a charm she had not previously known she possessed. Both Gillian and Katie had valiantly attempted to tutor her in the art of ladylike conduct before she left, but the opposition of Gillian's dainty shyness and Katie's saucy confidence had left Melantha hopelessly confused. It was dear old Magnus who had ultimately given her the most helpful suggestions, recalling how his beloved Edwina had beguiled him when he first wooed her in his youth.

"This is Tess," said Neill, gesturing to a plain dumpling

of a girl who was shaking out the coverlet in Melantha's chamber. "She will see to it that you have whatever you need."

Tess bobbed Melantha a respectful curtsey.

"If you find yourself wanting for anything during your stay here, please let either Tess or myself know," said Neill.

"I would love to have a bath." Melantha sighed wistfully. "Travel does make one feel so dusty."

"I will order one for you immediately," said the warrior, looking pleased that there was something more he could do for her.

"You are too gallant. I shall have to lie awake tonight and think of some way to repay you for all your kindness."

He blushed to the roots of his hair before hurrying out of the chamber.

"I think ye've lit a flame in Neill's heart, milady," remarked Tess merrily. " 'Tis not like him to be running about ordering baths and such when the warriors have strict orders to be on guard for the Falcon."

Melantha gasped. "The dangerous outlaw? Why—are you expecting him?"

"Indeed we are. He's due to arrive any moment now— that's why you saw so many guards at the gate and upon the wall head. The very instant he appears, he'll be surrounded by a hundred men and dragged before Laird MacTier. Then our laird is going to punish him for all his wicked robberies."

"But how do you know he is coming here?"

"Our men were clever enough to learn that the outlaw has friends among the MacKillons," Tess explained. "And so they went and captured two MacKillon lads, and told their clan that if they wanted to see them alive again, they'd best produce the Falcon right quick!"

Melantha looked appropriately dismayed. "They took mere lads as hostage?"

"They're not that young," the girl quickly assured her. "Actually, they're almost men."

"Ah, well, that's different," said Melantha, choking back the desire to correct her. *They're not men at all!* she wanted to scream. *Matthew is only ten, and Daniel is all of thirteen, although he tries to act much older.* "You've seen them, then?"

"No," she admitted. "But I've a friend who works in the kitchens who knows the warrior who takes them their food at night, and she told me."

Melantha went to the window and looked about nervously. "I do hope they're not being kept in a chamber near this one, lest the Falcon or the MacKillons decide to attack the castle and try to free them."

"The MacKillons haven't the strength to dare try to attack us," scoffed Tess. "Anyway, the lads aren't being kept here. They're in one of the dungeons below the east tower."

Melantha's heart broke as she looked at the dark tower on the opposite side of the courtyard. Somewhere, deep within its dank interior, Daniel and Matthew sat huddled upon the damp earth, cold and hungry and terrified. *Soon, my sweet lads,* she thought, trying to impart the strength of her love across the bailey and through the thick walls of stone. *Soon you will be free, and we will all be home, and we will sit together in the great hall and tell the clan the story of how wonderfully brave you were.*

"Your pardon, milady, where would you like your bags?"

She turned to see Lewis standing in the doorway. "Put them over there," she instructed.

He scurried over to where she was pointing and dropped them on the floor.

"Take care, you lazy fool!" she snapped.

Lewis blanched. "Forgive me, milady."

"Have the horses been attended to?" she demanded, going over to her bags.

"Aye," said Lewis respectfully.

Melantha unlaced the flap of one of her satchels. "Look at this!" she cried, outraged. "You've shattered my precious bottle of rose oil, you clumsy oaf! Not only have you ruined my clothes, but now there is nothing to scent the water of my bath!" She stalked toward him with her hand raised, causing Lewis to cower.

"Your pardon, milady, I'm certain I can find you some fragrant oil for your bath," interjected Tess quickly, clearly concerned for poor Lewis's welfare.

Melantha hesitated. "Really?"

"We've all kinds of lovely scents for the bath," the girl assured her. "I'll just run and fetch you some."

"I prefer rose oil. Not too strong a blend, mind, or else my skin will itch."

"I'll scarcely be a moment." The girl gave Lewis an encouraging smile as she hurried from the room.

"They're in the dungeon of the east tower," whispered Melantha urgently. Any moment more servants would arrive bearing her bath.

"Are you sure?"

"That's what that Tess said—you had best confirm it before you attempt to free them."

Lewis nodded. "The ale will loosen the warriors' tongues before it puts them to sleep. Already Magnus is whetting their thirsts with talk of the fine brew we have brought as a gift for their hospitality. He will keep them drinking and distracted with gambling while Colin, Finlay, and I get the lads. When you hear Magnus singing his favorite ballad about the warrior and the dragon, you'll know we have the boys and are leaving. Meet us at the gate as fast as you can."

It was Edwina who had cleverly suggested the use of a drugged ale to help them steal the boys back. She had developed a potent sleeping essence that did not affect either the scent or the taste of the brew, but had the effect of reducing a man to a state of deep slumber after scarcely half a cup.

"Did you find out if Roarke and his men are here?"

"They left a week ago for Roarke's new holding," reported Lewis. "They are not expected to return for months."

Relief poured through Melantha. Ever since she had formulated her plan to rescue her brothers she had been plagued by the possibility that Roarke might be here. The fact that he was gone would make everything simpler.

"I am to dine with Laird MacTier and his wife in their private chambers," she whispered quickly. Already she could hear the sounds of men in the hallway bearing a bathing tub. "Once I hear your signal, I will tell them I am weary and bid them good night. Then I will slip outside and meet you at the gate."

Lewis nodded.

"Now go!" she urged.

He went to the doorway, then hesitated. Looking back at her, his eyes were filled with trepidation. "You'll be careful, won't you?"

"Of course I will," Melantha assured him. She had not shared her plan to murder MacTier with any of her men. If she had, they would never have permitted her to come. She forced herself to smile.

Lewis looked at her with penetrating clarity. "Melantha—"

"Here is my bath," she said, severing any further comment from him as two men arrived carrying a heavy copper tub.

Lewis cast her a final look of concern before disappearing into the corridor, leaving Melantha to face her enemies alone.

The laird's chambers were brilliantly lit with dozens of candles, gilding the rooms in flickering ribbons of gold.

"I am pleased that you are able to join me this evening, my dear," said Laird MacTier, laying his hand against the small of her back as he escorted Melantha into his private dining hall. He had dressed for the occasion in a splendid tunic of crimson wool edged with gold thread, over which he had arranged a generous swath of his clan's tartan, which was secured by not one but two elaborately jeweled brooches. "I have been eagerly anticipating your visit, and hope you might be willing to grace us with your charming presence for longer than just one night." He pressed a lingering kiss to her hand, his lips slightly parted.

"Unfortunately, my dear cousin is anxiously awaiting my arrival," said Melantha gaily, restraining her impulse to tear her hand away. "We have not seen each other since she wed Laird Grant's nephew. I could not bear to disappoint her by delaying our reunion."

"Alas, then it is I who must be disappointed." Laird MacTier sighed, relinquishing her hand to seat her at the elegantly carved oak table. "Our visit will be brief, so we must be certain to make the most of it." He brushed his palms over her shoulders.

Melantha noted the table had only been set for two. "Is your wife not joining us this evening?"

"Unfortunately, my dear wife has taken ill," Laird MacTier replied, seating himself opposite her. "She sends her regrets, and hopes she will be recovered sufficiently to see you tomorrow."

"How distressing." Melantha was absolutely certain Laird MacTier had never intended for his wife to join them. "I hope it is nothing serious."

"Not at all," he said, closing the subject of his wife as he raised a magnificently worked silver decanter and generously filled her goblet.

Melantha swept her gaze over the table laid before her. Elegant silver platters offered what was easily enough food for ten people. Roasted venison, rabbit, partridge, and duck were flanked by colorful vegetables and blanketed in rich gravies, while plates of tender smoked salmon, heavy dark bread, tangy cheeses, and soft bannocks vied for their share of space on the crowded table. At home Beatrice, Gillian, and Edwina would work hard to stretch this food to serve thirty or forty people, she thought furiously. The realization had the perverse effect of making her feel sick.

Laird MacTier frowned. "Is the meal not to your liking?"

"It looks wonderful," Melantha said, forcing a smile to her lips. She swallowed a mouthful of wine, then served herself a chunk of bread and a morsel of salmon. If she could just get that down, she might be able to make herself eat a little more. It was vital that she keep Laird MacTier occupied while her men drugged his guards and freed her brothers.

Once she heard Magnus's signal, she would unsheathe the dirk strapped to her calf and plunge it deep into MacTier's heart.

"Was your journey here without incident?" he enquired conversationally as he piled his trencher with food.

"Nothing untoward happened at all." Melantha sighed, feigning girlish disappointment. "After hearing all these tales about the Falcon and his dreadful band of outlaws, I was hoping he would try to rob us, just so I could see if he is really as terrible as everyone says!"

"You are fortunate that you did not encounter him. 'Tis well known that the Falcon and his men have been the ruin of many a beautiful lass who had the misfortune to fall victim to their brutish ways." His gaze was vaguely predatory as he finished. "It is not a fate I would like to contemplate for one as lovely as you."

Melantha's eyes widened with appropriate shock. "The Falcon ravishes women? I had not heard that."

"You have nothing to fear, my dear, now that you are safe within my holding," he soothed, reaching out to lay his hand over hers. "However, you might consider delaying your departure to your dear cousin's home until I have had a chance to capture this depraved beast. I expect to do so within a day—two at the very most. Until then, I'm sure that I could find ways to keep you pleasantly entertained during your stay here." He languidly drew his forefinger along the flesh of her palm.

He paused suddenly, frowning at the thickened skin years of swordplay and archery had developed on her hand.

"I was told that you are expecting him," said Melantha, abruptly closing her fingers into a fist. "But with the scores of guards you have posted about the castle, do you really think he will just ride into your holding and announce himself?" She casually withdrew her hand to lift her goblet.

Laird MacTier took a swallow of wine and smiled. "He has little choice, I'm afraid. I have laid an exceptionally compelling trap."

"Because of the lads you have captured?" She was careful to keep her tone clean of contempt.

He nodded. "Until now, no one has been able to determine to which clan the Falcon belongs, or if he is, in fact, affiliated with any clan at all. That has made it impossible to determine his identity. His relationship with the MacKillons will prove to be his ruin—for it will force him to deliver himself to me."

Melantha regarded him over the rim of her cup. "But why do you believe he cares what happens to the lads? If he is as vile and depraved as everyone says, why would he sacrifice himself to save them?"

"If he doesn't come forward, then one of the MacKillons will reveal the secret of his identity," he replied impatiently, brushing aside the implication that the Falcon was less than utterly despicable. "The boys probably have parents whose love for them exceeds whatever regard they have for the Falcon. Either way, I will capture this bloody outlaw. And when I do," he finished darkly, "I will see to it that he returns every goddamn item that he has stolen from me—down to the last scrap of cloth."

No, it is you, MacTier, who has stolen from me, and from my brothers, and my people. And nothing you have could ever repay us for that which you have taken. She drained her goblet, feeling her pain and hatred begin to meld.

"More wine?" offered MacTier, smiling. It was clear he intended to get her drunk.

"Thank you," said Melantha breathlessly. If he believed her to be intoxicated, his own defenses would be dulled.

That would make him easier to kill.

Drunken laughter and singing wafted through the window. Melantha strained to hear Magnus's ballad, but could not detect his song above the chorus of raucous male voices.

Laird MacTier frowned. "What the devil is going on down there?"

"It sounds like your men are enjoying themselves," said Melantha dismissively, wondering why the MacTiers weren't falling asleep. Surely they had drunk more than a half cup of Edwina's ale by now? " 'Tis the reflection of a good laird when his men feel so inspired to indulge in song. Come, Laird MacTier, you have barely touched your dinner—"

"My men are not permitted to indulge in so much as breathing without my orders," he said in a scathing voice. "And at this moment they have been ordered to keep alert for the Falcon—which they can hardly do if they're blinding drunk." The singing and laughter grew louder as he moved toward the window.

Panic surged through Melantha. If Laird MacTier discovered that his men were either drunk or drugged, he might suspect the Falcon was within his holding, and immediately dispatch guards to bring Matthew and Daniel to him. Colin,

Lewis, and Finlay were probably at the dungeon trying to free her brothers this very moment. If they were discovered, they would be slain.

She had to stop MacTier from reaching the window.

It was this simple, desperate purpose, rather than the painful web of her hatred and fury, that caused her to stand and wrench her dirk from its sheath. There was no time to consider the morality of her actions, no time to torment herself with vagaries of right and wrong. There was only the absolute need to prevent the man before her from murdering those she loved.

She hurled her dirk across the chamber.

The blade flew in a straight, true line, slicing a clean path toward her target. But Laird MacTier, perhaps distracted by the action of her rising from her chair, turned at the last instant, altering her mark. He did not make a sound as the dirk burrowed into his shoulder, but merely stared at it incredulously, as if he could not quite believe how it had come to be there.

And then his eyes met hers, and his incredulity turned to rage.

"Guards!" he roared, taking a step away from her as if he feared she might have some other weapon concealed upon her. "*Guards!*"

The chamber door crashed open and four warriors of awesome proportions tore into the room, their swords poised for massacre. When they saw only Melantha standing there looking small and pale, they turned to their laird in confusion.

"Arrest her!" ordered Laird MacTier. "Take her to the dungeon and—"

"*Escape! The prisoners have escaped!*"

This new development had the effect of stripping Melantha of everyone's attention as both MacTier and his warriors raced to the window to see what was happening below.

"Stop them!" shouted a warrior who was staggering drunkenly toward the gate. After giving this directive he stopped, belched, then turned around and started to whistle, evidently satisfied that his contribution toward catching the prisoners was complete.

Another warrior gamely took a few faltering steps before collapsing to his knees. "Somebody close the gate," he murmured thickly. With that he fell facedown onto the ground and began to snore.

"Och, Ewan, ye're not lookin' very good, my friend," remarked a warrior who stumbled out of the stables carrying a jug. "Do ye want a drop more o' this fine drink?" When his friend didn't answer he drained the jug himself, then turned to relieve himself against the stable wall, singing at the top of his lungs, "Oh, there once was a lass with a bonny round ass...."

"Close the gate!" roared Laird MacTier, watching in frustration as Colin, Lewis, Finlay, Magnus, and the boys suddenly burst from the stables on horseback and thundered toward the open portcullis. "*Somebody close the goddamn gate!!*"

"... so I gave her my shaft and she near left me daft, with a hey, ho, come lie with me...."

"What the hell is the matter with them?" demanded Laird MacTier, watching in outrage as his prisoners escaped and the courtyard was littered with the staggering, falling, singing bodies of his finest warriors.

"They look drunk," observed one warrior.

"Maybe they've been put under some kind of spell," offered another.

Laird MacTier's face turned crimson. "I'll kill him! I'll catch that bloody Falcon and I'll see him torn to pieces—do you hear!!" He waved his arms in frustration, then inhaled sharply at the pain in his right shoulder. "You!" he snarled, his eyes narrowing at Melantha. "You're part of all this—and you know who he is, don't you?"

Melantha said nothing.

"Bring her to the great hall," Laird MacTier ordered brusquely. "And one of you find someone to take this goddamn dirk out of my shoulder!"

Misery was carved upon the face of every warrior who dragged himself into the great hall to face Laird MacTier's wrath.

Their laird's fury was awesome, but Melantha did not believe it could compare to the current effects of Edwina's powerful brew. Edwina had assured Melantha it would send those who drank it into a blissful slumber. What Edwina had failed to mention, however, was that once the pleasant euphoria began to wane, it would be replaced by a crushing headache and roiling nausea that might well make the sufferer pray for death.

It looked to Melantha as if an inordinate number of warriors were praying at that very moment.

"Fools!" barked Laird MacTier, his mood even nastier now that the dirk had been plucked from his throbbing shoulder. "Idiots! I should chain each and every one of you up by your wrists and leave you to rot in the dungeons!"

No one said anything. Either they were overwhelmed by their physical suffering or each had wisely decided it was better to remain silent in the face of their laird's rage.

"And you," he said, suddenly switching his attention to Melantha. "Just who the hell are you, and how are you associated with the Falcon?"

"It doesn't matter," Melantha replied coolly, enjoying his obvious frustration. "You'll never capture him."

Laird MacTier had tried to find some warriors who were not falling-down drunk to go after her men and her brothers. By the time he finally settled upon a handful who were still capable of mounting a horse, her men had the advantage of a lengthy start. She had no doubt they would be able to lose themselves in the shadows of the woods they knew so well.

"Your profound loyalty to this outlaw is as brainless as it is pathetic." Laird MacTier slowly circled her. "Don't you think it cowardly that he sent a mere lass to keep his enemy distracted while he had a force of warriors to protect himself? What kind of a man would expose a maiden to such danger and then callously leave you behind?"

"What kind of man would take two innocent lads and put them in a dungeon, using their precious lives to lure his enemy?" challenged Melantha scornfully. "It could only be the same kind of man who makes a sport of attacking clans that are weaker than his, stealing every scrap of cloth and morsel of food from them so he can drape himself in ridiculous robes and seat himself at tables ready to collapse beneath the weight of the food prepared solely for his gluttony!"

A horrified gasp rose from the stunned MacTiers.

Laird MacTier's face betrayed not a flicker of emotion as he clamped his hands on Melantha's shoulders. Slowly he began to squeeze, first bruising the tender flesh, then crushing against the bones until she thought they would shatter beneath his cruel grip.

"Beware the sharpness of your tongue, my little asp," he drawled, his breath hot and foul upon her cheek. " 'Twould be a shame to be forced to break such a pretty little neck." He released her shoulders to trail his fingers down her throat, his touch gentle yet menacing.

" 'Tis you who needs to be afraid, MacTier, for a man with nothing but enemies can never know an easy moment." She lowered her voice to the barest of whispers as she fervently vowed: "If the Falcon doesn't kill you, one of your own men will. That is the price of power wrought by tyranny and fear."

His hand froze against her.

She smiled, taking grim satisfaction in the spark of apprehension she saw kindled in his eyes.

"We've got him!" shouted excited voices from outside. "Make way—*we've got the Falcon*!"

It was Laird MacTier's turn to smile. "Now, this is a fascinating turn of events, don't you think?"

Abruptly he released her.

Alarm streaked up Melantha's spine. Affecting only a modicum of interest, she watched as several MacTier warriors stormed into the hall, roughly hauling not one but two captives.

When she saw that they were Colin and Daniel, her alarm turned to terror.

Laird MacTier walked slowly over to Colin, who was being restrained by two men. One of them she recognized as the fair-haired warrior who had led the recent attack on her holding. The other was Neill, who had been so chivalrous in his attentions when she first arrived.

"I have been waiting a long time for this moment, my outlaw friend," Laird MacTier murmured.

He drew back his fist and rammed it hard into Colin's face.

Somehow Melantha stifled the cry in her throat. Anything she did to reveal her feelings for either Colin or Daniel could only put them at further risk. And so she forced herself to watch with rigid calm as Colin spat a scarlet stream upon the floor, spattering red droplets upon the finely stitched leather of Laird MacTier's shoes. Then Colin raised his head to regard Laird MacTier once again.

"Is that how you welcome all your guests?" he enquired mildly. "I must say, it isn't very gracious."

"Oh, but you are not just any guest," Laird MacTier said, enjoying his position of power over him. "You are the man who has managed to vex me constantly by making a sport of stealing that which is mine. And now that you have been caught, I'm afraid you must be made to pay."

He struck him hard in the face again, causing blood to spurt from Colin's nose.

"Stop it!" cried Daniel, fighting to escape the grip of the warriors who were holding him. "Leave him alone!"

Colin shook his head, which had the effect of spreading the blood leaking from him across his cheeks, making his face look as if it had been beaten to a pulp.

Melantha clenched her fists, feeling her deliberately constructed calm begin to crumble.

"It seems your young friend does not relish the sight of you in pain," remarked Laird MacTier archly as he unsheathed Derek's sword. "That is a pity—I'm sure he is not going to enjoy what I am about to do to you now."

"Kill me if it pleases you," snarled Colin tautly, "but at least have the decency to let the lad and the lass leave."

"I'm not going to kill you," Laird MacTier informed him, testing the weight and balance of the heavy claymore in his hands. "Not when we still have so much to talk about. You, my Falcon friend, have taken a great many things from me over the past few months, and I mean to find out exactly what you have done with them. All I'm doing at this moment is making it eminently clear to everyone in this hall that I do not take the crime of stealing lightly. After all," he continued, moving behind Colin, "stealing is a sin."

He swung the heavy blade down with all his might, striking Colin on the back with the flat of it. It was a blow that would have felled any man, but with the severed muscles of Colin's back still in the painful stages of healing, the effect was devastating. He groaned in agony and fell to his knees, his head bent so that neither Daniel nor Melantha could see the depths of his suffering.

"Stop it!" cried Daniel, tears streaming down his face. "Stop it—*you bloody bastard!*"

Outraged by his insolence, Laird MacTier moved to strike him.

"Leave him alone," commanded Melantha, her voice like the lash of a whip. "Or I swear to you, you'll never see any of your precious possessions again."

Laird MacTier hesitated, disconcerted by the steely confidence with which she spoke. "What are you talking about?"

"The man you have there is not the Falcon."

"Is that so?" He skeptically cocked one eyebrow. "Then I suppose this sniveling lad is the one who has been plaguing me all these months?"

"No," returned Melantha. Her expression was deadly serious. "I am."

Stunned surprise rippled through the great hall.

"Don't listen to her!" yelled Colin, staggering to his feet. "I'm the Falcon!"

"No, he isn't," Melantha countered, her gaze intent upon Laird MacTier. "You may trust me, MacTier. I am the outlaw you seek."

"She's mad!" protested Colin furiously. "How could that thin slip of a lass be the Falcon? For God's sake, just look at her! She could scarcely lift a bairn, never mind wield a sword! She's just saying this to try to save me—you mustn't listen to her!"

"No one has ever been able to describe the Falcon because he always wears a helmet," continued Melantha calmly, ignoring Colin's outburst. "That was because I had to keep the fact that I was a woman a secret."

"I wear a bloody helmet because I want to keep my skull intact," interjected Colin, growing even more adamant. "Don't listen to her childish fantasies!"

"As you have already noticed, my hands bear the marks of years of swordplay," she continued, lifting her callused palms for Laird MacTier's perusal. "I have been trained in the use of a sword from the time I was six."

"Every country wife has work-worn hands," scoffed Colin, desperately trying to discredit her confession. "It doesn't make them a dangerous outlaw, for God's sake!"

"But not every country wife bears the marks of an enemy's sword." She jerked down the sleeve of her gown, revealing the jagged pink scar that snaked from her shoulder to her elbow. "Surely one of your men returned to boast of managing to wound the elusive Falcon, MacTier?" she asked scornfully. " 'Twas in the late spring and we had attacked a coach bearing a king's supply of silver goods and one overly fed priest. The guards assured us that the entire lot was on its way to you—"

Laird MacTier crossed to her within three strides. "Where is it?" he demanded fiercely.

Melantha regarded him in confusion. "Where is what?"

He slapped her with such force she was knocked to the floor.

"Don't give me a reason to finish off your gallant friend over there," he warned, his eyes narrowed into dark slits of fury. "If you truly are the Falcon, then you know exactly of what I am speaking." He leaned down and whispered harshly, "Where is the amulet?"

Melantha fought to clear her head from the dizziness his blow had caused. What was he talking about?

"Don't pretend you don't have it," he snarled. "That fool of a priest told me how you and your men threatened to disembowel him if he didn't turn it over to you. You knew he carried a sacred relic of great power—that was why you attacked the coach in the first place—wasn't it?" He kept his voice low, guarding his purpose from the rest of his clan.

He was speaking of the silver-and-emerald pendant, Melantha realized. The pendant Magnus had insisted she take for herself, instead of selling it or trading it in exchange for something useful like food or weapons. She had worn it constantly around her neck from that day forward. But the gown she had donned for her journey here had left the pendant exposed, and she had feared that either Laird MacTier or someone else within the clan might recognize it.

And so she had given it to Gillian to wear for safekeeping.

"It is hidden in a safe place some three days' journey from here," she said evasively, realizing that producing it was the only way of appeasing Laird MacTier's anger and securing Colin and Daniel's freedom. "Release these two, and they will retrieve it and bring it to you in exchange for our lives."

Laird MacTier studied her a moment, debating whether or not to believe her. "If you try to trick me, I swear to you, you will suffer beyond your worst imaginings," he warned softly. He plunged his hand into her hair, painfully jerking her head up by its roots. "Do you understand?"

"Yes," said Melantha, wincing beneath his cruel grip.

He released his hold, leaving her crumpled at his feet as he rose to face his clan.

"The Falcon and I have come to an agreement," he announced pleasantly. "I have decided to release you tonight," he said, speaking to Colin, "so that you may go and retrieve a few items of mine that your leader was foolish enough to take. She will tell you exactly what it is I seek, and where you may find them. Bring them to me within six days, and then you and this angry young lad will be released unharmed."

He paused for a moment, studying Daniel as if he were looking upon him for the first time. Then he turned to Melantha, his expression oddly triumphant.

"He is your brother, isn't he?"

"No."

Even as she said it, she knew her denial was futile. No one in that moment could mistake the striking resemblance between the two of them, especially given the cold hatred that glittered so fiercely in Daniel's green-and-amber eyes.

"A pity." Laird MacTier sighed. "A lad who burns with such loathing must be taught the consequences of defying those in power. It is only by teaching these lessons to the young that we can avoid having to punish them even more harshly in the future."

"If you dare so much as touch him," Melantha warned, her voice ice cold, "you will never see it again."

Laird MacTier arched his brows with mock surprise. "Do you really believe me to be such a monster, that you think I would harm a mere lad? Your brother cannot be held responsible for your actions. Therefore once your bleeding friend here returns with the items I seek, both he and the lad will be free to go—"

Relief poured through Melantha. Her own life did not matter so long as Colin and Daniel would be spared.

"—right after they have witnessed your execution."

The hall froze in shocked silence. It was clear even the MacTiers were appalled by the cruelty of their laird's gesture.

"Bastard!" screamed Daniel, flailing wildly within the strong grip of his captors. "I'll kill you, do you hear! *I'll kill you!*"

"Lock him up," commanded Laird MacTier.

Melantha felt her heart break as the warriors dragged her screaming, weeping brother away.

"Sometimes a leader must make difficult decisions," reflected Laird MacTier philosophically. "Your brother must be shown what fate awaits him should he ever decide to follow in your path, my pretty Falcon. It will be a hard lesson, but one that he will not forget easily. And neither will anyone else who dares to contemplate the idea of stealing from me." He frowned. "Why are you smiling?"

"I was just thinking, MacTier, about the day when someone will teach you the consequences of stealing from others."

"If that day ever comes, you will not be alive to see it."

"Whether I see it or not is of no consequence," she told him calmly. "All that matters is that it is inevitable."

"Go and tell your friend where to find what I seek," he

snapped. "And do not try to trick me, or I shall be forced to execute your precious brother along with you."

Melantha went over and whispered in Colin's ear. When she was finished, she studied him a moment, the corners of her mouth lifted in the barest hint of a smile. It was little more than a brief, quick gesture of reassurance that revealed nothing of the incredible devotion she felt toward this fine man who had been a lifelong friend. There was much she wanted to say, but she dared not, for fear Laird MacTier would use her feelings toward Colin against her. And so she simply held his gaze, feeling a profound tenderness fill her soul.

"Enough!" snapped Laird MacTier impatiently. "I give you six days," he said to Colin. "If you do not return within that time with what I have asked for, I will execute her."

"You will have it," Colin replied tersely.

"Take him outside and give him his horse," ordered Laird MacTier. "And take her to the dungeon where her brother is. I see no reason why they should be denied the pleasure of each other's company."

Melantha held her head high as she was surrounded by a ring of warriors, each no doubt anxious to prove to their laird that they were of some use this evening after all. The Mac-Tiers regarded her with a mixture of awe and pity as she walked past them. She kept her gaze frozen steadfastly in front of her, refusing to even glance at the faces of those who had brought her and her clan so much suffering and misery.

Whatever happened, Colin would not fail her. He would retrieve the pendant and return here within six days.

Beyond that, she could not bear to contemplate.

CHAPTER 12

"This place is a tomb," complained Donald, moodily filling his cup once more. "I swear I've been in battles that have been more amusing."

Myles gazed in bewilderment at the empty tables surrounding them. "Why does everyone leave the hall the minute they're finished eating? Don't they like to stay and talk?"

"They only dine with us because Roarke ordered them to," replied Eric irritably. "Once they have obeyed his command, they hurry away to be amongst themselves."

"Well, I wish you would command them to stop cowering every time one of us walks by," Donald grumbled to Roarke. "When I try to talk to someone they spend the entire conversation memorizing the details of the floor. Then they look like the devil himself has just delivered them from death when I finally give up and tell them they can go."

Roarke traced his thumb along the intricately worked stem of his silver goblet. How many MacKillon children would this feed? he wondered, feeling guilty for having such a costly object in his possession. "They're afraid of you."

Donald looked at him in astonishment. "Why should they be afraid of me? I can understand that they might be afraid of Eric—just look at him. He looks miserable enough to frighten a goblin."

"What do you mean by that?" growled Eric.

"I don't mean to insult you, my friend, but ever since you bid farewell to fair Gillian your mood has been insufferably black. You prowl around this place looking like you're just waiting for someone to give you an excuse to vent your rage."

"That's a *bloody lie*!" Eric roared, banging down his cup with such force the entire table shook.

"You see?" said Donald, looking at Roarke in exasperation. "I think he's got them all terrified of us."

"Eric has always been like that," remarked Myles. "The MacKillons didn't seem to be bothered by it."

"That's right," Eric said, pleased to have Myles come to his defense. "The MacKillons weren't bothered by it—even the very quiet ones." His chest tightened as he thought of Gillian. " 'Tis just this groveling lot that scurries away like frightened mice every time they see one of us coming."

"But that doesn't make any sense," argued Donald. "After all, we haven't done anything to them."

"No, we haven't," Roarke agreed quietly. "But the Mac-Tiers who came before us and forced these people to give up their freedom did."

"But now we'll make them stronger," pointed out Myles. "They have the whole MacTier army to come to their defense if they need it."

"Or to crush them if they dare to defy me." Roarke drained his cup and filled it once again, feeling weary and incomprehensibly melancholy.

Laird MacTier's gift to him had been generous. The lands were green and fertile, and were ringed by a dense growth of woods and several clear, fast-flowing streams. There was a deep, cold loch that was almost silver with fish. The people here were traditionally industrious, as was evident by the neatly planted fields of grains and vegetables. And he could not find any particular fault with the castle itself, although he would make some improvements to better fortify it. Inside it had been tastefully furnished with exquisitely stitched tapestries and painstakingly carved furniture. Because Laird Mac-Tier had decided to add this holding to his collection, he had chosen not to strip it or cause it any undue damage, the way he had the MacKillon castle. And so Roarke finally had the pleasure of sleeping in a handsome, comfortable bed, and eating his meals at a solid, polished table, and stretching out before the fire in a wide, elegantly carved chair. It was a fine holding of beauty and abundance, and the people who inhabited it were unfailingly dutiful and obeisant. Neither he nor any of his men were permitted to want for anything.

Why then, was he so bloody miserable?

It had been different at the MacKillon holding, he reflected. That decrepit, barren pile of pink rocks had always bustled with cheerful activity. The chambers were invariably drafty, yet he had never felt cold; the meals were simple and spare, yet he had never gone hungry. He and his men had been prisoners, but none of them had felt as isolated as they did here. The MacKillons had laughed with them and drunk ale with them, had even dared to make them the object of raucous jokes. How many times had Magnus goaded him about that arrow in his arse? he wondered, the corners of his mouth twitching at the memory. The MacKillons had not treated them like prisoners. And they had not treated them like enemies, except for their absurd propensity for locking them up at night. They had simply treated them as equals.

Until coming here, Roarke had not realized what an honor that had been.

Melantha had tried to warn him, he realized bleakly. She had told him the people here would have been terrorized into submission, and so they had. Whatever happened here had either shattered their spirit or beaten it into a badly broken resignation, which they only dared free on occasion, when they were certain no MacTier could witness it. That was why they all hurried away the instant they felt he would tolerate their absence. That was why they spoke to him with their eyes downcast, their shoulders hunched with the heavy burden of their fear and oppression. Nothing he could say or do would ever eradicate how he had come to rule them. Although he did not think anyone here would ever dare defy him, neither would they ever come to like him.

He drank deeply from his silver cup, wondering why the prospect was so completely dispiriting.

Then, of course, there was Melantha. He spent most of his time desperately trying not to think of her. This was a considerable challenge, when there was so damn little here to keep him otherwise occupied. The fields were planted and the larders were full. The castle was in excellent shape, and any improvements could be initiated tomorrow or next month or even next year—with the strength of the entire MacTier army at his disposal, it scarcely mattered. As for beginning a training program, Laird MacTier had been most adamant that Roarke not attempt to turn these people into a fighting force. They had only recently been conquered, and MacTier wisely did not want to run the risk of training and arming a force of angry young men, only to have them wield their weapons against their new masters. And so the holding hummed along on its own, with everyone mindful of their place and what they had to do to keep themselves fed and clothed and otherwise occupied.

Which left Roarke with ample time to reflect on Melantha, and the ragged, gaping hole her absence was tearing in his heart.

"These jugs are all empty," complained Eric, surveying the half dozen pitchers strewn across their table. "I'm going to fetch some more."

"I'll go with you," offered Donald, pleased to have a mission of some sort. He rose from the table, then paused and scratched his head. "Where do you suppose they keep the ale?"

"I'll find it," said Myles, pushing his chair out from the table.

"The two of you are incapable of finding anything," Eric noted scornfully. "I'll find it."

"More ale, milords?" asked a drab little figure of a man who suddenly appeared out of the shadows bearing two sloshing pitchers.

"I wish he wouldn't do that," grumbled Eric. "It's as if he's always listening."

"Thank you, Gowrie," said Roarke.

"Not at all, milord," said Gowrie, keeping his eyes respectfully low as he filled Roarke's cup.

"Is everything quiet?" Roarke asked him conversationally.

Gowrie kept his gaze fixed upon the goblets as he moved around the table to fill them. "Aye."

"Has everyone gone to bed?" Roarke pressed.

"Aye."

"Including the guards on the wall head?" joked Donald.

"No," said Gowrie, his expression utterly serious. "Not the guards."

"Do you wish to retire for the evening, Gowrie?" Roarke asked.

"Only if you wish me to, milord."

"Are you tired?"

Wariness flashed across his face, as if he feared that the question might be some sort of trick. "No, milord. I'm happy to stay and serve you."

Roarke gave up trying to engage the man in conversation. "You may retire, Gowrie."

"Thank you, milord." He was careful to avoid Roarke's gaze as he bowed and quit the hall.

Eric snorted in disgust. "I don't trust him."

"I don't trust any of them," added Myles.

"You don't trust them because 'tis clear that they do not trust us," Roarke said wearily. "Somehow we must overcome their fear of us."

" 'Tis strange," mused Donald, studying his brimming cup. "After so many years of battle, I had thought I'd enjoy a life of leisure. But now that I've tasted it, I find 'tis not as sweet as I'd imagined."

No, thought Roarke in gloomy silence. *It's not sweet at all.*

"You can't go in there!" Gowrie shouted suddenly from just beyond the doorway. "Come back here—stop, I say!"

Despite their ale-sodden state, all four warriors were up and had their swords drawn just as the intruders burst into the hall.

"God's ballocks, would ye tell these squawking geese that we're friends, not foes!" complained Magnus in exasperation. "I'm thinkin' 'tis easier to gain an audience with King Alexander!"

"I'm so sorry, milord," apologized Gowrie, wringing his hands as he bowed low before Roarke. "I don't know how they got in—I tried to stop them—"

"It's all right, Gowrie," Roarke interrupted, sheathing his sword. "These men are friends. Now leave us."

The servant obediently dropped his gaze and escaped the hall without another word.

"Milord, is it?" said Magnus, raising a brow as he quickly appraised the rich adornments of the hall. "Ye've done well for yerself, lad."

"What has happened?" demanded Roarke. Magnus's hair was a wild tangle of white, and both he and Lewis bore the smudges and scratches of a fast, desperate ride.

Magnus eyed him speculatively. "Ye told us that ye'd speak to your laird and tell him to leave us MacKillons alone. I thought ye to be a man of yer word."

"You know that I am, Magnus," Roarke told him impatiently, "otherwise you wouldn't be here. Now, what has happened?"

"They took Matthew and Daniel," burst out Lewis. "And then they attacked the holding and burned the cottages and fields. They wanted us to reveal the identity of the Falcon."

Cold fury surged through Roarke. Bastards. He had known his clan was ruthless, but he had never imagined them to be so vile that they would resort to using children as hostages. "Was anyone hurt?" he demanded tautly.

"No."

"Then let's get them back." He signaled to his men to follow as he strode across the hall.

"I'm afraid we already tried to free them, lad," said Magnus, any mistrust he may have felt toward Roarke shattered in the wake of his apparent concern. "But we weren't entirely successful."

Roarke stopped, struggling to appear calm as fear began to twist in his gut. "What happened?"

"Things didn't go quite as well as we'd hoped when we were leaving," began Magnus. "We got the lads, and Melantha was supposed to join us at the gate but—"

"Sweet Jesus," he swore. "You left her there?"

"We had no choice," said Magnus, his aged face lined with regret. "We thought we'd escape, then form a plan to retrieve her later. But when Daniel realized she wasn't coming, the hotheaded lad decided to turn around and go back for her."

"Colin rode after him to try to stop him," continued Lewis. "And they were both captured. But then Colin was released."

"Why?"

"Laird MacTier is looking for a pendant that we stole some months ago," explained Lewis. "Colin was set free so that he could retrieve it and bring it to Laird MacTier. He found us on his journey home, and told us what had happened. Once Colin has returned the pendant, Laird MacTier has promised to let Daniel go."

"What about Melantha?"

Magnus shook his head mournfully. "It seems Laird MacTier believed that Colin was the Falcon, and he decided to make an example of him before his men."

"And so Melantha convinced him he was beating the wrong outlaw," finished Roarke.

Magnus and Lewis regarded him grimly.

Roarke closed his eyes. Of course that is what she would have done. Melantha would never have stood by and let one of her men be tortured. "What is her punishment?" he asked softly.

Magnus cleared his throat, forcing himself to say the words. "She is to be executed before the clan in four days. Daniel will be made to watch. Once she is dead, the lad will be set free."

Roarke inhaled a slow, steadying breath, fighting the helpless rage roiling through him. *No*, he thought, trying hard to focus on what Magnus had said. *No, no, no.*

"What about this pendant?" asked Donald urgently. "Does anyone know where it is?"

"Apparently Melantha gave it to Gillian for safekeeping," said Lewis. "Laird MacTier believes 'tis an amulet—that is why he is so anxious to have it returned to him."

Roarke recalled the shimmer of silver against Melantha's pale skin. "Is it the silver-and-emerald bauble you stole from the priest that he seeks?"

"Aye," said Magnus. "Melantha told Colin that MacTier believes it has unnatural powers."

So that was it, thought Roarke. MacTier had been clear that Roarke was not to kill the Falcon—he had directed him to bring the outlaw to their holding for punishment. What MacTier had really wanted was to learn the where-abouts of his precious charm before he executed the Falcon. Not even Roarke, his most trusted warrior, had been told of the missing amulet.

Obviously MacTier had not had sufficient faith in him to believe Roarke wouldn't take it for himself.

"Assuming Colin rides fast and hard, he has barely enough time to retrieve the amulet and present it to Laird MacTier within the remaining four days," reflected Donald.

"But we can be at the MacTier holding within two days," pointed out Eric. "I say we leave now."

"And do what when we get there?" wondered Myles. " 'Tis just the four of us against an entire army."

"There's six of us," corrected Lewis. "Magnus and I may not be highly trained warriors, but we are still able to fight." He gripped the hilt of his sword, looking considerably older and more confident than the nervous youth who had dropped from the trees the day Roarke and his men had been caught.

"No offense, lads, but I was hoping there would be a few more than that," said Magnus. He regarded Roarke expectantly. "Now that ye've got yer own holding, don't ye have an army at yer disposal?"

"Unfortunately, the army at my disposal is the one we're going to fight," said Roarke.

Magnus's crinkled eyes widened in bafflement. "What about all the lads ye've got right here? They seem a wee bit fidgety, but I'm sure they could wield a sword fair enough if they had to."

Eric snorted in disgust. "We don't trust them."

"These people were conquered by the MacTiers," explained Roarke, "and they see us as their conquerors. I cannot ask them to join me against those who have already reduced them to the cowering servants you saw when you came in."

"Colin is going to return with Finlay and more men, but it'll only be twenty or so at best," said Magnus, looking troubled. "Do ye think that'll do us?"

"Even if he brought every single MacKillon fit to ride, it wouldn't be enough to defeat the MacTier army," said Donald. "We're talking about a deadly fighting force of some nine hundred warriors, each equipped with the finest weaponry available."

"They'll crush us like bugs the instant they see us coming," predicted Eric.

An idea began to unfurl in Roarke's mind. "Did you say Laird MacTier is planning to execute Melantha before the clan?"

"Aye," said Magnus. "Seems the wretch wants to make an example of her to any who are vile enough to watch."

Roarke considered this barely a moment. "Gowrie!"

The servant appeared so fast he nearly collided with him. "Yes, milord?"

"Rouse everyone in the castle and the cottages at once. Tell them to start packing."

Gowrie looked at him in confusion. "Now, milord?"

"Yes, now," said Roarke impatiently. "We must be on the road within the hour. Only the main detachment of guards may stay to guard the holding."

"Your pardon, milord, but may I be so bold as to ask where we are going?"

"We're going to see the mighty Falcon's execution," Roarke told him. "Now make haste!"

"Well, lad, I'm not sure what ye're about," remarked Magnus, watching in bemusement as Gowrie scurried out of the hall. "Did ye not just tell me that these people were not fit to fight?"

"They will not have to."

"What exactly are you planning?" wondered Donald.

Roarke reached for his silver goblet, then paused to study its elaborate artistry against the coppery flicker of torchlight. He had lived his life as Laird MacTier's devoted warrior, conquering holdings in an endless quest to expand his clan's power and riches. And ultimately he had been paid well for his service. This castle was everything he had ever longed for, he reflected, deriving no pleasure from the realization.

Except Melantha.

After a life of unfailing loyalty, he was about to lead a ragged band of outlaws against the powerful clan he himself had helped to create. He was betraying his laird and his people, and renouncing both his blood ties and the magnificent prize of this holding in the process. Once it was finished, assuming he survived, he would be left with absolutely nothing. It did not matter.

If Melantha died, then so would he.

"Laird MacTier has decided to make a show of Melantha's death by executing her before an audience." Roarke drained the silver goblet and hurled it against the hearth before finishing in a hard, flat voice, "I intend to make certain it is an event he will never forget."

CHAPTER 13

Melantha sat crouched upon the dank earth floor, intently grinding the end of her stick against the rough stone wall.

"If the wood is too dry, it will splinter easily," she advised Daniel, brushing away the fibers clinging to the creamy point. "You can wet it with spit to help keep it whole, but 'tis best to select a firm, young twig with moist flesh." She handed the twig to him. "You try."

Daniel obligingly took the stick and awkwardly began to scrape it against the slick stones. "Like this?"

"Press a little harder. You should be able to see the wood peeling away from the end."

The twig snapped in Daniel's hands. He regarded her with huge eyes, his expression crestfallen. "I'm sorry, Melantha."

"That's all right," she said cheerfully. "Now we can make two stakes. Here, twist off the broken length and you continue to work on that one while I start another."

"Did Da show you how to make these?" he enquired, watching her as she began to expertly grate her piece against the stone wall.

She nodded. "Da always said every good hunter always saves one last arrow for his journey home, in case he suddenly finds himself in need of it. But sometimes, in the excitement of the hunt, he will have used up all his shafts. If the journey home is long, he must know how to quickly forge something that he can use to protect himself, should the need arise."

"And that's what we're doing, isn't it?" His voice dropped to a whisper as he urgently demanded, "We're making weapons so we can escape and go home, aren't we?"

Melantha kept her gaze fastened upon the ragged end of her twig. It was easier to deceive Daniel if she didn't have to look directly at him. "Once Colin returns, I am going to convince Laird MacTier to release the two of you immediately." Her manner was deceptively confident as she finished, "Then I can escape without having to worry about you as well."

"But what if Laird MacTier refuses?" Daniel's fine dark brows puckered with concern. "That bastard said he was going to kill you and make me watch!"

"You mustn't swear, Daniel."

"For God's sake, I'm not a bairn, Melantha—I'm almost a man!"

She looked at him in surprise. His eyes were glittering with anger, but she knew it was not directed at her. It was an anger born of fear, coupled with a raw, naive determination. He was gripping his crudely carved weapon with murderous intent. In that moment Melantha realized that the innocent

little boy she had loved so deeply and tried so hard to be a
mother to was gone. In his place was this terrified youth, a boy
who was not quite a man, but was definitely not a child either.
Aching loss swept through her, leaving her feeling cold and
fragile. Sometime during this past year, the beautiful child she
had known and adored from his first tiny breath had vanished, forever lost amid a tide of suffering.

And except for these agonizing moments spent sharpen-
ing useless sticks against a foul wall, she would never know
the brave young man before her.

"You're right," she acknowledged, averting her gaze so he
would not see the depth of her pain. "You're not a bairn.
Swear if you like. But try not to do it in front of Edwina or
Beatrice—it will only distress them. And don't do it in front
of Matthew and Patrick either," she added, her chest tightening at the thought of her other two brothers. "They're too
young to swear."

Daniel sighed, looking as if he could not begin to understand such feminine nonsense, and continued to work on his
slender weapon.

It had been hard on Daniel, Melantha reflected, to not
have a father. She had tried her best to fill the role of mother,
but the role of father was one she had left untouched. After
her da's death there had been some whispers within the clan
about her marrying Colin so that her brothers could have two
parents. Even Colin had been noble enough to suggest that it
might be a good arrangement. But Colin was Melantha's closest friend, and she could not imagine forcing him into becoming a father of three at the tender age of twenty-two.
Moreover, she had never felt anything other than the purest,
truest friendship for Colin, though she sensed that he had
long felt something more toward her.

Only Roarke had managed to ignite a fire of passion
within her, and it had burned so hot she had thought she
would melt within its unbearable light and heat.

She had thought about Roarke endlessly these last few days. It was ironic, that having spent so much time after he left struggling not to think of him, she now indulged in his memory at length. Her attempts to imprison him in a tiny, hidden cell in her mind had failed miserably, and had only mattered when she had believed she was destined to live the remainder of her life without him. Now that her existence could be counted in brief hours, she permitted herself to reflect on him at will. The thought of Roarke was especially comforting as she lay huddled upon the frigid dungeon floor at night, her arm wrapped protectively around Daniel. The cell was a pit of sour blackness in those hours, filled with nothing but the soft whisper of Daniel's breathing and the oppressive weight of her own guilt and despair. Having examined the hopelessness of their situation from every conceivable angle, there was nothing left for her except to desperately try to forget, just for a moment, where she was.

It was then that Roarke came to her, washing away the stench and the black and the cold. His expression varied according to her mood; sometimes it was faintly teasing, sometimes it was sober and reflective. But most often it was the look of yearning etched upon his face just before he kissed her, that darkly powerful, magnificently heated expression he had as he drew the tip of her breast into his mouth, or as he thrust deep inside her, melding their flesh and their need until they were one.

She had been filled with fury when he left. Much of her rage had been directed at him, for after witnessing the suffering of her people, she could not believe that he could so callously accept a vanquished holding as his rightful prize. But even more of her anger was with herself. For deep within her heart lay an overwhelming desire to forget that Roarke was her enemy, and see him only as the man who had somehow reached inside and touched her very soul.

When he was her prisoner his presence had bewildered

and tormented her. But from the moment he left, she felt as if her heart had been ripped in two.

She prayed that Roarke would not learn of her capture until after she had been executed. He had been ensconced in his own holding the day she and her men arrived, but it was possible that Laird MacTier might invite him to attend her execution. She could bear anything but that. To have him watch as she stood waiting to be killed, knowing that he would have wanted desperately to help her, but that there was absolutely nothing he could do, would only deepen her torment.

I will not let you or your people suffer anymore.

How strong and sure he had sounded as he made that pledge, with silver drops of rain falling off his black hair and his wet shirt and plaid clinging to his massive frame. For one glittering moment she had almost believed him, had almost permitted herself to be lulled in the arms of his strength and his conviction. He had wanted to protect her, to shield her from the cruelty that seemed to fill the world around her. But that was before she had come to his clan and tried to sink a dirk into his laird's heart. There could be no illusions about Roarke's empathy for her now. He was a MacTier through blood and bone, and more, he was a favorite warrior of his laird, an honor he had fought his entire life to earn. Regardless of what had passed between them, Roarke's absolute, undying loyalty was to his laird and his clan.

If Laird MacTier ordered Roarke to kill Melantha himself, Roarke would have no choice but to obey.

Hinges groaned somewhere down the dark passage.

"Hide these!" she hissed, slipping her crudely worked stake into Daniel's boot, then adding the sharp one he had been holding into the other.

The heavy lock on their door turned, and a shaft of oily light spilled into the dungeon. Having grown accustomed to the dark these past six days, both Melantha and Daniel were forced to squint as they stood and struggled to make out the shadowy form of their visitor.

"Good afternoon," said Laird MacTier pleasantly. "I trust you both have been keeping well?"

He was resplendent in a magnificent robe of gold heavily embroidered with silver thread, the hem of which he had carefully draped over his arm in an effort to protect the costly garment from the dank, stinking floor of the dungeon. A weighty gold belt dangled from his waist, and several gem-studded chains of varying lengths had been positioned over his chest, making it clear that he was attired for an occasion of considerable import. Panic rippled through Melantha as her eyes slowly adjusted to the light.

Her pendant was not shimmering among his garish jewelry.

"Oh, yes, your gallant friend returned," Laird MacTier assured her, sensing her concern. "Although 'twas barely within the time I had allotted. I have no desire, however, to draw undue attention to the pendant he brought me, and so I am wearing it concealed beneath these robes. I'm not prepared to have someone else try to steal it from me—especially with so many unfamiliar faces milling about. It seems the occasion of your execution has become something of an event, my dear," he continued, idly polishing one of the gems resting against his chest. "I'm not sure whether 'tis because I have clipped the wings of the mighty Falcon, or because the Falcon turned out to be such a beautiful young woman."

Desire flickered hot within his gaze, despite her disheveled hair and the grimy state of her gown.

Melantha did not flinch beneath his nauseating scrutiny, nor did she expose the depths of her contempt. Were it only herself being held prisoner, she would have gladly pricked his temper. But she wanted to secure Daniel's release, and for that she needed to appeal to whatever sliver of compassion Laird MacTier may have had buried deep within his shriveled soul.

"Whatever the reason," he continued, returning his attention to his own attire, "a crowd has gathered to watch you take your final breath. The entire affair has become quite festive, with jugglers and minstrels strolling about, and food and ale being sold. Several troubadours have already composed ballads in which I am acclaimed for my role in bringing the terrible Falcon to justice." His robes finally arranged to his satisfaction, he lifted his eyes to her and smiled. "I have no doubt this momentous day will be talked about by all the clans for a hundred years or more."

"And so now you have everything you wanted," Melantha observed. "You have regained your precious amulet, and can enjoy being heralded as the laird who managed to capture the elusive Falcon. It is a moment," she continued, choosing her words carefully, "in which you could well afford to make a gesture of compassion."

"It is a most gratifying moment," Laird MacTier agreed. "But surely you are not suggesting that I disappoint the hordes of people pouring through my gates by not executing you. To do so would incite a riot."

"I'm not suggesting that," Melantha quickly assured him, squeezing Daniel's arm to keep him silent. Her voice barely wavered as she continued. "All I am asking, Laird MacTier, is that you spare my brother and my friend the agony of having to watch."

Laird MacTier gave an affected sigh. "I'm afraid that is not possible, my dear. I have said that this lad must be shown what fate awaits him should he decide to follow in your path, and as so often happens in matters of this kind, word of my decision has spread. Hundreds of people have traveled many miles to watch you die, but they are just as eager to see your dear brother as they are to see you. I have made arrangements for the lad to sit upon the dais with me, so everyone can be afforded a clear view of his tormented face."

Melantha's hand rested upon Daniel's arm in an effort

to restrain the anger swelling within him, but she was no match for the fury that Laird MacTier's cruelty suddenly unleashed.

"*You bastard!*" Daniel screamed, lunging at his tormentor and clamping his hands around his throat.

"Daniel, *no!*" cried Melantha. She tried to pull him away, but rage and fear had given her brother an awesome strength, and he was unaffected by her efforts.

The surprise of being attacked by a mere lad momentarily stunned Laird MacTier, giving Daniel a brief advantage. MacTier quickly regained his composure, however. He swept his arms around in a powerful circle, breaking Daniel's bony grip upon his neck, then drew back his fist and drove it deep into the boy's lean gut. Daniel doubled over in pain, enabling Laird MacTier to deliver a final, crippling blow with both fists to the back of his neck.

Daniel moaned and sank to the filthy floor.

"This ruffian needs to be taught to respect his betters," snarled Laird MacTier as he angrily rubbed his stinging neck. "I will have him executed along with you for daring to attack me!"

"No," pleaded Melantha, feeling utterly desperate. She could withstand any punishment Laird MacTier might choose for her, but she knew with agonizing clarity that she could never endure watching Daniel suffer. "I beg of you, Laird MacTier, spare him—he is just a lad—"

"Even more reason to snip the stem of his existence," interrupted Laird MacTier coldly. "I've no desire to let him grow into a man and come back to kill me later."

"But such an action could only be seen by those who await outside as unnecessarily cruel," Melantha argued. "After all, would you not expect your own son to fight on your behalf if you were sentenced to a fate such as mine?"

"I will never be sentenced to your fate," he snapped, but she could see that her question had affected him. "Just look at what he has done to my robe!" he complained as he gathered up the hem of his precious garment, which was now slimy with muck from the dungeon floor.

"Perhaps you have time to change into another—"

"There is no more time," he said, irritated. "Even as we speak the throng outside grows restless to see you. Can you not hear them calling your name?"

A chant had been swelling outside for some time, but it had been lost amid the general noise of the crowd, making it impossible for her to interpret it clearly through fifteen feet of stone wall and earth. There was no mistaking the words that they were shouting now, however. Hundreds had joined the chorus, giving the phrase a terrible rhythmic cadence.

"Kill the Falcon, kill the Falcon, kill the Falcon. . . ."

"I cannot possibly delay your execution a moment longer," said Laird MacTier, looking almost wistful as he assessed the condition of his attire. "However, I will let your brother live, for the moment at least." He gave Daniel a menacing look. "Do one more thing to vex me, and I will have you dragged onto the platform to stand beside your sister and join her in her fate. Now get up—I'm sending the guards to escort you outside."

He turned in a flurry of gold and gems, leaving Melantha and her brother alone once again.

"Are you all right, Daniel?" she demanded anxiously, sinking to her knees beside him.

"Here," he said, freeing the sharpest wooden stick from his boot. "Take this so you'll have a weapon to use when you escape."

Melantha shook her head. Already the guards were coming down the corridor to lead them outside. "You keep it," she said softly, putting it back into his boot. "You'll be able to use it better than I."

"No," he protested, trying to give it to her once more. "You need it—"

"Listen to me, Daniel," Melantha urged, feeling her heart begin to break. "I have used up all my shafts in this hunt—do you understand?"

He stared at her in disbelief. And then his eyes welled with tears. "No."

"Now it is up to you to go home and take care of Matthew and Patrick. You must get home, Daniel, so do whatever you have to do to get there. Do you hear me?"

"I won't go without you," he choked, throwing himself into her arms. "I'd rather die!"

"I know," she whispered softly, stroking the sweet tangle of his hair. "But you aren't going to die, Daniel. I need to know that you are going home, and that you are going to take care of Matthew and Patrick. You'll do that for me, won't you?"

He inhaled a shuddering breath. "Yes."

She pressed a kiss to his forehead, holding him as long as she dared, trying to pour her love and strength into him as she held him close. And then somehow she found the courage to break away, and to regard him with steady calm, when beneath her fragile composure she felt as if she were shattering.

"Here," he said, scooping up something off the ground and pressing it into her palm. "If you won't take the stake, at least take this."

Melantha felt the coolness of a stone press into her flesh. "Thank you," she whispered, swiftly closing her fingers over the pitiful weapon. If nothing else, at least it would give her something to grip as she faced the horror of her death.

"It's time," growled the guard who appeared at their door. His face was deeply pocked from disease and his chest and arms were webbed with scars at various stages of healing, giving him a truly hideous appearance. "You come first." He pointed a blackened finger at Daniel.

Melantha and her brother rose together. She gave Daniel a small smile, then watched as he straightened his shoulders and walked into the waiting grip of the monster at the doorway. Another guard roughly grabbed his other arm. Daniel did not look behind, but something in the sure, brave way with which he held himself as he disappeared gave her a fragment of hope.

She was about to die, but Daniel and Colin would make it home.

Somehow, that would have to be enough.

"And so the honor of leading the infamous Falcon to her death falls to me."

Pure hatred flared within her as she studied the handsome warrior whose enormous frame now blocked the doorway. He was the same MacTier who had held Colin steady to suffer Laird MacTier's beating the night they had been captured. He was also the one who had led the assault on her holding to retrieve Roarke and his men; the coward who would have torn her home apart piece by piece with his deadly siege machine. Magnus had told her that he had also led the subsequent assault on her home, where both Daniel and Matthew were taken and the cottages and fields were burned.

She tightened her fist around the stone nestled in her palm, wondering if she should make use of it now by hurling it straight into his face. It wouldn't gain her freedom, but she would derive immense satisfaction from being the one to permanently mar the perfection of this smug warrior's unblemished features.

"I'm baffled as to how such a pretty lass has managed to cause so much trouble," reflected Derek, looking at her as one might regard a naughty child. " 'Tis a pity our paths did not cross before now. I would have kept you so exhausted in bed, you'd have had neither the strength nor the inclination to go riding about playing outlaw."

Melantha regarded him with unmitigated contempt.

"Unfortunately, fate has not been kind to us," Derek sighed. "Come, milady." He mockingly extended his arm. "Your executioners await you."

Melantha stiffened her spine and walked past him, coldly ignoring his proffered arm. "By what method am I to die?"

"Laird MacTier has come up with something rather unique," replied Derek, walking alongside her. "As hundreds of people began to flock here from miles around, it quickly became apparent that a simple hanging wouldn't do. Too fast, and somewhat ordinary for an outlaw as notorious as yourself. And so MacTier held a tournament this morning, in which over a hundred participants competed for the coveted privilege of shooting the Falcon. Ultimately six archers were chosen. That way there is less chance of your surviving beyond the first volley."

A shiver of fear rippled through her. She had assumed she would be hanged, or perhaps burned, neither of which were appealing. But the prospect of being riddled with arrows by six overzealous archers filled her with an almost paralyzing dread. No doubt each participant had indulged in a cup or two of ale to help pass the long hours before their exhilarating performance. What chance had she that one or more of them might not succeed in cleanly piercing her heart, but would blearily send their shafts into an arm, or leg, or perhaps even her face instead?

She stumbled.

"You're looking rather pale, milady," Derek observed, deriving a perverse pleasure from her fear. "No doubt the fresh air will revive you."

They ascended the slime-coated stairs leading from the depths of the castle. The fetid stench of the dungeon was gradually replaced by the reek of greasy roasting meats and the heavy smell of charred breads and other hastily cooked dishes. The crowd that had poured through Laird MacTier's gates to see her slain would need to be fed, and it seemed the kitchens and bakehouse were working hard to make sure there was ample fare.

Up the narrow, slippery steps, along a dank, barely lit corridor, and then up another twisting staircase, until finally they had reached the main level of the castle. The chanting outside began to swell, pouring through the open windows of the holding in a hostile wave. Two guards stood on either side of a heavy oak door. When they saw Melantha approach with Derek, they regarded her with pity. Melantha did not know if their unexpectedly tender sentiments were aroused by the frailty of her appearance or the drunken savageness of the crowd awaiting her. Whatever the reason, their sympathy had the effect of causing her stomach to quicken. She inhaled a shallow breath, fighting the painful pounding in her chest as she forced herself to stare woodenly ahead.

Soon it will be over. Soon.

The heavy door crashed open, and the restless mob roared with anticipation. The sound was almost deafening, a ghastly cheer of animosity and bloodlust and pleasure merged into one. It was clear that copious amounts of ale had already been consumed, for virtually every man in the throng held a dripping cup, and the sickly stench of spilled brew permeated the air.

"Kill the Falcon! Kill the Falcon! Kill the Falcon!"

Their faces were screwed into hard, angry masks as they fought to catch a glimpse of her, each one looking as if he would relish the opportunity to carry out the deed himself.

Six enormous warriors instantly surrounded her, making a formidable ring of muscle and sword as they slowly marched her through the jeering, screaming crowd. Melantha suspected Laird MacTier had ordered this gesture purely for its theatricality, for it made it appear that the dangerous Falcon had to be vigilantly guarded right until the moment of her death, lest she suddenly decide to escape. Trapped in the midst of more than a thousand men, women, and children, each one of whom would scramble over the other for the honor of slaying her, Melantha could see no possibility of flight. Even so, she was glad of the circle of warriors, for they shielded her from the crush of the mob and the clawing, groping hands and fists that rained down upon them as they made their way to the high platform erected at the far end of the courtyard.

Laird MacTier had given careful consideration to his audience in the construction of her scaffold. The platform was positioned above even the tallest warrior, with a narrow stake rising from its center, ensuring that everyone would have an excellent view of her as she was riddled with arrows. Derek and another warrior painfully gripped her arms and hauled her up the wooden steps. Melantha was suddenly aware of the small stone hidden within her palm. An overwhelming sadness seeped through her. She knew Daniel was watching, expecting her to do something, anything, to hurl this tiny, ineffectual stone at Derek and somehow secure their freedom in the process. Her arms were wrenched around the stake and her wrists were bound with rough cord, the pebble still safely nestled in her hand. She kept her gaze low, not because she was afraid of facing the crowd who was calling for her death with drunken enthusiasm, but because she could not bear to look at Daniel and see the awesome anguish in his face as he slowly realized that her life was truly lost.

She suddenly found herself recalling how her father had looked at her just as he was about to die. It had been the most hideous moment of her life, intensified a thousandfold by the staggering grief she had seen in his beautiful eyes. Whatever happened, she could not burden Daniel with such a devastating memory. Summoning the last vestiges of her composure, she lifted her gaze to the splendidly draped dais across the courtyard, affecting an air of frigid contempt as she stared at the man who had so enthusiastically orchestrated her death.

Laird MacTier was seated in a handsomely carved chair of mammoth proportions, which had the unfortunate effect of dwarfing him somewhat, which Melantha suspected was far from his intent. He regarded her with bold triumph, then raised his hand to mockingly stroke his chest, indicating where the amulet lay safely hidden from view. To his left sat his wife, a sad, wrung-out figure of a woman who looked as if she had been crushed beneath the heel of his cruelty years ago. Beside her was a short, doughy boy of about ten years of age, who was furtively biting his nails when he thought his father wasn't looking. Melantha did not waste any of her last precious moments giving them any consideration, but immediately turned her attention to Laird MacTier's right side.

There sat Daniel, his lean face frozen with dread, his wrists bound before him so that all he could do was grip his hands tightly upon his lap. Beside him sat Colin, his own face shadowed with a despair so tearing it pained Melantha to even look upon him. There were other men chatting amiably in a row behind them, who Melantha supposed were the clan's council. To Colin's right was an empty chair, evidently for some honored member of the clan who had failed to arrive. She wondered if it had been reserved for Roarke. She hoped that it was, for its vacancy meant that he had not come to watch her die. There was a modicum of comfort in that, at least.

Laird MacTier stood and raised his hand in the air, calling for the mob's silence. But the sight of him in his sumptuous robes and jewels had the effect of exciting the crowd even more, and a deafening cheer rose into the air.

"Hail, MacTier!" they shouted ecstatically. "Hail, the captor of the Falcon!"

They raised their cups and drained them, then roughly

shoved each other out of the way as they surged toward the ale carts to procure more drink.

Laird MacTier smiled and waved, clearly relishing the moment. Finally he raised his hands again, and the mob obediently quieted.

"My friends," he began, "today is a glorious day in Mac-Tier history. Before you stands the nefarious Falcon, the outlaw who has stolen bread from your mouths and boots from your feet, who has callously stripped you of the very plaids you wear, so she could profit from your suffering, and laugh as you limped home to your families, naked and ashamed!"

Angry curses rose from the drunken throng.

Laird MacTier smiled and raised his hands to quiet the crowd once more. "For many months this thief has eluded us, hiding within the depths of the forest, using the cloak of the trees and the dark of the night to carry out her cowardly attacks. 'Twas not until I cleverly drew her into my trap that we were finally able to end the terror she has wrought. Now you can live your lives without fear of you and your loved ones being beaten, robbed, and viciously slaughtered!"

He paused again, giving his audience another opportunity to cheer him.

"She will stop at nothing to continue her evil war upon the innocent," he continued gravely. "Even I came close to death when she realized that I would finally bring her dark reign of the woods to an end."

The crowd gasped and murmured among themselves, speculating on whether Laird MacTier had been injured, and if so, where.

"It is my duty, as your laird and protector, to hereby sentence this outlaw to death," Laird MacTier finished with grand finality. "Her execution shall be carried out immediately." He gave Melantha a final look of smug triumph, then nodded to the archers below.

Melantha returned her gaze to Daniel and Colin. She

wanted her last glance at them to be filled with love and hope, and not with the terrible despondency that was now pulsing through her every vein. She tried to affect a smile, but immediately felt it quiver and crumble. And so she tore her eyes away and fixed them steadfastly upon the gray cloaked line of executioners who had silently assembled before her, each armed with a supple bow and a quiver full of arrows, lest the first volley not be sufficient to stop her pounding heart.

Dear God, she prayed, *please let it be over quickly.*

The archers nocked their arrows and drew back the strings of their bows in one fluid motion.

And then they spun around and released their shafts, neatly piercing MacTier guards in every direction.

"What the hell is happening?" roared Laird MacTier, watching in disbelief as the archers immediately sent a second deadly volley of arrows into the air, cleanly puncturing another round of MacTier warriors. "For God's sake, *somebody kill them!*"

Pandemonium erupted as the bleary mob surged in every conceivable direction, their frothing cups in one hand and their weapons in the other. Most of them could not see the archers and therefore were not quite certain who it was they were supposed to kill, but they were eager to join the fray nonetheless.

At that moment one of the archers threw off his cloak and easily leaped up the steps of the scaffold.

"No," Melantha whispered, her eyes blurred with tears. "No."

"I realize I'm not much," Roarke conceded mildly, slashing at the ropes securing her to the stake, "but I must confess, this isn't quite the welcome I had expected."

The other archers had also stripped off their cloaks by then. Eric, Donald, Myles, Finlay, and Lewis were thrashing at the enormous wave of MacTier warriors surrounding them with their swords. Each was fighting with powerful determination, but any fool could see it was hopeless. They were six against a thousand. They would be slaughtered where they stood, Melantha realized miserably. And she would be executed anyway.

It had been horrible enough that she was going to die. The added burden of their deaths was excruciating.

"You'll be killed," she choked, feeling as if her heart was being torn apart. "You never should have come."

"You know, there was a time when I might have been insulted by your utter lack of faith in me," mused Roarke, severing the last of her bonds. "Now I find it rather charming."

"Here, lassie!" called Magnus, his snowy head bobbing up from the crowd below. "Don't forget to keep yer eyes sharp!" He winked and tossed her sword to her.

"Stay close to me, Melantha," ordered Roarke as he crashed his blade against the weapon of a MacTier who had ascended the steps of the scaffold. "And see if you can't take care of that fellow over there."

Melantha lashed at a warrior who was climbing up the other side of the platform. Her swordplay was quick and true, but ultimately the enormous MacTier gained the advantage, deflecting her blow and trapping her blade against the wooden platform.

"Is the terrible Falcon going to run me through with her sword?" he taunted, vastly amused. His mouth split open, revealing a dark cave of rotting teeth.

"No," came a hard voice from behind. "I am."

The warrior started to turn, but found his movement severely limited by the silver shaft that suddenly burst through his gut. His rotting smile vanished as he groaned and fell to the floor.

Melantha stared in shock at Lewis. "You killed him," she said, unable to believe her shy, diffident friend was actually capable of such a feat.

"Aye," said Lewis, nodding. He whipped past her and

began to confidently clash with another warrior who was scrambling up to kill them.

"Damn it," swore Roarke, withdrawing his dripping blade from one warrior only to immediately begin fending off another, "what the hell is taking them so long?"

Melantha raised her sword high and hacked it deep into the shoulder of a MacTier who was almost up the steps of the platform. He bellowed with pain and clutched at his injury, enabling Melantha to shove him off the steps and into the roiling crowd below. Another warrior instantly replaced him, and she gripped her sword tight as she began to fight him. Whatever Roarke was waiting for, she hoped it happened soon. They were trapped in the midst of this mob, and could not possibly defeat every warrior who scaled the scaffold.

"*Fire!*" came a startled cry from across the courtyard, only to be echoed in every direction.

"Fire!"

"Fire!"

"*Fire!*"

Thick black smoke spewed from the bakehouse, the brewery, and every window of the castle, as well as from giant torches of flaming straw around the courtyard. Panic streaked through the horrified mob. Their efforts at routing the invaders were instantly abandoned, and the entire assemblage deteriorated into a crashing tangle of yelping, shrieking bodies. Some valiantly tried to douse the flames with their precious ale, but most seemed more concerned with quitting the MacTier holding altogether. They clamored over everything in sight as they charged toward the gate, upsetting heavily laden carts of food and ale, and sending dozens of enormous barrels rolling into the melee.

"Stop them!" bellowed Laird MacTier, waving his hands in helpless frustration as he watched a pair of men on horseback appear suddenly from the back of the castle leading two mounts. "Somebody stop those riders!"

Melantha watched in amazement as Ninian and Gelfrid rode toward them, completely unheeded by the crowd that was surging in the opposite direction.

"Jump!" said Roarke.

"No!" Melantha raised her sword to engage the warrior who had crept up behind Roarke.

"For God's sake—"

Roarke impatiently shoved her off the platform, watching as she landed with a thud upon her waiting mount.

"Roarke!" she cried, "behind you!"

Roarke started to turn, but it was too late. A hot slash of steel burned into his back, severing the flesh across his shoulder blade. He clenched his jaw and spun about, whipping up his blade to meet his opponent.

His eyes met the shocked gaze of James, a young warrior who had been trained by Roarke himself, and fought bravely in his army for nearly two years.

"What are you doing?" James demanded, appalled that he had injured his former commander, and unable to comprehend how Roarke could possibly be betraying the clan he had fought his entire life to protect.

"I'm freeing the Falcon," Roarke replied quickly, his sword poised to deflect another blow.

"Why?"

"Because she does not deserve to die," he answered simply.

James considered this for barely an instant.

And then he turned and rammed off the scaffold the warrior who had climbed up behind him.

Roarke wasted no time offering thanks, but turned and leaped onto his horse, which Ninian was holding steady for him below.

"We have to fetch Daniel and Colin!" said Melantha urgently.

"Myles and Finlay are freeing them."

"They can't get past the guards—look!"

Roarke turned his head to see Myles and Finlay valiantly trying to fight their way onto the laird's dais. Wounded Mac-Tiers littered the ground below them, but as quickly as they were felled, more guards appeared.

"Take Melantha out of here," he commanded Ninian and Gelfrid.

"I'm not leaving without my brother and Colin!"

"I will bring them safely to you, Melantha."

"And I'm going to help you—"

"All you would do is bring more MacTiers charging after you, which will only make things more difficult," Roarke countered impatiently. "I know it is hard," he conceded, gentling his voice on seeing the torment in her eyes, "but the best way you can help them is to ride out that gate."

It was impossible, what he was asking—surely he could see that? She bit her lip and stubbornly shook her head, struggling to gain control of her fear.

"Trust me, Melantha," pleaded Roarke, knowing he had barely seconds before the warriors coming toward them would be close enough to attack. "Just this once."

His gray eyes were large and imploring. In that instant she felt as if she could see into the deepest recesses of his soul. And suddenly she knew.

Roarke would honor his vow to her, or die in the attempt.

"Be careful," she implored, her voice a ragged whisper. "Please."

With that she dug her heels into her mount and headed toward the gate, with Gelfrid and Ninian flanking her on either side.

Laird MacTier was still roaring at the crowd, angrily bellowing orders that could not be heard. His poor wife looked as if she wanted to swoon but did not dare to without his permission, while his son was happily gnawing on his nails as he watched the magnificent chaos. Meanwhile, Daniel and Colin had loosened each other's bonds, unheeded. The council members behind them were preoccupied with swatting at the flames now licking up the scarlet-and-gold curtains of their dais, and all the guards had left the platform to prevent Myles and Finlay from advancing.

"Let's go!" said Colin, gesturing for Daniel to follow him.

Instead Daniel reached into his boot, withdrew his sharpened stake, and charged with murderous fury at Laird MacTier.

Sensing the attack, MacTier turned. The pike did not puncture his back as Daniel had planned, but burrowed deep into his shoulder, ripping open the still raw wound Melantha had created with her dirk.

"You little bastard!" swore MacTier, clutching at the stick protruding from his bloodied robe. "This time I'm going to kill you!"

He lunged at Daniel. Colin grabbed Daniel and threw him out of the way, then hurled himself into Laird MacTier, knocking him to the floor.

"You fools!" hissed MacTier, grabbing the dirk at his waist.

"Colin, Daniel—let's go!" shouted Myles, who had finally made it onto the dais.

Laird MacTier stared at Myles in complete bemusement. "Just what the hell do you think you're doing, Myles?"

"We're freeing your prisoners," he said in a flat voice.

A veil of smoke was swirling round the platform, forcing Laird MacTier to blink.

When he opened his eyes, Roarke was standing before him.

"Have you gone mad?" Laird MacTier demanded.

"I don't believe so."

"Then what in the name of God are you doing?"

"I am trying to right past wrongs," said Roarke. "Come here, Daniel." He extended his arm.

Daniel did not hesitate, but obediently went straight to Roarke.

"You cannot do this!" sputtered Laird MacTier, watching

in helpless fury as Roarke shepherded Daniel off the platform, with Myles, Finlay, and Colin following.

"Your castle is burning, Laird MacTier," said Roarke, lifting Daniel onto his horse before mounting behind him. "I suggest you try to engage whomever you have left here in trying to preserve it." He began to ride toward the gate.

"Stop them!" shouted MacTier, rising. "Somebody stop them!"

But Laird MacTier's crowd of admirers had all but vanished. Most of the throng had emptied through the gates, leaving the smoke-shrouded courtyard empty but for a sickly mess of spilled food, broken cups, leaking casks of ale, and countless groaning bodies.

"A hundred pieces of gold to the man who shoots them!" he bellowed wildly. "Two hundred!"

That generous incentive managed to bring four intrepid warriors scrambling after them. But their gait quickly became slow and uncertain, and their hands were clumsy as they positioned their arrows.

"What are you waiting for?!" Laird MacTier screamed. "Shoot!"

The archers dutifully released their shafts, which sailed crazily through the air.

Confusion gripped their faces.

Then panic.

Suddenly the four sprinted away, desperate to find a place to relieve themselves.

"Have you tried the ale we brought just for this occasion?" enquired Roarke cheerfully as he watched Colin, Finlay, and Myles ride through the gate. "You really should— 'tis simply marvelous for cleansing the bowels."

With that he galloped into the waning summer light, leaving the man for whom he would once have given his life staring in helpless rage behind him.

CHAPTER 14

"... it came off when I was strangling MacTier and so I gave it to you. I thought it might bring you luck," finished Daniel, shrugging his thin shoulders.

Melantha stared in bewilderment at the pendant shimmering in her palm. This was what she had gripped so tightly, thinking it was only a stone. The silver orb felt hot against her skin, and the green jewel in its center seemed paler, almost as if it were glowing from within. She shifted it slightly, and the glow vanished. Obviously it had just been a trick of the light, she realized. Deeply touched by her brother's gesture, she wrapped the broken chain around her wrist and knotted it, tucking the amulet inside her sleeve. She did not know if it held any mystical powers, but it had certainly been a comfort to hold as she faced her death.

"Thank you, Daniel." She wrapped her arms tightly around him.

"They're coming," announced Lewis from his perch in a tree. "Looks like about twenty riders."

"Either this lot has bellies of iron," Magnus quipped, "or they managed to avoid my fair Edwina's special new recipe." He furrowed his white brows in bewilderment. "What the devil is that thing flapping about in the wind?"

"That's Laird MacTier," said Donald. "It seems he didn't take time to change out of his fancy robes and jewels."

"Looks like he brought my fair-haired friend with him," Colin observed, referring to Derek.

"Good," said Finlay, withdrawing his sword. "We've a score to settle with him." He spat upon the ground.

"Everyone to their positions," Roarke commanded, "and wait for my signal."

Myles leaned over and clasped his hands together in a makeshift stirrup. "Come, lad, let's get you up into this tree."

Daniel regarded Roarke stubbornly. "I want to fight."

"There are different ways of battling an enemy," Roarke told him. "A warrior should not be afraid of attempting to outwit his opponent before he resorts to his sword and dirk."

"Fine," huffed Daniel, clearly unconvinced. He turned to Myles and permitted the burly warrior to hoist him up into the tree.

Fear coursed through Melantha as everyone quickly began scaling trees and burying themselves beneath mounds of branches and leaves.

"Why are you doing this?" she asked Roarke anxiously. " 'Tis nearly dark—we could easily conceal ourselves within these woods and the MacTiers would never find us. Why are you so determined to fight them?"

"Because we must bring this matter to an end."

"It will never end," Melantha countered. "Laird MacTier will not rest until he has killed me—especially now that he has been publicly humiliated." Her despair was nearly suffocating as she quietly finished. "He will make it his life's work to see me captured and executed, and to destroy my people as well."

Roarke reached out and tenderly brushed his fingers against her cheek. "No, Melantha, he will not. I will not allow it."

"You cannot stop him." Her fleeting exhilaration at escaping death was now eradicated by the knowledge that she had sentenced her beloved clan to destruction. "He will not listen to you, and my people do not have the strength to fight his army." Her eyes glistened with tears as she raggedly finished. "You should have left me to die."

He gripped her chin and tipped her head up, forcing her to look at him.

There was much he wanted to say to her, but he knew he would never find the words. A life of battle had not equipped him with tender words and sweet phrases. Muriel had never expected them from him, and he had not offered them to her. And although he had loved his precious Clementina, he had been away fighting for much of her brief life, and had not learned to speak his heart to the child who expected nothing of him except love.

How could he possibly make Melantha understand what she had come to mean to him?

"I could not let you die, Melantha," he ventured gruffly, "because I would have died as well."

Melantha stared at him, her eyes wide and silvered with emotion.

The pounding of hooves was drawing nearer, forcing Roarke to release her. "Now take your position," he ordered brusquely, "and try not to get shot."

She hesitated, studying him through the soft blur of her tears.

And then she looped her bow over her shoulder and silently melted into the shadows of the trees.

Laird MacTier and his warriors thundered toward them, their bodies bent low over their mounts. Their pace did not slacken as they approached, making it clear that they were determined to find the Falcon and Roarke, and had overlooked the possibility of a trap. The shoulder of Laird MacTier's robe was drenched with blood, but he was not permitting his injury to hinder his speed.

A little closer, urged Roarke silently, watching as MacTier rode past the trees where Ninian and Gelfrid were positioned. Utilizing the patience that had been painstakingly honed during twenty years of battle, Roarke waited until the very last MacTier warrior had thundered into the tight parameters of their ambush.

"Now!"

Three enormous nets dropped from the trees, instantly snaring a dozen warriors. Their mounts reared and tossed their startled masters onto their backsides, leaving the Mac-Tiers swearing and scrabbling as they tried to avoid being crushed by churning flanks and hooves.

The remaining seven riders and Laird MacTier withdrew their swords and wheeled about, vainly searching the darkness for their enemy.

"Now!" commanded Roarke.

A shower of arrows rained down upon them from the branches overhead, piercing them in their shoulders, backs, and arms, and reducing their numbers again by more than half.

"Damn you!" raged MacTier, jerking his horse round in an agitated circle as he impotently shook his sword at the tangled canopy above. "Come down and fight me on the ground!"

The earth exploded in response to his invitation, with mounds of branches and leaves suddenly bursting all around him. At the same time men began to drop from the trees. By the time he, Derek, and Neill had managed to regain control of their terrified horses, they were completely surrounded. The remaining MacTier warriors were either nursing their injuries or cursing in frustration as they crashed into each other ensnared in the nets.

"Drop yer weapons," ordered Magnus, aiming a quivering arrow straight at Laird MacTier's jeweled chest, "or I'll make a big, bloody hole in yer fancy gown."

Laird MacTier nodded at Derek. "Kill him."

The blond warrior looked at his laird in surprise. "We're surrounded and he has an arrow trained upon you."

"He cannot kill me," Laird MacTier informed his warrior calmly. "Kill him."

"I'm just as happy to put a shaft in you, laddie," said Magnus cheerfully, shifting his aim to Derek. "I've more than enough arrows for the lot of ye."

Melantha pointed her weapon at Derek. "If you're thinking he's likely to miss, I promise you I won't," she stated coldly.

"Nor will I," added Ninian, adjusting the string of his bow.

Gelfrid's face contorted with effort as he struggled to keep his shaking arrow from releasing prematurely. "Nor I."

"If they only succeed in wounding you, I shall be happy to hack you into bloody chunks for the wolves to feed upon," offered Eric, his sword gleaming through the darkness.

"And I'll take this stick and gouge your eyes out," threatened Daniel.

"I'll help," offered Donald gallantly.

Myles waved his blade at Neill. "And I'll take care of your shivering friend over there."

Derek needed no further convincing. He hastily tossed his sword onto the ground, then threw down his dirk for good measure, inspiring Neill to do the same.

"You cowardly fools!" raged Laird MacTier. "I'll have you both executed for disobeying me!"

Roarke moved into the lacy veil of moonlight now filtering through the branches. "I advise you to follow their example and relinquish your weapons, Laird MacTier."

"My God, Roarke," MacTier breathed, his face twisted with fury. "No man could have trusted his own brother more than I trusted you."

"Your weapons, Laird MacTier."

Laird MacTier maintained his grip upon his heavily jeweled sword. "How could you betray me and your clan, and sacrifice everything I gave you to help this ragged, filthy band of thieves?"

" 'Tis interesting," mused Roarke, "that in all the years we have stolen from others we have felt it was our right to do so. Yet when others stole from us, we branded them thieves and demanded retribution."

"It's not the same!" snapped Laird MacTier. "You and I have spent our entire lives leading the MacTier clan to ever greater power. We did it for the good of our people and for the generations of MacTiers who will come after us."

"But the prosperity of our clan has come at the suffering of others," pointed out Roarke. "No matter how much we take from others—their land, their homes, the very chairs upon which they sit and cups from which they drink, it's never enough. There is always another holding waiting to be conquered."

"Of course it is never enough," agreed Laird MacTier. "That is how a great clan is built—by constantly expanding its borders and increasing its wealth. It is the most basic law of nature that the strong will prey upon the weak."

"We are men," argued Roarke, "not animals. We have the ability to temper our actions with morality, compassion, and honor. It is wrong to prey upon the weak simply because they are weak."

"We are warriors," scoffed Laird MacTier. " 'Tis rooted in our very nature to conquer. It is what makes us great leaders."

Roarke shook his head. "You were in a position to help others build something, to make them stronger and ally them with your army so that everyone could benefit. Instead you chose to brutalize them and steal from them. Then when they, in turn, stole from you, only because you had reduced them to a state of near starvation, you became enraged and demanded vengeance. But vengeance was not your right to demand," he finished. "It was theirs."

"Enough of this foolish talk!" snarled Laird MacTier. "You have betrayed me, and for that you must die!"

He dug his heels into his horse and raised his sword, preparing to cut Roarke down where he stood.

Roarke's men sprinted forward with raised blades. The flurry of arrows released by Melantha, Magnus, Ninian, and Gelfrid arrived first. Ninian and Gelfrid's arrows sailed past their target and struck a perfectly innocent tree, while Magnus's shaft accidentally pierced Derek's shoulder, which was to the right of Laird MacTier.

Melantha's aim, however, was perfect.

Laird MacTier howled in pain and dropped his sword. His eyes round with horror, he stared at the shaft protruding grotesquely from his wrist.

"You cannot kill me!" he raged, clawing at the golden swath of fabric at his throat. "I have the amulet!"

One by one he cast his heavily jeweled chains upon the ground with his uninjured hand, desperately searching for the pendant. When the last necklace lay shimmering upon the earth and his throat was exposed and naked, his eyes widened with alarm.

"Did you lose something?" drawled Colin sarcastically.

"You're a MacTier, Roarke, by birth and blood," Laird MacTier blurted out, suddenly afraid. "Your sworn loyalty is to me and your clan. It is therefore your duty to protect me from these murdering outlaws."

"You did not earn my loyalty," Roarke countered. " 'Twas

given blindly, merely by the fact of being born a MacTier. But I can no longer follow you blindly—not when compassion and honor have finally opened my eyes."

"Only a madman or an idiot would forfeit the holding I gave to you over such nonsense," argued Laird MacTier, cradling his bleeding arm against his side. His eyes narrowed. "Whatever they're paying you, I'll double it."

"Now, there's a tempting offer," chortled Magnus, vastly amused.

Roarke shook his head. "There is nothing you could give me that would change this."

"Eric—Myles—Donald," called Laird MacTier. "You owe your loyalty to me before Roarke. Help me now, and you will each receive a fortune in gold."

"My allegiance has always been to Roarke first," Eric told him bluntly. "And no amount of gold could compare to the jewel that awaits me at the MacKillon holding."

"By all the saints, I knew it!" burst out Magnus, nearly releasing his next arrow in his excitement. "Ye may have fooled some with all that savage Viking business, but I knew our sweet Gillian would see through it!"

Colin regarded Eric incredulously. "Are you referring to my sister?"

Eric nodded.

"But she is terrified of you," Colin protested.

"No." A peculiar warmth flooded through Eric as he realized he was declaring his intentions before Gillian's brother and clan. "She isn't."

"Myles," pleaded Laird MacTier, dismissing Eric, "think of what you could do with all that gold!"

Myles shrugged his heavy shoulders. "I don't need any gold. If you gave me some I would just give it to the MacKillons."

"I'm afraid our Myles has been struck by the arrow of love as well," Donald observed, smiling. "Her name is Katie," he added, as if he genuinely thought Laird MacTier might find this information interesting.

"What about you, Donald?" demanded Laird MacTier, growing frantic.

"Alas, I haven't met the woman who will be my wife yet," Donald told him. "But thank you for asking."

Laird MacTier's eyes narrowed on Roarke. "By turning against your clan, you spit upon the graves of your own wife and child."

"My wife was devoted to both her clan and to me," Roarke replied, infuriated that MacTier would attempt to use their precious memory against him. "And my daughter was devoted to her mother. Were they alive today, I have no doubt that they would respect me for my actions."

"You cannot kill me." His tone was almost pleading.

"I have no intention of killing you," Roarke assured him. "As long as you agree to my terms."

Laird MacTier regarded him warily. "Which are?"

"I will have your word that you and your allies will leave the MacKillons in peace, and that you will cease your pursuit of the Falcon and her outlaws."

"She tried to kill me!" objected Laird MacTier. "Twice!"

"If I had wanted to kill you that last arrow would have punctured your heart instead of your wrist," pointed out Melantha. "I was merely trying to stop you from killing Roarke."

"Let us say you will both refrain from trying to murder each other," said Roarke. "In return for your assurance of peace, the Falcon will cease to prey upon the MacTiers and their allies, and I will spare your life and the lives of your men."

Laird MacTier hesitated, considering.

"If you do not agree, I shall permit my men and these outlaws to cut you and your warriors to pieces," said

Roarke. "I know that Derek here has managed to raise the ire of at least several members of the Falcon's band. They would take great pleasure in seeing scraps of him scattered throughout these woods."

Derek paled.

His face contorted with pain and defeat, Laird MacTier nodded. "Very well."

"You will also renounce any claim upon the holding you gave me—"

"I knew that was too sweet a gift for you to surrender." His tone was laden with scorn.

"—and you will grant complete freedom to its inhabitants and refrain from ever attempting to conquer it again."

Laird MacTier regarded him in astonishment. "You're not keeping it?"

"It is not mine to keep," Roarke informed him, "just as it was not yours to give."

"Fine."

"Swear it," insisted Roarke. "Upon your honor."

"I swear it!" he snapped. "Upon my bloody honor!"

"Well, now, I'm not sure what good an oath like that is," scoffed Magnus, "when 'tis a well known fact that ye have no honor."

Laird MacTier's face turned scarlet with rage. "How dare you!"

"How can we be sure that he will keep his word?" demanded Colin.

"He has no choice," Roarke told him. "He has made a vow in front of his own men. Were he to break his word, his army would never trust him. Knowledge of his deceit would quickly spread, until all his allies would sever their ties with him, and he would be left isolated and powerless."

"I suppose that will have to do," Magnus conceded. "But mind my words, ye'll be feelin' more than a shaft through yer wrist if ye try any more foolishness, do ye hear?"

"If you've all finished with your threats, would you kindly let me go before I bleed to death?" asked Laird MacTier.

"I'll remove that arrow if ye like," offered Magnus, suddenly feeling generous. "Ye'd not be the first MacTier to benefit from my touch." He winked at Roarke.

"I'd recommend trying to live with the arrow," Roarke advised dryly. "Your men will be stripped of their weapons and their mounts before being released. As you are injured, you may retain your horse."

"Thank you," drawled Laird MacTier, still cradling his dripping arm.

Roarke gestured for his men and Melantha's band to relieve the MacTiers of their weapons.

"I suggest you leave these woods quickly," he said, picking up Laird MacTier's sword and examining the heavily jeweled hilt. " 'Tis a known fact that they are filled with outlaws."

He tossed the sword onto a pile and turned away.

Melantha wove her way through the columns of trees in silence, leaving behind the low rumble of snoring and the smoky scent of dying fires. She had found a small stream to bathe in, and the night air washed over her damp skin as she followed the liquid path through the darkness. Finally the woods came to an end, and she stepped out beneath the crystal-flecked sky.

Roarke sat before an endless expanse of loch, contemplating its shimmering surface. He wore only his plaid, and his black hair was wet and curling against his damp skin, indicating that he had been swimming. He did not turn as she approached, but continued to study the rippling water. Melantha seated herself beside him and wrapped her arms around her knees. For a moment they sat together in silence, neither willing to break the stillness.

"How did they die?" Melantha finally ventured softly.

Roarke kept his gaze upon the ribbon of moonlight dancing upon the loch's surface. "My daughter succumbed to a fever at the age of three, and I was not there to help my wife endure it. She poisoned herself."

Melantha had always known he had endured a terrible loss. She had seen it shadowed in his eyes the first time she had looked upon him. Even so, she had never imagined his wounds to have been so deep. She had always believed her own suffering to be far greater than anything he could comprehend.

She had been wrong, she realized, feeling selfish and ashamed. The deaths of a wife and child were an agony of which she could scarcely conceive.

"Is that why you wanted a holding of your own? Because you couldn't bear to return to the place where they died?"

"In part," he admitted. "It was also why I stayed away for so many years. I had failed miserably as a husband and a father. But I never failed as a warrior. As long as there was a battle to fight, then I had somewhere to go."

She could understand that. Love and responsibility for her brothers had tied her to her clan, but she had sought refuge in the forest. Whether hunting for meat or stealing under the guise of the Falcon, the woods were a place where she could almost escape the pain of her past.

"Magnus told me the holding Laird MacTier gave you was very beautiful," she said after a while. "He said the hall in which he found you was filled with fine tapestries, and that you drank from silver cups."

Roarke's mouth tightened with contempt. "We drank from cups the price of which could have fed a child for a month, and slept on soft feather mattresses that made my back ache. And I hated it."

She looked at him in surprise. "Why?"

"Because it wasn't really mine. Everyone there knew it, and I knew it, and yet we played this idiotic game of their bowing before me and acting as though they respected me, when in fact they utterly despised me."

"They would have learned to respect you, Roarke—just as my people did. All you had to do was give them time."

"I didn't give a damn if they learned to respect me or not."

Melantha studied him in silence. Despite his efforts to denigrate the holding Laird MacTier had given to him, it had been his long awaited reward for a lifetime of dedicated service. The lands had been fertile, the castle solid and handsome. And regardless of what he said, Melantha was certain that eventually Roarke would have been able to win the trust and devotion of the people who lived there. He could have lived a comfortable life of stature and affluence, while maintaining his position in his clan.

Because of her, he had nothing.

"It was everything you have ever wanted," she whispered, unable to conceal her regret.

He reached out and brushed a dark strand of hair off her temple, then laid his hand possessively along the paleness of her cheek. "No, Melantha," he murmured quietly, "it was not."

He lowered his head, his eyes never leaving hers. His lips were barely a breath away from her own when he finished in a rough whisper, "I want you. You and Daniel and Matthew and Patrick, and the wonderful children we are going to create together. That means more to me than all the holdings and tapestries and silver cups in Scotland. Do you understand?"

She stared at him a long, anguished moment, trying to absorb what he was telling her.

And then she threw her arms around him and crushed her lips to his.

Roarke plunged his tongue into the wet heat of her mouth, tasting her deeply, absolutely, while his hands roamed the thick silk of her hair, the delicate span of her ribs, the lush swell of her breasts. He wanted her with a desire that was staggering, to bury himself inside her and make her his, until there was nothing but the clear cape of sky above them and the glorious heat of love between them. He pulled her into his lap, feeling himself harden beneath the coarse wool of his plaid as he began to ease up the fabric of her gown. Melantha pressed herself eagerly against him, splaying her hands across his back to steady herself.

Roarke winced.

"You're hurt!"

"It's nothing," he assured her, trying to bring her back into his arms.

Unconvinced, she wriggled out of his grasp and moved behind him. A long, dark cut marred the bronzed flesh across his shoulder blade. The wound had stopped bleeding and his dip in the loch had washed it clean, but it would have to be closed nonetheless.

"You need to be stitched," she announced.

"If you dare turn me over to Magnus, I swear I shall go after MacTier and beg him to take me back."

"I suppose Lewis could do it," she speculated. "He's very good at fixing things."

"Does he knew how to close a wound?"

She hesitated. "I'm certain he could figure it out."

"Well, he can figure it out on a scrap of cloth, not on my back." A nagging suspicion began to form in his mind. "Why don't you do it?"

She looked away, suddenly fascinated by the moonlight on the loch.

"Melantha?"

"I never actually learned to sew," she confessed.

"I see."

"I was too busy learning how to fight and hunt," she told him defensively.

"Those are valuable skills," Roarke agreed. "Unfortunately, it means I am going to have a wife who is adept at slaying beasts and enemies, but not at keeping her family's wounds tended and their clothes from falling apart." He sighed. "I suppose I shall have to teach you how to sew myself."

Her eyes widened. "You can sew?"

" 'Tis a skill every self-respecting warrior needs to have. You would be amazed at what gets slashed on a battlefield." He pulled her down before him. "Since you lack the ability to close my wound, perhaps you could do something to distract me from the pain and raise my spirits." He began to press slow, lingering kisses down her neck.

Melantha's hand grazed across his lap. "I would say your spirits have been raised already."

"You're a saucy lass," he chided, lowering her against the grass. "I can see that life with you is going to be exhausting."

She pulled away the rumpled length of his plaid. "You may be right," she conceded, wrapping her hand around his hardness.

She kissed him as she caressed the length of him with slow, teasing promise, alternating her rhythm and her touch until his entire body was rigid and straining with pleasure. Finally Roarke could bear no more. Pulling himself away, he quickly pushed up the skirts of her gown and nuzzled the creamy skin of her thighs.

"I like this gown," he murmured, "far better than your breeches."

It was much later that they lay twined together beneath the soft warmth of Roarke's plaid, listening to the gentle caress of the loch against the rocks.

"Do you think the amulet really possesses the power to protect its wearer?" Melantha asked, studying the silver sphere dangling against her wrist.

Roarke lifted the chain so that the emerald sparkled in

the moonlight. "If you had asked me before, I would have said no. However, it cannot be denied that you have had uncommonly good fortune while it has been in your possession."

"You nearly cut off my head, I suffered an arrow in my shoulder, and was almost executed by six archers," she pointed out aridly. "That scarcely seems like good fortune to me."

"Yet here you are, safe and well in the arms of the warrior who tried to slay you, and instead has come to love you above all else." He dropped the pendant and began to nuzzle the valley between her breasts. "You should know that it is not my custom to marry the outlaws I have been sent to capture. In the case of the Falcon, however, I am willing to make an exception."

He took the peak of her breast into his mouth and began to suckle.

"That is most chivalrous of you," observed Melantha. She closed her eyes and sighed with pleasure. "I shall give your proposal my utmost consideration, and will offer you my response in the morning."

Roarke paused in his ministrations to regard her with amusement. "In that case, my little outlaw, I shall do everything within my power to influence your decision." He began to press a lingering path of heated kisses down the soft flat of her belly.

It was not much later that Melantha whispered her answer into the velvet night.

About the Author

KARYN MONK has been writing since she was a girl. In university she discovered a love for history. After several years working in the highly charged world of advertising, she turned to writing historical romance. She is married to a wonderfully romantic husband, Philip, whom she allows to believe is the model for her heroes.